The Brotherhood of the Unicorn

The Brotherhood of the Unicorn

Wilfred L. B. Fraser

First published in paperback in Great Britain in 2006 by Hibiscus Publishing
a division of Hibiscus Communications

1 3 5 7 9 10 8 6 4 2

ISBN 0 9552665 0 5 (10 digit) and 978 0 9552665 0 8 (13 digit)

Typeset in Great Britain by SX Composing DTP, Rayleigh, Essex
Printed and bound in Great Britain by Bookmarque, Croydon, Surrey
Cover illustration by Louis Neubert, nowriter@hotmail.com
Cover design by Will Perrens, www.perrens.co.uk

Hibiscus Publishing
A division of Hibiscus Communications
www.hibiscuscommunications.net
admin@hibiscuscommunications.net

Dedicated to my sisters,
God bless them, every one of them.

There are stranger things in Heaven and Earth
Than angels without wings!

Part One

1

Jerry Slade was on his way to fetch fresh bread as he did every morning except Sunday. It was his last chore before breakfast, which he would have as soon as he returned. Then it would be a quick change and on to school.

Sister Ju had woken him as usual at seven o'clock, and he had already swept the yard clean of all the cedar blossoms that had fallen during the night and joined his older brother Ambrose for their morning dip in the river, which was mandatory except when it was raining.

This morning, he ran behind a metal hoop, which he propelled and controlled with the aid of a stick.

Running close behind and all around him was a white mongrel pup with occasional brown patches. His name was Sparkplug.

As they approached the crossroads of Salisbury and High Street, he saw a group of people standing almost in a circle, seemingly to avoid a part of the ground before them. His curiosity was immediately aroused. He grabbed hold of the hoop and ordered the pup to be quiet; he walked around the group but could not get a clear picture of what they were looking at.

Still holding on to his precious hoop, he squatted on his haunches to avail himself of a better view through their legs. He was very puzzled when he saw what the grown-ups were looking at.

Scattered on the ground as if flung into the crossing, was a

3

concoction of herbs, spices, fruits, flowers, and strangest of all, coins of different denominations.

So wrapped up was he as he tried to count the number of coins on the ground, which he now thought to be thirteen, that he was startled by someone standing very close behind him who was almost shouting to make himself heard.

"Make way there, stand aside!"

Jerry jumped out of the way to allow the speaker to pass. Walking towards the available space left by the small crowd was a white man who seemed to shuffle forward with an awkward gait. He was about six feet tall, with a long straight nose, bushy eyebrows and long brown hair. He wore a faded sleeveless blue shirt that left his arms bare from the shoulder. The shirt was very tight fitting and resembled a waistcoat. Khaki shorts and brown sandals completed his attire. The bath towel he was carrying in his hand, he now placed around his neck, holding on to the ends on either side.

Although he could be described as slim, he seemed fairly muscular and just about an inch or two from his shoulder he sported a brilliantly coloured tattoo of a huge bird that carried a fish in its talons.

The most noticeable thing about him was the way he walked, which suggested that he might have suffered a serious injury at sometime in his past. He seemed unable to bend his back either way.

As a result of this and to aid momentum, he swung his arms in an exaggerated military-like fashion.

"What is all of this?" he asked, and many voices spoke at once, each saying something different and consequently cancelling each other out.

The man eased forward a couple of places, which took him right into the middle of the thrown concoction.

"Don't!" shouted Miss Mala, who lived only a few doors away and had seen that sort of thing before.

"Get away man!" shouted Mr Poole, who was leaning heavily on his walking stick in an attempt to take the weight off his damaged right leg.

"Please don't stand in that thing," pleaded Miss Mala a second time.

"And why not?" said the man.

"Because," said Poole, "you'll be buying trouble."

The man muttered something in a language that nobody present understood, then unexpectedly, he bent both knees and with his head tilted slightly backwards, probably due to his inability to bend his back, he very slowly stooped towards the ground.

"Stop him somebody. Please!" It was Miss Mala again, but no one ventured in after him. By now the man's intention was quite clear to everyone.

"If you touch any of that mess, you'll be buying into whatever misery the bather was trying to get away from. This is obeah."

All the other voices had gone quiet when he started to speak. He was Ivan Pope, who lived near the communal cemetery and frequently carried a big book underneath his arm. Many of the locals saw him as some sort of a mystery man.

"What is this obeah? And what has it got to do with somebody's bath?" said the man, who incredibly, still held his stooping stance.

"It's a superstition mostly. The person who threw that mess there took a bath in it and probably chanted some incantation. He or she believes that anyone who takes all, or any part of what is on the ground, will be inheriting the troubles or whatever malady the person who threw it there might have," Ivan explained.

"Nonsense, stuff and damn nonsense!" said the man whose towel, loosely wrapped was still around his neck. He continued on his way to the ground. When he was close enough, he stretched both legs forward and placed his right hand on the ground to take his weight. Then, not unlike an acrobat, he bent his legs at the knees as if to aid elevation, and began picking up the coins around him, all the time, moving his body in a clockwise direction, negating the need for turning his head either way. In this way, he swivelled around until all the coins were picked up and with what seemed like a great effort, he rolled unto his side and slowly stood up again.

As soon as he had regained his balance, he slipped the coins into the side pocket of his trousers. Pulling hold of the towel still around his neck, he gave every indication of continuing his journey.

The crowd was now considerably larger than when Jerry first arrived, but now it parted in much the same way as their ancestors from the Middle Ages would have done, at the sound of the bell that warned that a leper was passing. No one wanted any physical contact with him, fearing possible contamination by touch. Everyone started talking at once, each voicing a different variation on the same theme.

All were agreed on one thing, one way or the other, the man was doomed. For the man's part, the look in his eyes, rather than anything to do with his legs, suggested a spring in his step.

"Damn mumbo jumbo," he said so all could hear. Taking one last look around as if to satisfy himself that he was finished there, he started whistling what sounded like a military march and continued on his way to the beach for his morning swim.

"Well, I tried to warn him," said Miss Mala, "he should put his house in order if he knows what's good for him."

Jerry waited until the man had gone about a hundred yards before going on to the shop for the bread, and just to be absolutely sure, he took great care to walk on the other side of the road.

That day at school, the spillage at the crossroad was the main topic of conversation between Jerry and his little friends, and he was the point of reference through which the story was checked and confirmed.

Lying in his bed that night Jerry had trouble sleeping. He could not keep his thoughts away from the event of the day. He wished that the man hadn't picked up those coins. What if the person who had taken the bath was going to die? Mr Poole as much as said afterwards that the man would most likely be dead instead of the bather.

Jerry knew the strange looking man; he had actually spoken to him once before, about a month earlier. It was a Saturday morning, perhaps his favourite day of the week; no school or going to church. So after he had assisted his brother with taking the animals to the pasture and had his breakfast, he had the rest of the morning to himself before he accompanied Sister Ju to the market.

Not long ago, Mrs Martin, who lived near the pasture, had had one of her chickens taken by the chicken hawk and Jerry, aided by Cousin Noah, had taken immediate steps to protect the chickens in his yard by making a slingshot. Actually, Cousin Noah made the slingshot with a lot of ignored tips from him. So, armed with his trusty weapon, he had gone into the small wooded area behind Mother Tina's house, hunting for birds or any dangerous animal he might come across.

He cut a comical figure as he imitated the stealthy approach he had seen in his one and only picture show of *Tarzan, Lord of the Jungle*, as a treat for his eighth birthday. Close on his heels, and making enough noise to incur the wrath of Sister Ju in church, was his dog Sparkplug.

The hunting party forged deeper into the woods. Jerry had his slingshot at the ready, the pebble pouched for a snappy shot should the occasion arise. All the time he listened and scanned the surrounding area.

"Quiet Sparky," said Jerry in a little over a whisper. Just about ten yards away a humming bird was hovering over a blossom, he took aim and fired but the bird flew off to another tree and another blossom a further six feet away. The dog was still active, but the bird seemed totally unconcerned by their presence. Jerry took another few steps forward and thought of Cousin Noah's instructions. "Take careful aim, then hold your breath, and release." This time, he followed the instructions to the letter.

He fired with spectacular success and the hummingbird fell to the ground.

"Bull's-eye!" he shouted, again aping the big game hunter. He ran to the spot where the slain bird had fallen, all the time expecting it to fly away, but of course it couldn't. He bent over the bird and after a little while tentatively picked it up and placed it within the palm of his other hand. He stared at it for a little while and instinctively, he began blowing over it in a vain attempt to make it breathe again. It was only then that he noticed the delicate pattern around its neck and the distinctive tuft at the front of the head.

The exhilaration he felt when the pebble impacted on the tiny bird had disappeared completely, replaced by a deep sorrow he could not understand or explain.

Sparkplug was now barking again and Jerry became aware for the first time of the strange looking man he had seen walking through the streets. He was leaning on a coconut tree nearby and was looking very carefully at him. He straightened and shuffled forward towards him.

"Well, Little Hunter, I think you've just had beginner's luck." He spoke in an unusual way that Jerry just about understood.

"But, but" stuttered Jerry.

"I know," said the man, "you didn't mean to kill it."

"No!" said Jerry quickly, "I didn't think I would hit it."

"The first rule of hunting, is never to fire at a prey unless you want to kill it," said the man. He rested his hand gently on the boy's shoulder. "Nobody can make it fly again Little Hunter."

"I was only practising for when the chicken hawk comes," said Jerry.

"The hawk, when it comes, will not stand like the hummingbird, he will circle slowly and when he picks his prey, he will fly down as quickly as you blink your eyes, and will fly away again just as quickly." He emphasized his point by snapping out his right hand and pulling it back again.

"To kill the hawk you must learn on moving targets," he advised.

"What's a moving target? asked Jerry.

The man smiled benignly and said, "you will learn Little Hunter, you will learn."

He could tell by the boy's body language that he was still hurting from having killed the bird.

"Now you feel bad for killing that bird but maybe it's worth it, if you learn not to take life away for fun."

He took the dead bird from Jerry's hand. "Nice dog you have Little Hunter," he said in parting and shuffled away whistling something that Jerry had never heard before.

The hunt was called off and the boy and dog made their way home to the big empty box underneath the house, which was now his den. Sister Ju was surprised to see them back so soon. After a little while, the silence began to make her anxious. She called him into the kitchen where she was busy kneading flour to make dumplings. "What's wrong Jer?" she asked. He said nothing.

"Whatever it is," she continued, "it can't be that bad."

"But it is!" The words came tumbling out of his mouth even as she spoke.

"Tell me about it," she said, and with a little further coaxing, he told her the whole story including his talk with the strange man.

"His name is Leopold," she said.

"That's a strange name," said Jerry.

"I know. They say he is from a place very far away called Portugal. They say he came to these islands with his ship and liked it so much, he decided to stay. They also said that before he came here, he was drifting from island to island."

"He speaks funny. Sometimes I have trouble understanding him," said Jerry.

"That's because of his foreign accent."

"What does that mean?"

"Well, where he comes from, they speak a different language, so when he is speaking English, he sounds a little like when he is speaking his own language, I guess."

He thought he understood what she meant, but he wasn't sure.

"Anyway," she said, "going back to the subject of the dead bird, Leopold was right, you should not fire on anything unless you mean to kill it, because if you end up wounding it, it will suffer a great deal, and I'm sure you don't want that, do you?"

"No!" he said quickly.

"Well, from now on, you'd do better if you practise on fruits hanging from trees, or even stones on the ground, if you are going to be ready for that chicken hawk when it comes."

Five minutes later the hunt was on again, only this time, it was in

9

his very own garden and there was no need for stealth, there were targets everywhere.

From an early age Jerry was made aware of the many superstitions common to his part of the world. His aunt Alicia, his dad's sister, was always telling him to be careful around mirrors, because if he broke one, he would have seven years of bad luck. Nor should he walk under ladders, because that too was bad luck.

"How many years bad luck will I get if I walk under the ladder?"

"Just never mind and see that you never do," she cautioned.

Then there was Mother Tina, as everyone called her. She was the local candy maker. She would always call Jerry or any other male around if her first customer of the day was a female. She said they brought her business bad luck, so she would hand the purchase to Jerry, who in turn would hand it over to the buyer. The buyer would then pay Jerry and he would pass the money back to Mother Tina. The object of the exercise being, that there would be no physical contact between her and the female customer.

After all that was done, he would be rewarded with a peanut cake, or stretch candy for his trouble. Also, he had seen that whenever Cousin Noah opened a bottle of rum or beer, he would always throw a little on the ground before drinking, and say, "to absent friends."

Then, there was old Mr Campbell who lived just a few doors away, for whom both Jerry and Ambrose ran errands.

"Stay away from silk-cotton trees," he had warned them on more than one occasion.

"What's wrong with silk-cotton trees," asked Ambrose.

"When I was a lad no bigger than you," he said, pointing at Jerry, "a man sheltering rain under the silk-cotton tree was struck by lightning and went mad. Evil spirits is what's wrong with it, they live there."

Even Sister Ju would always stop anyone at the dinner table from passing the pepper from hand to hand. She said to do so would cause friends to fall out with each other.

Earlier this year, when he'd been sick with chicken pox and was asleep during the afternoon, Aunt Alicia had woken him and helped him to sit up.

"You shouldn't be asleep while the dead is passing."

He could see the funeral procession through the window. Also, Miss Mala was quite sure that if food fell from a person's mouth while eating, that was a sure sign that they were cheating on their partner. But craziest of all, was old Miss Mable who lived alone and always kept a bowl of sand in front of her door at night, as a safeguard against being molested by 'loupgaroos'. This of course was a variation on the vampire theme, pronounced 'legaroos' by the locals. The theory being that once the 'legaroo' had entered the house, he must first count every grain of sand in the bowl before he can leave. Should the sun rise before he is finished counting, he would be stranded by the sunlight. To Jerry's knowledge, no 'legaroo' was ever caught on the entire island.

With all those confusing thoughts whirling around in his head, he wished that Mr. Leopold had not taken the coins at the crossroad. He wasn't sure why, but he liked him and didn't want anything bad to happen to him. More than that, he didn't want him to die as Miss Mala said he would. He had called him Little Hunter and he liked that. It had fitted in with his own idea of being a big game hunter, so when he said his prayers that night, he had asked Jesus as a special favour, not to let Mr Leopold die. He intended lighting a candle for him on Sunday when he went to church.

2

Father Raymond Devas checked his watch for the second time in the last five minutes. This time it was a quarter to six on Sunday morning, his busiest day of the week by far.

He was standing on Leapers Hill where he had stood every morning whenever his duties allowed, which fortunately for him, was almost all the time. He was waiting for sunrise.

He had been posted to the Caribbean in the early part of 1944, where he'd worked in St Vincent and enjoyed the island tremendously. He was pleasantly surprised to find it unspoilt and after the carnage he had recently seen in Europe, he took readily to the rugged, mountainous formation. One year on, he was transferred to Grenada. All he knew about it at that stage was that it was the most southerly of the Windward Islands.

He arrived in June 1945 and took up his appointment as parish priest of the Roman Catholic church in Sauteurs, a town in the most northerly parish of St Patrick. Where he found St. Vincent pleasant and enjoyable, Grenada simply took his breath away.

He was enchanted from the moment he landed on the pier at St. George's harbour. The more he saw of the lush vegetation and rugged terrain, the more in love with it he became. When asked by a colleague a few years on, how he liked the island, he said that someone had told him that in Grenada the stars hung much lower than anywhere else, and Father Devas had agreed.

From the tender age of five he had been a bird watcher. Up at five in the morning, armed with a pair of binoculars, he would sit in the church tower with his grandfather, who very carefully pointed out all the local species of birds.

He was hooked from then on and everyone including himself, thought that his career was in that direction. Later, he found another calling but he retained his passion for the study of birds. Now, he had the best of both worlds, with the opportunity to pursue his ambition to study tropical birds.

Years later, after his very prestigious and informative book, *Birds of Grenada*, he was regarded as one of the foremost authorities; some would say, the foremost authority on birds in Grenada.

On his first full day in the parish, he had risen earlier than usual, determined to get his bearings around his new home. After morning prayers, he stood in the yard listening to the dawn chorus of birds for a few minutes. It was still too dark to see the singers. Instinctively, he turned towards the cliff face of Leapers Hill, overlooking the ocean.

About a hundred yards away, he spotted a grotto and walked towards it. Inside was a statue of the Virgin Mary. A few candlesticks were placed at intervals around it, with two vases of recently wilted flowers on either side of them. He said a short prayer and returned to his former position. How long he stood there lost in thought, he had no idea.

He gradually became aware of a sudden increase in the light, realizing at the same time that the sun had broken the arc of the horizon. He stood rooted to the spot, totally lost in the wonder of the event. After that, his morning visits became a matter of routine.

Later that evening and every other evening since, he could be seen astride his B.S.A. motor cycle, making his way to Bedford Point, which offered an equally spectacular view of the sunset.

He glanced at his watch yet again and this time it was three minutes to six. He waited expectantly and once again he was surprised by the intensity of his excitement, given the fact that he had stood here every morning it had been possible during the last two years.

13

Any moment now, he thought, and his attention was drawn to the rays preceding the rising, prickling through the clouds and shooting upwards and across the horizon, forming a pattern not unlike the top part of the stone on which Moses received the commandments. It also reminded him of the incredible lighting that characterized the biblical paintings, which hung on the walls of the family home in Derbyshire and in the church where he served as an altar boy.

The magical moment had finally arrived. As the sun emerged as though from the depths of the ocean, the part of it that was visible resembled the moon in its first quarter. Yet, it projected enough light that spiralled along the surface of the water, as if someone had suddenly punched on all the switches.

In his mind's eye, he could see an angel, perhaps Gabriel, standing behind the sun and holding it up like an Olympic torch, signalling the start of the celestial games.

He felt some discomfort and realized that, overawed by the spectacle, he had been holding his breath. He breathed out slowly, allowing his gaze to follow the light across the land and eventually, over the mountains.

Ten minutes after the rising he was still on the hill, but now he was leaning against the wall that separated the cemetery from the schoolyard, as if the experience had drained some of his strength. He wondered, not for the first time, if the event that gave the hill its name, was pre-ordained or simply coincidental.

When Christopher Columbus arrived in Grenada in 1492, he named it Conception Island. Unlike any of the other islands in the region, it stayed un-colonized for about one hundred years, possibly because of its size; but many experts believed the real reason to be the fierce reputation of the Caribs, who, according to rumours, had driven away the peaceful Arawaks and were now in residence on the island. Later, the Spaniards changed the name to Grenada because the terrain reminded them of Granada in Spain.

The sovereignty of these islands was usually determined by who held the balance of military power in Europe, which at that particular time was disputed between the crown heads of England and France.

In 1651 the French were in residence in Grenada and it wasn't long before they discovered that the reputation of the Caribs as fighters was well earned. The garrison commander was fighting a war that was new to him. His men were constantly harassed in night forays by an unseen enemy. He decided to put a stop to it and to that end made the necessary arrangements.

Leaving a small force behind, he led his men in a running battle against a surprised enemy. Many skirmishes were fought. Gradually, the advantage swung the way of the soldiers who had carried rations, while their hotly perused adversaries who depended on hunting for their food were unable to do so in the face of such relentless pursuit.

Valiant as the struggle was, the inevitable happened and the Caribs were trapped with their backs to the sea. The soldiers decided to wait until morning when there would be more light and placed a cordon in semi-circular fashion, cutting off any means of escape.

The next morning at sunrise, maintaining the same formation, they converged slowly on their trapped foe. The Caribs held their position until the soldiers were close enough, as if curious to see them in the cold light of day. The soldiers moved closer.

With a signal from their leader, rather than being taken as slaves, the Carib men took the children in their arms and followed their women over the precipice, and unto the jagged rocks a hundred feet below. As a result, the town was named, Bourg des Sauteurs, which translated to, the Town of Leapers. The hill became, Leapers Hill.

As the priest walked the short distance back to the presbytery where he must prepare for the morning's high mass, his thoughts turned to the ritualistic dumping at the crossroad. Preachers of all the other churches in the parish had already addressed the disturbing practice. He had waited as long as he had, because he wanted to learn as much as he could before facing his flock.

He had never favoured the 'fire and brimstone' approach, but he was also aware that he was duty bound to address the practice of devil worship. He still had much to think about before mass.

On re-entering the house, he put out a handful of breadcrumbs and left-over rice for the birds and closed the door of the sacristy behind him.

3

Jerry was number ten out of a family of eleven children. His last sister, Millie, was born in Aruba shortly after his mother's arrival there and was his only junior. Indeed, by the time he came along, two of his older sisters had already been married and had their own families and homes and Jerry found himself in the embarrassing situation of having a nephew six years older than he was.

He had no recollection of his mother who had emigrated to the Dutch Caribbean island of Aruba when he was only eleven months old. Before travelling, she had been housekeeper for ten years to the then local magistrate, an Englishman by the name of Whitley. By way of a reward for her years of dedicated service, he had used his influence to secure for her a domestic contract with an American family in Aruba.

Embracing the opportunity, she had taken her daughter Beth out of school to look after Jerry. After bidding a tearful farewell to her family, like others before her, she set off to help them the only way she knew how.

As Jerry grew older and stronger, the highlight of his day was always the moment when his dad walked into the house after a long day searching for animals to slaughter. His dad was one of three local butchers.

Jerry and his brother Ambrose would stand at the window, staring through the glass in the darkening gloom, listening for the clip-clop of Gooney, the donkey that their father rode.

When at last he came in, he would embrace them all in turn, always leaving Jerry until last, pretending that he had forgotten him, then turning around suddenly, he would lift him up and cuddle him, pressing his face so close to his, that Jerry could feel the bristle on his cheek and smell the tobacco he used in his pipe.

"And how is my little man today?" he would ask, sitting him on his lap as he sat at the table, while his dinner was being warmed up. That being done, the boys would help themselves to something from his plate. Only then would he add pepper and begin eating.

After dinner, he would enquire into everyone's day. When it was Jerry's turn, he would again sit him on his lap and ask, "What did this little man learn today?" and the boy would show off with whatever nursery rhyme, or tables, or stories he might have learnt, waiting impatiently for the praise he knew would follow.

On Saturday mornings, the family went down to the stall in the market place where the meat and blood pudding was sold, all except Juliette and Jerry, who went in later in the day.

By the time Jerry got to the market, Ambrose would normally be finished with whatever chores he might have had and together they would explore the market. They heeded the customary caution from Sister Ju, to stay away from the main road, which now boasted continuous traffic with about one vehicle every ten to fifteen minutes.

Should Ambrose be occupied, Jerry would enjoy sitting on the waterfront near to the stall, watching the pelicans dive-bombing the fish in the harbour. Sometimes, he would concentrate on one bird and try to count how many attempts it made and how successful it was, by how many times it swallowed. By now he had become so familiar with the local fishing boats, he could identify most of them by their trim.

One of his favourite pastimes was watching the fishermen in the boat cast their net in a wide arc across the bay, and then pulled in slowly by two teams of mostly men, about one to two hundred yards apart on the shore.

On odd occasions, he and his brother, together with other children, would take hold of the rope behind the grown-ups as they pulled the fish in. Jerry liked to pretend that he was in a tug of war and always on the winning side.

As the net got nearer, it would sometimes bulge if it was a good catch and the captive fish could be seen jumping about in the net, in a vain attempt to escape.

Afterwards, still with his brother, they would wonder through the vendors, who knew them well and would sometimes give them small treats. The market abounded with everything for domestic uses, but the boys were only interested in things that were edible.

They always left the most exciting places for last; forbidden places such as McSwill's rum bar. They would hang around outside listening to the music from within played by an impromptu band, made up of different individuals, some of whom might be total strangers. On average, at least once during the afternoon there was the inevitable fist fight which was exactly what they hoped to see. And finally, on to Main Street which, by then, was bursting with activity.

As they entered the street they turned left to look at the Catholic church which sat on the south side of Leapers Hill and totally dominated that part of the town. At the bottom of the hill on the same side was Parks Produce Company, its main business being, cocoa beans, nutmegs, mace, cloves, and many other spices, leaving the visitor in no doubt as to why Grenada is known as the Isle of Spice.

The post office on the other side of the road leading to the market came next, and it boasted the greatest activity, as each Saturday, a different set of workers queued to collect their wages.

Further down the road was Bata's Store, which supplied shoes for all the family. Almost directly opposite was Gleans' Garage, the chief motor maintenance centre in the whole parish. Moving back up the hill, still on the opposite side of the street, were other big stores such as Supply, Grandby's, and Lalsingh's.

But all that was forgotten as the boys heard the familiar sound of

Dabo's bell. Dabo was the advertising man who nearly always wore a sandwich board, which featured whatever film was being shown at the cinema, or a dance, local concert, or even a cricket or football match.

Now he made his way to his usual spot in front of the post office, near the teachers from all around the parish, who were waiting to be paid.

During the past year Dabo had endured two embarrassing incidents, the second of which earned him enough notoriety to cause his dismissal from the job that some suspected he would have done for nothing.

Dabo had a wonderful rapport with his fans who very often showed their appreciation by buying him bottles of beer. The problem usually arose after he had consumed some or all of the gifts, when he would make really outrageous claims about whatever he was advertising, often in very risqué language.

In the first incident, he was jazzing up a feature film entitled *Tars and Spars*, concerning two dim-witted song and dance sailors, who attracted disaster like a magnet. After the beers, Dabo covered the official posters with blank paper and began selling the film as *Tarzan Spars*.

That night the cinema was crowded with locals eagerly anticipating the heroics of the ape-man. The scene that followed might have been funny if there were not so many angry people demanding a refund.

To pacify his customers the proprietor promised to allow ticket holders to attend a future programme of their choice.

The second incident occurred on the Saturday before carnival. Dabo had a far bigger audience than usual and got carried away after too many beers and the encouragement of rapturous applause.

He was advertising a dance given by the Forester's Lodge, which was one of the social events of the year. He waxed lyrically about everything including music to make you dance even if you were on crutches, the quality of the buffet, the attending musicians and even the condition of the candle-waxed dance floor and to top it off, he insisted that men, dressed only in their ties, and women, only in their stockings, would be admitted.

All of Dabo's listening fans knew this to be a comical embellishment, but the damage was done.

The vengeance of the members was swift, and they used their well developed moralistic muscles to see to it that Dabo never worked again, for bringing the Lodge into disrepute; least ways, not as an advertising man. But such was his charisma and influence, that he was reinstated on one condition. No more outrageous embellishments.

Some wit at McCloud's suggested that Dabo would most likely be on probation for the rest of his working days.

Back to the stall and the highlight of the day. Spending money. Jerry received the usual shilling and proceeded to spend it in the usual way. One Bain's soda and one roti for three pence each, one ice cream for two pence and four pence left over for stretch candy during the week. By the time he was tucked in that night, he was always exhausted, but very happy.

The Anglican church clock chimed six thirty, but Jerry was already awake. He loved Sundays almost as much as Saturdays. Ambrose was already outside and he could hear him urging Annie the cow along to the pasture. He stayed in his bed and listened to the street come alive. This was a luxury allowed only on those two mornings.

On these days, he was exempted from his mandatory dip in the river. He had a long, luxurious stretch, and wondered what they would be having for breakfast. Even now he could hear Sister Ju in the kitchen, as she took her breakfast preparations as far as she could for now. No one was allowed to eat before mass.

Jerry and his entire family had taken their seats in the third pew along from the pulpit. Sister Ju liked to hear what father had to say.

Father Devas stood silently on the pulpit for all of ten seconds. He had deliberately continued his silence even after the congregation had

21

settled down. At length, he cleared his throat and crossed himself while he intoned, "In the name of the Father, and of the Son, and of the Holy Ghost." The congregation answered, "Amen."

"In the two years that I have been serving as your parish priest," he began, "I always hoped that despite our daily fumbles, we were all of us striving to do God's work. I still do. But I would be failing in my duty as your priest if I did not convey to you the gravity of the sin of worshipping false Gods. I refer of course, to the ritualistic dumping at the crossroads of Salisbury and High Street not so long ago."

He continued to address the subject at some length and, unusually for him, he forcibly banged the pulpit on a number of occasions.

Jerry's interest had wandered. After a while, he started swapping eye signals with his classmate Wally. Sister Ju nudged him with her elbow and opened her eyes wide at him. He settled down.

All through the week the priest had agonized about finding a way to make his point so that they would all understand. Standing on the hill while waiting for the sun to rise, he had prayed for divine assistance. Now he continued.

"In a village near where I lived in England, there was an ordinary family, a husband, a wife, and one son. They were decent God fearing folks who attended church regularly, always doing their bit within the community. The war came and her husband did his duty to his country, and joined the army. Unfortunately, he was one of the early losses. Not too long afterwards, her son became ill and badly needed an operation but it was very difficult, as most of the doctors were also serving their country, doing what they could for the men wounded at the front.

"She was beside herself with worry. Her son was all she had left, so she spent a great deal of time on her knees, asking God to save him.

On one such occasion during a sudden thunderstorm, a stranger knocked on her door to seek shelter. She showed him into the parlour and excused herself, and resumed her praying.

When the storm was over, the man thanked her and left. Not long after, without the operation, her son died.

At the funeral the man introduced himself as her new neighbour. It turned out that he specialized in the very illness from which her son died."

"As painful as it is, there is a lesson to be learnt here. Ordinarily, that poor woman would have known about her neighbour. She would most certainly have offered him a cup of tea, and passed the time of day with him, but because of her preoccupation with her son's illness, perhaps understandingly so, she was not as civil to the man as she might have been; if she had, she may have saved her son. You see, the question we have to ask ourselves is, how much do we trust God or Allah or Buddha or Jehovah? Different people call him by many names, but in the end he is the same thing to all of us."

"The point I am trying to make is that if that poor, grief stricken woman had left her problem with God once she had told him about it, and tried still to be neighbourly, things may have turned out differently. After all, he has to listen to all the prayers all over the world."

Here he took the opportunity to lighten the mood just a little. "And many of them are in foreign languages." A flicker of a smile touched his face. "Seriously, we all of us pray to God for various reasons and we are always hopeful that our prayers will be answered but I don't think it's as simple as that."

"Take a simple example; there is one job available and it's now down to two young men, one as desperate as the other for the job that would make such a difference to their lives and that of their families. Both their mothers have prayed for her son's success. Even for God that would be a dilemma. He is all knowing and all seeing, but some problems are more urgent than others. If we allow him the time, he will get to us. He is well aware of all our needs and remember, he works in mysterious ways."

Once again, he took a lengthy pause and tried to make eye contact with as many of his congregation as he could. "Once you have told him your problems, allow him the time to answer. There may be some of you, who, in the interest of quick results turn to dark forces and surrender your immortal souls to the devil, but his message is quite clear. 'Thou shalt have no other Gods but me.' In the name of the Father, and of the Son, and of the Holy Ghost." As before, the congregation said, "Amen."

Jerry relaxed. Sunday was the only day when the family ate meals together, but more importantly, it was the only day he was allowed to help himself. As soon as they were out of the church, he asked, "What's for breakfast," and Sister Ju gave him the same answer he always got whenever he asked.

"I'm not running a hotel."

Finally, the call came, "breakfast!"

He stood for a few seconds looking at the table, and from his expression, one would have guessed that he wasn't disappointed with what he saw. On his plate he placed one piece of blood pudding, two fried bakes, and two fish cakes. He paused for a while. It was at this point that his dad used to say, "That's enough for now Jer, you don't want to be too heavy when you dive into the river."

He poured himself a cup of hot chocolate from the teapot, but before sitting down, he asked, "what's for dinner?"

Sundays were always kind of special to both Jerry and Ambrose; special because they always spent it with their dad. They always accompanied him down to the river where they joined their little friends and frolicked in the late morning sun. While they played their dad shaved and washed his hair. Then it was their turn to have their hair washed with the same cactus soap that he had picked at the roadside on his way down to the river and used on himself.

Afterwards, they searched underneath the stones for crayfish sometimes, having to dive for better access. Then it was on to Scotty for soda and coconut tart.

On this particular Sunday however, they bypassed Scotty. It was Jerry's seventh birthday, and the boys were told to prepare themselves for a big surprise. After dinner, the whole family except Millie, who,

24

because of the lack of space in the family home, stayed with their grandmother, made the short distance of a few hundred yards, to view the new three- bedroom house on High Street, which was finally completed and into which they could now move from the house on Salisbury Street.

He charged through his new home, revelling in the new found space that had been at a premium in the old house. Ambrose would never find him now when they played hide and seek.

4

Jerry's idyllic existence continued unabated for another year after they had moved into the new house.

Shortly after his eighth birthday, his dad came home with two goats and one kid about three months old. The odd purchase was a package deal; without the kid's inclusion, the old lady would not have sold.

A similar situation to this had arisen once before, where the boys had looked after a sheep that was little more than a lamb.

The conflict of interest came when it was time for the sheep to be slaughtered. By then the boys had very originally named it Baba, and made a family pet out of it. Their dad, trying to solve the dilemma, compromised by swapping Baba for some other animal from a rival butcher, taking a loss in the transaction. Even so, there was an atmosphere of gloom around the home for a few weeks. With that in mind, he gave strict instructions that the kid not be given a name.

Jerry adopted the kid right from the word go and his dad gave him total control of its welfare. One day, their dad heard Ambrose refer to it as Billy. He called him over and in a very serious tone, said, "I thought I said that this animal must not be given a name?"

"But, but Daddy," stuttered Ambrose, "we haven't given him a name, he is a billy-goat." His dad quickly got his handkerchief out and pretended to wipe his face, he didn't want the boy to see his smile spread all across it.

If you listened to the locals, Steadman Slade had one flaw, a flaw that all the children in the neighbourhood would have wanted their dad to have. He was obsessive about the welfare of his children and did not agree with the tradition of automatic physical punishment of an errant child by an adult, mainly because of his age.

The next Sunday followed the usual pattern but yet again they did not stop at Scotty's but they were not disappointed. There would be plenty of sodas and coconut tarts at the cricket match they were attending with their dad that afternoon.

The match was between the local team, Dreadnought, and the visitors, Buccaneers, both names suggesting the warrior spirit of the players.

The boys soon joined the other children in a game of softball, while their dad, in the company of his friends, cheered the home team.

In the early gloom of the evening, the home team emerged victorious and the three of them sang in celebration of the victory all the way home. Later, Jerry fell asleep on his dad's lap and the last thing he heard that night was his voice. "Come on little man, yours was a busy day." It was the end of another perfect day.

These halcyon days continued on in this way for a few more months, until one afternoon Jerry came home from school and saw Gooney in the yard.

"That can only mean one thing", he thought, "daddy's home".

He ran to the house calling out as he went. "Daddy, daddy, where are you?" But his dad was not sitting in the front room as he expected.

"I'm in here Jer," he answered from the bedroom. The boy found him lying in bed.

"Daddy, are you sick?"

"Not really son, I'm just a bit tired and need to rest for a while."

Jerry sat on the bed and asked lots more questions. His dad put his hand on his head and said, "And what did my little man learn today, eh?" All the time he was trying to keep the pain from his voice.

Jerry rattled off his four times tables but instead of the usual fuss, he patted him on the head and said, "Well done, I have a very smart son."

The next day Jerry rushed home from school knowing his dad was home. He ran into the bedroom but before he could speak, Sister Ju put her finger to her lips, signalling him to be quiet. Later, when he saw his dad he didn't ask about his day but instead, asked him to sing the nursery rhyme, *Twinkle, Twinkle, Little Star*. When he was finished, he said, "That's a good boy. Now Jer, leave me to sleep for a little while."

All that evening there were people in and out of the house, coming to visit his dad. That night before bed, they wouldn't allow him to say goodnight. His Aunt Alicia said daddy wasn't feeling too good at the moment and he would see him in the morning.

Lying in the bed next to his brother that night, he sensed that something was terribly wrong but he had no idea how serious it was. Thinking about his dad and how he looked, he cried silent tears, not knowing what to say to his brother if he asked him why.

Next morning, he was up much earlier than usual, but there were already lots of people in the house, but strangest of all, even though it was still dark outside, Ambrose was nowhere to be found. He got out of bed and went into the front room and Sister Ju, seeing him coming, ran forward and hugged him very tight. He looked into her face.

"What's the matter? Why are you crying?"

She just kept rocking him from side to side, all the time murmuring, "It's all right Jer, it's going to be all right, I promise."

After a while she led him away and sat with him on the stairs and took a long time telling him that daddy had passed on during the night. With a somewhat puzzled look on his face, he asked, "passed on where?" But before she could answer, Ambrose, who for the last hour had been sitting underneath the house, came forward slowly and said. "He is dead Jer, Daddy is dead."

"Dead, dead how?" There was a look of disbelief on his face.

"I'm so sorry Jer, the doctor said it was pneumonia and he couldn't make him better," Sister Ju said. He remained in her embrace for a while but the confused look on his face was an accurate reflection of his thoughts and neither went away for a long time.

Because everybody he saw in the house was crying, he cried himself, more in sympathy with the others than for his own grief, for as yet he had still to comprehend the full majesty of death. He had still to realize that the focus of his young life was lost to him forever.

The reason for his confusion was because he had often heard them refer to people who were dead, as, "having passed on," or, "that the person was finally asleep, or gone away," all of which suggested that the person might come back, just as his mom would some day.

He didn't have the miracle of modern day technology that his twenty-first century descendants would take for granted, and consequently lacked their worldly knowledge and wisdom. In his whole street there were only two radios, conspicuous by the long bamboo aerial, which at that time was the ultimate status symbol.

The technology which would deliver television, computers, and the most sought after of them all, the mobile phone, was still regarded as science fiction.

His confusion was deepened when he ran into Mrs Chase, who owned a store on Main Street and who helped out in the church.

"Never mind son, you'll see your dad again one day," she said to him. But it was a day or two before he truly comprehended the full enormity of what had happened; that his dad was gone forever, without him having had the chance to say goodbye to him.

Nothing that he had experienced before could have prepared him for the pain, turmoil and grief that he now felt.

Perhaps he may have understood had he been allowed to see his dad's body, but he was protected from that, just as he was protected at the cemetery from witnessing the actual burial. Sitting in his den, he let out a heart-rending scream, which echoed through the immediate neighbourhood.

When Juliette found him it took a long time in her embrace before his sobbing subsided and his body stopped shaking.

She spoke very softly to him, reminding him of how very much daddy loved him and this was the time for him to show that he was indeed 'his little man'. Although he felt somewhat calmer, it didn't stop him from vomiting all over himself, and his doting bigger sister.

Afterwards, a strange transformation occurred. He went from a very happy, healthy, noisy and active little boy, with a better than average appetite, to one who only spoke when he was spoken to. His school attendance that was always excellent suffered, as did his work.

When he was at home, he spent nearly all of his time in his den. Most worrying of all, he had to be coaxed into eating something at mealtimes.

For his part he didn't want to be a little man if his dad wasn't there. He missed the feel of his stubble against his face, the smell of his tobacco, the comfort and security of sitting in his lap, but most of all, he missed him coming home at the end of the day. He had finally realized why he loved the river so much on Sundays but hated it on other mornings.

Another month went by with no obvious improvement in his condition and his weight loss was a constant source of worry for his sisters. Juliette decided it was time to seek professional help and took him to see Dr MacSwing, whose reputation with the local people was one of prescribing powder, salts, and medicine as a cure-all.

He listened to her patiently, though he understood her problem. He was, after all, the doctor who had attended to their father. When she was finished, he muttered something unintelligible, at the same time sitting Jerry on his lap and gently stroked his head.

"I am so very sorry," he said. "The pity of it is that there is nothing that I can give you that will help him, but you must do all you can to get him to eat. The weight-loss in such a small boy is very worrying. What he needs is something or someone who can lure him out from wherever he has withdrawn to."

She pondered what the doctor had said for most of the night, but no immediate solution came to mind. The next morning, she saw Jerry standing at the window watching Ambrose as he took the animals out, and she had a brainwave.

She roused him at seven o'clock the next morning, and explained to him that the animals were too much for one person to look after and she needed him to help Ambrose by taking care of the two sheep and the lamb, as well as Billy. He was to tie them out in the morning, water them during the day and get them home in the evening.

Success was partial and gradual and Jerry's eating improved, but he ate barely half as much as he used to. He also spent less time sleeping or sitting in his den and even his school attendance was slightly better.

Juliette was delighted and thanked God for small mercies. On the debit side, he was still having bad dreams some nights and still didn't say much by way of conversation. Once or twice when she had made him say his prayers, from force of habit, he had asked God to bless his daddy. She knew he was on the mend but that there was still some way to go before he'd be the old Jerry again.

Sometimes, when the boys went to sleep Ambrose could hear his little brother mumbling in his sleep and occasionally cried out when he had a bad dream. Like the rest of the family, he was very concerned about Jerry and became even more protective towards him. He also allowed him unlimited time with Gooney and even gave him access to some of his things that were out of bounds before.

On the weekend, Jerry's sister, Marigold, was going to Miss Angeline's to collect a new dress. The house was very quiet and she thought the boys were in the pasture but as she was leaving she heard Jerry coughing from his den. She called out to him and despite his reluctance, took him along with her.

On arrival, they found Miss Angeline underneath the house feeding a bitch that only a few days before had given birth to a litter of seven puppies.

Jerry was fascinated with them and wanted to know why they

31

were all blind. Miss Angeline explained that all puppies were born this way but promised him they would all be able to see in a few days.

When the women went upstairs to fit the dress, he stayed with the puppies and was still there when Marigold was ready to leave. The women exchanged glances.

"I suppose", Marigold said, "that all these puppies are spoken for?"

"Not all," said Miss Angeline. "There are still a couple left," and hardly stopping for breath, she asked, "would you like one of the puppies Jerry?"

"Would I?" he breathed. "Oh yes please."

"In that case, you can choose one of the two that's left and you can collect it when it is old enough to leave its mother, in another month or so."

On the way home Marigold could hardly keep up with him, his enthusiasm for the pup had caught her completely by surprise. She knew that he just couldn't wait to tell Ambrose about it.

There was some urgency about everything he did in the month leading up to the time when he would take delivery of the pup. He woke up in the mornings without too much coaxing and his school attendance was almost back to normal. More significantly, he always got back early from school so he could spend an hour at Miss Angeline's with the pup every day. Every evening he would come home with a different name for him.

On the morning he was due to pick up the pup, he had taken the sheep to the pasture and was now taking Billy to the bottom of Mother Tina's garden where there was plenty of vegetation. He stooped to secure Billy's picket to the ground and stayed longer than usual in that position. He was daydreaming about the pup.

In the meantime instead of feeding, Billy was standing quite still as if measuring the distance between them. Suddenly, he leapt forward off a short run and butted Jerry squarely on the bottom, tossing him forward to land on his stomach. He remained still for a few seconds and despite the pain in his rear, started laughing. "Well," he said to Billy, "that's twice you have butted me; the first and the last time."

Fortunately, no real harm was done, although he remained standing in class all that day.

Marigold accompanied Jerry when it was time to collect the pup. She wanted to be sure that he thanked Miss Angeline properly as well as promising to take good care of it. On that night and many others that followed, the boys tried out names for the puppy on each other but none was considered appropriate.

In the meantime, Jerry and the pup were inseparable, except when he went to school or church. He tried his utmost to get the pup into the bedroom at nights but Juliette was having none of it. It was decided that he would sleep on the mat in front of the back door. For the first month, despite his protest, she forbade him from taking the pup with him when he took out the animals. She said it would distract him too much.

One afternoon after school, he had slipped quietly by the pup and went into the house to get out of his school clothes.

Juliette was in the yard spreading out the day's washing. Not only could he not find his clothes, more importantly, he couldn't find the contents of his pockets, which he wasn't allowed to take to school.

He called out to her to find out where they were and immediately, the little mongrel sat up and pricked his ears.

"Your clean clothes are on the sofa and your things are on the washing board under the calabash tree," she replied.

He went out to the tree and on the washboard were a few buttons, six transparently patterned marbles, four soda corks, and a small ball of twine. "My spark plug is missing," he shouted. At the sound of his young master's voice, the pup ran towards him.

"What was that?"

"My spark plug – it's missing."

The pup tilted his head and made a pathetic sound.

"I don't know, I left everything in the same place. What is that thing anyway?"

"It's a spark plug, they put them in the engines of cars."

This time the pup literally jumped up and down.

Jerry, who had noticed his antics, walked about ten feet away and said, "Sparkplug!"

The dog ran towards him and started jumping up and down again. He laughed, all the time running away from the following pup, and calling, "Sparkplug, come here boy!" Finally, the pup had got its name.

"What made you choose that name?"

"I didn't, he chose it himself," said Jerry.

"I declare," she said, shaking her head and smiling.

The frolicking continued long after the naming, inside the house and outside, down to the garden and back underneath the house, and all the time the sound of the boy's laughter intermingled with the pup's barking.

Juliette remembered how worried they all were about losing their little brother only a short time ago. He had become a sad little boy, now he was just a little boy again. She offered up a quiet prayer. "God bless you Sparkplug."

Jerry was exercising his recently gained privilege of riding Gooney while Sparkplug brought up the rear. Before long, there were four of his friends queuing for rides – Wally and Lynton from his class, and Billy and Elton from the Anglican school.

He very quickly realized that this was a lucrative opportunity and almost anything was accepted in exchange for rides. Fruits, marbles, skipping ropes and whenever possible, farthings, were all part of his bounty.

He further expedited matters so that up to four boys could ride the huge donkey at the same time. Gooney tolerated the intrusion into his feeding time for about half an hour, then without warning, broke into a fast trot that developed into a gallop and suddenly dug his front hooves into a stop and very effectively, ejected the intruders from his back. Far from being apprehensive, the boys looked forward to ejection time.

After he had counted his takings, it was time to take the other animals home, so leaving Gooney behind for Ambrose to take home he joined his friend Elton who was heading in the same direction.

The boys were playing catch, throwing the ball back and forth as they went, with Sparkplug somewhere in the middle trying to catch it. On one occasion, it flew above Jerry's head and he raced Sparkplug to retrieve it. The ball was lodged within an aperture underneath a fairly large stone and scattered all around the entrance were bird feathers. Jerry was immediately intrigued and called Elton over. "Look at all those feathers, how do you think they got there?"

"Oh, I thought you knew – that's where the General hides to catch the swallows as they fly by," said Elton.

"Who is the General?"

"It's not who – the General is a big one eyed, wild ginger cat."

He held up his hands on either side of his chest to indicate how big.

"Why is he called the General?"

"That's what everybody calls him," said Elton. "Every year when the swallows come, he appears and disappears when they are gone. Look over there at the telephone wire."

Jerry glanced at the telephone posts scattered all along the road. In all, there were six strands of wire attached to the poles and each strand sagged with the weight of the birds as they rested between forays while they fed upon the insects in the open field.

"Have you ever seen him?"

"No, but my dad has. He said that the General waits patiently and pounces as the birds fly close by. He says it's as big as a dog."

"Ah, come on," laughed Jerry, "you are telling a fat one."

"Well, that's what my dad says. He saw it and you never."

Jerry picked up a few of the feathers and put them in his pocket. "See you," he said, leaving Elton, having to run now to make up the lost time.

After he had taken the sheep home, because he needed to hurry

35

he locked Sparkplug in the kitchen and ran away to fetch Billy who was tied at a different location from the sheep. Even so, he was still running a little late so he decided to use the shortcut through Banana Hollow.

Halfway along he came upon Alfie's house. Alfie was a bachelor aged about thirty, who lived by himself and who was often in disputes with his neighbours for unsociable behaviour. He kept a black mongrel dog by the name of Atila, who had already bitten one child. The parents took him to court, where he was fined and told to keep the dog tied up until after dark.

Jerry had Billy on a short lead beside him for obvious reasons.

Suddenly, Atila started barking and Jerry's first reaction was to run but before he could get started, the dog came walking from around the corner and blocked his path. Petrified, he dropped Billy's rope without realizing it.

Atila came within six feet of where he stood. He bared his teeth and the hairs along his neck stood up, but most ominously, a low menacing growl came from deep in its throat.

Jerry was willing Alfie forward to call off the dog but he was nowhere to be seen. All that time Billy was standing quite still at Jerry's side. He had grown quite considerably from the kid that his dad had brought home more than a year ago. His big brown eyes and his horns, which were already about an inch long, dominated his face.

Jerry was close to panicking. He thought of running back down the track but was afraid of triggering Atila, who so far had been standing menacingly still.

The drama that unfolded around him over the next few seconds was like a dream. Billy, from a standing position, had moved quickly and butted Atila squarely on the nose. The dog, surprised by the sudden burst of violence, cowered his way underneath the house and to safety.

The butting ability Billy had displayed throughout his growth had finally paid off. Jerry, who learnt quickly from his mistakes, never used the shortcut again without Billy at his side and whether by design or good luck, they were never attacked again.

When they got home, he stole some of Annie's grass and fed it to Billy, for his courage in the face of the enemy.

5

Jerry was on a fast run to the game that was being played in the pasture when old Mr Campbell stopped him and sent him to Miss Murray's for tobacco.

"Such a shame about Leopold, nobody seems to know where he is," she said to Poole as she handed him his tobacco.

"Well," answered Poole, "them that will not hear must feel, everyone tried to tell him but he put mud in his ear."

"They say his back door is still open, but no one has seen him all week," continued Miss Murray.

"You mark my words, they won't see that one again. You cannot mock the spirits," Poole said with great conviction. Having had his say he pocketed his tobacco and left the shop.

The news that Mr Leopold was missing, maybe even dead, instantly depressed the boy. When he entered the kitchen, Juliette knew immediately that something had happened. "What is it Jer? What's wrong?" she asked anxiously.

He was staring at the floor in front off him, but didn't respond. She repeated the question, this time holding him by the shoulders. Still looking at the floor, he said, "Mr Leopold is missing, and Mr Poole said he might be dead."

"Oh!" She was instantly angry. "I could strangle that man and giggle while I'm doing it. He thinks he knows everything. Nobody knows what happened to Leopold. He comes and he goes as he pleases. Anytime now you'll hear him whistling and he will think everybody was crazy."

He gave her the suggestion of a smile but he was far from convinced.

That night, for the first time in a while, he had trouble sleeping. He thought about the time he had killed the humming bird and how kind Mr Leopold was to him. He had called him Little Hunter.

"Please God," he prayed, let Mr Poole be wrong, don't let Mr Leopold be dead."

Another week went by and despite himself he began to accept the popular opinion. Perhaps they were right and he was dead. He wondered whose place he had taken by picking up those coins.

The police had checked and found that most of his things were still in the house. No one could explain why the back door had been left open. That was what had started the rumours in the first place.

The Sunday following, Jerry and Elton had just climbed down from Mother Tina's plum tree with their pockets bulging. They were on their way to watch Ambrose's team play football.

They both heard the whistling at the same time and Jerry waited anxiously to see if Sister Ju's prediction was correct. Even though he thought he recognized the whistling, he was still a little surprised when Leopold came round the bend; very pleasantly so, in fact.

"Look!" said Elton. "It's Mr Leopold and they said he was dead."

In his excitement he had spoken much louder than he intended and it was clear that Leopold had heard him. He headed straight for them.

"And who is dead?" asked Leopold.

"They, they say," stuttered Jerry.

Leopold cut him off before he could continue. "And who is they?"

He was standing with both hands on his waist with his fingers almost meeting in the middle of his back and held his head at a tilted angle, the better to see the boys.

"Mr Poole said you were dead," said Jerry quietly.

39

"I don't know how that old fool finds his way home," said Leopold.

"Mr Poole said" began Elton.

"Stop!" Leopold seemed somewhat agitated. He had heard the news of his premature death the moment he stepped off the bus. "Do you think that Leopold dies so easily? Do you know who I am?" He pointed his finger at each of the boys in turn.

"How old are you?"

"Nine," they said in unison.

"When I was only two years older than you, I was hunting wolves through the snow with my grandfather. When I was seventeen, I hunt treasure ships in ocean filled with sharks."

He touched his chest with the index finger of his left hand. "I have looked into the eyes of the unicorn. Do they think some damn mumbo jumbo could kill me?"

For the first time, Jerry noticed that his eyes were piercing green. He had never seen anyone with green eyes before. "What's a unicorn?"

"It's a mythical creature."

Seeing the lack of understanding in their faces, he tried to explain.

"A magical creature like a horse, with a horn in the middle of its head. Well, I have looked into its eyes."

He poked himself in the chest again as if to emphasize the point. "And Leopold is still here. Do I look dead to you?"

They both shook their heads to indicate "No."

"Is it dangerous to look into its eyes? The unicorn I mean," said Jerry.

"Once you have looked into the unicorn's eyes boy, you will always best your opponents," replied Leopold.

"What is opponent?" This time it was Elton.

"Questions, questions! Always questions. Your opponent is . . ." he paused for a moment. "How do you say – ?" he prolonged say, as he searched for the word, "your enemy I think," he said at last.

Jerry felt a rush of pleasure to be talking to Mr Leopold again.

"When you were gone, I prayed for you to come back," he confided to Leopold. The man seemed visibly moved by the boy's sincerity.

"Well, thank you for thinking of Leopold."

He straightened up as if to leave and Jerry asked before he could move. "Where did you go?"

"More questions," he said, and walked a few paces, then he turned back and said to him,

"If I tell you, you keep secret, yes?"

"Yes, yes I promise."

"I was building a bakery in Carriacou, but it's nobody's business, you understand?" Once again, he looked at both in turn. They both nodded to indicate that they did.

"Bye little hunter," said Leopold.

"Bye Mr Leopold," said Jerry to his back as he shuffled away.

"Mr Leopold!" Jerry shouted at his back.

"What now?" Leopold's voice intimated that he was losing his patience.

"Why did you leave the back door open?"

Leopold smiled for the first time. "I forgot to close it little hunter, but Leopold has nothing worth stealing."

That night, after he had said his prayers, he thought of the day's events, about Mr Leopold's reappearance and what he had said about the unicorn and looking into its eyes.

Jerry was sure that Mr Leopold's eyes had turned green when he gazed into the unicorns', now he can best any opponent, even the person who dumped the coins at the crossroads.

If only he could look into the unicorn's eyes; no, he might not live to tell the tale. After a little while he thought to himself. "But I have looked into Mr Leopold's eyes". Though he couldn't explain it, he felt that by association, he had inherited some of Leopold's invincibility. Now all he had to do was to find a way to defeat Jake Antoine.

6

It was the start of the August school holidays, and Jerry and his friends shared most of their spare time between the beach and Mrs Thyne's back yard.

Her house was one of only two on the street that boasted a lawn. Because of school closure, the bigger boys had exercised their right to the two pitches in the pasture. Mr Thyne who was a keen watcher of all sports had invited the smaller kids to use his yard, which had a huge tamarind tree. His wife had no objection to the arrangement.

Recently, a Mr Jake Antoine had moved into the vacant house that shared its boundary with Mrs Thyne's. Since then, Puff Jake, as he was called locally, had confiscated six balls, one spinning top and one metal hoop. Jerry, whose hoop it was, had also lost one ball.

Antoine, who got his nickname because the locals thought him 'puffed up', was about five feet ten inches tall, and was very well built. He sported a well-trimmed moustache and always carried a cane when walking, more for effect than necessity. His pride and joy was his shiny B.S.A. motor cycle which he treated like a national treasure.

There was a shortcut behind Jake's house that linked Salisbury Street to High Street, access to which was always taken for granted. Now however, he was insisting that children would only be allowed to use it when in the company of an adult.

Jerry was sure that he had left his hoop leaning on the bush on Mrs Thyne's side but Puff Jake claimed it was lying in his garden and if

Jerry wanted it back he would have to sweep his yard for one week, including Saturday.

He agreed, as did the other kids, who all had to perform some chore or another for however long Puff Jake decided. This way he got everyone else to do his work for him for nothing.

As a result of their recent losses, the games lost their competitive edge. Everyone was worrying about the consequence of the ball ending up in Puff Jake's property and the game broke up about an hour earlier than it normally would have done.

Just a few days after Jerry recovered his hoop, Puff Jake struck a vicious blow.

Grandby's had recently put some plastic footballs of different colours on show, their special feature being that there was none of the lacing that had been essential to its predecessor.

Admiring the balls in the window, the boys salivated about getting one of them for the remaining two weeks of the holidays. There was a big problem however. Seventeen shillings and six pence was a lot of money. Even after they had pooled all of theirs together, they were still twelve shillings short of the asking price.

After a hurriedly arranged get together, they decided to go around the neighbourhood to see if they could raise the money by doing odd jobs. At the end of the day, when the rewards of their labours were counted, it totalled nine pence.

They all tried again the next day, but there was one major drawback; they were approaching the same people they saw the day before.

After four houses without success, Jerry and Wally ran into Leopold who was coming back from his morning swim. Jerry approached him tentatively. "Good morning, Mr Leopold."

"And good morning to you, little hunter. Have you killed anything lately?" There was a hint of a smile on his face.

"No", answered Jerry,"

"I have been practising, but not on anything living."

"There are many living things you can practise on, such as rats, mongooses, and of course, the hawk. You need a moving target," advised Leopold.

He turned to leave and Jerry ran around him. He spoke very quickly.

"We are trying to get a new ball, so I am wondering if you have any jobs that we can do."

"Jobs, what is this job?"

"Oh, work!" said Wally, speaking for the first time.

"This ball you speak of, what is it for?"

"To play football," said Jerry.

"Are you sure it is not for that damn cricket?"

"Oh no, it's for football," Jerry reassured him.

Leopold put his hand into his breast pocket and handed them a ten- shilling note, and without waiting to be thanked, he waved the boys away and continued walking.

Jerry ran all the way home where he found Ambrose sitting on the veranda. Very excitedly, he explained to him what was going on, careful to leave out how much more they required. Ambrose gullibly took the bait, well aware that he was being scammed.

"If you can tell me in ten seconds how much more you need, I'll give it to you."

Jerry waited as long as he thought was decent, then shouted, "one shilling and three pence!"

His big brother pretended to work it out by counting his fingers. "Well what do you know," he said, and gave him the money.

"Done it!" he shouted and gave his brother an instinctive hug before running inside to his secret hiding place.

They picked a red ball, reasoning that it would be easier to spot in the undergrowth. As an extra precaution, they arranged that someone would patrol Puff Jake's garden in much the same way as a player patrols the boundary ropes at a cricket match.

The tactic proved successful for the rest of the holidays while someone was available. But afterwards, without that protection, the

44

inevitable happened. The precious red ball was impounded and this time Jerry had to wash Puff Jake's motorcycle for one week. Saturday included of course.

After he had completed the last day's wash, he ran up to the house to collect the ball. Puff Jake came out and looked at the heavily clouded sky, while making a big show of his only inspection of the week.

"I'm afraid this won't do, this won't do at all. The back wheel is still dirty," he said. When Jerry reached for his cloth, he waved him away. "Not now, there isn't enough time. You can do it tomorrow."

The boy was furious he could not believe that a grown-up could tell such a fat one, but he had no choice so he did one more wash before Puff Jake grudgingly returned the ball.

Ever since his introduction to the cinema, Jerry's spending habit had changed drastically. He restricted himself to Mother Tina's stretch candy and directed the bulk of his savings towards his next opportunity to go back to the pictures.

He would never forget the initial impact the images had on him. All the big wild animals that he had read about and the pictures he had seen in the schoolbooks had been right there in front of him. When the huge lion bared its yellow teeth, shook its shaggy mane and roared, he was terrified and briefly hid his head behind Ambrose seated beside him. Cheetah's antics had him in stitches and Tarzan, with his amazing strength and agility, was an instant hero. Like so many other kids the world over, he was completely seduced by the silver screen.

The last time he had been to the pictures was when he accompanied his sister Marigold and her boyfriend George to see *the Music Box* with Laurel and Hardy.

He wanted to see Gene Autrey and *Champion, The Wonder Horse*, but Marigold pleaded with him to trust her. "If you don't like it, you can choose the film next time," she promised.

Stan and Ollie were at their comical best and Jerry laughed so much that he complained afterwards that his face was tired.

On the way home he could not keep the excitement from his voice as he talked about the trailer he had seen for *Sinbad the Sailor*, which was coming soon. He had two weeks to amass the fee.

On the afternoon before the matinee, after a good day selling rides on Gooney for a farthing a go, he had just enough for his admission and one snowball.

That same afternoon, he was having something to eat when Sparkplug started barking and a man's voice shouted, "Hello the house!"

Jerry went to the door and saw Sister Ju talking to Puff Jake, who frequently pointed at him.

"Mr Antoine says that Billy had eaten all his young corn trees. Was Billy loose today?" Her voice was stern.

"No," said Jerry. "He was in the same place I tied him this morning."

She sent him back to his snack but continued talking to Puff Jake.

She later informed Jerry that she had to pay ten shillings for the damage that Billy had done and since he was responsible for looking after him, his pocket money for the next two weeks, plus his matinee fee, would be confiscated.

He was gutted. He couldn't believe even Puff Jake could be so spiteful. Not only was Billy still tied to the same spot, but any and all vegetation within his reach had been devoured. Ample proof to him that Billy hadn't strayed.

That night, when he was in his bed where he did all his best thinking, he wondered at length what he was going to do about Puff Jake. "I must talk to Cousin Noah," he thought.

When he got home from school the next afternoon, his cousin was sitting at the table smoking his pipe and he was alone.

Sparkplug was running around Jerry's legs seeking attention, but it was clear to the older man that the boy had something else on his mind. "Well", he thought, "he'll get to whatever it is in his own time."

"Cousin Noah," Jerry almost shouted and sat at the table at the same time. He took his time thinking about what he wanted to say. "What do you do when your opponent knocks the chip from your shoulder?"

He took the pipe slowly from his mouth, raising his eyebrows at the same time. "Opponent?" He said, clearly not understanding. "Do you mean your friends?" He seemed a little surprised.

"Oh no!" exclaimed Jerry. "He is not my friend."

Noah was convinced that the reason the boy sought him out was that he didn't ask too many questions.

"Well, when someone knocks off your chip and you do not accept the challenge, they will think that you are a coward. If on the other hand you accept the challenge, even if you lose, they will still respect you. It's the same as picking up the gauntlet."

He went on to explain what he meant to the boy. Jerry's resolve to even the score with Puff Jake was further fuelled by the glowing reports he heard from his friends who had seen the film; he was so mad, he could bite a porcupine. "Soon", he thought, "soon".

Next morning, chasing his hoop to the shop with Sparkplug in close attendance as usual, he was a little preoccupied. Because of the war in Europe there was a scarcity of some goods in the shop. As a result, all the shopkeepers had banded together and introduced a system whereby the three 'specials', flour, rice, or sugar, could only be purchased when one other item was bought as well. Furthermore, if you wanted all three specials, then six items in all must be purchased.

Not surprisingly there was now a scarcity of all the cheaper items, such as needles, matches, thimbles, cubes of blue for washing, and so on.

His preoccupation was trying to think of two things he could buy with the two specials, so he wouldn't have to make another trip.

Due to his lack of concentration, the hoop got away from him and

47

it was only smart work by Sparkplug that stopped it bumping into Puff Jake's motorcycle.

"You are a very lucky little boy. If that thing had scratched my paintwork you'd be in big trouble."

Days turned into weeks and still Jerry hadn't thought of a plan to even the score with Puff Jake. He had just tied out Billy and was on his way to the river to meet Ambrose for their morning dip before school, when he heard someone whistling. It was Puff Jake and he still hadn't seen him.

Instinctively, he ducked behind the bushes. Puff Jake was carrying an open basket in the crook of his left hand; he was out picking up mangoes that had fallen during the night.

Jerry was very quiet as he rested on his haunches, watching Puff Jake bending over every now and again to avail himself of his choice of mangoes.

The idea, when it came to him, almost made him shout and give his presence away. It was like the last piece of a puzzle falling into place.

Very quietly he backed away to put his plan into action, thankful that because he was running late he had locked Sparkplug up that morning.

Five minutes later he was back hiding behind a cluster of banana trees, with Billy on a short lead standing quietly at his side. Puff Jake was halfway along the riverbank and the basket was nearly filled.

"Not much time left now," Jerry whispered to Billy whose rope he had already slipped from around his neck.

Puff Jake was now about fifteen feet away from where the boy and the goat were hiding. In his path was the stem of a large fallen tree, behind which there were some mangoes he seemed to be considering. Putting down the basket he bent forward and with the aid of his stick pulled the fruits towards him.

Jerry kept urging the goat forward. It made no move but it never took its eyes from the target.

48

Puff Jake stood up with two mangoes in his hand and, after a quick inspection, threw one back to the ground. He picked up the basket and resumed walking slowly, roughly in Jerry's direction.

The boy almost panicked. He was trying to think of what to say when Puff Jake saw him. He couldn't understand it. Since he was a kid, Billy had butted anything that stood still. Now, when he really needed him, he didn't move a muscle. His panic receded rapidly as Puff Jake changed direction having spotted another mango that he wanted.

He must have tripped. He stumbled slightly, but even so a few of the mangoes fell from the almost full basket. After he had recovered his balance, he bent over to retrieve the fruits and presented Billy with the perfect target. This time, Billy didn't hesitate. He very quickly covered the distance and hit a bulls-eye, which sent Puff Jake tumbling and screaming all the way to lie face down in the river.

The suddenness and the speed of the attack was such that he did not know who, or what had hit him.

Jerry crawled forward and peeped over the edge of the riverbank. Puff Jake was still on his belly and looking anxiously around with a bewildered look on his face. His eyes stopped at the empty basket that was being driven by the current pushing against it.

Jerry backed hastily away from the edge and took hold of Billy, who by now seemed to have forgotten all about the butting and was busy munching away at a fallen mango nearby, his tail constantly shifting back and forth as if to indicate pleasure.

He quickly retied the rope and hurried away from the scene, before he was recognised by Puff Jake or anyone else. After he had retied the goat, he ran the two hundred yards to where his brother was waiting for him further up the river, screaming and shouting all the way in celebration of a victory over his opponent.

When at last he met his brother who was somewhat apprehensive about all the noise he was making, he had to be calmed down before Ambrose could make any sense from his story. Once he was aware of the facts, they abandoned the idea of the dip and left the area in a hurry.

"One thing," said Ambrose as they walked home together. "You say nothing about this for the time being to anyone, now promise me!"

Jerry promised.

For the rest of that day and a few others following, he waited anxiously for Puff Jake's shout or knock on the door, but it never came. Even so, he decided it was best to keep away from him and let him make the next move. He was quite sure in his mind that Puff Jake must have guessed where the attack came from.

They were walking back from church on Sunday morning and Juliette decided as usual to use the shortcut. Normally, he would be delighted as it meant a quicker breakfast. This morning however, he was very reluctant, but couldn't give a good reason not to take the shortcut.

As they approached Puff Jake's house, they saw him standing in the middle of his garden with a watering can in his hand. After the 'good mornings' were exchanged, they were about to walk on when he said. "Oh Jerry, I was hoping to see you. Come by later you and your friends and pick up your balls. Oh, and there are a couple of spinning tops and a few marbles."

"Thank you Mr Jake," said Jerry hesitantly.

They started walking again when he called after him.

"And Jerry, in future I'll allow only you to go into the garden and get the balls, but you must be careful."

"I will," he promised, wanting to jump and shout and proclaim his victory for all to hear. Instead, he showed the restraint of a much older head and walked quietly beside his sister. He thought about Mr Leopold and what he had said about defeating your enemy, once you have looked into the eyes of the unicorn. He must remember to look into the mirror to see if there was any change to the colour of his eyes.

"What's all that about?"

Juliette's question roused him from his thoughts. He thought for a little while. "My prayers have just been answered," he said with a straight face.

"I won't be a bit surprised," she said with just the hint of a smile across her face.

That night the brothers revelled in the victory over Puff Jake.

"I think he surrendered Jer. I think he gave back the things he seized because he doesn't want anyone to know about the butting. I think he is ashamed."

Jerry had checked his eyes in the mirror, and he was almost sure that there was just a hint of green in the corners. Just before he succumbed to sleep, he thought, "I have looked into Mr Leopold's eyes and lived to tell the tale."

7

Jerry was used to changes in his life and there were going to be more. Five years after his mom had left, Martin his oldest brother had joined her and now worked in the oil refinery.

The following year two of his sisters, Beth, who had left school to look after him together with Marina, had also joined her. His oldest sister Ella was married before he was born, and Dolly, the one after her, lived with her husband in Trinidad. Worst of all, his dad had died and was gone forever. Now, another change had taken place. Ambrose had started his secondary education at the Presentation Boys College (PBC) in St. George's two weeks ago, at the start of the January term. The college opened its doors in 1947, and together with its senior brother, the Grenada Boys Secondary School, (GBSS), provided the only secondary education for boys in Grenada.

As a direct result of that move, Juliette had decided that all the animals were too much for Jerry to look after alone and had agreed on a price for both Annie the cow and Gooney the donkey.

He was sad to see them go and argued that he could mind them all but Juliette's decision was final. He would especially miss Gooney, not only because of the profit he made from the rides, but because he was genuinely fond of the big jack.

He was on his back in the dark, staring up at the ceiling he couldn't see while he pondered these things. There was only one bright spot in the middle of all this, for the first time ever he had a room all to himself.

He was roused from his reverie by a synchronized sound of voices that sent a slight chill through him. It was the chant of 'The Wailers'.

They were a small group of people numbering anything from nine to sometimes twice that number, depending on their standing and popularity, and perhaps more importantly, how much rum the family of the deceased was willing to donate.

At a time when speed was the main consideration for dealing with the recently dead, and given the difficulty of communication and refrigeration, the services of the Wailers was invaluable.

If someone died before nine o'clock in the morning, that person was buried on that same day. Any later, and the burial would be scheduled for the next day and then it became a job for the Wailers.

Armed with their flambeau and libations, they engaged in a rhythmic chant with a combination of French patois and English. They travelled the parish taking all the available routes and informed the community that someone had died and of the time and place of the burial.

This was the first 'wailing' since Ambrose went to his new school and given Jerry's fear of all things pertaining to death, his anxiety increased as the chant got nearer.

"Wake! Wake!" shouted one voice.

"Sa ki tan parlay lut," shouted another, as each took it in turn.

"Sa ki bas tan manday lut."

Here, they would use the name of the deceased person, making sure to include whatever nickname he or she may have been known by.

"Wood-nose Smith, e allay, e coupay."

The burial information would then be passed on.

Roughly translated, what it said was that Wood-nose Smith was dead. Those who hear should tell others and who didn't hear, should ask others. He's gone! He's cut!

As they got nearer to the house, he covered his head with his pillow in a vain effort to silence the noise, but the sound of their 'wailing' carried long distances through the quiet of the night and he could hear their chanting long after the words became unintelligible.

He was startled by the hooting of a passing owl that normally he would have been pleased to hear. His heart thumped loudly and his nerves were raw. He waited until the voices were silent and quietly let in Sparkplug. Then together, they curled up on the bed and very quickly fell asleep.

The next morning when Juliette came to wake Jerry up, she found them still asleep together. She looked down at the dog and marvelled at how big he had become. Then she thought of the little pest that he was when he first came. She didn't wonder why he was in the bed, as she had already made the 'Wailers' connection. Smiling, she went back to her room and started moving things around, giving Jerry the chance to get rid of the dog before he was discovered.

That Saturday morning, with his slingshot already in hand and his pocket filled with pebbles, Jerry took another of his trips into the small woods behind Mother Tina's house. Sparkplug trailed behind him.

They were hunting for moving targets such as rats or lizards. He had come close to hitting one or the other many times, but he had never actually succeeded. Now, with a specially selected pebble in the pouch, he was ready.

Suddenly, Sparkplug went straight for a nearby bush and barked continuously.

"If you want to help, then be quiet!"

He reprimanded the dog sharply, but instead of obeying, Sparkplug ran to the opposite side of the bush, still barking loudly. Jerry was about to shout again when a mongoose jumped out of the bush and ran straight at him, then changed direction and headed for some nearby vegetation. Getting over his surprise, Jerry eventually managed to get one shot out, but the mongoose had disappeared as quickly as it came. He felt a belated surge of adrenaline within him, his heart beat loudly and he was flushed with excitement.

"A fine hunter you are," he chided himself. "The chicken hawk will come and go and you wouldn't even know."

It was then that he noticed Sparkplug sitting on his hind legs staring up at him with his head to one side, waiting to be congratulated. He got down on his knees and took the dog's face in his hands.

"Well done Sparky, good boy. You are a real hunter." He was still praising the dog when they walked into the yard.

Easter came and with it brought a new joy into Juliette's life. The BBC Overseas Service started broadcasting a radio programme called, *Mrs. Dale's Diary.* The family consisted of the doctor husband Jim, his wife Mary, a son, Bob, and a daughter, Gwen. Juliette became such a fan, she would check to make sure that there was no rain to disturb the radio signals. Before long, they became her adopted family.

Ambrose came home for his first holiday and Jerry could hardly wait as he got off the bus. When he appeared, they ran towards each other and embraced.

"Let me look at you," said Ambrose, holding his little brother away from him. "I swear you are much taller than when I left."

They spent a lot of time together, each asking and answering the other's questions, until they were both up to speed.

A couple of afternoons later, Jerry went to the pasture to watch Ambrose's team play football. When it was time to start, they were a man short. Ambrose called him over. "Get in there on the right and do your best. You can do it."

He must have had a good game, because he continued to be picked on odd occasions, even after Ambrose had left.

One morning shortly afterwards, he was playing softball with his friends when the team captain, McKay approached him.

"We are a man short today. Be there at three o'clock if you want a game." Jerry could hardly contain himself. He went home earlier than he would have done to clear up anything he had to do before the appointed time.

He woke with a start. Someone was pounding on the front door.

"Who is it?" asked Juliette anxiously.

"It's me," answered Carol, her neighbour from directly across the road.

"Look out your window at the church."

Instead of heeding the advice, Juliette went to open the door. Jerry, who on waking, believed that it was already morning, opened the window at the foot of his bed to be greeted by two surprises.

Firstly, it was still night and secondly, he was able to tell the time by the church clock, which should have been impossible at that time on a moonless night.

He was often told by most of the older people on his street that he had very good eyes. He had threaded needles for most of the women. Even so, this had to be something else. It was only then that he became aware of the reddening sky and billowing black smoke. Juliette called out to him to see if he was awake. "Get changed quickly Jer, there's a big fire on Main Street."

He snatched his school trousers from the bedpost, but could not find his shoes.

"Coming!" he shouted back, but by the time he ran bare-footed into the street she was already escorting his two nieces, aged five and four, to stay with Carol's daughter.

They set off at a brisk pace and headed for the shortcut through Salisbury Street, which was partially lit from the reflections of the flames over half a mile away. The group was getting larger as more and more people came running from their houses.

They quickly emerged on Main Street but were still some way from the fire.

They continued along, being joined by still more people, whose curiosity had triumphed over their need to sleep.

Drawn like a moth to a flame, they advanced ever closer. When they were about two hundred yards away Juliette's attention was drawn by someone gesticulating furiously in her direction, it was a friend of the family, who lived in a two storey building on the other side of the road. She invited them upstairs. She was Alice Kingsley and she shared the house with her mother.

Once upstairs, Jerry was allowed a window with a perfect view of the fire all to himself. He looked down and was surprised at how quickly the street had filled up with people and many were trying to get still closer. Away from all the noise and distractions on the street, he gave his full attention to the blaze coming from St. Louis' drug store.

The wind must have died down because even though he was much nearer with a clearer view, he could not now see the church clock, which was obliterated by a huge column of black smoke.

His attention was again drawn by a commotion going on in the street below. It was the fire-wagon, whose bell clanged continuously, being drawn along by the fire fighters. There was lots of shouting and running around, as they strove frantically to get the hose connected to the water hydrant. Hardly had they started pumping when the pressure dropped.

The equipment was very old and badly in need of repairs. At intervals along the hose were patches of canvas, stuck with glue and bound very closely with twine.

The speed of the pressure drop had surprised the firemen and it was soon obvious to all those watching that the fire was quickly gaining momentum. By now, the flames had penetrated clean through the roof and roared upwards.

The chief of the fire fighters, realising the futility of their attempts to make any impression on the blaze, embarked on a strategy of prevention and concentrated all their efforts on soaking the buildings on the other side of the road.

Suddenly, there was a sequence of loud bangs as some of the chemicals within the drugstore exploded. The flames shot high through a hole where the fire had penetrated the roof. There were shouts and screams everywhere as the crowd panicked briefly in a confused attempt to get further from the sparks that the wind had blown in their direction.

Somehow they had managed some successful repairs on the hose and now had enough pressure to direct the spray onto the roof of the timbered structures. Inevitably the flames jumped the six feet to the neighbouring building, Hosten's Produce Company.

Despite its walled exterior, the curtains in the window of the first floor caught fire, quickly followed by the rest of the room.

It wasn't very long before flames shot upwards through the hole in the roof. Other than Gleans' Garage with its petrol pump, the most dangerous building to catch fire in the entire parish was Hosten's.

It housed a combination of spirits, spices, kerosene, paints and accessories. It was easily the biggest store of its kind in the town.

Hosten's consisted of two floors. The ground floor boasted an impressive office and all available space was taken up by groceries, household appliances paints, and even gardening tools.

At the back, at the end furthest from the drug store, was a liquor bar; but easily the most lucrative part of the business was the huge amount of spices in which they traded.

On the first floor they stored hundreds of bags of cocoa beans, nutmegs, mace, cloves, and other spices, each stacked neatly in their separate areas. Each bag weighed fifty pounds. Hosten's bedroom was directly above the bar.

Most lethal of all were several giant demijohns, specially designed to hold up to ten gallons of spirits. In this case they held the locally made and greatly over-proofed River Antoine rum. This famous distillery is said to be the oldest in the Caribbean.

There was a loud crash as burning rafters fell to the first floor as part of Hosten's roof collapsed, smashing some of the bottles on the floor beneath.

Almost immediately the fire shot through the hole and merged with the blaze from the drugstore. The heat intensified rapidly, fuelled by the spillage of the spirits below. So hot was the fire that the bystanders were forced to retreat further to relative safety. The fire fighters, none of whom had ever witnessed a blaze of such intensity, took the same precaution, thereby rendering the antiquated apparatus redundant.

A massive explosion erupted and was clearly heard despite all the other noises of the night. Another portion of the roof collapsed; now the fire was a raging inferno against the night sky.

Two more explosions almost in unison and the watchers gasped as different coloured lights, probably the result of the coming together of the chemicals and alcohol, shot into the sky.

A gust of swirling wind blew across the blaze, catching the sparks in a whirlpool effect and giving the impression of a frenzied mating dance of a swarm of fireflies.

Another loud crash as the rafters from the first floor plummeted below. Once again, the fire intensified as the spillage of the remaining bottles broken by the crash ignited. The only consolation was that the centre of the fire was now contained on the ground floor, protected from the wind by the concrete walls that were still standing.

Every now and then a bottle exploded and although it was still frightening, did not match their earlier counterparts for volume.

Gradually, the explosions subsided and although the flames could still be seen from the top of the burning buildings, the fire seemed at last, to be well on its way to burning itself out.

After a little while, a few spectators began slowly to walk away and then it happened. By far the biggest explosion of the night, dwarfing anything that had gone before it, staggered and frightened the bystanders who watched with disbelief, as the great main door was wrenched from its hinges in the wall, and flung, as if by some avenging terrorist into the street. The blaze that was trapped inside came billowing out through the opening.

A huge drum of kerosene almost filled to capacity had gradually overheated and began slowly to expand from the pressure building from within. Finally, it tore itself apart, having the same effect as a thrown grenade, shattering the windows of the buildings opposite.

So spellbound was the crowd by the spectacle of the fire, hardly anyone noticed that the tiny wooden parlour near to Hosten's had completely disappeared. Miraculously, after three and a half hours of the biggest fire Sauteurs had ever seen, no one had been killed or even injured.

It was the closest Jerry had ever been to a fireworks display and now that the danger had passed, only the excitement remained.

Next morning even as the sun was rising, many parishioners, most of whom had seen the blaze and reddening sky from as far away as the mountains, were eager to get a close up view. Others who had witnessed the disaster as it happened were just as eager to see the after effects in the cold light of day.

Even now, odd wisps of smoke could still be seen drifting away on the soft morning breeze and those who had advanced to the police barrier could still feel the warmth of the heat that was trapped and was now emanating from the skeletal walls that remained standing.

The road leading to both the Roman Catholic school and church was cordoned off until it was decided that it was safe for use. Everywhere there was a strong smell of burning matter dominated by nutmegs and alcohol.

In the school garden across from the church at the back of Hosten's, a goat that was tied there during the night was found barbecued from the intense heat of the previous night.

A small crowd of people had gathered around the dead animal and speculated about its ownership, but having already lost the goat and fearing a reprimand for tying it in forbidden territory, no one had claimed it.

Almost unnoticed, a man eased himself in front of the small crowd and rubbed his hands together.

"Well now," he said so quietly, that only those close around him, heard him. "What have we here?"

If he expected an answer, he didn't get one. He walked slowly around the goat, never taking his eyes from it.

"Whose goat is it?" he asked.

"Nobody knows, no one has claimed it," somebody said from the back. The man took a small but very sharp hunting knife from a canvas case hanging from his belt and with the tip of the knife, he moved one of the roasted hind legs around. Satisfied, he straightened up and took out a brown paper bag from one of the many pockets on his clothes. He opened the bag and smoothed the creases from it.

"As soon as it cools down the dogs and the flies will come and then it will be too late," he said, more to himself than to anyone else.

"Too late for what?" Somebody close by wanted to know.

"This here animal is real goat meat. Would be a shame to leave it all to the dogs and the flies and the maggots. Besides, they'll only have to bury what's left of it. You know what they say, waste not, want not, so if nobody minds, I'll be cutting myself a small slice or two."

He bent over the burnt animal and very diligently, cut two ample slices of the thoroughly cooked meat, before straightening up again. Placing the meat in the paper bag he gave it time to cool down before depositing it into one of his pockets and almost as unobtrusively as when he appeared, he disappeared. His name was Jimsey Crow.

School was reopened one week later and as expected the kids talked of hardly anything else. The teacher noticed that Jerry was always in the thick of all the discussions and decided that if she couldn't stop it, she may as well control it. She called the class to order and explained that since Jerry had viewed the fire from a vantage point, he would stand in front of the class and tell them all that he had seen.

He was very nervous to start with and haltingly narrated what he saw. So successful was the exercise, that some of the other teachers requested and received his help. This time around though, he was much more relaxed and a lot more graphic. By the end of the week, he had attained something nearing celebrity status among his peers.

Following the fire, speculation prevailed. There were those who suspected foul play, believing arson to be the cause for personal gain. One school of thought favoured was that Hosten had the most to gain, since there was talk of him expanding.

Another thought that the drugstore owner might have started it himself, because he may have been facing bankruptcy. If there was ever an investigation, nothing was ever found.

A few months later, Hosten acquired the spot and the drugstore owner travelled to Europe to be trained as a doctor. He was nearly forty years old. A few months on, Hosten's was rebuilt. Only this time it was twice the size it was before the fire.

8

Shortly after Jerry's eleventh birthday the rainy season began, bringing with it emotional experiences that threatened to overwhelm him. It had rained all during the night and most of the morning and as a result, there was no school. The rain finally stopped at around eleven o'clock.

An hour later, after all the clouds had been blown away, the sun was out in all its glory. Sister Ju called from outside with a hint of urgency in her voice.

"Jer! Close all the doors and windows, quickly!"

Sensing there was something wrong, he went to the window and for an instant, stood dumbfounded at the sight that greeted him. He was astonished to find that the sun had been obliterated by what seemed to be thousands of swarms of flies, all rolled into one as far as the eyes could see.

Very quickly he closed all the doors and windows, but even so some of the winged visitors were already in the house. He ran into the kitchen to get an empty jam jar, then outside to see how many he could catch.

Once outside, he found that his idea was easier said than done. For one thing, he could hardly breathe. The flies were everywhere; up your nostrils, in your mouth, but most of all, in your eyes.

He ran back into the house and returned almost immediately, wearing one of his sister's old stockings over his face. Problem solved, he ran along the street trying to fill his jar.

When he got to Mother Tina's, Mr Fletcher the sanitary inspector, who was always seen taking books from the library, was standing in the road near to his motor cycle.

He was wearing goggles and a scarf much in the way that the pilots seen in the newsreel did whenever he was riding. He looked up and then all around him. He held both his hands up and said a name that Jerry didn't know.

"What's that?" asked Mother Tina.

"Oh," answered Mr Fletcher, "that's the Latin name, they are just rain flies. One of nature's little miracles; they are born, live, lay their eggs, and die. All in one day."

"Well, that's a big shame if you ask me," she said, as she closed the door, running the risk of losing a sale.

He ran around trying to fill his jar and before long was joined by some of the other kids, who, one way or another, had part of their faces covered. After the hunt was over, he went back home to find that the jar was still nearly empty.

More and more now, Jerry had been getting into the bigger boys' team. Initially, his selection was based mainly on his size and strength, now he was picked for his ability, as many thought him to be a promising left-winger.

Though he had been playing fairly often, today he was very nervous before the start. It was the first time the captain had come to him on a Friday to tell him he was playing on a Sunday. Now he was a regular.

The first half went badly for his team; they trailed by one goal. Halfway through the second half he noticed Sister Ju among the few spectators and was immediately alarmed. She had never been to any of the games before. He started walking towards her but she waved him back. They did better in the second half of the match that ended in a draw at seven all.

Right after the game he ran to his sister.

"What's wrong? What's the matter?" he asked, a little apprehensively.

"Nothing is wrong, but I want you to come home with me now," she said with a reassuring smile.

As they walked along, his curiosity got the better of him. All his instincts were telling him that something was up.

"Please Sister Ju," he pleaded, "won't you tell me what is happening?" he asked again.

"I have a surprise for you. You'll just have to wait and see," she said, still smiling. As they approached the house she turned to him.

"Let me look at you . . . fix yourself up."

She took her handkerchief from her pocket and wiped the sweat from his face. When she was satisfied, she said, "that's better," then they walked through the door.

Jerry walked into the room first and stopped abruptly, causing Juliette to bump into him. Sitting in one of the chairs in the front room was a lady that he had never met before, but knew from photographs he had seen that she was his mother.

He had not moved from the time he had entered the room, his gaze never leaving the face of the stranger. She put her hand quickly to her mouth, at the same time catching her breath and smiled brightly.

She was about five feet, eight inches tall, on the plump side with hair that was halfway grey. She wore a blue two-piece suit, with stockings and black high-heeled shoes and completed the outfit with a white top. She weighed about a hundred and fifty pounds and looked as smart as the women he had seen in his sister's old magazines.

Although the resemblance between her and the photographs was unmistakable, he thought there was a difference about her that he couldn't explain. Then he noticed her large, soft, dark brown eyes and he understood the difference.

Apart from the movement of her hand, she had sat quite still mirroring his gaze. After what seemed like a long time she rose slowly from the chair and opened her arms. He hesitated an instant longer, then rapidly covered the short distance into her embrace and shouted, "Mother!"

She hugged him tightly, rubbing her face on top of his head. The strength of her embrace made him flinch.

"Oh, I'm so very sorry, it's just that I have really been looking forward to this for such a long time." She had spoken for the first time. After a little while she held him away from her.

"Let me look at you. I can't believe how tall you are. Turn around," she said, without stopping for breath. Juliette walked backwards through the door and pulled it quietly after her.

For the boy that month went by like a blur. It was as if his mother was trying to accomplish all of the things they should have done in the last ten years into this single month. On average, she kept him out of school about two days a week, saying that there were many things to learn about, and not all of them at school.

In the days that followed Jerry was to do many firsts and all of them with his mom. He went with her to the capital, St. George's, where they took a water taxi from the pier to Grand Anse beach. Perhaps most exciting of all, they went into a restaurant and had lunch.

He was very nervous when they sat down at the table and the waiter came to take the order.

"We'll have the lobster, stew peas and rice," she told him.

"But Mom", said Jerry after the waiter had left, "I don't eat lobster."

"Don't you?" Well never mind, we'll fix up something when he comes back."

The food was served and the waiter moved quickly to a new customer.

"Go ahead," she urged, "you might like it."

He liked it so much that he ate everything on his plate while she watched him without touching her food. When he was finished, she swapped the plates around and smiled at him. "Have some of mine."

Then it was up to the Annandale Waterfall before catching the bus home.

He especially enjoyed going to church with her so that all the other kids could see them together. She never took the short cut near to Puff

Jake's house. Instead, they walked the long way along Main Street, meeting and talking to people coming from the Anglican church.

After breakfast, he was listening to one of his favourite shows on the radio; *The Auntie Kaye Show* from Radio Trinidad. The programme was for children of all ages, who were encouraged to exhibit their talents.

He heard his mom call and went out to find her leaning against the banister at the top of the stairs. She pointed to two roosters that were fighting in the yard.

"Look at this," she said.

He looked at the cocks fighting, but didn't understand why she wanted him to watch.

"I've seen lots of cockfights before Mom," he told her.

"Just watch," she said, laying her hand on his shoulder. The fight continued for another two minutes. For a time, they seemed evenly matched, then one of the cocks turned away and ran a few feet before stopping to forage.

"Now look closely at the winner," she said to him.

Soon afterwards, the winner flapped his wings and crowed a couple of times, before settling down to scratch for insects.

"That is what I wanted you to see. Whenever animals of the same species fight, it is very seldom to the death, and then they die from the wounds sustained in the fight. Once one surrenders, the fight is usually over."

She paused for a moment before going on. "Unlike man, who often carries on beating his opponent long after he is unable to defend himself. If we had the animals' compassion, we wouldn't even need policemen."

Jerry was surprised that although he had seen many cockfights, he had never noticed before that the winner always crowed and he told her so.

"It makes me laugh when someone behaves badly and people say he or she behaved like an animal. Animals only do what they are supposed to do."

"Do all animals behave like that?" he asked.

"As far as I know, yes. You see, if they are well matched, there is nothing to say the loser today may not be the winner tomorrow and then it would be his turn to crow. They coexist and there is no intended cruelty. Man on the other hand always looks for revenge."

"Mom, are you saying we shouldn't ever fight?" There was a hint of incredulity in his voice.

She smiled openly and rubbed the back of his neck.

"I'm not saying man shouldn't fight. He should fight for his honour, his good name and his self-respect, but most of all he should fight to protect his family. Even so, it should be avoided as much as possible. Sometimes, it is harder not to fight, but man is cursed by his pride."

"Why his pride?" he asked.

She thought for a little while.

"Because he is afraid to be thought of as weak, but there are all kinds of strength and I don't ever want you to forget that."

This timely lesson was to stay with him and influenced his thoughts throughout his adult life.

Jerry stood and waited impatiently as his mom exchanged greetings with the other adults after mass. In his hand he carried a bunch of wild lilies that he had taken from Sister Ju just before she hurried on in front towards home and breakfast.

Eventually his mom joined him, and together they turned left at the bottom of the steps, onto the road that led to the cemetery. He was taking her to visit his dad's grave.

On arrival she took the flowers and placed them on the grave, then took his hand. They stood quietly for some time, each with their own thoughts. After a little while she spoke as if more to herself than to him.

"This isn't how I thought it would be."

"How did you think it would be?"

"Well," she smiled ruefully, "I always thought he would hold on to me, look me in the eye and tell me we did the right thing."

They walked slowly along the way back from the cemetery, both seemed preoccupied; eventually, the boy spoke.

"Mom?"

"Yes?"

"Why did you leave us? Why did you go away?"

He stared at her. She turned around and held him by his shoulders and bent forward, so that her face was only six inches from his. Her voice was little more than a whisper.

"Jer, I know that you have been waiting all your life to ask me that question, yet, now that it's time, I'm still not sure how to answer."

She took his hand and they walked on to the church steps, where she sat and patted the spot beside her. After he was seated, still holding on to his hand, she attempted to explain.

"There were seven of us living in a one bed roomed house, then I became pregnant with you. The thought of bringing another life into that house took all the joy out of the pregnancy. Your father and I spent a lot of time thinking and talking about how to improve our situation, but nothing came to mind.

"The money we were making between us just about covered food and clothes. There was hardly anything left over for medicine, let alone a bigger house, so in desperation your dad reluctantly decided to stow away to Trinidad.

We argued a great deal. I was afraid that he would be caught, thrown in prison and, like those before him, be deported, leaving our situation worse than it was before he left. In the end he agreed with me and we had a bit of luck.

"Mr Wheatley, my boss, arranged through a contact for me to go to Aruba to work for an American family. It was a great opportunity.

"This is what I meant by all kinds of strength. Most men would have been too proud, arguing that the man should provide for his family and the woman's place was at home, but they wanted women, not men, and we both wanted what was best for our children. My going was the best way to do that. That's why I left, so that my family could have somewhere decent to stay and my children have a good education."

As if the explanation had taken a lot out of her, she sighed heavily. The boy surprised her with his next statement that she thought was way beyond his years.

"I'm sure had dad been here, he would have been very happy and told you that you both did the right thing."

She hugged him so closely he could smell her lavender water.

"Lord, I do declare, only eleven and you already know how to comfort a woman. Come on," she said. "I could do with some breakfast."

"And I'm starving," said Jerry.

All too soon, that magical month raced by. He accompanied her to Pearls Airport, where, before boarding, she gave him a long hug and got his promise to write to her often. Then as an afterthought, she said, "Don't forget to take a picture with Sparkplug for me."

At the top of the stairs, she turned and waved before disappearing into the bowel of the plane.

That day, he saw an airplane land and take off for the first time. He remembered thinking that it was not nearly as graceful as the birds, but he was exhilarated by the sheer power as it took off.

9

The rainy season continued unabated and football was the only game being played. There was a match scheduled for that Wednesday afternoon against Redhead Street, but maybe due to all the rain, they didn't turn up.

Most of his friends stayed behind for a game of sorts but Jerry decided to take the opportunity to bring the animals in early. As he walked away from the others, his friend Wally, who'd also decided to leave, joined him.

"Wait up Jerry," he called, catching up to him. "Where you off to?"

"Thought I'd bring the animals in."

"Kinda early, eh?"

"Thought if I left early I could raid Miss Mann's," he explained.

"You mean the grafted mango?" Wally seemed clearly surprised by the suggestion.

"All I have to do is keep the pig busy long enough, then I'll go to work with these," he said, touching the pebbles in his pocket.

"But as soon as you pick them the pig will eat them and even if it doesn't, how will you get them without her knowing?"

"Two problems, one solution," he answered, holding up the weighted brown paper bag he carried in his hand.

"Over ripe bananas. They will keep the pig busy long enough for me to pick and gather the mangoes before he starts grunting and sound the alarm."

71

"Let's go!" said a clearly impressed Wally.

They approached cautiously and spoke in whispers. They chose a spot close enough for their purpose, but also well hidden from the track that ran alongside.

As previously arranged, Jerry threw the bananas one at a time, making sure to spread them apart to keep the animal occupied longer. Wally quickly took his place under the tree so he could pick up the fallen mangoes as quickly as Jerry could pick them off with his slingshot.

There were no fallen mangoes on the ground, but even if there had been, Jerry would not have picked them up. A hunter always picks his own. His many months of diligent practice had paid off handsomely and now he had more successes than he had failures.

Soon, the brown paper bag began to bulge with the picked mangoes just as the sentry had eaten the last banana and given the alarm.

Mission accomplished, they ran as fast as they could away from the garden, so that by the time Miss Mann came running, armed with the usual bamboo pole that she was adept at throwing underhand, they were long gone. There were many who would testify to her accuracy.

As they ran away laughing, Wally struck his foot against the root of an avocado tree and stumbled to the ground. Lying on his back, he noticed that a swarm of bees had taken residence in a hole in the tree. Safe from the clutches of Miss Mann, Jerry joined his friend on the ground and studied the bees at length, while they enjoyed the mangoes. The very next day they drafted in another friend, Lynton, and together they planned a strategy for extracting honey from the avocado tree.

On the Saturday around noon, they arrived at the tree fully prepared. Wally carried an empty paint can into which they had put burning charcoal, the theory being, that they would cover the coal with green leaves, which in turn would provide enough smoke, which would then be fanned into the hive, rendering the bees passive enough to allow them to extract the honey.

As the one who would go into the hive, Jerry donned some

headgear; a piece of cloth with two holes cut into it to allow him to see, tucked underneath his cap to keep it in place. When he was ready, he gave the word.

The leaves were then dumped into the pan and for a moment, provided the desired effect but because of the heavy shower of the late morning they were wet, and soon doused the fire to the point where there was very little smoke to be seen.

What followed was never clearly understood. The intrusion naturally agitated the bees and made them angry. The first to shout was Lynton, who had taken a sting at the back of the neck. Then Jerry, perched on a branch that allowed him access to the hive, was stung three times by bees that had got in underneath the cloth, on his right cheek, on the bridge of his nose and his left temple.

Such was his pain that he released his hold on the branch, lost his footing and fell the seven feet to the ground. Wally sustained a single sting on the back of his right hand.

After running into each other and the avocado tree over and over again, without anyone giving the word, they all ran as fast as they could from the angry bees and even as they ran, Jerry took leave of his friends with a promise to see them later. He then ran all the way home.

As he came into the yard, he slowed and walked casually past his sister, where she was taking advantage of the break in the weather by hanging the washing out to dry.

His face felt as if it was on fire and he had a throbbing headache. Without removing his shoes, he climbed into the bed and covered himself all over.

On the stroke of six o'clock, Juliette, together with Millie and her two nieces were getting ready for supper. The sound of the church bells had reminded her of the time and she wondered openly as to his whereabouts.

"That boy pays no attention to time, he knows I like him here for supper."

73

"But Jerry is in Aunt Ju. I heard him coughing just a little while ago," Anna informed her.

"Then go and get him," her aunt insisted.

A few seconds later, Millie who was closest, went in to check his room. The quiet of the household was shattered by a frightened scream.

"What is it Millie," Juliette asked anxiously as she made her way to the room. She opened the door and was just able to see through the gloom. Her hand went to her mouth with a gasp.

"My God, Jerry, what's the matter with your face?" she asked in horror.

Very slowly, she drew the story from him and forgetting all about supper for the time being, she marched him down to the surgery, where nurse McMillan gaped in horror at his face. He was barely recognisable, as all three stings had swollen into lumps that almost merged, leaving him with a grotesque appearance.

"What in God's name happened?" demanded the nurse. With her magnifying glass and tweezers, she worked diligently, removing the stings while she listened to a graphic account of the incident. She then covered the spots with iodine, warned Jerry and Juliette of the probability of a fever and reassured them that the swelling, as hideous as it looked, would disappear in about two or three days.

Two mornings later, Juliette held her brother by the chin, turned his face this way and that as she examined him.

"I see you've decided to stop frightening children," she smiled.

He smiled back but said nothing. She went into her bedroom and returned with his slingshot that she'd confiscated two days before and handed it to him.

"I'm sure the bees have taught you a far better lesson about meddling than I ever can."

"I promise I'll never meddle with the bees again."

With that assurance, he ran into the yard calling for his dog. It was business as usual. Collecting the sheep, he tied them out for the day and hurried down to the river for his morning dip.

Having missed two days of school, Jerry was determined not to be late, and stopped to admonish the dog for straying on their way from the river. Sparkplug, head tilted to one side, listened attentively to the rebuke.

"Now look! I don't have time for you to chase lizards and everything else that moves. I can't be late for school, so come on!"

The dog tucked his tail between his legs and followed meekly on.

Halfway along, the track narrowed because of the large trees growing on either side of it, and standing right in the middle of it was Alfie, closely followed by his dog Atila. Jerry stopped dead in his tracks and instinctively placed his hand on his dog's neck. He looked behind him to see if there was somewhere he could stand to allow Alfie the space, but before he could do anything about it, Sparkplug began to growl deep in his throat and moved a couple of paces forward.

Alfie was standing with his feet wide apart and in his hand was the fallen branch of a tree which he was using as a walking stick to better handle the rugged terrain. He had a big grin on his face.

"You better get that flea-bag out of the way and let a real dog pass," he said mockingly.

By that time, both dogs had assumed an aggressive posture with their eyes fixed on each other. Jerry looked at Sparkplug. He was nearly three years old and fully-grown with a glossy coat and a tail that wagged almost continuously. He knew of Atila's reputation and feared the worst for his dog.

"Please let us pass," he pleaded with Alfie, but he wasn't listening. He placed his right hand on Atila's neck and shook it vigorously, arousing the dog's fighting instincts. "Go get him boy!" he urged, smacking it lightly on the backside.

The dogs rushed at each other, each growling menacingly as they collided. There was instant pandemonium; they fought savagely for early advantage, while the boy shouted for it to be stopped and the man shouted encouragement to his dog.

It wasn't long before blood was drawn, as Sparkplug sustained what appeared to be a nasty gash on the side of the neck. For a while they matched each other in ferocity and the advantage swung this way and that. All the while, Jerry was shouting continuously for the fight to be stopped. "Please Alfie," pleaded the boy again, "my dog is hurt, please call Atila off."

Instead of complying, Alfie was urging on his dog. "That's right boy, finish him."

Suddenly, Sparkplug was on top of the fallen Atila. He looked as if he was about to savage him when Alfie lifted the stick in his hand and started towards the angry animals. Very quickly, the boy got his slingshot from his pocket, and before Alfie could land the first blow, he struck him on his right leg, just above the knee.

Alfie looked up in surprise. He had a look of thunder on his face but Jerry had already loaded another pebble into the pouch, and taken aim.

"You touch my dog and I won't be aiming at your leg this time," he said threateningly to the older man.

Alfie froze. In the meantime, Atila had assumed a submissive stance. Sparkplug stood over him for a long time, growling through bared teeth before slowly backing away, all the time with his eyes on his vanquished adversary.

When they got home, Cousin Noah washed the wound with Jeyes disinfectant and applied a mixture of aloes, ashes, and sulphur. Within a week the gallant Sparkplug was back to normal. Atila on the other hand had sustained several nasty bites and was out of action for a while longer.

Because of Atila's dubious reputation there was a lot of interest in the outcome of the fight and the result went right through the neighbourhood.

Afterwards people would give Jerry treats for Sparkplug. It seemed that he was a hero.

Before Jerry went to bed that night, he had another look at his eyes in the mirror. He still wasn't sure. Once again he had faced and defeated an opponent. Was the colour of his eyes changing he wondered. He'd have to wait and see. As he thought about the fight, he heard his mom's words in his head.

"Whenever animals of the same species fight, it is seldom to the death, and then only from the wounds sustained in the fight. Once one surrenders, the fight is usually over."

He remembered Sparkplug standing over Atila then slowly backing away. He could not imagine Alfie doing the same thing in a similar situation.

The next day after arriving from school, he changed into his home clothes and was about to run out of the house before he could be intercepted when Juliette called, "Here you are Jer."

She handed him his own letter from his mom. Very excitedly, he unfolded the page and read.

> *My dear son,*
>
> *I meant to write to you long before this, but there were a million things waiting for me to do when I got back. I miss you very much, and I'm already wondering about my next holiday. One thing I can promise you is that it won't be as long again before I see you.*
>
> *You are a fine boy Jer and I'm very proud of you. I want you to write to me and give me all the news about yourself, and whatever else is happening at home and in the neighbourhood. One more thing, don't forget to have that picture taken of you and Sparkplug and send one to me. Please be good for your sisters. I love you. Mom.*

That reminder by his mom to take a picture spurred him into action. Having had had his hair cut, he changed into his Sunday clothes and together, he and the dog made their way across the river to Mr. Mark's photo studio. They found the door closed. A weather beaten note attached to a string which hung around the handle read, 'Back in a few minutes.'

They were running around and romping together in the yard when Mr Mark rode up on his motorcycle.

77

He watched the boy and the dog as they played together and decided against a studio shot. Instead, he chose a spontaneous close up as they frolicked. Jerry was surprised when he was told to come back after a week for the pictures. He hadn't realized that Mr Mark had already taken the picture.

On the way home, they had to cross the La Fortune Bridge that spanned the river. When they got there, he took some leftover rice from his pocket and threw it into the river below. Hardly had they touched the water before the mullets came up to feed.

He always liked looking at the fish which never missed a chance to feed. As he watched, a sudden breeze caught underneath the peak of the red cap that his mom had brought him and blew it over the rail into the river below.

Even as he looked, he knew it wouldn't be long before it drifted into the strong current to be lost to him forever.

He was brought back to the moment with a start. To his horror, the dog had followed the cap into the water.

"No Sparky!" he screamed as he ran as quickly as he could around the railing and onto the riverbank and through his rising panic, he scanned the river for any sign of the dog. Relief flooded through him. For swimming towards the bank a few yards away was Sparkplug, with the cap firmly in his grasp.

He was both relieved and overjoyed, but above all, he was very proud of his dog. He started jumping up and down and shouting, "Come here boy, come to me, good dog!"

Without allowing him time to shake himself dry, he hugged the dog tightly and together they rolled all along the ground. Soon they were covered with mud. By the time they had stopped fooling around, Jerry was soaking wet and his Sunday clothes were filthy. At that moment he felt as happy as he thought he was ever going to be.

Right from day one, like every other kid everywhere, Jerry had tried to teach the dog to do tricks to show how smart he was.

So far he had learnt how to shake hands, how to sit when told, and how to catch, but nothing he had done would have led him to expect the heroics of jumping off such a high bridge. That night, for only the second time, Sparkplug was allowed to sleep in the bed.

Shortly afterwards, Jerry was asked to keep an eye on his year old nephew, Johnny. He was the first son of his sister Marina. The baby became grumpy and Jerry gave him his rattle as a distraction.

Throwing a minor tantrum, he threw away the rattle, which was promptly returned by the dog. Several times he repeated it, only to have it returned by the tireless pet. After about five or six attempts, the baby, who by then had turned it into a game started to laugh and gurgle. Jerry could hardly believe what he had seen. Smiling, he stooped to stroke and cuddle the dog.

"You are so smart, you keep surprising me. Who's a smart dog then?" The affectionate animal responded by wagging his tail furiously and licking his young master's face. After that, looking after Johnny was a breeze.

Because of all the rain of the past few weeks, the vegetation every-where was lush and green, and the pasture was thickly carpeted with grass. It was the lambing season. That evening, when Jerry brought in the animals, Cousin Noah was sitting under the calabash tree smoking his pipe. He cast an experienced eye on the two pregnant ewes and suggested that it would soon be time. He also promised to be close by until after the event. In preparation, he sent Jerry to the shop for candles and kerosene for a flambeau should it be needed.

Next evening on the way home, one of the ewes had to be urged on by Sparkplug and on seeing her condition, Cousin Noah was sure she was going to deliver that night.

In order to be ready, Jerry had gone to bed still wearing the clothes he had on. Despite his determination to stay awake, he was sound asleep when Cousin Noah knocked on his window.

He jumped out of his bed and rushed downstairs. Underneath the house the flambeau was already alight. It was his first time at a birth and he didn't want to miss anything.

On arrival, he was told to wash his hands properly and be sure to dry them on something clean. After he had complied they sat down to wait, but with the impatience of youth, the boy began to have doubts that anything was going to happen that night. His thoughts were disturbed as Cousin Noah asked. "Have you got your slingshot with you?"

"No, it's in my room."

"Go and get it, and when you have done that, take Sparkplug with you and bring me some bu-cu-sou from the garden," said his cousin.

"Do you mean the wild beans that grow along the fence? Because she won't eat them?"

"She will tonight – trust me. It will help her to pass the afterbirth."

When he got back nothing seemed to have changed, but his cousin was sure that something was going to happen soon.

"Why did you want me to get my slingshot?"

"Because the smell of the afterbirth might attract wild dogs and they would need to be discouraged."

After a little while the ewe started bleating.

"I think she is ready boy", the older man said.

As he watched, the lamb was already on its way, he could see what he thought were tiny hooves. He could hardly curb his impatience as the minutes ticked by without obvious progress.

"Why is it taking so long?" he asked impatiently.

"Have some patience boy. You will learn that there are some things you cannot hurry. Sometimes, these things take time."

As Noah spoke, the ewe started grunting and the lamb was eased a little further forward. Jerry could feel his heart pounding in his chest, and his excitement was at fever pitch. To his surprise, just as his cousin had said, the ewe began munching on the vine.

"I don't understand," he said. "I have never seen her eat that before."

The older man smiled for the first time. "I told you so," he said with satisfaction.

The ewe grunted again and suddenly the head appeared. Jerry was so engrossed in his eagerness not to miss anything he carelessly held the flambeau too close to the floor above him. The smell of burning wood alerted them.

"Pay attention to what you are doing before you burn the house down!" Cousin Noah said sharply.

Another grunt from the ewe and yet again there was more forward movement. Cousin Noah moved closer to the ewe and squatted on his haunches. Very gently he took hold of the proffered limbs and waited, and as the next movement started, he pulled the lamb free.

"There you are girl, it's all done. That's a very good girl," Cousin Noah said.

"Oh boy!" shouted Jerry. "Look!" he said pointing.

The older man smiled as the ewe began to lick the lamb all over. Unbelievably, less than ten minutes later, the lamb started moving around in an attempt to stand on spindly, rubbery legs.

"Isn't it just beautiful?" the boy enthused. "Just look at it trying to stand up already."

"I agree, said his cousin, "I think all new life is good."

After the ewe had done her licking, she turned once again to the vine and started eating.

"What did I tell you," Cousin Noah said. Jerry followed his gaze and saw a couple of dogs prowling around in the shadows.

"Well! What are you waiting for? discourage them."

The boy needed no further encouragement. He whipped out his slingshot after putting down the flambeau, took careful aim and fired. The dog yelped as the pebble found its mark. With hardly a pause, he repeated the process with the same success.

Another half an hour went slowly by before the ewe finally dropped the afterbirth, which Cousin Noah buried in a hole he had already dug in the garden.

As he walked back, Jerry cried out to him excitedly. "Come an' see, Cousin Noah! come an' see."

The man saw just what he expected to see. The lamb, just over half an hour old, was already standing on shaky legs, suckling its mother.

Seeing the excitement on the boy's face, Noah allowed him another ten minutes before sending him to bed.

"Off you go now to your bed. Sparkplug will help me take care of things here. Don't forget you have school in the morning."

Unable to sleep straight away, Jerry was lying in the dark thinking of the wonder he had just witnessed, when, to his utter surprise he heard the ewe bleat and a few heartbeats later, the lamb answered.

He wished the ewe could have waited until daylight so he would have been there the first time that the lamb bleated.

As he replayed the events of the night in his mind, he could hear his cousin saying, "I think all new life is good."

His thoughts went back to that awful day he had killed the humming bird and once again he was filled with remorse. Mr Leopold was right, he thought. It should never be an option to kill for fun.

Though he had slept for only a few hours he was already in the playground, surrounded by some of his friends, a full ten minutes before the assembly bell was rung. Once again, they hung on his every word as he graphically described the birth of the lamb. He could hardly wait for the turn of the other ewe.

It was about that time of day, between the sun going down and that brief period that passes for sunset in the tropics. The evening was still, with hardly a breeze, suggesting a shower or two later on. The playful sound of children's' laughter was briefly interrupted by the squawking of a large flock of birds as they flew low over the trees in V formation.

Having brought in the animals and had his dinner, Jerry hurried to join the other children of his age in Mother Tina's yard, where they were busy helping to shell raw peanuts.

No one knew for sure when it started but over the years the younger children had taken to congregating in the yard of an evening and assisted with whatever chores there were around. The activity was seen as a marker for determining their places in the hierarchy and an impatient child who insisted on participation got the answer, "Next year darling, next year." The practice was fast becoming established as tradition.

After the helpers were finished they were rewarded, and on this particular evening it was with lemonade and Marvin's biscuits.

Afterwards, the games that usually lasted for about an hour began. Sitting at the table with Mother Tina were Wally, Lynton and Billy. They were playing a board game called the *Grand National*. Each player was represented on the board by red, green, yellow, or blue discs and their progress along the course depended on the number thrown on the dice. The six obstacles included the famous jumps, the *Chair* and *Beecher's Brook*.

Any player unfortunate to land on any of these would be penalised and, in the case of *Beecher's*, would be relegated back to the starting line.

The excitement generated by the simple game amongst both players and spectators alike would have baffled an outsider.

Sitting on the floor near to the screen that separated the front room from the working area were another two of Jerry's friends, David and Elton. They were playing with a deck of cards that was so old and familiar that one or the other would call, "Snap!" long before turning over the card.

A roar went up at the table. Lynton was a long way in front of his competitors but throwing a four would land him on *Beecher's* and send him back to the beginning. Both the players and spectators willed him to disaster.

"Come on, hurry up," Mother Tina urged, "I've got my evil eye on you."

Meanwhile, Elton, who was sitting on the floor, had pulled the short straw earlier, when they drew to decide who was going to lift some of the tastier roasted nuts that were designated for next day's peanut cake from its protection behind the screen. Taking advantage of the commotion, he edged up as close as he could and reached behind the screen in his search for the tray. Suddenly there was a loud

83

snap accompanied by Elton's screech and all eyes were tuned on him. There was total silence. He withdrew his hand in near panic, and attached to two of his fingers was an old rattrap.

"Oh dear! How on earth did that happen?" said a seemingly surprised Mother Tina. She promptly bathed the offending fingers in cold water and applied a generous covering of Canadian Healing Oil and declared the games closed for the night. Without a word of rebuke, they went merrily home with her customary, "Sleep tight darlings, and?"

"Don't let the bedbugs bite," they all answered in unison.

Mother Tina had a long look at the old trap and smiled.

"Come on Snappy, let's put you back to sleep until you're needed again."

10

It was the last football game between the schools. The big game between the Roman Catholics and the Anglicans. As with all neighbouring foes the competition between the two teams was always fierce. They were due to meet on the Friday before Whit Sunday and a victory would convey bragging rights to the winners for one whole year.

Picked to represent his team for the first time, Jerry, at eleven years old was the youngest player on the field, but his exploits at left wing with the High Street team were well known to Mr Jerome, who was in charge of sport.

The game when it started was fast and furious, with quite a lot of bunching in the middle of the field, but what it lacked in technique, it more than made up for in enthusiasm. At half time the teams were even at three goals each but Jerry was far from happy with his performance.

After they had all returned from a drink at the tap in the playground, Mr Jerome got them together and congratulated them on their efforts so far and made one or two suggestions for the second half hour.

"Try not to hog the ball. Remember it's a team game, so pass it to your team mate. Now do you think you can do that for me?"

The Roman Catholic team started better, but the Anglicans made the score four – three against the run of play. A few minutes later,

Jerry's team was awarded a penalty and tied the score at four goals each. The game ebbed and flowed and ended in a lucky win for Jerry's team, after the goalkeeper fumbled a shot from Jerry. The moment the game was over he grabbed his books and ran most of the way home. He could hardly wait to tell those who'd missed all the action.

When he was almost there, the run, plus the exhaustion of the game kicked in and he slowed to a brisk walk. Halfway up the short cut along Cross Street through Banana Hollow, he started running again and as he approached the house he called out for Sparkplug like he always did. "Sparky! Where are you boy? Come to me boy," but the dog didn't respond to his call.

As he got nearer to the house, there was a small group of people gathered in the street in front of it and without knowing why, he felt that something was wrong.

He headed straight for them. Juliette saw him and she moved to intercept him before he could see the reason for their loitering, he eluded her easily and barged into the front of the little group. What he saw confirmed his worst fears.

The dog was lying in the middle of the road in a pool of blood and part of its entrails was lying on the tarmac. He heard a loud scream but wasn't aware that it had come from him.

He rushed over to the stricken animal, who in recognition of his young master, started wagging its tail and attempted unsuccessfully to rise.

"No Sparky, please don't try," Jerry sobbed pitifully as he sat down in the street, bent over and gathered his friend into his arms, barely aware that he was covered in the blood of the dying animal.

"Oh Sparky, Sparky, how could this happen? Who did this to you?" he asked over and over again, his sobs making his shoulders shudder.

After a while, one of the men wrestled his arms from around the hurting animal and gently passed him over to his sister, who by now had tears streaming unashamedly down her cheeks. Very gradually, she led him towards the house as Noah hastened in their direction.

"What happened here?" he asked, directing his question to Juliette.

"I was in the house when I heard a car screech to a stop and Sparkplug howled. By the time I got out, he was lying in the street in a pool of blood. The driver of the car said that he ran out in front of him and there was nothing he could have done to avoid him. He said he was willing to pay."

"He did! I'll give him pay," said Noah, all the time watching the boy.

"No Noah!" Juliette said, fearing a violent outcome. "There are two people who saw what happened. It was just an accident."

Noah turned abruptly away and approached the dog, which by now was lying motionless in the street. Sparkplug was dead.

Without saying another word he picked up the dead animal in his arms, quite mindless of all the blood, and he carried it into the garden before going into the kitchen for the spade.

During all of that time Jerry had stood motionless, leaning on the shoulder of his comforting older sister. Without warning, he pulled away from her embrace, ran underneath the house and threw up, just as he had done when his dad died.

Juliette, still leaning against the house half whispered, "Oh dear Lord, not again."

That night the joy of scoring the winning goal for the school was completely forgotten as the boy mourned his friend.

He laid in the darkness thinking of Sparkplug and all that time, though he never made a sound, his pillow was saturated with his tears.

In the days that followed, all of Juliette's fears came true. The pattern was the same as when his dad had died. Once again he went off his food and spoke only when he was spoken to. This time, although his school attendance did not suffer, his work did.

One Sunday morning shortly after that terrible accident, Miss Angeline walked back from church with Juliette and a very silent Jerry.

After a lot of small talk, she intimated that the bitch would soon be having another litter, but the boy did not show the expected response. Still persevering, she asked him if he would like to come by and choose one of the pups after they were born, and sweetened the offer by promising that he could have first pick. Very politely, he refused the offer. He thanked her but said he didn't want any other dog.

"Well, if you change your mind, the offer is still there," she said hopefully.

Since the accident, he went to the pasture only to tie the sheep and bring them home in the evenings, never staying as he did before to join in any games. Somewhere in the back of his mind, he was convinced that Sparky would still be here if he hadn't stayed after school to play football.

More and more, he was spending his time after school, sitting against the grotto on Leapers Hill, where he did his homework and sought escape in the comic books that his mom had brought him.

However hard Jerry tried, he couldn't stop thinking about Sparkplug. Nor could he stop the bad dreams he had most nights with Sparky lying in a pool of blood but still wagging his tail and trying to get up. Without him, life just wasn't fun any more.

For the first time in a long time, he wished his mum was at home, at least when Sparky was killed. He missed her now more than when she left.

"Give Sparkplug a big hug for me," she had said to him at the airport, as she was getting ready to leave. In her letter, she had reminded him to take a picture with the dog and send her a copy.

"The photographs", he thought, sitting up. He had forgotten all about them. Then he relaxed once more into his bed, surprised by the realization that he had no great desire to collect them.

In the next room, Juliette and Marigold were also awake and conversed quietly, as they tried to figure out a way to get their little brother back to his old cheerful self. At the moment that day seemed a long way away, given the bad dreams he was having almost every night, exactly as when their father died.

Juliette and Marigold were very close. Their dual efforts looking after the rest of the family had bounded them closely together, even for sisters.

Juliette was the third offspring and ten years the senior to Marigold. She was only about five feet tall, her hair was short and her lips were full. Her best feature by far, was her soft dark eyes and long lashes. In her devotion to her family, she was single-minded.

Marigold was taller by about four inches. Blessed also with those long eyelashes, she had an abundance of rich black hair and a slender figure, which all combined to make her a very attractive young woman.

It was Marigold's idea that Miss Angeline should make the offer of another pup, and she was both surprised and disappointed at its failure.

"I just can't understand why he doesn't want another dog, I thought he would jump at the chance to have first pick," she remarked.

"It's not really so hard," said Juliette. "He thinks he will be unfaithful to Sparkplug, if he chooses another."

"He never laughs or even smiles anymore," said Marigold, unable to keep the hopelessness out of her voice.

"I just wish he would start eating properly again," said Juliette.

"I don't think he has taken part in any games since that dreadful day," Marigold said.

"Come to think of it," said Juliette, "he doesn't enjoy anything anymore. Do you know, I almost had to scold him into going to the matinee the other day?"

"He loved the pictures. He laughed so much when I took him to see Laurel and Hardy, that afterwards, he said his face was tired," Marigold said.

"He has been spending so much time by himself, his friends have nicked-named him, Lobo," Juliette said.

"That's a funny kind of name, why Lobo?"

"Well, like I said, plenty of time by himself. You know – lone wolf Lobo?"

Despite the gravity of the situation, Marigold smiled. "Boys will be boys. I just hope something happens soon to change things."

"He keeps having those bad dreams, so if at anytime during the night you hear him mumbling, wake him up. In the meantime, we can just hope and pray," Juliette told her sister.

Time was passing slowly, with still no improvement. If anything, he was eating less, and Juliette was certain that Sparkplug's demise had reawakened the hurt of their father's death. Funny that the remedy for the first malady should now be the cause of another, she thought to herself.

She was still trying to decide what to cook for dinner when the sound of the fisherman's conch shell signalled a catch. The fact that the shell was blown for only a short while indicated that the catch was a small one. The shell, used since the days of the pirates to announce their presence was now used to advertise a catch.

Although it was just after nine o'clock in the morning, it was already quite warm and her experience told her that it was going to be another scorcher.

She was a little preoccupied as she walked along the bay making her way back from the frenzied activity of buying the fish. It was always the same when the catch was limited and everyone was trying to get the fisherman's attention.

She looked to the sea and saw there were already a few bathers catching a morning swim. As she walked along she saw Leopold stretched out in the sun.

She smiled. She would never understand the obsession the white people had with the sun. As for this one, he was as mad as a bat and yet Jerry thought he could walk on water. She walked all of fifty yards or so before coming to a dead stop.

"That's it!" she said aloud to herself. "It's got to be worth a try."

She turned around and walked towards where the man was lying on his back. As she got nearer, she could see that his eyes were closed.

The sand masked the sound of her approach and the sound of her voice startled Leopold as she greeted him.

"Good morning Mr Leopold."

He opened his eyes and looked at her and his stern look suggested a hint of annoyance at the intrusion. He rose slowly to a sitting position.

"Good morning yourself, young woman," he said. "I'm afraid you have the advantage of me."

"Oh! I'm sorry, I am Juliette, Jerry's sister?"

"Jerry?"

This was proving more difficult than she expected.

"Yes, he talks about you a lot, he admires you a great deal," she told him, but his expression said quite clearly that he still didn't know who she was talking about. She was beginning to get nervous, but persevered.

"Small boy," she said, "always went around with his dog. He . . ."

"Ah!" drawled the man as he interrupted her. "You mean the Little Hunter?"

His expression had changed to one of affability.

"Leopold is at your service. What is it that I can do for you?"

Her flagging confidence returned by the change of his expression.

"Three years ago, Jerry lost his dad, he died of pneumonia. He took it very badly and we nearly lost him. Then he got the dog and everything was all right again. A few weeks ago the dog was killed in an accident and now he is that way again," she told him.

"I am sorry. I heard the people in the shop talking about it. He was a good dog, very good for the boy, but I still don't understand why you speak to me about it," said the man.

"Well, like I said, he admires you a great deal and I thought that if you had a word with him, he might listen to you. He has no interest in anything. Before the accident they had a picture taken together. That was weeks ago, but he still hasn't collected it. I have tried everything and I really don't know what else to do."

He stroked his chin for a few moments. "Yes, yes I see. You think he will listen to Leopold, yes?" He held up his hand as she was about to answer, "I will see the Little Hunter and I will speak with him."

"You can find him any evening after school by the grotto," she informed him.

"I know the place," he said. "That's the hill looking out to the ocean, I speak to him for you. Leopold will try," he smiled at her.

Jerry had talked of his green eyes, but it was the first time that she had been close enough to see them. She wasn't sure she had believed him. For her also, this was a new experience.

"One thing though, he mustn't know that I asked you," she pleaded with him.

"He will not know. You not tell him and Leopold will not tell him."

She tried to thank him, but he waved her away.

"No bother to thank me, I have done nothing as yet."

As she walked away, she felt a lot better. It might not work, but there's a chance and if that's what it takes, she was willing to try them all.

Left alone once again, Leopold eased himself back onto the sand and reassumed his position in the hope of continuing his meditation, but he found it difficult to concentrate.

When he came into the region he had made a few rules for himself, the chief of which was never to get involved on a personal level with the affairs of the locals. Now, here he was, having just given his word to talk to the boy, without understanding how or why.

He remembered their first encounter vividly and despite whatever misgivings he might have, he smiled as he saw again in his mind's eye, the comical scene of the boy mimicking the demeanour of the hunter and the pup which followed behind, making enough noise to rouse a drunken sleeper.

The boy had been unaware of his presence as he fired his first shot from his slingshot and missed. After a mild rebuke to the pup for excessive noise, he'd taken careful aim and fired a second time, this time with deadly accuracy. The stricken hummingbird had fluttered briefly before lying quite still.

He had witnessed the horrific look on the boy's face as the full enormity of his act had dawned on him. In desperation he had started blowing over the dead bird in a futile effort to breathe life back into it. It was then that Leopold had approached him and tried to help him to understand and possibly come to terms with what he had done.

It was not quite true that he did not understand why he had agreed to help. In some uncanny way, his young life had paralleled the boy's very closely. Although he would not readily admit it, he had been deeply touched for the first time in many years, when the boy told him that he had prayed for his safe return when he thought he was in trouble. He had stopped praying for himself a long time ago.

He waited for an hour after school, by which time there was very little activity in the yard. The grotto was situated about two hundred yards from the school and afforded a panoramic view of the ocean.

He deliberately walked along the cemetery wall, quite near to where the priest was standing at sunrise and came up on the boy's blind side. His tactic was to walk casually by and pretend surprise at having met him, but as he strolled by, he realized that his attempted stealthy approach was unnecessary.

The boy was sitting on the grass with his legs stretched out before him, the top part of his body relaxed against the grotto, and both his eyes were shut as if he was dozing.

"The sea breeze, it is good for sleep, yes?" Leopold's speech was slow and deliberate. The boy opened his eyes, coming awake with a start. He seemed surprised to see the older man.

"Hello Mr Leopold." His greeting was low and non-committal. Leopold got his pipe out and very slowly, filled it from a tobacco pouch he took from his shirt pocket.

He needed time to form his strategy which he had deliberately left until he had seen the boy and gauged his mood. On completion, he cupped his hand around the flame to shield it from the strong wind.

"I'm glad that I meet with you, Little Hunter. I heard about your dog. I wanted to tell you that I am sorry." His voice was even and sympathetic.

"Thank you Mr Leopold," said the boy.

"This is going to be harder than I thought" the man thought to himself. This was one of the most talkative boys that he had ever met yet remarkably, he was having trouble having a conversation with him. He tried again. "I understand how you feel," he said.

The boy looked at him for a long time but said nothing for a while. Leopold began to feel that his ploy had failed. Finally Jerry spoke. "Everybody keeps telling me that they understand how I feel, but they don't." He paused yet again, then said much quieter "They can't."

Now it was Leopold's turn to linger. At last he took the pipe from his mouth and blew the smoke into the wind.

Very slowly, he walked to within four paces and directly in front of his young friend and very awkwardly, sat himself on the ground. Once there, he crossed both legs and tucked them close to his body, allowing himself to sit very straight without support.

"I do," he said. "You see, when I was thirteen, just about your age —"

"I am eleven years old," the boy interrupted.

"Really? I thought you were older," said Leopold. "As I was saying, when I was thirteen, I too, lost my dog."

For the first time Jerry showed interest, both by his manner and his questions.

"Did you? What happened? What was his name?"

"That's better," thought the man. "To answer your last question first, his name was Lancelot."

"Why did you call him that?"

"My granddad named him after Sir Lancelot, King Arthur's bravest knight of the round table." He now had the boy's full attention.

"My father died at sea when I was only four years old. My mother took me to live with her parents on a farm in the country outside Braga —"

"How did your dad die?" interrupted Jerry.

"He was a sailor in the merchant navy"

"Was he in the war?"

"Ah! Now the questions," thought Leopold. "One night, in a bad storm outside Madagascar, his ship must have struck a rock. Pieces of it were found floating in the sea. There were no survivors."

He paused for a while. To his surprise, the boy said earnestly, "I'm sorry Mr Leopold."

"Long time now," the man said quietly. He continued, "On my fifth birthday, my grandfather gave Lancelot to me. From then on we were always together. You could say we grew up together.

Grandfather said he was a cross between a Labrador and a Collie. He grew into a beautiful black dog. I taught him lots of tricks. He was very smart and a very good hunter.

"That winter was very cold and the snow came early and stayed on the ground for a long time. The wolves, they started to kill the odd animal on the farm. One morning, when grandfather went out he found one of the sheep killed and half eaten by wolves."

"He said the kill was recent, so we set out after them, the fresh tracks in the snow making them easy to follow. Lancelot led the way with grandfather and myself following behind. After about a mile we could tell we were getting nearer to them."

"The scent was getting stronger, because Lancelot ran on ahead. We could not keep up with him due to the thick snow on the ground, but we knew he had caught up with them. We could hear him growling and snapping and we knew they were fighting."

"When we caught up to them, there were about six wolves and they had overpowered Lancelot. He was lying on his back by then and they were all around him. Grandfather and I shot one each and the others ran off, but we didn't go after them."

"He had bits taken out of him and there was a serious wound on his neck and he was bleeding badly. When he saw me, he started wagging his tail and even tried to get up, but he couldn't."

Leopold paused. He had a faraway look in his eyes, as if he was once again on his grandfather's farm watching the wounded animal.

"That was exactly what Sparky did when he saw me," said the boy.

He turned his head to the side to hide the tears that flowed freely down his cheeks, but a few drops fell on his shirt and betrayed him. The man sensed they were for Sparkplug more than Lancelot. Pulling his shirt tail from inside his trousers, Jerry dried his eyes and blew his nose quite vigorously.

"After a while," continued Leopold, "my grandfather said to me, 'it's your dog boy, you know what must be done, or would you like me to do it?' I told him that I would do it. I don't know how long I sat with him, with his head on my lap, so Grandfather reminded me that it was time we were getting back. Finally, I put the gun to his head, his tail was still wagging when I pulled the trigger."

Jerry put his hands quickly to his mouth and a small cry escaped from him. After a while he broke the silence.

"I don't think I could have done that Mr Leopold, I just couldn't."

"I heard how your dog died, boy. Are you sure you would not have done it if you'd had a gun? Would you rather see him suffer? Of course not, you would have done anything to stop his pain. "Afterwards, my grandfather put his arms around my shoulders. 'Try not to feel too bad son,' he said to me.

'That dog loved you more than anything or anyone, and he also knew that you loved him and would never hurt him – he understood'

'Your dog was smart, brave, and a very good hunter. Now, you must also be brave and show respect to his memory. You owe him that much.'

"Afterwards, we carried Lancelot back home and buried him in the vegetable patch. I know it's painful now, but after a while, after a long while, the pain of that loss would become less, unless you forget him."

"I will never forget him!" protested Jerry loudly.

"Then you will never lose him, as long as you remember him. Your Sparkplug showed a warrior's spirit and now, so must you."

He looked up and met Leopold's gaze. The strength of those piercing green eyes was almost physical.

"So," he said, "there are trees to be climbed, football to be played, and game to be hunted," he smiled benignly at Jerry. "Your Sparkplug, he will not like you to be sad."

The boy wiped his still wet cheeks with the back of his hand.

"Yes," he said, "I know you are right. He was the best dog ever."

Just as he had at the crossroads after picking up the coins, the man rolled unto his side and stood up. Once again, cupping his hands around the flame to protect it, he re-lit his pipe, which had gone out while he was talking.

"Do you still miss him? Lancelot I mean," asked the boy.

"All the time. It took me a long time before I stopped looking around for him," he smiled sheepishly.

With his pipe clenched firmly between his jaws he started to walk away. He took a couple of steps and turned all the way around to face the boy again. Taking the pipe from his mouth, he added, "Sometimes I wish I had a picture of him."

"I do!" said the boy enthusiastically, who for the first time during the whole conversation, actually smiled. "We took a picture together."

"Then you are lucky." Also smiling, he pointed the pipe at the boy. "Take care."

After Leopold had departed, Jerry remained in his sitting position for about five minutes, while he mulled over everything that he had said. Only, now he was sitting with his legs drawn up and both hands hugging his feet, his chin rested comfortably on his knees.

Mr Leopold was right he thought. There were lots of things to be done. He was overdue a visit to the photo studio. Gathering himself, he ran all the way home to deposit his books and most importantly, to collect whatever money there was in his hiding place.

He was surprised to find that he had over eight shillings then remembered he had been staying away from the matinees.

Collecting his hoop, which he used for the first time since Sparkplug's death, he ran all the way without once stopping and was pleased when he saw the bike in the yard. Mr Mark seemed very pleased to see him enter the studio.

"Good afternoon Mr Mark," he greeted.

"Hi Jerry," he answered cordially, "I thought you had forgotten all about the photos."

"I'm sorry sir, I," but the older man interrupted.

"No! No son. I am sorry. I heard about your dog and I know how painful it must be for you."

He opened a drawer in front of him and took out a framed photograph about six inches by four inches, and handed it to the boy.

The picture showed Jerry with his head thrown back laughing and the dog standing on his hind legs, with his two front paws resting on his young master's chest and his tail wagging. He stared down at the picture for a long time without a single utterance. When he did speak, there was a hint of surprise in his voice.

"Sparky! What a beautiful picture," he said it half to himself, half to Mr Mark.

"Yes," agreed the photographer. "In all modesty, I think it is a great picture, which captures exactly the way you felt about each other."

The boy put his hand into his pocket and started taking the coins out. Mr Mark put up his hand in a stopping gesture and said to him, "No need for that. I want you to accept it as a gift."

He returned to the drawer and handed him another unframed print of the same shot.

"Thank you Mr Mark, thank you very much," said Jerry.

"It's my pleasure, I'm sure it will look very nice on your front-room wall."

"Yes sir, thank you sir."

He put the pictures face to face and placed them inside his shirt and did up the buttons.

On the return journey, he stopped at the bridge and took the pictures out. He leaned against the rail and stared down at the river and the memory of the photo shoot less than two months ago was so clear in his mind. He could almost feel the warm breath of his panting comrade.

His gaze stayed on the water and he marvelled all over again at the bravery of the dog. Mr Leopold had called him 'smart, with a warrior's spirit'. He was the best.

As he replaced the photos inside his shirt, he thought to himself. "I too, have a warrior's spirit."

Eager now to hang the picture, he picked up his hoop and hurried home.

For the first time since that dreadful afternoon, he breezed into the house in much the same way as he did of old, startling Juliette into asking from the bedroom, "Is that you Jer?"

"Yes," he answered. "I didn't know you were in."

"It's all right. I just didn't expect you," she said as she came into the front room.

He took the pictures from within his shirt, the glass in the framed photo was smeared all over with his body heat. He placed it on the table and hurried into the kitchen, returning almost at once with a stone, which he used as a hammer. Juliette picked up the picture and started cleaning the glass with the tail of her apron.

"My, oh my," she said, holding it at arm's length in an attempt to see it better. "Isn't that a beautiful picture?"

"Mr Mark said it was a great picture," said the boy proudly, as he began hammering the nails just between and underneath the two holy pictures already hanging on the wall. "And he wouldn't take any money for them. He gave them to me as a gift."

"That was very Christian of him. I hope you thanked him properly," she said.

"Oh yes I did," he answered, as he took the picture from her and placed it on the wall. They both stared at it for a while, shifting positions to make sure it was in the right spot.

Juliette said, "He looks so alive, I –" but he interrupted her.

"He was the smartest and the best, and –"

Now it was her turn. "That he was Jer. As smart as they come. He used to pick up the fallen clothes pegs for me when I hung out the washing. We'll all miss him very much. Mr Mark was right, it's a great picture."

He left her still admiring the picture, went into his room and changed quickly into his home clothes. On returning, he said, "I'm going over to the pasture for a little while before bringing the animals home."

"I'll see you later then," she said.

As he turned to leave, she noticed his slingshot in his back pocket. She hugged herself and on her face was the biggest smile she had given in just over two months. When he was almost at the door, he suddenly stopped, turned around and covered the few steps between them. As if on impulse, he threw both arms around her and very quickly, kissed her on the cheek and was gone before she could react.

Placing her hand on the spot that he had kissed, she sat heavily in the chair nearest to her and was still hugging herself when the tears rolled down her cheeks; only this time, they were tears of joy.

Fumbling around in her apron pocket for a handkerchief, she wiped away the tears and blew her nose. Looking skywards, she prayed in little more than a whisper, "May the good Lord bless you, now and forever, Leopold."

As he got nearer to the pasture, he could hear the thump of the heavy football and the shouts of his friends.

His excitement built and suddenly, there was an intensity to be part of it. When he got there, the penultimate game of the day was in progress, waiting on a goal by either side to decide the winner. Also waiting was his friend Elton, who seemed genuinely surprised to see him. He called out to him in greeting.

"Hey! Lobo, what's up man?"

Jerry knew of the nickname and ignored it at first, but had finally bowed to the inevitable. As they were talking, the game ended and while all the additional players were taken on for the last game, which on occasions had fielded as many as thirteen a side, the captain of the senior team approached Jerry.

"There's a game against Marli on Sunday. You in?"

"Yes, sure," he said eagerly.

"Three o'clock then. Don't be late."

Without waiting for an answer, he ran off for the start of the last game.

The game finally began. It was his first game of any kind for two months and he revelled in it. He ignored his position and just chased the ball. He was hit by a fierce tackle which sent him sprawling, but to the bystander, judging from Jerry's reaction, one might have thought that he'd just been handed a juicy mango or a piece of stretch candy. He was up and chasing again in no time, laughing his head off as he went.

As he ran alongside his friends demanding the ball, he felt for the first time that the invisible cloak of gloom he had been wearing for the past few weeks had been lifted from him and he devoured the feeling of freedom and camaraderie that recently had been missing from his life. For the first time ever, he didn't care if the game was won or lost.

After supper that evening, he sat at the table and wrote a long letter to his mom that was to set precedence for all the letters he would write to her in the future. He told her of Mr Mark's generosity, what Leopold had said, what Father Devas said in his sermon last Sunday, and the exciting news of him following in Ambrose's footsteps to be an altar boy. He enclosed the picture of himself and Sparkplug and sealed the envelope.

"Will you please post this for me?" he asked, handing the letter to Juliette.

"Why don't you post it yourself?" she pointed to the dressing table. "Look in the vase, there are stamps there and you know the address."

Six o'clock on Sunday morning and Jerry was already wide awake.

He was too excited to sleep late. Later that morning, he would be serving in his first mass since becoming an altar boy, where he would be seen by all his friends.

He liked everything about being one, but the reward of half a crown every time he served at a wedding or a funeral, was a powerful incentive.

Later that afternoon, he would be playing football for the senior team. "What a difference a few days can make," he thought. The tears that were forever behind his eyes had suddenly dried up and the constant weight in his chest had disappeared. Best of all, the bad dreams had all but gone away. Mr Leopold was right. There were things to be done and games to be played. He bounded out of bed to meet the day.

11

Time passed as it inevitably does and with its passing came an abundance of testosterone to the recently teenaged males of the town. Childish pursuits that were so vitally a part of preteen years were abandoned in favour of more robust and dangerous replacements, more ambitious challenges.

Gone were the hoops, spinning tops, slingshots, hide and seek and marbles, substituted by point to point swimming, mongoose trapping, teasing, cricket or football, depending on the weather or the equipment, but most of all, male posturing, and girls.

The eagerly awaited August holidays had finally arrived and the boys revelled in the activities, sporting or otherwise, but most of all, they enjoyed the camaraderie which would link them together for the rest of their lives.

Jerry rose early that first morning and rushed through his chores and breakfast, and headed for the beach. As early as he thought he was, he found that a few of his friends were already there.

The plan for the morning was a point to point swim from Rathan Bay, designated point A, to The Boucheree, point B, a distance of just over a mile and fanatically competitive.

The event was nearly always won by the same person, Lynton Cross, nicknamed Ahab because of his obsession for all things connected to the sea. Even now, he was already standing at the Table repelling all comers in a game of free for all.

The Table is a rock situated about a hundred yards from the shore. It is about six feet in diameter and can only be seen when the tide was very low. It was so called because of its smooth flat surface. On this particular day, those on it were standing shin deep in the water.

The idea of the game was to gain and keep possession. While up there you were fair game, the only rule being, that there were no rules.

The most effective, and so the most popular form of attack was to come in with the wave, generally referred to as 'a riser', using feet, hands, and even one's head to clear the Table. Even armed with the knowledge of your intent, they were disadvantaged against the waves.

It became more tactical when played by teams. Usually, one or more of the team in attendance would be left in the water to ruin interference, thereby, helping to nullify the success of any intended attack.

On the Table, whether in free for all or team game, Ahab had no equal. Jerry who was no mean performer himself swam eagerly to join the fray. He did not have long to wait for a decent riser, and decided on a frontal attack.

Using both hands and head, he charged in. Ahab anticipating the move, very quickly got down on his side and using the momentum of the wave and his feet, he tossed Jerry about four feet into the air and into the water on the other side.

After each of the others had tried and failed, they initiated the rush and overwhelmed him by sheer force of numbers. Before leaving for the swim, Ahab stood at the Table and beating his chest like Tarzan, shouted his usual victory cry.

"Out here I'm king, and the Table is my kingdom. I shall repel all boarders. Come one, come all!"

The rest of the stragglers had finally arrived, swelling the number to eleven. The safe way to Rathan Bay was around the cliffs and over the top, but the journey took about an hour. They opted for their customary route along the rock face, which was at least half the time, but laced with danger.

They proceeded in single file, doing a fair imitation of mountain goats and uncharacteristically for them, keeping the conversation to a minimum.

Rathan Bay was a small out of the way beach, just over a hundred meters long and because of its inaccessibility, was nearly always deserted, and for that reason suited their purpose perfectly. After raiding the sugar-apple trees nearby that were just coming into season, they got down to business.

The race was started in the usual fashion. A stone was thrown high into the air and they waited for the splash. At the given signal the competitors ran into the sea and swam as fast as they could for as long as they could. Jerry, determined not to repeat his mistake of the last swim by trying to stay with Ahab, settled down in the middle of the pack, hoping for a strong finish in the last two hundred yards.

By the halfway stage, Ahab had already established a considerable lead. Free styling from the word go and breathing every second stroke, his strength in the water and his technique, took him further and further away, until at last he came to the Table. There he did his usual victory dance to rub in his superiority over the pack, then swam the short distance to the shore, a full three minutes ahead of his nearest pursuer.

Jerry's plan worked almost to perfection. He was denied the second place he was hoping for, but managed a close third. When at last he made the shore, he found Ahab engaged in conversation with two giggly girls from the Anglican school.

For Jerry, the best part of the holidays was having Ambrose home for six long weeks. On his very first week home, one afternoon, he hired a bike for two hours and spent the time teaching Jerry how to ride.

The next day, Jerry, together with Elton and Wally, went to the pasture to look for a game. With some other friends, they were on the verge of starting a game of football when they were muscled out of the playing area by the older boys with a promise to give it back after one game. The boys were outraged but could do nothing. When the game was over their tormenters reneged on their promise and started another. Devastated, they sat under the huge cedar tree and hung their heads.

Just then Ambrose came walking up with his football boots slung around his neck.

"What you fellahs looking so happy about?"

Jerry told him what had happened.

"We'll soon see about that," his bigger brother said.

He took his place under the tree and waited until the ball was kicked in his direction and he picked it up. Only, instead of throwing it back, he proceeded to undo the laces and removed the inner tube.

"Hey, Ambrose!" shouted one of the players. "Just what the hell do you think you're doing?"

"Taking back my property. You asked me to buy you a tube with a promise of payment on delivery. It's now almost a week and I'm still to see a red cent. If you want it you know where it will be." He threw back the casing.

Without a ball, the bullies gave up the pitch, and the boys had their game.

Later on that afternoon, Jerry picked up his school bag and headed for his favourite spot by the grotto. His homework for the holidays was to write an essay of not less than five hundred words on superstition. He was determined to finish it early so he could concentrate on his holidays. He was scribbling furiously when he was startled by a shadow falling over the page.

"Sorry if I frightened you," said Leopold, who was standing a few feet away holding a paper bag.

"Oh, hello Mr Leopold, I just didn't see you coming," said Jerry.

"I was hoping to see you here," said the man.

"Is something wrong?" asked the boy anxiously.

"Oh! Nothing like that, I was looking through my things today and I found something I would like you to have."

He handed over the bag that he was holding.

"I picked it up in Cape Town, but never used it. I hope you like it."

The boy's excitement was instant and his hand shook slightly as he accepted the bag. He opened it eagerly and withdrew a coiled leather belt with a large silver buckle, upon which was the carving of a bird similar to the one in the man's tattoo.

He unfurled the belt and gasped in surprise, for at intervals along it were coloured pictures of four large animals.

"It really is beautiful," he said almost to himself. Then he said louder, "Thank you very much, Mr Leopold, I'll take good care of it."

"I'm glad you like it. It is better that you have it Little Hunter," he said. "But now," he smiled as he continued, "it is time not to call you Little Hunter anymore."

Jerry stood up and measured the belt around his waist.

"I'll need to put another hole in it. I'll take good care of it," he said, for the second time.

"If you rub some oil into the leather and polish the buckle, it should last you a long time," the man advised.

Jerry looked into those piercing green eyes.

"Thank you again, for everything."

Leopold's face crinkled into a rear grin.

"Goodbye hunter. You take care of yourself."

"Goodbye," answered the boy absentmindedly. He was so taken by one of the pictures on the belt, that when he looked up, Leopold was nearly half way down the hill towards Lance Coteau.

Later, admiring the belt, Juliette had a strange far away look on her face.

"Your Leopold is a strange one. He is never rude, neither is he very friendly. He makes a point of keeping his distance yet, here he is taking the trouble to walk all the way to the grotto to give you this beautiful belt. Perhaps you remind him of someone."

Couple of days on, Jerry was rummaging, trying to find something in his room and was a bit distracted as his sister tried to talk to him. "Make sure you get a haircut before school starts," she said.

"I will," he answered.

"Your cassock is done. It's in the basket."

"Thank you."

Somewhere in the middle of what she was saying next, he heard the name Leopold, which got his attention.

"What was that you just said?"

"I said, I heard from Mother Tina today that Leopold was gone. He hasn't been seen for two days and all his things are gone."

His mind raced back to their last meeting by the grotto and suddenly everything made sense. Mr Leopold was saying goodbye.

"Goodbye Hunter. You take care of yourself," he had said.

"I should have guessed," said Jerry. He went into his room and returned with the belt.

"That was his going away present to you," said Juliette.

"He really said goodbye, but I thought."

She was surprised to see him smile, if anything, she expected the opposite reaction.

"Good old Mr Leopold. He left just as he came. I wonder where he went?"

"Well," said Juliette, "wherever that is, he'll be all right. He is that kind of man."

Left by himself, Jerry remembered those piercing green eyes, so clear, so alive and those words, 'I have looked into the eyes of the unicorn, do you think that damn mumbo jumbo could kill me?'

"Good luck to you Mr Leopold, wherever you are," he said to himself. He would never see, or hear anything of Leopold's whereabouts again, but he would never forget him.

In years to come, whenever he saw someone with green eyes or a tattoo, he would smile in remembrance of him.

Part Two

12

> *While there are children anywhere*
> *Who reach for goals even when in fear*
> *Even with dirty faces*
> *In the most unlikely places*
> *There will be heroes yet!*

The town's very successful women's cricket team, the Suffragettes, was playing the Amazons from Rose Hill. As expected, the locals easily won the match. Afterwards there was a mixed match and the boys stayed behind to watch.

One of the organisers called them over and very generously shared their refreshments with them. The afternoon wore on and the game came to an end. Most of the spectators had drifted away and the boys found, as on many occasions, that they were the same group of seven remaining.

Together with Jerry there was Elton Manley, alias 'Atlas', the tallest of the group. He lived with his grandmother, and because of her rheumatism, had done the washing and ironing since he was eight. He was called 'Atlas' after the character of the same name in the famous ad and was looked upon as the wimp who had the sand kicked into his face, before his amazing physical transformation to the famous Charles Atlas. He was a good wicket and goalkeeper.

And there were more.

David Barnes, alias "Gatlin". Lived with his mother, grandmother and twin sister. Had a gentle nature and was perhaps the most sensitive of the group. Good footballer, useless at cricket. He was named after, and compared to the Gatling gun because of his accurate imitation of it. He stuttered badly, especially when excited, or agitated. Yet, within the camaraderie of his friends, one would hardly notice his impediment.

Wally Tate, alias 'Nugget'. Lived with his grandmother and two sisters and had done the man's work within the family since he was ten. Good dancer, renowned for his diving skills. His outstanding feature was his extremely smooth, very dark skin, which contrasted sharply with the white of his eyes and his teeth. Named "Nugget", after the boot polish company. The suggestion was that he was covered all over by the product.

Billy Glass, alias 'Optic.' Lived with his father who worked as a porter at Pearls Airport. Spent most of his time over at his grandmother's, where he took most of his meals. An avid reader of all the old sports magazines that his dad brought home, but most especially, anything on boxing.

One of the smallest in the group, but easily the most accomplished with his fists. The reason for his proficiency began from his first day at school, when other children teased him about his eyes, which were very badly crossed. The taunts resulted in fights, which his dad hoped would be temporary, but they never stopped. After a while, he became the best. His name stemmed from a combination of his surname, plus the glasses that he always wore.

Lynton Cross, alias 'Ahab.' Lived with his grandparents. Tall for his age, he had well developed shoulders from swimming since he was five. Did his share of the washing and cooking. Named after the great

Then there was Clive Rawlings, alias 'Brains.' He was the third of eleven children, the last being the only girl. He became his mother's main helper in her dress making business and frequently helped with both the washing and ironing. The time he could spend with his friends was restricted because he was thought to have an asthmatic condition. The name was because of his obvious intelligence and sharp wit. Easily the most mischievous of the group, whenever free, he was always game for a prank or a challenge.

Nicknames play a big part in Caribbean culture. Once a name has been established, it is used to the exclusion of that person's proper name. The given name is only used when talking to an adult about that person. The importance of the nickname can be seen by its inclusion in the Wailer's chant.

As they chatted, Optic noticed Lobo's belt and commented on it. They all had a good look at the shiny silver buckle with the bird engraved on it, but ignored the rest of the images on it.

"It was a gift from Mr Leopold before he left," he explained.

"You mean the crazy white man?" asked Nugget.

"Crazy! Did you say crazy? He has looked into the eyes of the unicorn and lived to tell about it."

"Right," said Brains, "and I'm the Flying Dutchman, roaming the ocean seeking forgiveness."

"Do you remember when Puff Jake was taking all our stuff and making us do chores before we could get them back?" asked Lobo. "Why do you think he gave everything back and allowed me to go into his garden afterwards?"

He then gave them a graphic account of everything that passed between him and Puff Jake and at the end they were all shedding tears amidst their laughter.

"Why have you not told us this before?" asked Brains.

"Because Ambrose told me not to, to be on the safe side."

113

"But if he was the one who looked into the unicorn's eyes, how come you bested Puff Jake?" Nugget wanted to know.

"Well," said Jerry, "he looked into the unicorn's eyes, and I looked into his."

"So what you're saying is that by association, you inherit some of the magic?" Brains sounded a little incredulous.

"Exactly!" said Lobo. He went on to remind them of the confrontation with Alfie and Atila and what Mr Leopold had said about defeating your opponent. Elton confirmed it. He finished by asking as he looked at each in turn.

"Have you ever seen his eyes? Have you ever seen eyes like that before?"

They talked until the sun went down, and all the other people had gone home, and once they accepted his theory, they decided by association also, that they too would inherit a little of the magic, if they looked into Jerry's eyes. With a feeling of togetherness, they vowed to assist each other, should the time ever come to defeat an opponent. The Brotherhood of the Unicorn was born.

All too soon, it was the last week of the holidays and every effort was made to fill those final few days with as many activities as possible. The main event of the day was a cricket match against Low Town. The temperature was in the high nineties as it had been all that month. On the roads the tarmac was beginning to melt and the vegetation was sparse and brown from lack of recent rainfall.

Due to play in the game, four of the boys had left the beach early and were the first to arrive at the pasture. Wanting to conserve their energy, they made their way to the calabash tree, which offered the only available shade nearby.

As they walked along, they came upon a hen that was teaching her six chicks the art of foraging. One of the boys had strayed close to the chicks, provoking the hen into an aggressive stance. Fluffing her feathers to make herself appear bigger, with outstretched neck and flapping wings, she looked as if she was going to attack and relaxed only when he moved away.

Close by, there were some other animals grazing on what little they could find and they all had one thing in common. They were all frantically swishing their tails around in a vain attempt to rid themselves of the pestering insects that constantly harassed them.

As they waited, they discussed the day's most interesting occurrence, the rare defeat of Ahab at the table.

Optic was fully stretched out with both his hands underneath his head, paying more attention to the fluffy white clouds that were drifting by than the ongoing conversation.

As he watched, a large bird entered his field of vision high up above. It circled languidly with fully extended wings that appeared to be quite still.

"What do you think Optic," asked Lobo.

"What?" replied Optic, who was clearly not listening? They looked at each other.

"What's up with you?" asked Gatlin.

"Do you see that bird?" Optic pointed upwards. "I've been watching it for the last five minutes and so far it hasn't flapped its wings once."

"That's the chicken hawk," said Nugget.

"Something else," said Optic. "When I started watching, it was just like a shadow, now it's almost close enough to see its colour."

Are you sure you could see all that?" asked Gatlin, who couldn't resist having a dig at Optic's eyes.

"Liss- liss- listen you," said Optic, getting back at him.

"Cut it out you two," said Lobo, who was clearly intrigued. As they watched, the bird was still lazily circling, feigning indifference to any and all suspecting prey in the area.

"Do you think he is going to attack?" asked Nugget, addressing himself to no one in particular.

"Naw," said Lobo, "he's just hanging around."

So caught up were the others, that they missed his attempt at humour.

As the hawk continued its deceptive circling, its shadow passed over the hen. Suddenly, she became very agitated and started clucking around, in what seemed to the boys, an attempt at getting her chicks from out in the open, and into the nearby brush.

Lobo forced his eyes to the bird that was now close enough for him to see its dark brown feathers.

"They are almost there," said Optic, but in fact, the hen and her chicks were still about ten yards from the brush and she was still frantically urging the fledglings to safety. As Lobo looked on, the hawk had stopped moving and seemed literally to be just hanging there.

Very suddenly, with a speed that he was barely able to follow, the struggle of life and death that had gone on for thousands of years before was re-enacted before their very eyes.

The hawk, with stiffened wings pointing backwards, swooped down at an angle which allowed it sufficient momentum, to climb smoothly back into the sky after what seemed a successful strike. The hen was still about ten feet from the safety of the brush.

He sat motionless as if spellbound by the speed and accuracy, of what he believed to be a magnificent strike.

"He missed!" Shouted Optic.

"I hope he di- di- did not get the chi- chi- chicken," said Gatlin excitedly.

Without saying a word, Lobo got up and walked the fair distance towards the hen and when he was close enough, counted the chickens. Where a few moments before there were six, now there were only five.

Incredibly, the hen seemed to know that for the moment at least, the danger was over. Staying much closer to the brush, she resumed the lesson in foraging.

His mind went back to the time when, armed with his slingshot, he had practised diligently for the time when he would bring down the chicken hawk, now, relief flooded through him.

The thought of hurting, let alone killing such a magnificent hunter, horrified him. He never would have been able to live with himself. It's not that he didn't sympathise with the hen; he simply admired the perfection of the hawk's endeavour. Hopefully next time, the chicks would be stronger and more experienced and with a little luck, the hen might win the day.

Sitting there afterwards discussing the strike, Lobo's excitement was obvious, provoking Gatlin into seeking an explanation.

"Why are you so damned ha- ha- happy?"

"Who says I'm happy? I just think it was one hell of a strike," he answered with admiration written all over his face.

"You didn't think so when you spent all that time practicing to kill it?" Nugget reminded him.

"That's because the chicken is not his," Optic observed.

"Now hold on one damn minute. The hawk has just as much right as any of us to feed itself and its chicks. Who is going to feed it? you?" He looked at them all in turn. The argument continued until the match began.

The cricket season started sensationally and for once it had nothing to do with the men. The Suffragettes had become so successful, that instead of playing teams from within the parish, they were playing teams made up of the best of the other players from different teams across the country. They were without doubt, the best women's team on the island.

Just about the time that Father Devas came to Sauteurs, a couple from the country had also taken residence in the town and opened a parlour where soft drinks and refreshments were sold. It also doubled as a shoemaker's shop. They were Duffy and Olivia Charles. It was pure coincidence that they shared the same surname; they were still unmarried and from time to time, received a visit from the Mothers Union who discarded subtlety and advised the couple to set an example by getting married, they saw themselves as the guardian of the morals of the town.

They were the perfect argument for those who believed that

117

opposites attracted each other. Duffy was in his early forties, five feet, six inches tall, and weighed about a hundred and twenty pounds in his coat. He spoke with a gruff voice that many believed to be affected for manliness and occupied the shoemaking part of the operation. He also kept an eye on the shop when the attendant was absent.

Olivia on the other hand, was a strong, strapping woman of forty. She was about five feet nine inches tall, and though she still retained her shape, weighed about a hundred and sixty pounds.

While she worked in the parlour on occasions, her real job was that of a trafficker, a name attributed to traders in fruits, vegetables, and spices trading among the other islands. Olivia confined herself to the Port of Spain markets in the neighbouring island of Trinidad. On the return trip she'd bring back things like textiles, groceries, even spare parts for cars and everything that would make her a profit.

Duffy, who greatly admired and always watched the games, approached the Suffragettes with an offer. He told them that during his ten years stay in Trinidad he had advised a successful women's cricket team. With his contacts he could arrange a tour of that island if the girls would put themselves in his hands. Eager to show their talents on the big stage, they readily agreed and true to his word, Duffy delivered on his promise.

The players had to find their own fares and numerous events were organized. They were well attended and very well supported by the locals.

They were to travel by the schooner, *The Island Queen*, on the first of week in August 1944, returning on the same boat three weeks later. They played six matches and were successful in five of them; they lost the last game to a combined team.

The manner of their successes had earned them great reviews in some of the local papers and even earned them a mention on Radio Trinidad.

Back at home in Grenada, the news of the team's victories in Trinidad was greeted with peripheral interest by a people in shock.

After dropping its cargo, human or otherwise, the *Island Queen* returned to Grenada for an overhaul, in preparation for her impending voyage; a once in a lifetime event and easily the most exciting venture ever attempted by the islanders, a sea cruise for the rich and beautiful people of the region.

When the trip was announced, there were many who opposed it on moral grounds, claiming that the extravagance was wrong with the war still on.

The organizers argued that with all the carnage of the war, life should be celebrated. Such was the response to the event that another ship, *the Providence Mark*, was brought in to carry the extra passengers.

On the evening of departure, after the guests were assembled, the young people of the *Providence Mark* swapped their tickets with their elders of the *Queen*, where the music and dancing had already started.

The two ships weighed anchors together on their way to the nearby island of St Vincent. The more luxurious *Queen*, recently fitted with a diesel engine that was the envy of all the other captains, sailed on ahead and was never seen again.

All 'sixty seven' people on board, the crew included, were lost. There were rumours of some debris found, including shoes and clothes on an out of the way bay, but they were only rumours. Despite a joint sea and air search by the military in the region, no wreckage was ever found of the ill fated schooner.

Many speculated that because of the *Queen's* diesel engine the schooner was mistakenly torpedoed by an allied submarine. Others suspected that she had struck a mine in the dark and a few even suggested the Bermuda Triangle theory, but nothing was ever proven one way or the other.

The news, when it came, had devastated the town of Sauteurs, and in particular, shattered the life of Mrs Molly Hill, a local resident. She lost all three children on the ship, a son and two daughters. Reggie, the rugged, handsome outdoor type was very active socially within the community, and was the assistant scoutmaster and teacher.

119

On his last meeting with Jerry and the rest of the troop, he had promised to tell them all about the cruise on his return. His two sisters worked in the capital.

In the days following, Mrs Hill, previously a devout catholic, enlisted the aid of every medium and spiritualist she could find in an attempt to put her in touch with the souls of her dead children, but to no avail.

Afterwards, very gradually, through the intervention of Father Devas, she seemed to have regained her faith, but the loss had taken a great toll. Less than a year later, she died of a broken heart.

Still in a daze, the locals walked about avoiding conversations with friends whenever possible for fear of having to discuss the tragedy. Perhaps it was divine intervention, as suggested by Mother Tina, which brought about the comical incident on Main Street on a busy Friday afternoon.

Walking out of Hosten's shop was a local boy recently returned home after ten years in the neighbouring island of Trinidad. He had been cursed since birth with the name Freddie Fist.

For as long as he could remember people had told him he had a boxer's name. After a while Freddie believed that fighting was his destiny. To that end, he stowed away to Trinidad when he was only seventeen. He did whatever jobs came his way but concentrated all his efforts on getting into the illegal fights held in the bars at weekends.

One promoter was so impressed with the name that he gave Freddie his first break, after adding 'the Iron', extending it to, 'Freddie the Iron Fist', changed by the fans to 'Ironfist Freddie'. His only claim to fame was that he trained in the same gym as the famous Jeffrey Stollmyer, future West Indian cricket captain and opening batsman.

Freddie stood on the pavement and was busy stuffing some cheese into a bread roll when Dabo came up the hill from Low Town. The sandwich board back and front of him proclaimed the forthcoming

Anglican Church harvest festival two weeks hence. Dabo's usual showman's expression was missing, probably due to the boring nature of his product. He passed Freddie on his way to Hosten's bar for a quick one. He came out again just about the time that Freddie finished his snack. He proceeded slowly up the street. He rang his bell for attention and a strange thing happened. 'Friendly Freddie' went through an amazing transformation; he became 'Ironfist Freddie'.

The sound of the bell had triggered off the fighting instincts of a punch-drunk Freddie, taking him back to the ring. He assumed the boxer's stance and shuffled his feet around, all the time throwing punches in union with his nasal breathing, as if he was sparring with some invisible foe.

The spectators, alerting each other started laughing at the spectacle. A stranger from the bar staggered forward to see what the excitement was all about. Seeing, he decided to add to it and made his way to the pavement and Freddie's imaginary boxing ring. He took his stance and started sparring with Freddie.

"Show me what you got," he taunted, swaying around on unsteady legs. The inevitable happened when 'Ironfist' landed squarely on the stranger's chin and knocked him out cold.

Some of the spectators had tears in their eyes as one of Hosten's workers came running out with a bottle of smelling salts and revived the stranger. Dabo promptly rang his bell lustily to celebrate the knockout, and 'Ironfist Freddie' became 'Friendly Freddie' again, his expression clearly puzzled as he wondered what all the excitement was about. It was in fact a timely distraction for a people in shock.

"You can't take all those punches and not learn how to throw a haymaker," Dabo said excitedly. Always the opportunist, Dabo used the fight to promote the harvest festival and swore that 'Ironfist' would be taking on all-comers.

Unfortunately for Freddie, he became a prime subject for 'the tease', as every kid who could get his hands on a bike went in search of him, in the hope of triggering his next fight when they rang the bell.

Very gradually, the community returned to normal, and interest slowly returned to the successful Suffragettes tour. Rumours began to circulate that Duffy had started an affair with one of the players while away. She was Betty Bell, twenty-two years old, five feet, eight inches tall, and weighed about one hundred and fifty pounds. She was not unattractive. According to Otto, Duffy had a serious case of, 'tabanca'. In local jargon, he was besotted.

The afternoon sun was merciless. There was hardly a breath of air and the reflected heat along the road gave the illusion of wetness in the distance.

Atlas wanted to go to Duffy's for the Sunday games of draughts of which he was a keen observer and player, but Lobo declined in favour of his place by the grotto.

The familiar players had gathered for the afternoon session but Duffy excused himself.

Ever since his return, he had been behaving like a man six feet tall and weighing a hundred and seventy pounds. Like most short men, he had a great desire to project himself.

"Sorry fellahs," he said, "but I have some business with the girls, I'll see you all later."

He returned sometime after, looking very dapper in a pair of sharply creased light brown trousers, a tan shirt and brown sandals. There was a gold chain and cross around his neck. Olivia looked up as he approached and gave a low appreciative whistle.

"That you Duff? You look like a real saga boy." The phrase indicated that he was dressed as the designer man of the day.

"Won't be long girl," he said. "I'll be back as soon as I get things straightened out."

He turned and was walking towards the door when Olivia called after him. "Oh! Come here a minute Duff."

"Make it snappy woman, I don't want to be late," he said, with every intention of impressing his friends.

Olivia smiled as she inclined her head, as if she wanted to say something to him that she wanted no one else to hear.

"This won't take long," she promised.

As Duffy approached her, Olivia reached out as if pulling his head closer for secrecy but instead she took hold of his jaw in her right hand. The muscles in her wrist tensed as she squeezed until his top denture popped from his mouth into her hand. Very calmly, she folded it in some wrapping paper and placed it in her apron pocket. The smile never left her face.

Duffy, rooted to the spot seemed dumfounded and said nothing.

"Well, don't let me keep you from straightening out your problems, I don't want you to be late," said Olivia sweetly.

Duffy, diminutive by normal standards, seemed to visibly shrink further in stature.

Without saying a word, he turned, and very slowly made his way out of the shop with his feet barely leaving the ground.

Afterwards, Duffy, instead of keeping a low profile, was busy rebuilding his image within the community, by roughhousing the younger customers.

He was playing a game of draughts with Donald Bannerman, nicknamed, Bulls-eye, because it was his favourite toast with every drink. He was considered an excellent player when he was sober.

They had equal pieces on the board, but Bannerman seemed to hold the stronger position. Duffy, a capable player, realized this and introduced one of his favourite ploys. He attempted to move several of the pieces without actually making the move, thereby distracting his opponent from the obvious next move.

The move, when it came, was to offer up one of his pieces in an attempt to strengthen his position. A sober Bannerman would have spotted it and removed the proffered piece, but in his tipsy condition, Bulls-eye missed the ploy and was about to forfeit his own piece by making another move. Atlas who was watching the game broke the cardinal rule of non-interference. By clearing his throat he alerted Bannerman to the danger so that he changed his move and Duffy lost one of his pieces as a result.

Duffy bounded out of his stool and grabbed for Atlas and was almost on top of him, before being restrained by two of the men in the shop. He struggled violently to free himself, his teeth were bared, and he had smoke in his eyes.

"Let go of me!" he shouted. "I'm going to poke those fast eyes from his head," he threatened.

The voice was pitched just over the noise in the shop, but everybody heard it.

"Let him go!" said Atlas, who had assumed the stance of a boxer with both his fists clenched and held up to protect himself. The whole place had gone quiet and Duffy had suddenly relaxed with a look of disbelief on his face.

"Well, come on. What are you waiting for?" asked Atlas, but there was no response from Duffy, who was by then released.

"Take it easy son," slurred Bannerman soothingly to Atlas, who didn't show any sign of having heard him. His voice was calm, and filled with menace. "You got yourself into trouble, now you want everybody else to pay for it."

Atlas lifted his voice for the first time. "So come on Paperman, what are you waiting for?"

Just as with his previous humiliation, Duffy walked away from the shop.

In the past, Atlas would have scampered out of there to avoid his wrath. Today he had stood his ground and faced his opponent and remained untouched. More than that, the name of paperman would haunt Duffy for the rest of his life. Later, the boys met and celebrated.

It mattered not that there was no physical exchange. The important thing was that Atlas was willing to stand and fight.

Shortly afterwards, the Suffragettes disbanded and most of the players including Betty Bell, who had made contacts on the tour, followed the trend of the time and left for Trinidad. With the breaking up of the team, the captain Glando, emigrated to Venezuela to join her mother. No future team, male or female, would ever match the Suffragette's success.

13

Jerry was in the garden weeding some yam beds when he heard his sister directing someone to him. It was Brains.

Brains, right from the start had been the proverbial thorn in the side of Principal Adams. Because of his condition, his school attendance record was always poor but due to the help he had from his father at home, he was always able to keep up with his class.

At the beginning of the school year, when he was eight, he went home to lunch and was quite visibly upset. It turned out that he had been denied promotion to a higher class, even though he had done reasonably well in the tests held in the previous term.

His father, clearly enraged by the school's decision, was waiting to see the principal. In front of the entire school where all could hear him, he demanded to know the reason for his son's failure.

The principal agreed that Brains' school grades were reasonable, but insisted that his attendance was unacceptable.

"But this is madness," said Mr. Rawlings, loudly. "How can a boy who knows his times tables backwards and reads the Trinidad Guardian, not be promoted to a higher class? Answer me that."

"You must try and see it from the school's point of view," said the principal.

"All my other children attend regularly, as well you know. Clive's condition is delicate, but he does not waste his time at home. I would like you to hear him read from this newspaper."

The principal, probably believing Brains to be coached, tested him with a National Geographical publication. Afterwards, Mr Rawlings, determined to prove his point invited him to question the boy, to see if he understood what he had read.

"Go on," he said to the principal, "see if he's really got brains."

The next morning, Brains was escorted to his new class by the principal himself. At the end of that school year, Brains' attendance record was just as awful, yet he still finished top of his class. From then on, everyone just naturally called him, Brains.

"Hey Lobo, what's up?" shouted Brains as he came down the garden.

"Just clearing up some beds. What's happening?"

As Brains got nearer, he noticed he was carrying a pail of wet clothes.

"You've been washing," Lobo asked easily.

"Yeah, it was my turn."

"You coming to the pasture later?"

"I don't know but I'll try. You know what mother is like. If not, I'm on for tomorrow. She is going to Chantemelle to measure up some people for dresses. See you," said Brains.

The rain started early next morning and fell on and off through the rest of the day, but nothing was going to deter Brains from making the most of his time out. A little after one o'clock, he called for Lobo as arranged.

They debated at length what activities to pursue, but given the handicap of the rain, it was proving somewhat difficult. Suddenly, Brains jumped up from his chair.

"I know! Let's go and tease Big John."

"No dummy, Big John is not on holiday, he's at work."

Brains closed his eyes and sat back down in his chair. Never having being blessed with the good health that his brothers enjoyed, he had even less the playtime than they did. Consequently, whenever he was allowed out, he was a bundle of nervous energy and invariably found ways of releasing it. Quite often in one fracas or another.

Juliette opened the door and gave her umbrella a good shake.

"Be very careful what you ask for. Yesterday I was crying for rain, because it was so hot. Today, I'm not so sure. It took forever at Miss Murray's because of all the people from the court."

After she had left the room, Brains had another idea and exclaimed, "I know, I think I've got it. Yes, that's it!"

"What's it?"

"We can go and listen to Ole' Heligar. They say he is the best."

"Are you crazy?" They'll never let us in the courthouse."

"You worry too much man, we'll think of something when we get there."

On arrival, they saw the people filing into the court for the afternoon's session. Sergeant Philip was on duty, resplendent in his uniform with white helmet, white tunic with shiny silver buttons and red stripes on the arm, black trousers with broad red stripes at the side, and highly polished black shoes. A tall man, about six feet two, with a military bearing, he was very highly regarded throughout the parish.

"Come on, let's go, said Lobo. "It's no use us hanging around here, he'll never let us in."

"Not yet, wait," said Brains. "I think I have it."

On mounting the steps they came face to face with the sergeant, who approached them and placed one hand on each of their shoulder.

"What are you boys up to? You know you shouldn't be here."

"Sorry sergeant, said Brains. "I was hoping to tell you in advance, but when I came to the station, you were out. We're doing a school project for Mr Mark," Brains lied.

"Mr Mark eh," said the sergeant, who quickly made up his mind. "Off you go then, find yourself a seat and be quiet."

As soon as they were seated Lobo whispered to Brains, "The sergeant is going to tell Mr Mark and when he finds out, we're dead."

"No man, no! I keep telling you, you worry too much, I'm going

127

to see Mr Mark and explain before the sergeant speaks to him. He is all right and he won't mind if I promise to write an essay on what we saw."

After that, they relaxed. Brains took a shopping list from his pocket and turned it over to the clean page.

"What are you doing?"

"Taking some notes, just in case."

The courtroom was very impressive, built almost entirely in oak. On the right side as you entered, was the podium where the magistrate sat, with the witness box at the far end. Hanging on the wall directly opposite, at a tilted angle, was a large mirror, strategically placed, some say, so that the duty officer could see anyone coming up the stairs when he was facing the court.

The gallery was made up of six rows of benches on either side, with ashtrays scattered at intervals. There was a small bunch of hibiscus flowers in a vase on the left side of the magistrate's table and high on the wall behind his chair was a faded framed picture of, 'King George VI'.

At exactly two o'clock, the door of the magistrate's room opened and out walked a handsome looking man in his early thirties. Caucasian, about five feet, ten inches tall, he had brown hair, blue eyes and was clean-shaven. He wore a grey single-breasted suit, with white shirt and black tie, and completed his attire with black leather shoes. As he entered the sergeant stood to attention and shouted, "All rise!"

The magistrate sat down and surveyed the room slowly, seeming to look into the eyes of each spectator. His eyes seemed to linger on the two boys. He glanced at the sergeant who nodded assurance. At length, he banged his gavel.

Mr Heligar was completing his second year as circuit magistrate, and sat in the town of Sauteurs once a week on Tuesdays. His appointment to the job surprised many, as it was generally believed that the post would have gone to a more senior magistrate. Many of the town's people speculated that the timing of his appointment, which coincided with a sensitive community matter, marked him as a fall guy. The smart talk however, from McCloud's was that he was the future and was the only man capable of bringing this matter to a satisfactory conclusion.

About three years previously, what had started as a simple bar room fight between two men, had soon escalated, through ignorance and stupidity, to occasional running battles through the streets, between supporters of both sides. The rematch, which happened on carnival day, resulted in several of those participating, and innocent bystanders, being hurt, a few badly so.

In the following two years, carnival day, which had always been an occasion for cultural expression of joy, of happiness, and wonderful togetherness, was marred by outbreaks of violence.

Heligar started his job about three months before the start of the next carnival festival. While looking through his workload for the next few weeks, he noticed that the remaining disturbance cases stretched up to and beyond carnival.

He instructed the clerk to reschedule all those cases on the same day, one month before the festival.

A keen diver, he spent most of his spare time exploring the local coral reefs in the company of two fishermen brothers with whom he often exchanged banter and as a result, had managed to capture the nuances of the local jargon.

On the day of the trial, all the defendants were assembled before the court and Heligar was determined to make this case a benchmark and send a clear message. After the verdict, five of the fifteen men on trial were released on insufficient evidence. The other ten were all given custodial sentences. First time offenders were given six months and the remainder, one year.

The gallery was stunned. Before Heligar, all of the previous offenders were fined and all the present offenders expected to be fined. The sentence sent a shock wave through the community. It was totally unexpected. Heligar was scathing in his address.

"The festival of carnival," he said, "is an institution that was enjoyed long before any of you came along and hopefully it will continue to be so long after you are gone. I intend to do all that is in my power to make it so. I hope you all understand what has happened here today."

He waved his hand to include everyone in the line.

"You will all spend the next carnival locked up. From here on, all perpetrators of disorder or any more violence committed on the run up to, or the actual day of carnival, will be held in the cells until after the festival. The trial will then be set for about a month before the following carnival and anyone found guilty will be imprisoned. In plain words, once you're found guilty for disturbances during that period, you will spend the following carnival behind bars. Your brand of behaviour will not be tolerated."

The following year, only four offenders were found guilty. Some said that the culprits had actually put their houses in order, before going to trial.

His message was very clear and well understood. McCloud's crowd was giving odds that there would be no offenders found guilty the following year. Three years on after that momentous decision, Heligar still managed to surprise them with his verdicts.

In the courtroom, after Heligar had ensured that all was in order, he told the sergeant to call the next defendant.

"Read it out sergeant."

"The defendant, Mr Benette Mosley, is alleged to have assaulted Mr James Morris in a public place at a prayer meeting, as a result of which Mr Morris lost a tooth."

"How do you plead?" asked the magistrate.

"Guilty with a cause your worship," answered Mosley.

"And what might that be?" he asked. There was a hint of irritation in his voice. This was something new to him since coming to the region, people admitting to be guilty with a cause.

Mosley was only about five feet, eight inches tall but his build was massive. He probably weighed a hundred and seventy pounds. He was dark with a large, cleanly shaven head.

Apart from small eyes that seemed too close together and gave the impression of meanness, he had the irritating habit of frequently blowing his nose very noisily. He fidgeted slightly and ran his forefinger between his collar and his bare skin, as though he felt uncomfortable.

"He is not a righteous man, sir," he answered.

"Go on," encouraged the magistrate.

"Well sir, I think he is a hypocrite. He never practises what he preaches. He is not righteous, sir."

"I still don't understand. Are you saying that's why you struck him?"

"I was just doing him a favour sir," said Mosley. "The bible said, that if your enemy strike you on the right cheek, give unto him also, the left. I tried to teach him a little humility," he said with a satisfied look on his face. "Instead of saying thanks, he brought me here."

The magistrate fixed his gaze on his notes as he spoke.

"Mr Morris may or may not be righteous, but he preaches *The Word*, which suggests he is heading in the right direction. You, on the other hand, chose to go to the meeting. If you disagreed with him, you could have left, so where is your cause?"

"I was just saying sir, that James was too proud to offer the other cheek," answered Mosley.

There was restrained laughter from the gallery and Heligar himself smiled fleetingly.

"And do you think he was unreasonable?"

"Well, yes sir. The bible said, 'Let not the sun go down on thy wrath'. I was just trying to help," said Mosley seriously. This time there was raucous laughter from the gallery, which brought swift response from Heligar. He banged his gavel sharply once.

"Any repeat of that sort of behaviour and I'll clear this court."

He made eye contact with all of the spectators until he had absolute quiet. He retained his silence for a long time and when he spoke, his eyes were a better indication of his mood than his voice.

"And what do you say to that, Mr Morris?"

"It was after eight when he struck me sir, and the sun was long gone," said Morris. His answer indicated his literal interpretation of Mosley's statement.

The sniggers from the gallery withered under Heligar's stern gaze. He turned his attention back to Mosley.

"What were you expecting from Mr Morris?"

"He could have said thanks, sir," said Mosley.

"Mr Mosley, the law of the land formulates rules by which we are all bound and as long as we obey these rules, we are left alone to carry on with our lives. It said nothing about a man's righteousness. That is a matter for his conscience and his creator, not you Mr Mosley. I think you should spend more time with your bible and try to understand it better instead of interpreting it for your own convenience. I am sending you to prison for six months, with the recommendation that you spend as much of that time as possible with your bible. It is my hope that at the end of your time, you will be more charitable to your fellow men. Case closed. Take him down please sergeant," instructed Heligar.

They had walked a few paces when the magistrate called out, perfectly imitating the singsong lilt of the locals, "Mr Mosley! You forgot to say thanks, man."

Mosley glared at him, then sucked on his teeth and emitted the most typical of Caribbean sounds, "Stupes". This expresses exasperation or that something is thought to be beneath contempt. Then he blew his nose vigorously into his handkerchief and walked away with the sergeant.

Both boys found the whole thing fascinating and were determined to return.

The next day, Brains went to see Mr Mark and told him everything, then handed him a five hundred word essay, and requested a note of entry in the future, which he readily granted.

From that day on, even when they had classes, they never missed an opportunity of catching the last hour and a half of the day's proceedings.

The last case of the afternoon concerned the defendant, a part time carpenter named Jacob Jordan and known to his friends as JJ. He was charged with the malicious wounding of John Pullman the plaintiff, who was in a wheelchair and accompanied by a lawyer and four witnesses. Jordan was alone.

Jordan's story was that he had gone to the Telescope Sands Races with his guitar that had taken him six months of his spare time to make. He accompanied all the other singers, but when Pullman sang they couldn't harmonise. Jordan thought he was singing in the wrong key but Pullman disagreed and put it down to bad playing. He asked to play the guitar himself but Jordan refused, on the grounds that he never allowed anyone else to play it.

Pullman who was with four other friends, wrestled the guitar away from him. When Jordan tried to get it back, Pullman smashed it against a coconut tree close by. They started to fight, but every time Jordan got the advantage, Pullman's friends would pull them apart.

After being knocked down the second time, he picked up a stone that was nearby, and threw it at Pullman who was coming back at him, because he felt threatened by his friends.

Pullman's lawyer said that his client treated Jordan as a friend right from the word go. He even offered to buy him a drink, which he refused. He described Jordan as a sullen, unsociable man who didn't play the guitar very well so his client asked to borrow it, but while he was playing, Jordan, in a pique of jealousy, tried to get the guitar back and they fell onto the tree in the scuffle, and the guitar got smashed. Then Jordan picked up a stone and hit his client at point blank range, breaking two of his ribs. At that point, he presented a paper from the hospital to confirm the injury.

Afterwards, Pullman's four witnesses were called and confirmed the lawyer's account almost word for word.

Given the recent custodial sentences that were handed out to the

133

carnival offenders and others since, everybody including Jordan was convinced that he was going down.

Once again, as was his habit, before giving his verdict, the magistrate took a long pause, allowing the gallery plenty of time to quiet down. When he spoke, his voice was clear and even.

"When the discrepancies in any case are as far apart as they are in this one, the truth usually lies somewhere in the middle and it falls to me to try and find it, based on the evidence. In order to do that successfully, there are some questions I would like clarified. So tell me, Mr. Jordan, why did you refuse Mr Pullman's offer of a drink?"

"He was with friends sir, if I had accepted his drink, I couldn't afford to buy him back one," said Jordan.

"You say you felt threatened. Why?"

"Because every time they pulled me away from him is when I fell sir."

"So, it wasn't Pullman who put you down?"

"No sir," said Jordan.

A brief smile flickered across Pullman's face.

"And how was it he was able to get the guitar from you?"

"I was afraid that if we struggled, it might get smashed," answered Jordan.

"And you Mr Pullman, why didn't you walk away?"

"We were just having a little fun, I wanted my friends to hear me sing."

"How close were you to the tree where the guitar got smashed?"

"Quite close sir," said Pullman.

"Thank you, both of you."

In his customary manner while summing-up, he paused at certain points, as if to emphasise what he was saying.

"Here we have a man, who took time from his busy schedule . . . six months it took him to make a guitar for his own amusement. Is he unsociable?" He asked rhetorically. "The fact that he was willing to play for all the other singers suggests otherwise. He refused the offer of what many would consider a free drink, because he couldn't

134

afford to buy one back. That shows him to be an honourable man not an unsociable one. I also believe the accused when he said he felt threatened by your friends.

One last thing, the evidence suggests that you did indeed smash the guitar. If it had been broken in a struggle, it would hardly have splintered like that."

He pointed to what was left of the smashed instrument.

"Between your bodies, it would have been better protected. You said he licked you down without provocation," he paused briefly. "While I wouldn't recommend that he makes a habit of it, I don't think he had any option but to lick you down on this occasion, as you yourself put it. You are free to go Mr Jordan, case dismissed."

After they left the courtroom, as soon as they were passed the door, Jordan leaned against the wall, clearly relieved but very surprised. That morning before leaving for the courthouse, he was quite sure that he was prison bound. Even if he was fined, he had no way of paying, so he had taken the trouble to fix up his affairs. Now, unbelievably, he was going home. "God bless Heligar! May there always be someone like him around," he thought.

Pullman, sitting in his wheelchair was being carried down the stairs by a couple of his friends, halfway down, he jumped out of the chair and in a rage, threw it down the stairs, and walked away cursing.

Brains was clearly very impressed with the verdict.

"I tell you man, Heligar is the boss," he said. Lobo had to admit that he found it far more interesting than he thought it would be.

The courthouse had become a place of major interests, not only to Brains and Lobo, but also to all the other boys.

Months later, after Jordan had built another guitar, the first thing he did was to honour Heligar in the traditional way. He composed and sang a calypso, projecting him as 'Boss Heligar, the Man Who Could See Round Corners.'

135

14

Any visitor getting off the bus and seeking the whereabouts of McCloud's would encounter no difficulties. It was as well known as any of the churches in the area, or the post office, and by some of the men in the town, it was more frequently visited than the post office or the churches.

McCloud's was one of three tailor shops in the centre of town, and Jerry had worked there every Saturday since he'd turned thirteen. Juliette had made the arrangement, saying he should learn a trade. One year later, all he had learnt was how to run errands and press trousers.

Matias Tailoring catered mostly for the farm workers and labourers. Peter's Bespoke Tailoring catered for the conservative older businessmen. And then there was just McCloud's with no explanation, as though everyone should understand its exclusivity. It catered for the young fashionable men of the town.

The establishment took its name from the owner Jack McCloud who was about five feet, ten inches tall and about a hundred and fifty pounds. He was clean-shaven, dark brown in complexion, had an athlete's physique and large dark eyes which many believed to be the cause of his success with women. Some people had trouble trying to decide whether he was handsome or just attractive.

His biggest obsession was showing off his craftsmanship. He considered himself a clotheshorse for his work.

His was the largest of the shops and boasted two permanent assistants. In the back room that doubled as a kitchen, there was the cutting table and the presser, with a single cot in the corner.

In the front, there were three foot-pedal machines. There was one on the left side of the door as you enter and one on either side of the kitchen door. The right side of the shop was reserved for playing draughts.

On a shelf above the kitchen door was probably the establishment's most treasured possession, one Marconi radio.

Fair sized crowds gathered to listen to cricket, BBC news broadcasts and the many singers of the day that featured on 'Voice of America.'

There was another priceless asset, Otto Bell, no relation to Betty. Those who frequented McCloud's had a saying. "If someone told you a story and said, 'Otto said', it lent that story authenticity."

In a perfect world Otto would have been an entertainer. He had a good singing voice and would often accompany the popular singers of the day, like Nat King Cole, Ella Fitzgerald, or Frank Sinatra. He also told the most amazing tales.

This particular Saturday, teachers were being paid and there was a buzz of activity as most of the young men of that profession came in to settle their financial affairs with McCloud.

One of the men, more an acquaintance than a friend, seemed animated and indicated that he would like to see McCloud privately in the other room. It seemed that McCloud had fathered two children one month apart, by different mothers.

With Christmas coming, he had purchased two postal orders of equal value, but mistakenly placed them in the wrong envelopes, sending each woman a postal order written in the other's name.

The women lived about five miles apart and though they knew of each other, had never met.

The one called Mavis flew into a rage when she discovered McCloud's mistake. She ripped the contents apart and threw the pieces into the wind. The other woman, Sarah, on discovery of the

137

error, remained calm and calculating. She kept Mavis's, but refused to hand it over.

Later, even as the man was still trying to warn McCloud of her impending visit, Mavis still managed to surprise him. Visibly nervous, McCloud emptied the shop of all those within, staff, customers and spectators alike.

Half an hour had gone by and his friends began to relax in the feeling that if violence had been intended, it would already have been inflicted. A bus came by, forcing the evicted crowd to the side and stopping about twenty yards from the shop. Otto, also standing outside, took one look at one of the passengers and ran back inside. McCloud, who must have been making progress in calming Mavis, was openly annoyed.

"I thought I asked you to wait outside?" he said a little angrily.

"Sorry Boss, but this won't wait," said Otto, who was clearly anxious.

"Please Otto, later," pleaded McCloud.

"Boss, I want you to think of yourself as out of ammunition and surrounded by the Indians and think of me as the cavalry," he said, rolling his eyes wildly.

The urgency of the matter was finally picked up, just as Sarah, the other mother, entered the shop. Whatever emotion McCloud was feeling before was replaced by panic. He turned around and flapped both hands but could say nothing.

Sarah gave Otto a gentle push through the main door and locked it. Still not having said a word, she walked past McCloud and headed for the back room, unaware that Mavis was waiting.

Excitement ran high in the expectations of the spectators, given the locals' capacity for gossip. What with Mavis's volatile nature and Sarah's quiet determination, they thought they were in for one hell of a scrap. They were very afraid for McCloud's safety.

As the minutes ticked by, they became more panicky, and someone ran off to fetch constable Wells.

The constable's first action on arrival was to disperse the crowd who shuffled around, but reformed a few yards further away. He knocked on the door and demanded entry. The crowd became restive as he entered and closed the door after him.

In the few minutes following the constable's entry, speculation was rife as to the condition in which McCloud would be found. Ten minutes later the door opened and there was a big surge forward by the inquisitive spectators.

The constable was the first to emerge; the crowd held its breath as if bracing itself for the worst.

The two women emerged next and the crowd gasped in surprise. They had their heads together and were actually giggling, either because of some joke they shared or in reaction to the crowd. McCloud for his part, reopened the shop and very leisurely invited his regulars back in.

Walking between the women, he accompanied them down to the post office to rectify what he would later refer to as a misunderstanding.

To most of the crowd waiting, the whole thing had turned out to be a bit of an anti-climax and some of them, probably touched by jealousy, were even disappointed that McCloud had gotten away with it. Even so, the story was told and retold in the bars and even around the dinner tables and as easily as that, McCloud passed grudgingly into local folklore.

In the years that followed, Otto would tell the story of his boss's dilemma over and over again, mimicking the walks and facial expressions of the women, each time embellishing the role of the cavalry.

Finally, it was the night of the big dance, the social event of the year, certainly as far as the women were concerned. Without doubt it was the biggest event of its kind of the year and the members of the Mechanic Lodge were duly proud of its status and insisted that admission would be strictly by ticket only. Its exclusivity was emphasized by the last line on the invitation – Admittance strictly by tickets. Indeed, to the different factions, the event represented different things.

To the wives, it was a splendid opportunity to remind any and all interested parties of their standing in the hierarchy.

To the unmarried women, among whom there was fierce rivalry, almost anything was done to get the nod to accompany their escort, secure in the knowledge, that whoever went to the dance would very likely get the ring.

To the errant husband, it was an opportunity to be absolved of all recent indiscretions, provided he was attentive and considerate.

It was a beautiful tropical night, warm, with a gentle sea breeze blowing off the ocean and to cap it all, there was a full moon. Outside, the large crowd of spectators which almost rivalled those inside, had assembled early enough to be sure of good vantage points and were very forthright in their comments on anything from fashion, to attitudes, and especially the couples.

Notable also, was the large number of cars parked in the courtyard, a clear measure of the stature of the event. There was an impressive round dozen, an unprecedented number for any event of that nature.

As always, most of the revellers had arrived on foot and had to run the gauntlet of the spectators' scrutiny.

The large clock on the Anglican church tower said nine o'clock and there was a steady trickle of couples and small groups who left the fragrance of their cologne in their wake.

A middle-aged couple came by and readily invited laughter as the plump woman, handicapped by her high heels in which she was clearly uncomfortable, tried to keep up with her escort.

One female within the crowd offered some advice.

"Take it easy Miss Pwence-ce-wen. He's yours if you can catch him."

Everybody roared with laughter. A few minutes later another couple passed by. This time, the woman who was quite slim, wore a long, loose-fitting blue gown that boasted a hint of elegance, but the rabble-rouser was equally scathing.

"Hi Mopsy! You forgot to take your nightie off."

Once again, they roared. Inside, the band was warming up and already most of the seats were taken.

On the stroke of ten, a buzz of excitement ran through the crowd and for a moment masked the sound of the church bell.

Strolling towards the school was Ivan Pope, flanked on either side by the two women who lived with him. They each held on to an arm. The women were dressed in identical material, but sewn in different styles, to compliment the wearer.

About a year earlier, Ivan had returned from one of his trips accompanied by a woman in her early thirties. She was about five feet, eight inches tall, plump, with ample breasts, and very softly spoken. She was known simply as Vi.

Six months later he repeated the process, only this time she was petite. At only five feet, three inches, slim and small breasted, she was the complete opposite. If that was insufficient contrast, where Vi was quiet, she was loud. She also was in her early thirties and known as Emily.

After the crowd had recovered, there were loud whistles, clapping and shouting, all of a complimentary nature.

"That's right son," shouted a man who was an obvious admirer. "Show them you are the sheriff."

A true extrovert, Ivan waved back in the manner of a celebrity to his fans. After that night, he became known locally, as the sheriff.

An undercurrent of excitement went through the other dancers as they entered. Like a man who had come out to play, Ivan wasted no time in taking to the dance floor, taking it in turn to dance with his two companions.

At first, maybe because they were still in shock, there were few other dancers on the floor. If Ivan noticed, he gave no indication. Throughout the night, he behaved like the perfect gentleman. He was thoughtful, considerate, attentive, and in buoyant mood. Next day, Ivan and his ladies were the talk of the town.

The organised women of the town were scandalized and for the first

141

time in the history of Sauteurs, the Mothers' Union of the Anglican Church and the Legion of Mary of the Roman Catholic Church got together to address the subject of morality.

After a short discussion, Mrs Blakely, who had in the past headed many committees, was elected spokeswoman for the group.

In her acceptance speech, she spoke at length about the women taking up the mantle by being the conscience of the town, and gave her solemn promise that things like 'the McCloud incident', as it was called, would not be tolerated and all such matters would be nipped in the bud.

First it was McCloud, with what she could only call his circus act with those questionable women, and now, Ivan Pope and his harem. After that she took suggestions as to how best to proceed.

After a lengthy discussion, it was decided that McCloud's would be put out of bounds to all the husbands and sons who frequented that den of iniquity and the ban would remain in place until he did the right thing and married one of the women.

Ethel, who worked at Nelson's almost directly opposite, volunteered her services in keeping a record of all those who broke the boycott.

Ivan Pope however, was a different matter. He couldn't be boycotted in the same way.

Mrs Baker who lived only a few doors from him complained that his lifestyle was a personal affront to her and suggested a no-nonsense confrontation with the monster.

At the dinner table that night, Gerald Blakely noticed that his wife was preoccupied with something and resisted the urge to turn on the radio for the BBC newscast. He knew if left alone she would talk about it in her own time far quicker than if he asked her. He poured himself a drink, filled his pipe and sat down to wait.

Experience paid off because a few minutes later, she said, "I'll not be home when you get in tomorrow. The ladies of the joint committee have business with mister high and mighty Ivan Pope."

"Does he know about the appointment?"

"This is not a laughing matter Gerald, as well you know, but Mr. Pope is in for a nasty shock."

He picked up his glass and excused himself in the hope of catching what was left of the news. There was a wry smile across his face as he said softly to himself, "Better you than me Casanova. Short shrift is what you're going to get."

At exactly five o'clock the following afternoon, the ladies led by the formidable Mrs Blakely climbed the stairs leading to Ivan's door, which was already opened. Mrs Blakely called out. "Is there anyone at home?"

Bringing up the rear of the eight women, one from each organization, were Lucy Brown, a spinster who lived with her sister and Angie Bannerman, Bulls-eye's wife. They were admiring the small well-kept flower garden at the front of the house. The hedges were covered with brilliant red hibiscus and scattered everywhere within the small patch were many varieties of croton.

"I have to say," said Mrs Bannerman, "the garden is well kept."

"So would mine be if I had two men sharing my bed," said Lucy.

"Lucy! Remember to wash your mouth out with Jeyes," said Mrs Bannerman, who seemed clearly shocked. She must have spoken louder than she intended and Mrs Blakely was swift with her rebuke.

"Ladies, let us remember why we are here."

Jerry was sitting at the table of Ivan's kitchen drinking ginger beer when the call came. He had delivered two packages given to him by the postman, which was not unusual.

Approaching footsteps brought Vi to the door. She was drying her hands on the tail of her apron and if she was surprised by the ladies presence, she didn't show it. Smiling, she asked in a voice that barely carried, "Can I help you?"

"Good afternoon," answered Mrs Blakely. "I wonder, is Mr Pope in?"

"I'll get him for you," said Vi before walking away. Another minute went by before he came to the door.

He was naked from the waist up, his body drenched in sweat and he was in the process of drying himself. Satisfied, he hung the towel around his neck.

Ivan was an attractive man and had an easy assurance. He looked at the deputation and thought, "Jesus, that's all I need, a flock of vultures."

"Good afternoon ladies I'm sorry for my appearance, but grinding corn is hard work. Is there something I can help you with?" He was at his most charming.

Mrs Blakely had pumped herself up for this meeting, her dander was up, but his courtesy surprised her. Quickly, she brought herself under control not taking her eyes from his still sweaty body. Forcing herself to concentrate, she chose her words carefully.

"Well, there is a matter of grave importance that we ladies are greatly concerned about and we would like to discuss it with you."

His manner was still easy. He shifted his weight to his other foot, causing her to look down at his bare feet.

"So! I repeat, how can I help you?"

Mrs Blakely was slowly gaining momentum.

"You, and others like you can help us all by setting a good example for our young people and –"

"What do you mean, people like me?" The warmth was gone from his voice.

"Well, I'm sure you heard about the debacle at McCloud's the other Saturday."

"And what has that to do with me?"

Mrs Blakely was beginning to get flustered. "Oh, come now Mr Pope! You know very well why we are here and what I am talking about."

"Suppose you tell me how I am setting such a bad example." There was an icy edge to his voice.

A plump attractive woman, always well groomed, Mrs Blakely, despite her resolve, was beginning to feel intimidated by this man who was so sure of himself.

It was understood that the presence of the other ladies was for moral support only and that she would do the talking but Mrs Bannerman could contain herself no longer.

"Don't you call marching into the dance with your two concubines on your arms a bad example? To say nothing of the fact that the three of you blatantly live together," she said, a little breathlessly.

For the briefest of moments, there was fire in his eyes. Then surprisingly, a big toothy grin spread across his face.

"I came to the dance with two ladies and conducted myself as a gentleman should, and by the way, we had a wonderful time. As for us living together, blatantly or otherwise, I must remind you, that whatever happens under the privacy of my own roof is nobody's business and if you can find someone in the entire town to look me in the eye and accuse me of an immoral act in thought, word, or deed, in any public place, then I give you my word to follow any solution you suggest to the letter."

Mrs Blakely jumped in quickly to try and retrieve the situation.

"Surely you must see how it looks, Mr Pope."

"No, I don't," he said a little mischievously, "but I'll tell you what I'm prepared to do. I would invite you all to come and spend some time with us and make up your own minds, but I lack the accommodation. But anyone of you ladies may feel free to come and stay as long as you like."

His face was serious, but his eyes twinkled. He continued before Mrs Blakely had recovered.

"Just let me know in time so I can make the necessary preparation."

"That will not be necessary, Mr Pope," said Mrs Blakely quite firmly. "You may mock if you choose, but you have not heard the last of this matter. We will do whatever we have to do."

She gave him a look she was sure would let him know what she thought of him.

"Anyway," said Ivan, "even if what you said was true, is that such

145

a bad thing, after all?" He bent forward to Mrs Blakely's ear and whispered something.

Whatever was said must have had the desired effect. Her face reddened and her "Good afternoon Mr Pope," was almost unintelligible.

"Ladies!" she said. Blooded, but unbowed, she led the retreat with her head held high.

Ivan strolled back into the kitchen, the semblance of a smile covering his face.

"Did you hear all that?"

They all nodded in agreement.

"The thing to remember here Jerry, is, always be polite to righteous people, but never take them seriously."

When his wife returned home, Mr Blakely was enjoying his evening rum punch but could hardly contain his curiosity regarding the confrontation. He asked, "How did it go?"

When she answered, he was surprised by the passion in her voice. "I tell you," she said, "that man's conceit is unbelievable. He will continue to flaunt his promiscuity in our faces, and there is not a damn thing we can do about it". She gave him a brief account of what went on and her anger surprised him.

"Take it easy dear, I'm sure you and your committee will think of something."

"Do you know what that- that womaniser said to me?" Her agitation was clear. "He said that even if it were true, Jesus wouldn't begrudge him two women, since he himself has thousands of brides, all over the world," she fumed.

Mr Blakely who was in the process of swallowing almost choked on his punch, with most of it ending up on the front of his shirt.

"What did the others say?" he asked, when he had regained his composure.

"They didn't hear him, he whispered it in my ear."

"Well," thought Blakely grudgingly, "you're a better man than I am. You must really be the sheriff".

Like the great fire, that Christmas also became a marker and the locals would refer to it as that crazy Christmas.

15

In 1949, the Eastern Caribbean, which consisted of the Windward and Leeward Islands, changed currency from pounds sterling to dollars and cents, and as is often the case when such changes are made, both shopkeepers and shoppers had problems with the conversion. The Treasury granted a three months' grace period, after which sterling currency had to be taken all the way to the capital to the only bank.

One such shopkeeper was Samson Bellows, locally known as Sam. He released his wife from the shop every evening about eight o'clock, to oversee the liquor bar at the far end of the building.

The boys were treating themselves after a kick-about underneath the gas lamp near to the Cutrate store, with sodas brought from Sam's shop. Gatlin, the provider on the night, was counting his change when he called out excitedly.

"Hey fellahs! Ole Sam gave me forty-seven cents too much."

"Count yourself lucky," said Optic. "He short changed my dad thirty seven cents."

"And my mom had to send my sister back to the shop, she was twenty three cents short," said Gatlin.

"Don't tell me ole Sam is trying it on," said Ahab.

"Now hold on there Ahab," said Gatlin, "Sam is not like that, it must be a mistake."

"Right! Listen. When it happens once it's a mistake. Four, five, six times? No," said Ahab. Lobo got in quickly. "Hold on fellahs, I think Gatlin has a point. Was Sam always the one giving the wrong change?" In each case, the answer was affirmative.

"Don't you see?" said Lobo. "I think ole Sam is having trouble with his sums. Think about it. He must have given lots of people too much change, like Gatlin here, but they just haven't advertised it."

"Perhaps we should tell him," said Gatlin.

"Hold on," said Brains, who up until then had been quiet. "We're talking about money here and he won't thank you for telling him he can't count. Besides, I think he knows that already, but he'll get it right soon."

"Jesus!" breathed Optic. "What do you say we put ole Sam through the test? We'll wait until he comes down before buying anything."

"Now wa- wa- wait a minute," began Gatlin, who was beginning to get concerned.

"Hold it!" said Brains. Optic has got something there. We'll make sure we use pound notes," he hesitated slightly. "We should also make the purchase an odd amount."

"What do you mean an odd amount?" asked Nugget.

"You know, like forty three cents instead of fifty. Only Gatlin objected, so it was on.

The experiment proved Optic right. Out of seven attempts, they were disadvantaged twice. They decided to take the rough with the smooth. All proceeds from the experiment were placed in an emergency fund to subsidise cinema fares.

Every Wednesday and Saturday night, Bonaparte's mobile cinema came to Sauteurs and transformed the Anglican school into a cinema. The previous week, a trailer of *The Spanish Main* was shown for the coming Saturday. A swashbuckling film that promised lots of action on the high seas.

A couple of the boys, including Nugget, were short of a few cents but he had the most to make up. Ordinarily, that would not have been difficult, but fate had taken a hand. Sam was confined to bed for at least a week with a bad cold. Nugget threw himself into getting the money, offering to do jobs at half the price, provided he could be paid in advance. He succeeded with less than three hours to go.

He walked towards Main Street freshly washed and changed. The excitement of the forthcoming film was already building within him, even though it was still over two hours away. He turned the corner and ran straight into Lily Frame, one of his classmates and the object of his affection. Lily's smile matched his as they said, "Hi."

"You're looking very nice," said Nugget.

"Are you saying I don't usually look nice?" She tilted her head and gazed at him sternly.

No!" he replied quickly, his eyes and teeth shining in his dark face. "I said very nice," he emphasized the word very. "That means, you always look nice," he hesitated slightly. "Least ways, I think so."

Her expression brightened, "And you're lucky that you are a fast talker," she said. They both laughed.

"Listen," said Nugget, "I have an hour before I have to do something for my mom." He wasn't taking any chances on being late. "Would you like a walk on the beach? If anyone asks, you can say you were checking to see if there was any fish."

She laughed. "That would be nice, but I can't just now. I'm going to Rose Hill for my mom. I'd ask you to come, but you've got an errand of your own to run." She turned as if to leave.

"Aren't you going to take the bus?"

"No, I can't, no money, she admitted. He reached into his pocket and handed her the dollar bill that would have paid his fare. "Take this", he said.

"Are you sure about this? I thought you were going to the cinema," She seemed genuinely concerned.

"Are you crazy girl?" He asked with his eyes bulging, "I wouldn't miss *The Spanish Main*. Please take it. I'm sure."

She thanked him and threw in a big bonus smile.

After she had left, he groaned aloud. Afterwards, he made one last attempt to persuade his grandmother to lend him the money from her emergency jar.

"When you have a real emergency, come back and see me." Her answer was final.

As the time got nearer, Nugget became more desperate and by starting time, had decided on a desperate measure. He would scale the dreaded trap window. It was so called because, while attempting to reach it, you saw nothing on the inside until your eyes broke the surface, in much the same way as if you were coming up through a trapdoor.

The school consisted of two floors. The ground floor housed the juniors and the first floor catered for the senior students, and doubled as the cinema.

Like many of the buildings in the region designed to house large numbers of people, instead of anything solid, it was surrounded by steel diamond shaped netting, which allowed maximum ventilation.

The trap window was conveniently located at the back and was covered by the shade of the big mahogany tree nearby.

In order to gain access through the trap window, it was necessary to get a foothold through the netting. Having got as far as it would take you, you must now reach up, grab hold of the windowsill with one hand and then with the other, complete the difficult task of hauling yourself up, unless of course, you were fortunate enough to arrange assistance, which Nugget had done.

Once in, if you were caught all the lights were turned on and you would be forced to do a walk of shame, accompanied by cheers and jeers from the pit.

A second offence would result in an audience with constable Wells, who read you the riot act and always concluded with the very real threat, "You don't want to know what will happen if there is a third time." There never was.

Ahab, whose idea of the ultimate in entertainment was an action film on the high seas, was preoccupied as he waited for Nugget's tap on the window.

151

In the semi-darkness, someone pushed pass him. It was Pato. Almost immediately, there was a tap on the window that Pato promptly opened. Nugget reached up with one hand and then the other. He took hold of the windowsill and held on firmly.

Pato pushed Ahab out of the way, reached out and took hold of both of Nugget's wrists, wrenched his hold loose and held him suspended in mid air.

"Let go of me so I can get back down!" exclaimed a clearly frightened Nugget, but Pato was having none of it.

"You are going back down all right, only much quicker than you think." He released his hold on Nugget's wrists and he screamed in fear all the way as he plummeted the fourteen feet to the ground. Amazingly, Nugget suffered one fractured and one very badly sprained ankle, but was up and about with the aid of crouches, as soon as the swelling went down.

The one thing Nugget was dreading happened, a visit from Lily. After the customary greeting, she said, "I am still trying to decide whether I should be angry with you or not. Why did you do something so silly?"

"I had decided not to go. I didn't want you walking all the way to Rose Hill and back, but when the time came I weakened. I feel like a real fool and don't know where to look. It was a stupid thing to do," he agreed contritely.

"You have to promise never to do anything that stupid again, you could have been badly hurt," she said fairly sternly, but her eyes were soft and the hand stroking his swollen ankles was very gentle.

When he was mobile again, he joined his friends under the light, and naturally, the conversation got around to the incident at the trap-window. To a man, they agreed it was a fair cop, but that Pato had overstepped his mark.

They felt that Nugget should have been given the usual punishment of ejection under lights. The conclusion was unanimous. Pato had crossed the line. He had knocked off Nugget's chip.

Brains asked the question that everyone was thinking.

152

"What are we going to do about it?"

"The first thing to do, is to ask him to apologize," said Optic.

"And what if he refuses?" said Atlas.

"If he refuses, then it's up to me to face him. After all, he is my opponent."

"So when are we going to approach him," asked Atlas.

"What about next Saturday," suggested Brains, already a little excited at the prospect of the confrontation?

They met as arranged in the courtyard about seven o'clock, in the hope of confronting Pato before it got busy with the expected crowd that would be seeking entrance. They stood at a vantage point where they were able to watch him as he made the necessary preparation.

At whatever age in history, or whatever country Pato lived, he would have been thought of as a giant. Had he been a gorilla, he would have been a nailed down silverback. He was about six feet, eight inches tall and weighed nearly three hundred pounds and there was no excess fat anywhere on his body.

Five years before, he had been picked and given a contract for farm working in the United States. Normally, the contract was for three years, but Pato's was extended for another two, because of the high quality of his work. Ever since his return a year earlier, he had been working for Bonaparte. According to Otto, he was bouncer first and handyman second. Prior to his return, it took two men to lift the generator that provided the electricity for the show. Now, they watched as he lifted it effortlessly from one place to another, as if he possessed an extra source of energy.

Satisfied that everything that had to be done was done, he washed himself using the water tap provided for the kids and replaced the man standing at the door, to keep out all undesirables. He sat on the chair and rested both feet straight in front of him, then lit a cigarette and relaxed. He tapped the side of his leg, keeping time with the music that was blaring out to attract customers.

The boys walked closely behind Nugget who had some difficulty negotiating the stairs. As they got nearer to where he sat, Pato heard

153

their approach. Without turning his head to look at them, he said. "Come back in half an hour, the door will be open then."

"We don't want to go in, we want to have a word with you," said Brains.

He looked at them for the first time and if he had any idea what it was about, he kept it to himself.

"What is it? What do you want?" he asked without appearing particularly concerned.

Nugget limped forward to stand just in front of the group. Pato looked at his crutches and for the first time seemed vaguely interested.

Losing patience while Nugget tried to collect his nerves, he said, "Well, what's itching you fellahs?"

They all looked at Nugget and eventually, so did Pato.

"Well?" he asked again.

When Nugget was able to speak, his apprehension quite visible for all to see, he said, "Two weeks ago you dropped me from the window. I could have broken both my legs or worse."

Pato focused on him.

"So it was you, was it? I couldn't see your face in the dark, but even if I did, it would have made no difference. We needed an example, and you were it."

"What I did was wrong, but so were you. You owe me an apology," Nugget said, with more courage than he'd ever shown before.

"Like I said, we needed to make an example and we did. Now get out of here before I make another one and toss you fellahs down the steps."

"Is that all you have to say?" asked Brains.

"Damn right! Now stop blocking the door," said Pato sternly, as he went inside and closed the door sharply behind him.

They left the courtyard and walked the short distance up the hill to High Street and sat under the light. They wanted to know how Nugget was going to handle it.

"There is plenty of time for me to think of something. I want my ankles to be better first," he said.

That night, like Lobo before him, he pondered his dilemma at length. He couldn't believe how frightened he'd been while facing Pato. Perhaps the sensible thing to do was to take it to constable Wells and accept his punishment for his part in the affair, but he discarded the idea before it took root. His mind went back to the trap window and he shuddered slightly. He had never been so afraid before. More than that, he felt terrified while he was falling, and he was ashamed for screaming. As yet, he didn't realise that anyone falling from a dangerous height would scream as a matter of course. Now he wanted Pato to experience that same fear. He had knocked off his chip and that made him his opponent, he had to find a way to stand up to him, but so far, that way eluded him.

Another month went by, and as far as anybody knew, Nugget had got no further in solving his problem, but at the last lime, he set the time. The term, 'liming', which is still used in the Caribbean today, is exactly the same as 'hanging out', as is used today in Europe and North America.

Now, as they gathered in front of the school, he was the last to arrive. There was still an hour before the programme began.

Nugget walked very slowly, and as he got closer, they could see beads of sweat on his forehead; they could not tell that there was sweat also on his palms. In his right hand he carried a brown paper bag that was tied at the top.

His colleagues crowded around him and started talking all at the same time, Optic held up both hands and literally jumped up and down to get their attention.

"Now," he said, his still upheld hands begging to be heard, "let's take a walk."

They stood in the shadows away from those standing around. Optic who had the floor spoke again.

"One at a time fellahs. I'll go first. Is it on for tonight, or not?" All eyes were turned to Nugget.

"It's on," he said simply.

Once again, they had to be calmed down. Everyone wanted to be heard.

"I think we should wait and think a- a-about it some more," said Gatlin, the most cautious among them.

"No!" said Nugget. "I think I have found a way to get even with him."

He held up his hand to stall any questions. "It's going to take too long to explain, but I think it's under control, so stay close. Just remember, I want my shot. This is between me and Pato. Let's go, now all I need is a break."

There was a lot of activity around the school. Wires ran all the way from the generator outside to the school. Speakers were placed to the best advantage, a rope barrier was provided to separate the rest of the house from the pit, an area renowned for its bawdy behaviour, and where the people sat on benches instead of chairs.

They climbed the stairs and walked slowly down the corridor facing the cemetery. On the far end, they could see Pato under the big mahogany tree. As always, when he was working all his concentration went into whatever he was doing. Not wanting to alert him of imminent danger, Nugget, who was by then leaning on the rail directly above him, waved them back.

Pato looked at his preparations and seemed satisfied. He walked over and got into the back door of the van. Lobo took advantage of talking to Nugget.

"You sure you won't tell us about the plan? We might be able to help."

"Don't worry Lobo. It's a very simple plan, but if it doesn't work, you fellahs better run like hell." Nugget smiled nervously.

"That's dumb advice. We're always ready to run like hell," said Lobo.

"You'd better get back, he's backing up," Nugget warned.

Lobo walked a couple of paces, then stopped.

"One thing man. The reason everybody still talks about David beating Goliath is that it happens like once in every hundred years. If it goes wrong, I hope your ankles are as good as you claimed they are."

Nugget watched Pato as he got out of the driver's seat and walked to the back of the van. Once again, he checked the prepared stand and with a visible effort, lifted the heavy generator unto the stand. The muscles of his hefty arms rippled impressively, enough to draw grudging admiration from Nugget, whose resolve began to weaken as he watched his formidable opponent below.

Nugget carefully placed the bag on the ground between his legs, and noticed that the place he was holding was wet with nervous sweat. Then he thought of Lobo and Puff Jake and Atlas and Paperman and he picked up the bag. Pato, having completed the move, was still crouched over the generator making some minor adjustments.

So far, everything had gone just the way Nugget hoped, but now at the moment of truth his doubts felt like they were going to overwhelm him.

What if the plan backfired and Pato got hold of him and put him through another humiliation? Then he heard again the sound of his voice as he fell to the ground, and the adrenalin kicked in.

"Pato!" he shouted. "Catch!" And he threw the package at him.

Very vital to Nugget's plan, Pato instinctively reached out and caught the package, just as one would catch a football. Then the power of those mighty arms came into play and ruptured the bag, releasing a mass of angry wasps, and he was the single target for each one of them.

He started flapping his arms about in a vain attempt to drive them away, then realizing the futility of the tactic, tried to run, and tripped over one of the tree roots. Pato, still not sure what was happening, started thrashing about defensively.

Everywhere he turned, there were rampaging wasps. He rolled

157

around in agony and made frantic efforts to clear his face of those crazy insects. He was undoubtedly a big man, but a man nonetheless.

In the face of such torture, he let out an agonizing scream, as he ran to the nearby tap to wash away his tormentors from his head and face.

By then, all the others had joined Nugget and watched as if hypnotized by the unfolding drama.

"I think we shou- shou- should get ou- out." Gatlin's suggestion was urgent.

"Yes," agreed Optic, "let's get the hell out of here."

They found out afterwards that Pato had visited the surgery just like Nugget had done, and as a result, the programme started half an hour later than advertised, amidst speculation as to the origin of the marauding wasps.

To celebrate, they went to one of the local parlours and Ahab suggested that for such a momentous occasion, they should order real beer. But that would have entailed too many problems, so they settled for ginger beer.

They decided wisely to leave all discussions on details until the next day but there was enough excitement and nervous energy to ignite a spark.

Later, Nugget lay awake well into the night. His mind was racing, going over and over again through the events of this amazing night. He heard again Pato's scream and his actual whimpering, after he had successfully washed away the wasps from his head and face and he smiled. Just as quickly, he sobered and contemplated the possibility of reprisals from Pato.

If it came, he would just have to deal with it, but he knew that there was nothing Pato could ever do to undo what had happened. When sleep finally claimed him, he had a smug, satisfied smile on his face.

They assembled on the beach the next evening when there was hardly anyone about. By a stroke of good luck, Brains had made it.

His mother was in the country attending the wake of a distant relative.

It had been a hot day, and the gentle breeze blowing from the ocean was greatly appreciated.

They sat around in a circle and talked and Nugget brought them up to speed on how he got the idea for the wasps.

"I went looking for golden apples," he began, "but there weren't any on the ground. I climbed the tree and almost butted the nest. I panicked and jumped right off. I remember thinking at the time, even Pato would run from them and then the idea hit me."

"Once I'd made up my mind I decided to wait until dark to give them time to settle down for the night, but when it started to rain in the morning, I knew they would be just as quiet. Wearing granddad's old dungarees and long sleeved flannel shirt and one of my mom's old stocking to cover my face, I went to work. I didn't want to get burned like you Lobe," he said in reference to the honey-extracting debacle. He continued. "I climbed the tree and very carefully, cut the twig on which the nest hung, dropped it in the bag, and tied the neck to keep them in. Even when I got there last night, my plan was to walk right up to Pato, crush the nest, throw it at him, and run like hell."

"As I watched him working with his bulging muscles, I had to admit he looked in good condition, as if he would have good reflexes, so I threw him the bag while he was still in the crouching position. The rest you know."

They hooted and clapped as one and toasted Nugget's guile and courage in facing his opponent.

Brains took the floor as the laughter died.

"You realize that this thing is far from over?"

"He started it, he crossed the line," said Atlas.

"Yes," agreed Gatlin. "And I'm sure he intends to finish it. He's mean."

"Perhaps we should give it a couple of weeks," suggested Atlas.

"I have already decided, we're going to the next film night. I'm not going to let Pato keep me out. Nothing he can do will change what happened last night," Nugget's tone was determined. That settled, they sat and picked the bones of the previous night's adventure dry. By then it was much darker and there were sounds of the night everywhere. From low over the nearby trees a passing owl hooted and a bullfrog croaked loudly at intervals, in the hope of a response from any nearby females; but most impressive of all was the mesmerising, intricate ballet of the night by the ever increasing numbers of the fireflies.

Saturday night the boys stood in front of the school as they were eager to accompany Gatlin to see, *The Plainsman*, a western starring Gary Cooper, they were all very apprehensive.

The plan was simple, just like with Ahab at the table, if Pato attacks Nugget, they were going to try and overwhelm him with numbers. All seven were present.

The doors were opened and as usual you could hear Pato's voice as he urged the crowd along. "Let's have your tickets! Move it along now."

They hung back until the latecomers were the only ones around.

"Are we go- going in, or what?" asked Gatlin.

"It's Nugget's call," said Ahab.

After a slight hesitation, Nugget said quietly. "Let's get it done."

They approached slowly and once again Nugget led the line. As recognition dawned in Pato's eyes, his right hand went up very slowly and involuntarily and touched his still partly tender face. Nugget told later how he tried to advance, but his feet wouldn't move.

The seconds ticked by slowly, while Pato looked at each in turn. When he got to Nugget, he held his gaze until the others started feeling uncomfortable. His mouth seemed as if he was about to say something, but then he changed his mind. Abruptly, he looked around to see if there was anyone else coming. He accepted their tickets as he resumed his chant.

"Let's have your tickets! Move it along now".

160

The usual irritation of Pato's chant was transformed into a melody, as it signalled the end of hostilities. Nobody else was ever dropped from the trap window ever again.

16

Constable "nip it in the bud" Jerome Wells made his way along Main Street, timing his arrival at the Roman Catholic school ground to coincide with the afternoon dismissal.

Just under six feet tall and of medium build, his benign appearance masked a steely resolve to prevent crime. He had what one of his bosses called, "the dubious distinction of never having logged an arrest."

Married, with four children he had been a policeman for twenty years, and would testify to the fact that he had disciplined two generations of young males, from most of the local families that he knew well and had served in one capacity or another, during those twenty years.

Twice during his long and dutiful career, he was summoned to headquarters in the capital, St George's, to defend his record.

In his defence, Constable Wells explained at length his absolute belief in prevention being better than the cure. Most significantly, however, was the report forwarded by three of the most influential members of the parish, both Roman Catholic and Anglican priests and the very highly regarded, sergeant Phillip. They strongly supported his strategy. After that, the constable was left to plough his own furrow.

Later that same year, he requested and was granted a shift, which as near as possible, coincided with school hours. He directed a lot of his time towards the kids. Over the years, he had devised his own punishment in dealing with truancy, bullying, destruction of property, or any other misdemeanour.

For a first offence, the culprit was given a stern warning, which he would be told was a promise, and not a threat. If he re-offended, he would receive the mandatory four strokes from the regulation belt that he wore around his waist.

A third offence would meet with the same result, plus, he would be escorted home and a full explanation given to the parents, who would without exception add their own punishment.

Under his watchful eye, truancy and bullying, which was rare, disappeared. Any use of a weapon would result in a court appearance. He encouraged the boys as a last resort, to settle their differences with their fists, the target being from the head to the belt, and always afterwards, the mandatory shaking of hands. The parishioners would swear that he prevented more crimes than most of the other policemen together had made arrests.

In the last three weeks the constable had noticed an increased number of boys with bruises that suggested they could have been involved in fights.

On investigation, he discovered that the injuries were all inflicted by young William Glass, Optic, as his friends called him. His first thought was that bullying had reared its ugly head, in which case it would be nipped smartly in the bud.

His timing was perfect. He arrived at the school ground about three minutes before the kids came tumbling out.

He leaned against a palm tree near the church, waiting for an opportunity to speak to the possibly errant boy. It wasn't long before young Glass appeared in the company of a very pretty girl, whom the constable knew as his cousin Pamela.

He thought it prudent to wait until he could get the boy by himself. As he waited, he saw another boy detach himself from a small group of children and approach young Glass. His body language suggested a confrontation. He knew that the boy was a stranger because he couldn't identify him.

163

The stranger walking up to Glass was spending two weeks with his Grandmother, while his dad who worked as a stevedore, was away in Trinidad.

Coming from St George's, he was very fashion conscious and generally regarded the country kids as backward. He was fair complexioned, about five feet, eight inches tall, with an athlete's build. He sported a fine gold chain around his neck. In his school, where he was the hundred yards champion, he had more than a fair reputation with his fists. He weighed about a hundred and ten pounds and seemed full of confidence.

Constable Wells' instincts told him that a confrontation was imminent. He moved behind the bole of the tree to better observe, without being seen himself. Hopefully, this should tell him all he needed to know.

Glass, although he was still talking to his cousin, was concentrating most of his attention on the newcomer. The constable hoped that he was wrong but deep down he knew otherwise; the newcomer was looking for a fight.

He could see three of Glass's friends, who were tossing a cricket ball around playing catch while they waited for him.

Ahab looked towards Optic to see if he was ready and sensed right away that a fight was about to take place.

"Look fellahs, it looks as if Optic has another challenge."

All of his friends had challenged him at some time or other sometimes more than once, always with the same result, victory for Optic. Usually, they retired hurt.

"Who is the dandy?" asked Ahab.

"I think he is staying with Mrs Thorn," Atlas informed them.

"Let's go and watch the lesson," said Ahab. They laughed together as they anticipated an easy victory for Optic.

"Hi," said the boy quite casually, when he was close enough to be heard. "Can anyone join in?" There was no doubting his arrogance.

"This is a private conversation or didn't you notice?" asked Pamela who was clearly annoyed.

"Can't he speak for himself? I thought his eyes were a mess, not his mouth," said the stranger with a smirk.

Optic, who regarded insults to his eyes in much the same way as Cyrano de Begerac reacted to slants about his nose, could feel the anger rising within him. It was in his voice. "Who the hell are you?"

"My name is Terence Thorn, but my friends call me TT."

He had the confidence of someone sure of their ability. The other kids who knew the signs drew nearer to hear what was being said. TT turned his attention to Pamela. "What's your name pretty girl, can I carry your books? Eyes here won't mind."

His words may have been meant for Pamela but his eyes were on Optic. Before she could answer, Optic snapped.

"Why don't you just go away from here?"

"Are you going to make me?"

They stared at each other for a few seconds then Optic relaxed.

"Come on Pam, let's leave this tough guy to himself."

As he made to walk away TT moved to block his path.

"I heard you were the boss in this yard. They must be liars."

The look on Optic's face said he was resigned to his fate. One of the kids in the yard approached with two pieces of twigs. The protagonists stood about three feet apart. He placed the first on TT's right shoulder and the other on Optic's left. Normally, whoever knocks off the other's chip, whatever the outcome of the fight would be thought of as being courageous, as being brave enough to seek justice. That's why there was a gasp of surprise from the kids when Optic brushed away his own chip.

"I'm not going to fight this clown," he said. Even as he spoke the chip was replaced and as before, he brushed it away.

"It looks like ole poom-eye here is just scared," TT taunted; poom being the local word for passing wind.

The chip was replaced for the third time and Optic remained perfectly still. TT leaned forward, his gaze locked with where he thought Optic was looking and knocked the twig from his shoulder.

They circled slowly, both held their fists up protectively. Optic, who always made a point of staying calm through his fights, was consumed with anger. He moved straight in and telegraphed a big left swing which TT slipped easily, landing squarely on Optic's jaw with a big right hand of his own.

For the first time in a long time, Optic found himself sitting on the ground. The kids became excited and started yelling encouragement. Surprisingly, the support seemed equal for both boys.

From his hiding place behind the tree, the constable could see that the new boy was at least ten pounds heavier and three inches taller than young Glass. Perhaps he should nip this in the bud. As he approached the boys, he saw Glass go down and promptly returned to his hiding place.

"This is a good opportunity to see what the boy is made of," he thought.

Optic remained on his backside for a few seconds. In every fight he had seen at the cinema, the fallen fighter, if he was smart, always took a count to clear the cobwebs from his brain. He backed away slowly on hands and heels before standing up about four feet away from TT. The punch had knocked the anger out of him and started him thinking again.

They circled once more and Optic remembered the maxim of his grandfather, who gave him his first boxing lesson.

"His hands are what he is going to hit you with, so keep watching them."

Optic, imitating his all time boxing idol, Jersey Joe Walcott, moved his feet as if dancing, in an attempt to confuse his opponent. He hoped that coupled with his awkward southpaw style, this tactic would confuse him still further. TT for his part found the whole thing quite comical and smiled broadly. "You dance, and I'll hit," he said.

Optic feinted with his left and landed his first jab on TT's nose, but took one on his left ear as he backed away.

"So that's it," thought Optic, "a counter puncher."

They continued to trade jabs, Optic being easily the more successful. He moved in again and took another glancing blow to the side of his face after hitting TT twice in the stomach.

After that, he made that spot his target. Gradually, TT's hands began to drop, instinctively trying to protect his tortured midriff. Optic moved in and connected to the face with a two handed combination, and it was TT's turn to sit on his backside.

In a rage, TT promptly jumped up and swung with his right and that was his last mistake. Optic hit him twice more in the face, all squarely on the target without reply and for the second time in as many minutes TT was on the ground, only this time, he was flat on his back.

He retained that position long after he was able to get up and then very slowly, got to his feet. Optic still maintained his aggressive posture. TT came forward with his right hand extended, he had a wry smile on his face and blood was trickling from his nose.

"For a meagre fellah, you punch like hell," he said. It was only then that Optic relaxed and took the proffered hand.

"You're not so bad yourself, what are you, a blacksmith?" There was more than the hint of a smile.

"Listen Optic, is it all right to call you that?"

"Sure man," Optic said, all traces of anger gone from his voice, he threw TT's words back at him "All my friends call me that."

TT hesitated for a while. "I didn't mean any of the things I said, I was just trying to impress your cousin, then the kids started telling me what you were going to do to me and I got the idea of picking a fight. It was a dumb thing to do." He touched his face gingerly, and smiled.

As the kids started drifting away, they agreed as one that it was the best fight ever seen in the schoolyard.

Constable Wells, about to confront the boys, realized that both his hands were knotted into fists.

"Well I'll be damned, that was one hell of a fight," he thought to himself, smiling.

He approached slowly and for an instant Optic was tempted to run, but the constable's slow walk, plus his recent exertions changed his mind.

"Who are you?" asked the constable, addressing TT when he was close enough.

"Terence Thorn, sir. They call me TT," he answered.

"Well TT, after what I just saw, you're welcome here anytime. And you young Glass," he said to Optic, "I came to see you. I wanted to know if you were a troublemaker and if you played by the rules, but again, after what I saw, both my questions are answered. "Remember!" he said loud enough so all the kids still around could hear. "From the face to the belt, and always, the handshake."

He turned and walked briskly towards the cemetery, his whistling an indication of his good mood.

In the next three years, TT availed himself every opportunity to holiday with his grandmother in Sauteurs, most of it in the company of Optic and by extension, the rest of the group. Not only did he become close to Pamela, he depended on Optic to keep all other suitors well away from her in his absence.

The very next morning after the fight, the principal J.V Redhead addressed the school at assembly to make two important announcements. He was very enthusiastic about the first.

"Mark this year well," he said, "and remember that in 1952 a company called Grundig invented the recording machine." He went on to explain the capabilities of that incredible bit of technology, and the difference it would mean for education. The second was a problem of such magnitude that some of the more superstitious suspected a curse on the island. A rat infestation of such proportion forced the Ministry of Health to become immediately involved.

In the schools, children were encouraged to carry whatever rats they may have caught to their respective schools for which they were promised the princely sum of two cents for each rat presented. For reasons of hygiene, they were told that only the rat's tail needed to be shown. The teachers keeping the log stayed as far away from them as was possible.

It wasn't long before Optic saw the opportunity and went for it. He approached one of the boys from the country that nearly always brought in rats, and offered him three cents for every rat he could deliver. Next, he employed five other boys including Lobo. The very next morning Optic took delivery of four rats tails and presented them to the teacher. After she had logged them she ordered him to get rid of them. He took the tails away and handed them to each boy in turn to be logged in, thereby turning a handsome profit. It was easy. It wasn't long before the operation jumped across to the Anglican school where it worked equally smoothly in the capable hands of Atlas.

For the duration of the infestation period, they financed the refreshments on movie nights. They mourned the epidemic's passing like a long lost friend.

When Jerry got back from the beach Juliette was in the front room dusting the furniture. She called out to him.

"Is that you Jer? There's some buns and lemonade in the kitchen. Come back here when you're finished."

On his return, she said, "I went to the cemetery today and grandma's grave was all covered in weeds, so I'd like you to clean it up as soon as you can make the time."

That Sunday afternoon he left the beach early, collected the cutlass and made his way to the communal cemetery in Marli where the dead of all denominations were buried. As he entered the gates, he walked straight to the little summerhouse and opened his shirt to catch the breeze. He was about to head for the grave when he suddenly stopped. Approaching from the far end of the cemetery to his right, was a young woman as yet unrecognised, but who somehow seemed familiar.

He continued to watch and slowly realization dawned, it was Leona Skye. All at once he became nervous. Flustered, even before she was in earshot, he said too quickly, and too softly, "Hi."

She showed no sign of having heard him, but continued to walk straight towards him. She slowed as she got within talking distance and greeted him as someone she was glad to see.

"Hello!" she said, smiling broadly to reveal gleaming white teeth. "I was beginning to think that you didn't live here anymore."

"Hi," he replied. "It is a long time since I've seen you, you look very well."

He thought of the image of himself standing there with the cutlass to his side and still wearing the shirt that Brains had torn earlier, and chided himself for not changing back into his Sunday clothes. Then he saw himself all dressed up and wielding a cutlass and despite the turmoil within, he actually grinned.

"Thank you, you also look very well," she smiled mischievously. "So, tell me, what have you been doing with yourself?"

"Same as ever, school, liming, football and of course the cinema," he said.

She smiled again. "Don't you mean liming, football, the cinema, and school?" They both laughed easily.

"Did you really think I was gone?"

"Well, this is almost my second week home and I've gone past your house almost every day."

"That's because I've been spending most of my days on the beach. Sister Ju says she hopes when school reopens, I'll continue to rise without any help from her," he hesitated for a while. "Perhaps one day, you'll drop by," he said hopefully.

They talked for a little while longer and just as she was about to leave, he asked, "Is it ok to walk with you? I want to stop by my grandma's old house." He hid the cutlass in the hedge and they turned left on the main road and walked leisurely in the hot afternoon sun.

"Were you visiting someone?"

"Yes, I always try to take my grandma some flowers whenever I'm home. She died when I was a little girl."

They walked past two small boys that were hunting lizards. The one in front carried a slingshot that he held at the ready. A little further on as they turned the corner, the road offered a picturesque panoramic view of the valley below and even at this distance, there was a suggestion of colour as the yellow of the nutmeg pods heralded what promised to be a bumper harvest.

From the road the land dropped sharply to merge with a ravine about eight feet below. From there it sloped steeply downwards, before flattening out to extend all the way to the main road along the seafront.

"I never get tired of walking through here," she said.

"I know what you mean. It really is beautiful."

Just then, a sudden gust of wind swept across them and blew her hat along the ground, until it flew upwards where it came to rest on a dead branch of a tree in the nearby gully.

"Oh no!" She cried. "My hat is gone."

"Just one minute," he reassured her.

Reacting quickly, he ran after the boys and snatched the slingshot with the pebble already in the pouch and shouted over his shoulder as he ran, "You'll get it back in a minute!"

Taking aim, he fired, but only grazed the offending branch. He searched around until he found a stone that filled the pouch. Composing himself, he held his breath, took aim and fired.

It was a perfect hit, it broke the branch and sent the hat floating gently until it landed about fifty feet away.

As he was handing her hat back, the boy shouted, "Hey Lobo, I want my sling back."

The faces of both boys were filled with admiration.

"Will you teach us to shoot like that?" He promised that he would. Afterwards, she thanked him profusely.

"This is my favourite hat, I couldn't bear to lose it like that. Thank you."

"I'm just glad I was around to help."

At which point she explained that the delay had made her late and she must go. He stood and watched her around the bend before turning back to retrieve the cutlass and complete his chore.

Thinking about her later, he relived the entire incident from the moment he had entered the cemetery to the time she left and for the life of him, he couldn't understand why he felt so tongue tied around her.

From as far back as he could remember, he had watched her passing his house almost every day, going either to church, or school, or to her sister's and although they always greeted each other politely and had the occasional small talk, he had not thought about her one way or the other. She was just a girl.

When she was eleven, she went to one of St George's secondary schools and came home for the holidays. Lately however, he had seen less and less of her, catching only occasional glimpses, nearly always in the distance.

In his mind's eyes, he watched her approach with an easy grace that made you want to stare and for an instant, he wondered if her walk had transformed gradually, or if she simply woke up one morning imitating a swan instead of an ugly duckling.

Somewhere along the line, she had made the proverbial change from caterpillar to butterfly. She was beautiful, slim, and weighed just about one hundred pounds. She had long dark hair tinged with brown, probably the effect of the sun. Dark largish brown eyes with long lashes, delicate straight nose with the merest hint of a bend where her glasses would rest if she wore any, and lips free of lipstick that made him think of kissing even when he didn't have it on his mind. Her breasts were of average size and her legs, probably the reason he liked watching her walk in the first place, were long and shapely. She'd worn a white blouse, with a blue flared skirt and black sandals, completed by her favourite hat, which sported ribbons the same colour as her skirt.

He couldn't understand why he found it difficult saying things to her, since he was as vocal as anyone when liming. Still, perhaps they'd meet again before she left. The next time, he'd be ready.

17

Juliette was putting her washing on the line when Atlas ran into the yard.

"Morning Sister Ju," he greeted. "Is Lobo around?"

"Morning Elton," she answered, "Jerry's at the bottom of the garden getting me some calaloo."

He thanked her over his shoulder as he hurriedly sought his friend.

"What's up," asked Lobo, who had heard the enquiry.

"Got any board? I must build a trap. The mongoose got another chicken this morning."

Later that afternoon, under the guidance of Cousin Noah, they put the trap together, baited it with fish gills and set it near to the ravine at the bottom of Atlas's garden.

The next day, as soon as they had changed from their Sunday clothes, they hurried to check the trap and found to their disappointment that it was still open. The only movement was a colony of ants, doing a good imitation of two giant motorways, as they very orderly went in on the left side and came out on the right.

After talking about it, they decided that mongooses didn't eat fish and went in search of a dead chicken.

The following day after school, they found the trap closed and with great jubilation, they carried it through the street towards the pasture, shouting as they went, "Mongoose, mongoose!"

Soon there was a crowd of rowdy boys, each armed with a stick and the shout became a rhythmic chant that kept time to their footsteps.

They chose a spot where the nearest vegetation was some distance away, then formed a circle and released the mongoose.

Amidst the confusion and the noise, the frightened animal frantically searched for escape, while the worried boys tried to maintain a safe distance as they trashed away with their sticks. Eventually, in a panic, the mongoose headed straight for Nugget who got smartly out of the way, allowing it the freedom and the safety of the nearby bushes.

Two days later another mongoose was caught and as before, it got away. Something had to be done.

That very afternoon, Lobo and Atlas paid a visit to the Villa, a lavish building that mirrored the architecture of colonial times in the twentieth century and housed the resident magistrate. Since then policy had changed, placing the parish under the jurisdiction of the circuit magistrate.

Left uninhabited, the house quickly deteriorated. It was at this point that Jimsey Crow became its self-appointed guardian.

Jimsey was a bachelor in his mid thirties with the easiest of lifestyles, who, with uncanny insight, had carved a niche for himself within the community. If he was anything, he was a survivor.

He could not be called a vagrant, as he always had somewhere to stay and always fed himself. Nor could he be called a beggar, because he never verbally begged but would readily accept anything that was volunteered after it was enticed from the giver.

He was not lazy, since he was always willing to perform any task of which he was capable and would accept any reward that was given. He also spent some of his time on Saturdays fetching shopping for the elderly, for which he never took any reward.

It was probably that sort of ingenuity which drove him to boarding up the Villa's broken windows, trimming the hedge and cutting the grass, after which he moved into the servants quarters. Not long afterwards, he came to an amicable agreement with the lawyer in charge and became the caretaker.

The boys approached casually to where, stripped from the waist up, he was cutting the hedge.

"Jimsey!" shouted Lobo, much louder than he needed to. "What's up man?"

Jimsey took the opportunity of a breather.

"Oh hello boys," his manner was easy. "What you boys doing in my neck of the woods?"

"We brought you these," said Atlas, handing over two large avocados.

"Damn, this is my lucky day," he said with a big grin. They talked for a while.

"Well", said Jimsey eventually, "no rest for the wicked as they say. If there is any way I can help, any time, just let me know." There was a knowing look on his face.

"You know, said Lobo, "you can do us a big favour."

"I somehow thought I could. You know me boys, if I can help, I'm all yours." He was smiling broadly.

The boys gave him a detailed account from the time the chicken was taken, to their present dilemma.

"So you see why we need the outhouse?" Lobo finished.

The outhouse was a large building about fifty yards from the main house, with gate designed doors placed right in the middle of its long side. It was heavily padlocked.

"I'm sorry boys, but as you can see, it's all locked up and I don't have the key. Everything that was in the house is covered up or packed away in there. The outhouse is out." He laughed at what he considered a clever pun and watched as their faces dropped.

"But I tell you what, why not use the garage? There's enough room in there. It's empty, and the door is unlocked. One thing, try not to damage the timber."

The next catch and once more the call of "Mongoose!" echoed along the street, as they made their way to the Villa. This time, they numbered eleven in all, more than there had ever been before. One of the newcomers was leading the way and was determined to get a result.

"I'm telling you fellahs, just keep out of my way and let me deal with the vermin," he said.

"We'll deal with it the way we always do, only this time, it's not running anywhere," said Lobo confidently.

As they approached, Jimsey was sitting on the veranda mending a torn mosquito net that somebody had given him. Lobo waved at him and he waved back.

"Good luck and try not to throw down the garage," he said.

They removed the bar that was against the door and entered, disturbing the many bats that were taking refuge there.

The garage was filled with ten excited boys. They placed the trap in the middle of the floor and formed a circle around it. Atlas was just about to release the prey when Nugget warned him, "we should close the door first."

Someone pulled the doors together but the moment they were released, they swung back to leave a gap wide enough to allow the mongoose to escape.

"That's the best I can do," he said. "It just won't stay."

"Then go outside and put the bar on the door," said Atlas firmly.

"Do you th- think that's wi- wi- wise?" asked Gatlin cautiously.

"Anyway," said the doorman, "I'll be locked out, I won't even get one lick at it."

"Then wait for the next time," said the eager newcomer, taking his place right in front of the trap. He shouted.

"Now, open the trap!"

Atlas pulled on the string that lifted the door and instead of the usual pandemonium, they gasped in shock.

Instead of the expected mongoose, a huge wild ginger tomcat with only one eye crouched as far back into the trap as he possibly could.

176

It was the General. The fur on his body stood up sharply all around, giving the impression that he was bigger than he really was. There was no denying his fierceness however. With bared teeth, he hissed almost continuously, until the newcomer threw his stick at him.

The sharp sound of the missile hitting the trap must have frightened him. He sprang out, jumped on the shoulder of the newcomer, ripping his khaki shirt in the process. The plan, tenuous at best, was now awry.

Lobo, eager to get out of the way after what he thought was an attack on the newcomer, slipped on the wet droppings of the bats and skidded into Ahab, bringing him down in the process.

The garage was in panic as everyone including the General looked for a place of escape and found none. The space that before seemed ample was now very confined and with no safe place to back into. Still hissing, the crazed animal attacked all in its path.

The newcomer screamed for the door to be opened, but amidst all the noise, the doorkeeper put it down to the excitement of the kill. Atlas ran for one of the corners and folded himself into a ball. Before long, he was completely protected as several other bodies, Lobo's among them, joined him on the floor. Gatlin was brave enough to aim a blow at the fleeting cat, but mistakenly struck the newcomer on his arm.

Two other boys collided and one of them sustained a nosebleed. After what seemed an eternity, the door was flung open and Jimsey entered with the bar, and very cautiously prodded the General towards the open door and safety. Afterwards, everyone had a story to tell. Jimsey, ever alert, rounded up the wounded and escorted them to the surgery.

That very afternoon, the trap was dismantled and the timber put to other uses. The hunting season was over permanently.

When Jerry got home, Juliette took one look at him, and said. "You look a little flushed. What have you been up to?"

He played down what really happened in the account he gave to Juliette.

"Don't you ever get tired of all that excitement? Why don't you read one of your books instead."

Given his recent exertion and apprehension, he thought it was a very good idea but instead of reading, he decided to write a letter to his mom. He picked up his school bag and headed for his favourite spot near the grotto.

Ever since he started writing to his mother, he had got into the habit of sending her long letters with all the news of the town. Everything from Father Devas's sermon, Heligar's judgments, Ivan Pope's dance escapade and especially those who died.

Today, he gave her a detailed account of the hunt, including the important fact that it was now over for good. Halfway through, he looked up to see Leona approaching, all at once he felt the feeling of inadequacy he felt before.

She wore a yellow summer dress, which hugged the top part of her body snugly, with the bottom half wide around her. In her hand she carried a single white frangipani flower, which she twirled around between forefinger and thumb, and every now and again lifted it to her nostrils and inhaled its delicate fragrance. A large white handkerchief covered her head and was knotted beneath her chin.

"Hi," she smiled.

"Hi," he replied, already tongue-tied.

"This is really very beautiful," she said, waving her arm in an arc to take in the scenery

"Yes, it is. It's my favourite spot."

"I know. I have seen you here before."

"I like to come here to study, write letters to my mom, and sometimes, just to be here, he said. "I can't ever remember you passing here before."

"I'm not really passing, I was looking for you. I wanted to give you this to say thank you."

She took a pencil from her waistband and was in the process of handing it to him, then stopped.

"Oh look, the point is broken," she said disappointingly. He searched for the penknife that he carried in his schoolbag and took the pencil from her.

"Let me do it. It's a poor enough present as it is." She placed the pencil against the grotto wall and worked a point into it.

"Thanks," he said accepting it. "You really didn't need to bother."

He couldn't take his eyes from it. He caressed the smooth ridge running the length of it, knowing it would be a keepsake, rather than a writing tool.

"I told you, it's my favourite hat," she said.

Still facing the grotto she chose a smooth surface and started carving into it.

"What are you doing?"

"Why not come and see for yourself."

Facing him was a single letter etched deeply into the wall 'L' for Leona. She handed back the knife.

"Why don't you put yours beside it?"

Looking over his shoulder, she saw that he was carving what looked like a J for Jerry.

"No," she said, shaking his shoulder, put an L, for Lobo."

She moved to within six feet of him into the shade, gathered her skirt around her, knelt to the ground, and rested easily on her calves.

"Why do those boys call you Lobo?"

"It's a nickname."

He was sitting with his back against the grotto and twirled the pencil between the fingers of his right hand.

"I know it's a nickname, but why do they call you that?" She had a look of exasperation on her face, which made him laugh.

"I was spending a lot of time on my own, so they said I was a lone wolf, hence, Lobo," he explained.

"I like it," she said. "It's kind of nice, it sounds strong," she smiled. "Is that when you were spending so much of your time here? Was there a special reason?"

He told her all about Sparkplug and his antics, of the tricks he had taught him, and they laughed together, until he came to the dreadful

179

part of his demise and the manner of it and Leopold's part in his rehabilitation. Without realizing it she had slumped, her shoulders sagged and her head was tilted to the left side. Her eyes shone brightly, but if there were any lingering tears, they never flowed. She sympathized and added belated words of consolation.

"I saw you sitting here once for almost two hours, but I had no idea what you were going through," she said.

"When? How?" He was genuinely puzzled.

"Midway through the term I had a fever. I was staying with my sister over there." She pointed to a green painted roof about three hundred yards away, in the direction of Lance Coteau.

"When the sun wasn't in my eyes, I could see the grotto from my bed. I saw when you came and I watched you leave."

They talked a little while longer then it was time for her to go.

"I'm leaving on Friday. I want to spend the weekend getting ready for the start of term. If I don't see you again before I leave, take care."

She floated away before he could think of something else to say.

He didn't move for a long time after she left. He kept looking at the pencil as he twirled it between his fingers and he heard her voice full of gratitude.

"Thanks for bringing it back," she had said. "It's my favourite hat."

He was glad he'd had the opportunity of rescuing her hat. He hoped one day he would get the chance to win her heart.

He took a last look at the etching, gave it an affectionate pat, then whispered the given name, Lobo and wondered why it was that he had never realized before, just how great a name it was.

18

It was just before four o'clock in the afternoon and the town was still reasonably busy as the last of the school children walked leisurely by in small groups, oblivious to everything except the gossip that was circulating.

The big stores, such as Grandby's and Bata, were open until five, in a hopeful attempt to catch any last minute sales from people getting off the buses from the capital that were due within the next half hour.

Sitting on the wall on the side of the road, which ran along the courtyard that housed the Anglican school and the police station, were five people. The locals referred to them as the Committee.

They had become a feature of the place, every day of the week except Saturday and Sunday, unless of course, an occasion presented itself on either of these days.

Normally there would be six of them, but one of the group had suffered an accident and was missing. She was Matilda.

Always in the same place and in the same order, they considered themselves the eyes and ears of the town. Starting from left to right, they were, Viola, in her mid–forties and recently married for the first time. She was especially vociferous when watching at social gatherings, such as weddings, dances, political meetings and the like. She was the candy and peanut vendor.

Carla was about forty, five feet, ten inches tall and very slim. She was the complete opposite of Viola in her manner and for a vendor, could be considered demure. She sold ice cream.

Vernon was a little man about five feet, six inches tall, with a goatee beard that was already speckled with grey. He was a married man of ten years, though he was still to see forty. He was about a hundred and thirty pounds and what he lacked in height, he more than made up for with banter. He was one of four local barbers.

Clifford was in his mid–forties with a noticeable paunch. He lived with his two sons on their smallholding. About five feet, ten inches tall, he weighed about a hundred and eighty pounds. He had a reputation for being able to hold his liquor. He was the obvious challenge to Poole's chairmanship.

Poole was a married man in his early fifties but looked older and lived with his wife. He took early retirement due to a serious injury. His belief in God changed as readily as the weather, depending on the outcome of whatever dilemma he was in. Many jokingly referred to him as, the Chairman.

Opinions varied as to the real reason they were there and what it was that held them together. According to Otto, each of the women had turned up on occasions when they had nothing to sell.

Of the group, only Poole had travelled to the neighbouring Windward island of St Vincent. The others had never been further than St George's, yet they all shared a passion for far away places, but appreciated it was unlikely they'd ever be going anywhere. So every day, they watched the buses come in, hoping that there would be someone getting off who was from a faraway place and who by association had brought a little of that place to them.

Another of the things that they would do was to try to pin down the person's personality, something that would be hotly debated in the future.

They were speculating about the welfare of the absent member, Matilda.

"Well," said Poole with an air of total boredom, his chin resting above cupped hands that held his stick between his legs, "she is not missing anything by being away."

Amazingly Clifford didn't contradict him. Instead, he appeared to be listening.

"Here comes the first one now," he said, indicating by direction of his head. "It's *Excelsior*."

The bus climbed the hill slowly and turned into the courtyard, it was about half full.

"She must have left first today and caught most of the workers getting off early," said Vernon.

They gave their undivided attention to the passengers as they alighted.

"Just the same old faces of people working in St. George's," said Viola disappointedly.

The other buses came in at short intervals but yielded nothing out of the ordinary. Only *Western Hope* was outstanding.

"It will be dark by the time it gets here if she doesn't come soon," Poole said impatiently.

"There you go making things grand again. It's only half past four but as usual, everything must be done to suit you," said Clifford. He continued, "The *Sea Nymph* came in from Trinidad this morning. She must have a full load but you'll just have to wait like the rest of us."

"You are one hell of a windbag," said Poole. "As you said yourself, The *Sea Nymph* came in this morning, so what has one to do with the other?"

The irritation in Clifford's voice was clear. "I'm a lot more than a windbag, and if it wasn't for that bum leg of yours, which you wave like a flag and hide behind, I'd be glad to show you."

"Enough you two. Stop blowing smoke and upsetting yourselves, your fighting days are done," said Viola, who had plenty of experience ordering her husband around.

Poole had placed his stick beside him and was busy filling the bowl of his pipe. After he had tempted it several times, he attached it to his mouth and lit it. He drew hard on it three or four times and allowed the wind to blow the smoke towards Clifford.

"Anyway," he said, "there's nothing for me to get upset about. Like I said, Cliff here blows a lot of wind. Besides, I whooped him once before and if it wasn't for my bad leg, I'd do it again."

"Only if I'm asleep, old man. One of these days, I'll forget about that leg, bum or otherwise and give you what I should have given you years ago."

"Come now boys, take it easy," said Carla soothingly.

They heard the sound of the engine as it laboured up the hill in first gear, long before *Western Hope* turned the corner and came into view. There were a couple of rows of cardboard boxes, and battered suitcases lashed to the top. Clifford grinned smugly. "Told you!" he said.

Poole refused to concede, he made no reply. Once again, they were all focused on those getting off.

"I mean," said Poole, "it's not too much −." He stopped in mid sentence and straightened himself for a better look.

"Not too much for what?" asked Carla.

Poole ignored her and instead he took hold of his stick and strained upwards. After a brief pause, he said. "Just for a second there I thought −" his voice trailed off for a little while. "No! Forget it," he said. "Impossible!"

Hardly had he settled back down before standing up again.

"Jumping catfish, it's him! It's Ben Crabb!"

"What are you stewing about? It can't be. He was doing five years in that bad Trinidad jail, last time I heard."

"You must be right," said Poole grudgingly agreeing with Clifford about something, perhaps more out of fear than conviction. Suddenly, unaided by his stick, he almost sprang up.

"Speak of the devil!" Poole's voice was little more than a whisper. About fifty yards away, a bulky man about five feet, ten inches, was standing with his back to the group while he appeared to be paying the conductor. Gradually, Olivia and her fellow traffickers, together

184

with their helpers drifted away and only a few people were left around the bus.

The man, having finished his business with the conductor picked up a box and held it under his right arm. He carried it with little effort. He turned and headed out of the courtyard and into the direction of the group.

"As I live and breathe," said Carla.

"They say if you look for trouble, sooner or later it will find you. Well, here it comes," said Vernon uneasily.

"Keep your voice down!" There was a hint of apprehension in Viola's voice, which was little more than a whisper.

The man walked slowly towards them, all the time looking around him as if he was checking that everything was still the same. As he came alongside, he stopped and turned to face them. There was recognition in his face.

"Well, what do you know," he asked rhetorically. "I see the coven is still active."

"And I see your manners are still the same," said Vernon defiantly.

"Ah, Vernon. I see you still have all that sand in your craw. Mind it doesn't leave a nasty taste in your mouth one of these days," he smiled only with his face. "Do you still keep that 'house call' sign on the door in your shop? You must be, because you're making a call right now. Are you still afraid of that wife of yours? Do you really think she believes it?"

"What I do or don't do is my business."

"Oh I see. What you do is your business, but you sit out here every evening watching other people's." He turned his attention to Carla.

"Sister Carla, you still going to church every morning in the hope that God wouldn't know what you are doing in the evening?" His voice was mocking.

"That," said Carla, "is between me and my God. You should worry about your own soul." Her voice was pitched just loud enough for him to hear. He moved one step to stand in front of Viola, his gaze taking in her wedding ring, "You finally trapped a man, eh Viola? Or did you cut your losses and marry Clifford here?"

"No such thing!" said Viola sharply. "I'm married to Allan." Her look was smug.

"You mean the cripple? You carry him to church on his bed?" He laughed loudly and there was no doubting his sincerity.

"Of course not!" she said indignantly. "He walked with his own two feet."

"You gave him one of your potions. Then it was, 'yes Vi, no Vi, I will Vi', he laughed again, heartily.

"Why don't you leave her alone?" snapped Clifford.

Benny gave the impression that he never heard him.

"Wait a minute," he said, "the last member of the coven is missing. Don't tell me, skinny Matilda kicked the bucket?"

"No," said Viola. "She had an accident, she should be back soon."

"Is she still with that saga boy, Hayling? Still buying him shirts in the hope that he'll pop the question? And does he still ride that bike of his with all those other women holding on to him so tight, he could hardly breathe?" He took them all in with his eyes. When no one volunteered an answer, he continued. "Don't tell me, after all the shirts and hot meals, he married another woman?"

"He was transferred to another place if you must know," said Viola.

Benny laughed as if something had just been clarified for him.

"So he did the decent thing by moving to another place before he got married, eh? One of these days, this place will get into the papers."

"Don't tell him any more, none of it is his damn business anyway," said Clifford.

"So Clifford," he said, as if he had noticed him for the first time, "you still stinking up the place with those pigs?"

"Listen," said Clifford, but he was cut off before he could go on.

"And you wonder why you can't get a woman to live there with you?"

"What's the matter with you, not back five minutes and you're already upsetting people?" said Clifford a little angrily.

"Just calling it as I see it."

Benny walked past in front of Poole, rested the box on the wall beside him and sat down, keeping it between them. He reached into his shirt for the makings of a cigarette and took his time rolling it. An uncomfortable silence prevailed.

He allowed his gaze to wonder as he took in the familiar scene.

Across the road and to his right was the dispensary, where he had whiled away many an hour, waiting to collect medicine for a mother that was always poorly. Behind it was the surgery, where he had spent more time waiting to be mended than he did in church.

To the left, as you cross High Street, was Miss Murray's little shop and just in front of it as you approach the road was Miss Nomo's house, directly opposite from where they were sitting. Just beyond was Aunt Minnie's parlour, followed by Hucky Hill's two-storey house, which seemed badly in need of a fresh coat of paint.

His gaze swivelled to the left as it took in the police station directly opposite and it surprised him that he immediately compared it favourably to the place where he had spent the last three and a half years in captivity.

Without looking, he knew that the Anglican school was to the left of it and between them, the entrance to the church and cemetery.

Locked away in that pit of desolation, whenever despair threatened which was often, he would allow his spirit to soar to this place, this very spot, the only place he ever felt that he belonged. In his tortured mind he always interacted with one of this pathetic group, perhaps the purchase of a roti from Matilda, peanuts from Viola or an argument with Poole. Now he was back, and already he felt as though he had never left.

He crushed what was left of the cigarette under his shoe and turned his attention to Poole, whom he had deliberately left for last and broke the silence.

"So Chairman, last, and very much least, are you still telling tales of the great things you saw in St Vincent?" he asked with obvious sarcasm.

"I never thought that my luck was so bad I'd ever have to look on your face again, Ben Crabb, but I was wrong. At least, I got to see most of St Vincent and left of my own free will, but I see they still didn't teach you any manners in that place. You're not yet back five minutes and here you are upsetting your betters," Poole said with all the contempt he could muster.

"I see you are still drinking bush for other people's fever old man and still using that leg as a shield. Well you can stop now, the war is over and you won't be called up. It's a pity though, the Germans would have died laughing." He was deliberately spiteful.

"You have no respect for anyone or anything. They say the possum knows which tree to climb, but one of these days, you'll climb the wrong one, and I'll be there to hear you beg for mercy." There was plenty of conviction in Poole's voice. Ben Crabb grinned.

"You can take my word for it old man, two things you will never see. Me begging for mercy and a green donkey," he said with a gloat.

Again, with little effort, he lifted the box and replaced it underneath his right arm and followed the road down to the family home.

In all the years that Clifford had known Poole, he had never seen him so rattled.

"What is it with the two of you anyway? It looks as if you hate each other," he observed.

Poole was a while in answering and there was an edge to his voice. "Just under five years ago there was a card game at McSwill's. There were five of us playing and the game was very amicable until Ben Crabb sat down and right away the spirit of the game changed. Ben was losing heavily, mostly to one fellah from Bequia. He accused him of cheating, but no one else agreed. The argument got heated, then without warning, Ben picked up a bottle and smashed it over the fellah's head. He did a lot of damage. He got frightened and ran. He went into hiding and a few days later his mother bribed one of the sailors on the *Sea Nymph,* and wearing all his clothes Ben stowed away to Trinidad.

"It wasn't long after, about six months I think, before news of his arrest came back. That's when his mother started crying and said she wished she hadn't sent him away."

"The story goes that he was staying with a woman he met where he was working and one day he came in and saw a man sitting there without his shirt. Without asking for an explanation or waiting for one, he attacked the man with a knife and put him in hospital.

It turned out he was the woman's uncle who had gotten caught in a heavy shower of rain and was waiting for his shirt to dry. According to the Trinidad Guardian, he was given five years in Carrera Island Prison. What I don't understand, is how he could be out already, I thought he had about another year to do," Poole said disappointedly.

"You could be right, I'm sure I heard someone say that a prison year is nine months," said Vernon.

"He has a vile tongue in his head, that one," said Viola.

"A vile tongue is the least of your troubles," Poole said gravely. "This one is pure evil. You mark my words, it's just a matter of time before he starts throwing his weight around."

"Perhaps his time inside has changed him," said Carla hopefully.

"I hope you're right, but I wouldn't bet on it," said Poole.

Normally, they would sit until dusk and depending how active the town became, would even wait for the gas lamp to be lit, but less than ten minutes after Ben Crabb had left, Poole picked up his stick, offered a lame excuse, and limped himself homeward.

Having got there, without waiting for supper or a word to his wife, he got into bed and covered his head with the sheet.

189

19

As they moved into the middle of the second school term, time passed lazily, and for the most part was uneventful. One night, Nugget introduced a packet of ten phoenix cigarettes to the lime.

"Where did you get these?" said Lobo.

"My granddad spent the whole afternoon looking for them. He thought he lost them outside, but after he left I found them under the chair."

"So you thought we might have a smoke, are you crazy? Do you know what will happen to us if we get caught? Have you got any matches?"

They all congregated into the shade and handed the cigarettes around. Only Brains abstained because of his condition.

Whatever it was the boys expected, they were disappointed. All they succeeded in doing was starting a coughing epidemic, and amidst the tears and laughter of relating their experiences, they quickly came to one conclusion. Cigarettes never again featured in their plans.

On another night, the novelty was provided by Optic, only this time instead of seeking refuge in the shade they needed light. Whatever it was Optic was holding could not be viewed under the gas lamp in full view of passers-by. Very quickly, Lobo ran to his house nearby for a flashlight and in the bushes behind the wall, they huddled together to admire a coloured centrefold of Betty Grable in a skimpy bathing suit. In the weeks following, that picture would ride in a different school bag every day until finally, it disintegrated from excess handling.

It was around that time that rumours started circulating about Benny Crabb imposing his will on others.

Cecil May was a post office clerk with a passion for sailboats of all kinds. To better enjoy his hobby he had over many months saved enough to buy a pair of binoculars all the way from Barbados and could often be seen from vantage points along the banks following the progress of any passing sailboat. It was easily his most prized possession.

As June the twenty-ninth got closer, he was in a high state of excitement. The date was a public holiday on which Fisherman's Birthday, was celebrated. It was also one of the biggest days of the sporting calendar, the highlight of which was the annual boat race.

The race was always held in Low Town bay, which stretched all the way to Mount Rodney, about a mile away.

Having both won the race over the last two years captains Berry and Burke, the respective captains of The Dolphin and The Kingfisher were expected to fight out the finish yet again. Both men had taken to the sea from an early age and had often been heard to talk about the other's ability in glowing terms. On the day of the race, there was a buzz of excitement from the large crowd who seemed equally divided between the two.

Scattered among them were the vendors, providing a wide choice of refreshments. In front of the fish market, which was in use as a public gallery, a tug of war contest was in progress between twelve skinny men on the one side, and twelve strapping women on the other. The men, though they pulled valiantly, were unceremoniously dragged along the beach to cheers and jeers of 'shame'. Further along, a group of girls and boys played a game of softball cricket, while another group of boys played football.

The great majority of revellers, however, could be seen and heard as they frolicked in the surf.

191

At last, it was time to start the race. All the boats got in a straight line and they were off. On the shore, there was a burst of activity as the spectators jockeyed for the best places from which to watch. The rules were simple and easy to follow. They all start together and first one past the post after navigating the course was the winner.

Cecil was straggling a coconut tree that he had picked out on high ground long before the beach got crowded. As they set off, one of the spectators asked him which of these he thought was going to win.

"Well," he said, enjoying the attention, "most of us agree that it's likely to come down to two boats. In this light wind The *Dolphin* has a slight advantage when they sail into the wind, but I think that could change when they sail with the wind. My guess though, if the wind stays the way it is or drops, The *Dolphin* will win. If however it starts blowing, it'll be easy for The *Kingfisher*."

Right from the word go, the captains began tacking in an attempt to catch the wind and already, Fred Berry had The *Dolphin* in a clear lead as Captain Burke headed towards the land.

"What's Burke doing now?" asked the same spectator.

"Captain Burke is a great tactician, he is trying to catch a land breeze," Cecil explained.

"And how far do they have to go?" he asked.

Cecil was amazed that the stranger did not know the course.

"From here they would sail east and turn around London Bridge, the direction of the turn being optional.

Then they come back past here on their way down to Gouyave about ten miles away, turn around the buoy in the harbour and back up. First to pass the jetty is the winner."

London Bridge is a large rock formation just North-East of Levera. The English sailors bestowed the name on the rock because they said, "It reminded them of London Bridge."

The crowd watched with bated breath as the boats went out of sight, curious to see who would be in the lead as they appeared on the return journey. In an attempt to catch the leaders, The *Kingfisher* skimmed the shoreline all the way up to Levera before heading out to open sea, by which time The *Dolphin* was long gone, rounding the "Bridge" a full five minutes before its main rival. When they reappeared, the Dolphin had retained a clear lead and The *Kingfisher* was not yet in sight. A huge roar went up from Captain Berry's supporters.

"I think it's all over." The stranger sounded disgruntled at what he saw as an anti-climax.

"Oh, I think it's far from over my friend," Cecil said enthusiastically as The *Kingfisher* came into view.

"The *Dolphin's* lead should be a winning one but they still have a long way to go and the wind may still change in *Kingfisher's* favour.

Cecil, an admirer of Captain Burke, was in his element even though his hero looked to be on a hiding.

Once again, still searching for that illusive breeze, Captain Burke headed for the shore but the tactic was only partially successful, as The *Kingfisher* maintained her position, but failed to appreciably close the gap.

The *Dolphin* rounded the buoy a full ten lengths ahead of its rival, and with the last leg into the wind, Berry looked home and dry. Then two things happened and dramatically reduced the certainty of victory. The wind had not only freshened appreciably, it changed. Immediately that happened, Captain Burke changed his tactic and tacked for the open sea. With a full sail, he rapidly began to overhaul his rival. Yet again, he tacked landwards towards Copeland point.

"What's happening now Cecil?" asked another spectator.

"I can't believe he is going for it," said Cecil, sounding puzzled.

"Going for what?" asked the man impatiently.

"Well," said Cecil, "he is heading into the breakers. The water there is shallow in places and he risks being grounded. If the turn is not accurate he could end up on the rocks. If he makes the turn though, he might just surprise Captain Berry."

"Hey, you! Let me see that glass!" said a gruff, discourteous voice. It was Benny Crabb.

"That's not a glass, if you must know it's a pair of binoculars and right now I'm using them," said Cecil testily, a little annoyed at being interrupted. All the time he was talking, he had the instrument fixed to his eyes.

"I said, let me see that," said Benny, grabbing the binoculars from Cecil's eyes and pulling it towards his.

The strap was still around Cecil's neck and his head was pulled violently towards Benny's, who yanked the straps from around his neck and placed the instrument to his eyes.

Cecil, not wanting to miss the manoeuvre lunged after the binoculars but Benny pushed him hard and he tumbled into the sand. Then Benny quickly lost interest and threw the binoculars into the sea.

Cecil who was of a timid nature was twenty-eight years old, five feet, eight inches tall, and weighed about a hundred and thirty pounds. It was a massive mismatch when compared to a man of Benny's bulk. He allowed him to walk away without offering further confrontation.

Ahab, who was in the crowd watching the race in his bathers, dived into the sea and retrieved the thrown instrument after a little while, and returned it to Cecil.

By then, Captain Burke had used his knowledge of the shallows, sailed as close to the rocks as he dared and executed a successful precision turn. Despite this strategy, The *Kingfisher* was beaten into second place by half a length.

Cecil was deprived of a moment he would long have treasured and talked about for many a moon.

In the bars that night and many future nights, more would be spoken about Burke's tactics than the actual winner of the race.

As one local wit enthused, "He passed so close to the rocks, he left some of her paint on them."

Any visitor would have been excused for thinking that The *Kingfisher* had won the race.

Such was the publicity given to the binoculars incident that

Benny's mounting notoriety began to take on an ominous aspect. Any kid who thought he was being taken advantage of unfairly, would be heard to challenge his aggressor, "Who do you think you are, Benny Crabb?"

Later, giving an eyewitness account of what he saw to his friends, there was a hint of disbelief in Ahab's voice.

"I tell you man, this fellah is mean through and through. Whatever you do, stay out of his way."

20

About the first week in July, police constable, Edgar 'Movealong' Vibert, came to Sauteurs, and like all new brooms, he was determined to make a clean sweep. Within a few weeks of his coming, most of the people around had either met him, or heard of him.

He was dark with smooth skin, about five feet, nine inches tall and wore his cap with the peak very close over his eyes and in the words of Carla, was broodingly handsome. Otto, on the other hand, observed that he only smiled at the members of the opposite sex.

He was christened, 'Movealong', by one of the locals, because of his obsession for moving people along.

Before his arrival, on the understanding that they kept the peace, the bars that were supposed to close at nine o'clock, were allowed to stay open later on special occasions like public holidays, political rallies, and so on. Despite advice to the contrary, Movealong, whenever he was on duty, insisted on regular hours under threat of prosecution.

Payday revellers who had over-indulged and would normally be allowed to sleep it off in the cells and released the next morning, would, when arrested by constable Vibert, be prosecuted for being drunk, which in a way was slightly ironical, since the constable was a strong drinker himself.

The group's first encounter with Movealong came one night after they had attended a local talent show at the Anglican school, where local celebrity, teenager Lillian Blake had won the star prize. The boys were occupying the very spot used by Poole and his friends and were debating among themselves the judges' decision. So engrossed were they, that no one noticed the constable until he was standing almost directly in front of them.

"That's a hell of a racket you boys are making. Do you want to tell me why?" he enquired by way of introduction.

Surprised by his sudden appearance, they were taken aback. It was a while before Brains reacted.

"We were arguing about the judges' decision," he informed him.

"Well," said Movealong, "the judges have made their decision, now so must I. I doubt though, that you're going to like it any better. So, disperse!"

Once again, the boys had trouble finding their voices and again it was Brains who answered.

"But we're not doing anything wrong, we're just talking."

"I know what you are doing, you're creating a public nuisance. I could hear you halfway up the hill," said Movealong. His voice was deliberately pitched very low.

"But we sit here all the time, we're not doing any harm," Brains persisted.

"What's your name," he asked, "because the next time, and I hope there will be a next time, I'm going to be talking to you." He bent slightly towards Brains to make sure of eye contact. "Now, move!"

Reluctant to end the lime, they took their time as they walked away and a curious thing happened. Although they all lived in different directions, without previous agreement, they all headed in the direction of High Street, together. When they were far enough away, they stopped to reassemble, keeping the constable in sight as he made his way to the station at the end of his shift.

Lobo, aware of Brains' dark mood, tried to placate him.

"Listen man –"

Brains snapped, "What the hell just happened?"

197

Quick as a flash, Gatlin said, "We were just run out- outta town man."

All eyes were turned on him. Suddenly, they started laughing and eventually, even Brains joined in.

"So," said Brains, "what are we going to do about him?"

Lobo knew that Movealong's threat to deal with Brains first was like waving a red flag in front of a bull.

"Why do we have to do anything? It's not as if we're surprised. He's hassled everybody else, so why not us?"

"Because we're not everybody else," said Atlas arrogantly.

The turn that the discussion had taken started to worry Gatlin.

"We are ta- ta- talking a- a- about a po- policeman you know." His speech indicated his rising agitation.

"So what?" said Atlas.

"Just hold it, hold it for a minute, Gats is right. He is the police and we were arguing, so all we have to do is keep out of his way." Lobo's look said he wasn't prepared to argue.

"That's right," said Gatlin, pleased for the support.

"We'll just keep out of the sher- sher —"

"The sheriff's way," Nugget concluded.

Gatlin turned on him with wide eyes. "Shut up you"! he shouted.

"Leave him alone," said Atlas. "You know he hates that."

Ahab spoke for the first time.

"Listen, we just have to find out when he is doing that shift and keep out of his way for that week."

It seemed the best thing for the moment and they agreed to leave it like that.

Having concluded their observations, they found out that with the exception of constable Wells, who worked the children's shift from 8 a.m. to 4 p.m., the police worked a three-week rotation.

The first shift started from 6.0 a.m. to 2.0 p.m., the middle from 2.0 p.m. to 10.0 p.m. and the night shift, from 10.0 p.m. to 6.0 a.m.

"It's quite simple," said Optic, "we just stay out of the way on his shift."

198

"Are you saying we should break up the lime?" asked Atlas. The tone of his voice suggested that wasn't an option.

"Well, I don't know," admitted a confused Optic.

"Wait a minute," said Lobo, "we could meet someplace else."

"Such as?" asked Brains.

"What about the pasture? He won't bother us there," said Lobo.

"Well, I don't know about you, but I'm not an owl. How are you going to see in the dark?" asked Nugget.

"You could smile and your teeth would light up the dark," said Gatlin, who couldn't resist the opportunity to have a dig.

They all agreed. It was settled, they'd just have to figure something for when it was dark.

That night, Brains brought some popcorn to the lime and was very grumpy about having to meet in the pasture.

"I still say we have the right to be on the street," he said.

"Let's give it a little more time, then maybe Movealong will leave us alone," suggested Lobo.

All except Brains agreed. The suggestion was carried.

Brains had read somewhere that 'fools for argument used wagers'. Since then had used it as his watchword. Yet, he was a sucker for a dare.

Nugget dared him to walk into Nelson's store and buy a condom. Brains knew that if word of the purchase got back to his mother there would be hell to pay but he found the dare irresistible, provided they paid for the condom. They agreed to meet outside the store at half past one the following day at Brains' suggestion.

Unknown to the others, because of Brains' frequent visits to the store on his mother's behalf he was familiar with the working arrangements of the staff. Every day at precisely one o'clock, Ethel the cook, relieved Mrs Nelson from her duties in the shop for one hour.

They assembled as planned but all of the others decided to stay well out of sight. Brains walked confidently into the shop. After his eyes had adjusted to the sharp contrast of the light, he stopped dead in his track. Sitting at the far end of the counter in the middle of her lunch, was Mrs Nelson.

"Hello Clive, what can I do for you?" she asked as she approached him. It took a little while for him to collect himself.

"Good afternoon," he said haltingly, "where is Ethel?"

"She heard the fisherman's shell, so she went to the market to buy fish. Did you want to see her?"

"No, no! I'm used to seeing her here this time of the day."

"So how can I help you?"

"Yes, I'm, I'd like one reel of number nine black thread, and, two soft candles to keep the pressing iron from getting rusty, please." He was close to babbling.

She smiled as she handed him his purchase, putting his manner down to preoccupation, rather than skulduggery.

He had failed the dare and had to repay the money. Far more embarrassing, he was Nugget's slave to perform one demeaning task. That was the least of Brains' worries as he waited anxiously for Sunday when Mrs Nelson would see his mother in church. Only then would he know his fate.

That Sunday afternoon, his relief was obvious as he repeatedly attacked Ahab with gusto. Lying on the sand afterwards, he said.

"Mother told me once if Big John ever catches me, he's going to skin me alive. If Mrs. Nelson had told her I was up to no good –" His unfinished statement hung ominously in the silence.

Nugget was still trying to work out the best way to embarrass Brains when he fell for yet another dare. As they sat about talking, Optic was the first to notice the beginnings of a freak tropical storm.

"Look at all that rain falling over there fellahs," he said, pointing in the general direction of the ocean.

Not more than three or four hundred yards away, the rain deluged. Yet, the beach was drenched in brilliant sunshine. It was as if there was a transparent curtain that prevented the rain from coming any nearer, and amazingly, a rainbow ran all the way across it.

"Look how near that rainbow is. I've never seen one this close," said Atlas.

"Me neither," echoed Nugget.

"Listen fellahs," Ahab said excitedly at the far off sound of thunder, followed by the flash of lightning much closer. "What do you say we swim out there inside that rainbow?"

"Are you out of your mind? said Lobo. "Haven't you noticed how dark it's getting over there?"

"Let me guess, you're going to look for the gold at the end of the rainbow," said Brains sarcastically.

"What gold?" Atlas's interest quickened.

"Legend has it there is a pot of gold at the end of each rainbow," Brains explained.

"Don't forget to tell him it's just a myth," said Lobo.

"And while you're at it, don't forget to say you're all just too chicken to go out there." He held his hands so that they were bent at the elbows and flapped them against his ribcage. There was no mistaking the contempt in Ahab's voice.

"Damn right I'm chicken. There's no way you're getting me out there," said Gatlin.

They each agreed in turn until it got to Brains.

"I'll race you there," he said, setting off at a dead run and plunging into the water ahead of Ahab on his way to the rainbow.

Despite his early lead Ahab soon caught up to Brains and together, they swam towards the rainbow. As they approached where they thought it should be, there was no visible sign of it. Believing it to be further in, they swam into the rain, which according to Brains, was falling so heavily he had to dive beneath the water to avoid the stinging drops.

Blinded by the storm, they became disorientated. The heavy rainfall, the mist and the darkness conspired against their sense of direction. They tried shouting to each other but to no avail.

Suddenly, it ceased being an adventure and became frightening. Lightning, far more impressive cut through the gloom and amidst all the noise, the thunder that followed was deafening. Blinded for an instant by the bright lightning, both boys had trouble locating each other. For the first time in his life Ahab was afraid of the water and regretted his bravado, now all he wanted to do was find Brains and get out. Brains was in a panic when he couldn't see Ahab and promised God that if they got out of there intact, he would never accept another dare; he started thrashing about with both hands in the hope of attracting Ahab's attention. With adjusted vision plus Brains' splashing, Ahab found Brains, tapped him on the arm and indicated that he shouldn't move then he took a deep breath, closed his eyes and dived. When he judged he was deep enough from the turbulence at the top, he opened his eyes and had a good look around and thought he discerned a brightening in the water to his left, where there was light just outside the downpour. He hurried back to Brains all the time trying to remember his bearings, tapped him on the shoulder and together they swam into the sunlight.

Without either saying a word, they swam together back towards the shore.

Back on the beach Ahab asked if the rainbow had disappeared while they were away. The others confirmed it was constant all along and in fact was still to be seen. The mystery of the vanishing rainbow was a major subject of discussion for a long time afterwards.

The tactics employed by the boys for avoiding Movealong worked well for a while, until the local football team, Crusaders, played Corinthians from St George's. Crusaders celebrated with a 4-2 win and the boys were in hearty spirits as they discussed it. They were walking up Main Street when the rain started to drizzle. They ran towards shelter under the awnings of the Cut Rate store. This time, they caught sight of him when he was about thirty yards away.

"Here comes Movealong," Ahab warned.

"Just take it easy, keep the noise down," advised Optic. With an effort to be quiet they continued talking.

The constable, who was strolling with his hands behind his back, seemed oblivious to the rain. He was looking straight ahead. He kept on walking until he was halfway past the awnings and despite their resolve, the conversation among the boys gradually dried up.

Movealong turned slowly around until he was facing them, but chose to remain standing in the light rain.

"So, I was beginning to think we weren't going to meet again, but I see you haven't disappointed me. Just as before, you're making a hell of a racket and I hate repeating myself."

The only good thing about this encounter thought Lobo, was that Brains was missing. Remembering his threat to Brains, Lobo wondered which of them Movealong was going to start with.

"Look officer, we're not doing anything, we're only sheltering from the rain," he heard himself saying.

"So, you expect me to believe that tough boys such as yourselves are afraid of getting wet? You must think me very gullible." He looked as if he was beginning to enjoy himself. "Anyway," he continued, "I didn't ask what you were doing, because I know what you were doing, but I'm very interested in what you're going to do."

As he spoke, the rain changed from a drizzle to a steady downpour but the constable made no move towards shelter.

"We're not causing any trouble, we haven't done anything to you," Ahab said defiantly.

"I disagree."

"We'll go as soon as the ray- rain stops off- off- officer," Gatlin promised.

Movealong ignored him. His gaze was on Ahab.

"You're causing a public nuisance. This is your last warning. Next time, I'm going to arrest the whole bunch of you. Now disperse!"

The boys looked at each other in disbelief. The rain was falling harder than before. Instinctively, they moved closer together and Movealong smiled for the first time.

"One way or the other, you're going to get wet. Either going home, or to the station, I don't much care which. So, GET A MOVE ON!"

This time, they scattered in different directions and made their separate ways home at a dead run. The same thought was in each of their minds, that Movealong had crossed the line.

At both schools, the word went around.

"The calabash tree at six o'clock."

For Brains' benefit, they went into the details of the night before and from his reaction, Lobo was glad he'd been an absentee.

"He can't do that!" Brains said emphatically. "My dad says, to cause a public nuisance you have to be causing a public disorder, or wilful destruction of property or person. We didn't do any of these things; he has overstepped his authority. He crossed the line. Something has to be done."

"We could tell Constable Wells about it," Gatlin suggested. Everyone was quiet for a while. Atlas broke the silence.

"If we tell, it would be our word against his. Who do you think Nip would believe?"

Before anyone could answer, Nugget asked, "Since when did we go to others to fix our problems?"

"But he is a policeman," Gatlin reminded them as he did the first time.

"I thought we agreed he crossed the line?" queried Brains.

Everyone nodded in the affirmative.

"Then he is an opponent first and everything else afterwards," he said, looking straight at Lobo.

After a little while, Lobo nodded in agreement.

"Brains is right, he is an opponent. He has offended every one of us."

Gatlin, a devotee of Western jargon groaned. "I hope they have pillows in the hoosegow," preferring the western slang word for jail. Everybody laughed and they relaxed.

They discussed it at length and decided to take time to think of a

204

plan. In the meantime, they were going to keep a close eye on Movealong, even though they had no idea what they were looking for.

It was two weeks to the August holidays, but the shadow of Movealong hung over their plans.

"I say we settle it before the holidays," said Brains.

"We'll settle it when we have a plan with a chance. If we think of one before then we'll do it before," Lobo answered.

"Is that why we wasted three weeks watching him, only to do nothing?" Brains was clearly reluctant to let it go.

"Then what do you suggest we do?" asked Optic.

Brains took his time thinking and the ruptured expression of his face was a clear indication of another crazy scheme. Then he did a curious thing. He lifted up both hands as if he was asking for quiet even before he started to speak. "Now listen, I've been thinking. The next time that Movealong hassles us, why don't we allow him to arrest us?"

Despite his raised hands, he was easily shouted down.

"Are you ma- ma- mad?" asked Gatlin, who had waited until things calmed down.

"You're damn right he is mad," said Lobo.

"Will you just listen for one minute?" pleaded Brains. "Say he arrests us, we go before Heilgar and we tell our side, including being dispersed in the rain. If Heilgar believes us, we'll never have to worry about Movealong again."

"That's one hell of a big if ," said Ahab sceptically.

"And what if he believes Movealong, what then?" asked Optic.

Gatlin who became anxious with all that aggressive talk around attempted to introduce some levity to the proceedings. Like all would be comics in the area, all of the jokes he told, most of which were his own creation were credited to a farmer named James John, who had told one ridiculously silly joke while drinking with his friends and had been paying ever since.

"Have you heard James John's latest?" he asked, and without waiting for an answer he hurried on.

"It seems his wife complained that he kept her awake with his snoring. 'All right Nell,' he said, determined to settle things once and for all."

At this point, the thought of delivering the punch line triggered Gatlin's excitement and his stuttering.

"Tonight, wa- wake me up so I cu- cu- cu-"

"Could hear how loud I'm snoring," finished Nugget.

Gatlin turned on Nugget with bared teeth and wide eyes.

"Right"! he shouted and started chasing Nugget. The others, who were used to the routine, ignored them.

They returned about ten minutes later and Gatlin was still brushing dirt and dry grass from his clothes.

"What took you so long?" asked Atlas whose curiosity usually got him blasted.

"Because this fool followed me down the hollow."

"I'm surprised at you Gats. He can run through that place with his eyes closed," said Atlas.

Gatlin, who because of his passive nature, was usually shouted down at suggestions time, waited for his chance.

"Why don't we get Movealong to chase Nugget down the hollow?"

The hollow was a beaten track that served as a shortcut, sloping downwards from High Street and connected to Main Street and existed long before any of the boys was born. While it was frequently used by some of the locals, it was avoided by most during nightfall, or after a shower of rain, except by the brave or the foolish.

The silence must have lasted all of four or five seconds after Gatlin's suggestions before anyone spoke. Lobo, who did not share Brains' enthusiasm to be arrested, jumped at another possibility.

"That's not a bad idea, not bad at all," he said thoughtfully.

"Aren't you forgetting something?" asked Ahab. "He never comes past Salisbury Street and the hollow is another two hundred yards at least."

More silence. Then Optic.

"Well, you know what they say. If Mohammed won't come to the mountain – . We just have to think of a way to bring him to the hollow."

They discussed it further but with no more progress they committed it to further thoughts. With only one week to the holidays, they still hadn't found a way to resolve their problem.

"All we have to do, is dangle Nugget as bait to lure him to the hollow, then we'll be waiting with a rope across the track," suggested Optic.

"Now wait just one minute," said a clearly perturbed Nugget. "How do you mean, bait?"

"We know that every night he leaves the station, he turns left on High Street and walks to Salisbury Street, where he either goes down it, or turns back for Main Street," Lobo reminded them.

"So perhaps Nugget could wait for him there and get him to chase him to the hollow," said Optic.

"And how do you suggest that I get him to chase me?" Nugget wanted to know.

"Perhaps you can shout at him, or stick your finger at him. He'll chase you then for sure," said Atlas.

"If he did," said Gatlin with conviction, "he'll catch you, like I would have, if you hadn't been so close to the hollow."

"Why do you think I always run there? I'm useless out in the open," said Nugget.

"So we just choose somebody else to use as bait," suggested Brains.

"But nobody else knows the track like Nugget," Gatlin explained.

"What I think Gat is trying to say," said Optic, "is that whoever he chases is going to have to run the hollow, or he might suspect something."

Once again, they were left seeking a solution.

It was the last week at school before they broke up for the holidays, and Brains, frustrated with the delay, was just waiting to unload on somebody.

An ex-pupil of the school Vera Lajee, who now attended one of the secondary schools in the capital, was home a week early, and had decided to spend it at her old school. As often the case so close to the holidays, the attendance of the senior class was less than fifty percent, as most of the country kids were busy helping their parents to harvest the corn before the birds and the insects decimated it.

Left to their own devices, they were expected to behave like young adults. Vera, because of her secondary education claimed the right to lead the class. Brains claimed that she disqualified herself since she was not even a pupil of the school anymore. After a lengthy debate, they compromised. They split into two groups. Brains headed the boys and Vera the girls. They decided on a game of abbreviations. The rules were simple, the questioner would spell out an acronym and the person answering would decipher it. No contestant on either side was allowed to answer more than two consecutive questions.

By the time Brains' turn came around, Vera had had her two answers and was disqualified from answering the next. Well aware of that, Brains still addressed his question to her.

"Vera, this one is for you," he said.

"I can't," said Vera, "I've already answered two."

"Well, this one is for you," he insisted. And sailing as close as he dared to the F word, but leaving Vera in no doubt what he meant, he said, "F.O.C.K."

He received the exact effect from Vera that he sought. He expected her sense of outrage, her embarrassment. What he didn't foresee was the drastic action she would take. She went directly to the principal.

"Vera!" he hissed. "Please don't," he implored her receding back, but to no avail.

Gatlin who was standing close to Nugget, whispered, "She's delivered him to Pilate."

"Be quiet!" said Nugget.

The principal's instinct for sensing trouble was finely tuned. He folded the page he was reading from the National Geographic magazine and placed it on the table in front of him to coincide with Vera's arrival. In all the time that she spoke he never once interrupted. The only visible sign of his displeasure was the rapid winking of his eyes.

His jacket, which he habitually took off every morning, was cradling the back of his chair and his shirtsleeves were rolled up to the elbows. He picked up his instrument of correction, the strap that rested like a coiled snake on the table, and stood up.

Without any encouragement from any of the teachers, the school gradually became very quiet. They knew an example was about to be made.

With the prospect of confrontation looming, Brains felt a rush of adrenalin run the entire length of his body. From where he sat, the principal looked like he was ten feet tall, instead of his six feet, three inches.

Brains' mind was in a whirl; at the back of it, he wondered if it was a nightmare.

"Well," he thought, "if it is, the belt would soon wake me up." But it was daytime and he knew he wasn't asleep. His heartbeat quickened, he wiped his sweaty palms on the back of his pants.

The principal towered above him even when he was standing.

"So Rawlings," he said, "like the moth you simply had to get too close to the flame, but then it was only a matter of time. You have a fine brain, but instead of concentrating on scholarly pursuits, you indulge in pranks and mischief. I'm sure you're going to tell me your question was innocent, but answer me this. Vera didn't qualify for the question, so why did you single her out?"

He walked slowly around him all the time he was talking. Gatlin, sitting two rows behind, was reminded of the chicken hawk circling slowly, just before it struck.

"I knew it wasn't her turn sir, but I didn't think she knew the answer, I saw it as a chance to embarrass her," he said, as he struggled desperately to isolate part of his mind, to try and think of an answer.

"Vera is a model student. Does the fact that she obeys the rules offend your sense of conformity?"

Brains took his time answering.

"Must be careful here," he thought. "The wrong answer could bring two extra for dumb insolence."

"Not at all sir," he answered.

The principal stopped directly in front of him. The strap was wound around his right hand like a knuckle-duster. He bent forward and put his head to within four inches of Brains'.

"I know that you must know the answer to your question, so will you now share it with the rest of the school?"

Brains was close to panic and stalled for time as he said haltingly, "Why, yes sir, of course sir."

"Well?" said the principal, straightening to his full height. "I haven't got all day."

He allowed the belt to become uncoiled.

"This day has been a long time coming," he said with smug satisfaction.

Brains heard it in his voice and saw the triumphant look in his eyes. He closed his own eyes. When he spoke, his voice was clear and his words precise.

"Foreign Orders of the Christian Kings, sir!"

The principal stared at him for a while, and the four fingers of his left hand, almost imperceptibly, visibly moved, as he checked the letters.

The silence lasted longer than expected. At last the principal spoke.

"Have you ever heard of Icarus, Rawlings?"

Brains knew the story of the man who was given wings and flew so close to the sun that they melted, but he had no intention of tempting fate.

"No sir," he answered.

"The book is in the library. I suggest you read it sometime. You sailed very close to the wind today. I have waited a long time and I can wait a little longer. You can't help yourself. My day will come and when it does —"

210

He turned and walked away without finishing the sentence, leaving Brains to ponder the consequences of another infringement.

That night in celebration, they had ginger beer and roti, as the story was told over and over again, from different perspectives, depending on who was telling it.

Afterwards, Lobo said to Brains, "Seriously though, you've got to stop taking dumb chances. He meant every word he said about having his day."

"I'll try and bite my tongue every time it looks like getting me into trouble," Brains promised.

They were in jubilant mood. Even the threat of a future encounter couldn't dampen their spirits. Keeping cool under pressure of a certain thrashing, Brains had prevailed.

Just two days later, it was Gatlin who fell foul of the principal.

He was standing on the school veranda with Atlas, just about where Nugget was standing when he threw the wasps at Pato. Suddenly, a shower of rain started and all the pedestrians around started running for shelter, including a plump, but pretty girl called Penny, who worked at the telephone station. Her most notable asset was an ample bottom. Unaware that the principal had come up behind them, Gatlin observed, "that Penny is a real lobster, man."

"And what makes you say that Barnes?" he asked, announcing his presence. Gatlin jumped as if someone had cracked a whip, much to the man's satisfaction. After he overcame the surprise, Gatlin went into an exaggerated stutter, for the first time taking full advantage of his disability to allow himself time to think.

"I- I- It's just a pro- pro- pro- project I'm wo- wo-working on su- su sir."

The principal held up both hands in a calming gesture. "Take it easy boy, calm yourself and tell me what your project is," he said reassuringly.

Gatlin by then was so nervous, he was no longer sure that he was pretending. "To wri- wri write a p- p- p- piece on the Sa- Sa- Saint

Val- Val-Valentine's day Ma- ma- massacre su- su-sir," he said eventually.

The principal was getting a bad feeling about his, just like with Rawlings.

He knew this boy was hinting at something vulgar and he was determined to get to the bottom of it. He persevered more in hope than in expectation.

"And what has the massacre to do with lobsters?"

"I was thin- thinking of wri- wri writing a po- po- po- poem. The word mob- mob-mobster rhy- rhy- rhymes with lob, lob, lobster su- su- sir."

"Why can't they apply themselves with the same zeal and imagination to their schoolwork?" the principal wondered. He could still see the look of triumph on Rawlings's face and hear the giggling of the other kids. He had thought of punishing him anyway, but the thought of his over zealous father writing to the newspapers, as he had threatened to before, was too much of a deterrent. If discipline was to be maintained, an example had to be made, and while he would have preferred Rawlings, Barnes would just have to do.

"Who is the project for?"

Gatlin had a brainwave. "Mis- mis- Mr Jerome s- s- sir," he answered.

"Do you mean the scout master?" asked the principal. Mr Jerome was also a teacher at the Roman Catholic school and frequently involved his troop in various projects.

"Yes s- s- sir, said Gatlin.

The principal rubbed his chin, "I see," he said. "Now you boys run along, we'll speak again later."

The principal was suspicious; he didn't think that it was a coincidence that the boy had chosen a teacher from another school. That night he made a rare midweek visit to Alexander's Bar, frequented mostly by the town's businessmen. Ordering himself a brandy, he invited the landlord to join him. It was a quiet period, the barman poured himself a drink and leaned towards him with both elbows resting on the bar. "Is this a celebration? You don't normally call during the week," he observed.

"No, nothing like that, but there is something you may be able to help me with. I would like to pick your brain."

"No prob," said the barman. The principal related the incident word for word, exactly as it happened. The man listened with an amused expression on his face.

"Who was the girl," he asked and when told, he sought verification.

"Do you mean Telephone Penny?"

The principal nodded, the barman had a real belly laugh. After he composed himself, he said. "Well, he is right, she does carry all her meat in her tail."

Once again he collapsed on the bar and banged it a couple of times with his right fist. He was doubled up in laughter. "You do know that all the lobster's meat is in its tail?"

As comprehension dawned, a knowing look entered the principal's eyes.

"That little degenerate," he said under his breath, "that settles it."

The next morning, without dismissing assembly, Gatlin was summoned to the stage and the entire school knew his fate was sealed. A flogging was imminent.

Taking advantage of his captive audience, the principal spoke at length about the value and importance of discipline and how the only way of achieving this was through obeying the rules and if that meant the occasional punishment, flogging or otherwise, then so be it.

Brains, who was standing close to Atlas groaned.

The principal was in full flow.

"Your parents have sent you to us with great sacrifice to themselves, so that we may concentrate your minds on learning such things as we teach here, but there are the odd few and it only takes a few," his eyes lingered on Brains for a while, "who choose to disregard our efforts and instead, indulge in malingering, mischievous pranks, disorder, and telling lies. This we will not tolerate. Be warned, when you break the rules and you are caught, there is a consequence."

He never specified Gatlin's crime, but the apprehensive boy knew that he must have spoken to Mr Jerome. Calling him to account before assembly was dismissed had confirmed it. He accepted that he was going to be flogged and decided to take it like Gary Cooper.

The principal concluded. "I assure you Barnes, that this will hurt me a lot more than it will you."

Gatlin, even in the bind that he was in, could not resist an inclination towards comical defiance. In the stoic mode of his idol and without a single stutter, he spoke clearly. "I'm sure you'll do your best, sir."

"Shut your mouth!" hissed Brains. He held his head in both his hands as the enraged principal said. "That's two added for dumb insolence".

He reached for the strap that was on the table and Nugget said to no one in particular, "ATP."

"Assume the position!" the principal ordered sharply.

Gatlin bent over the table and took six of the best and despite the principal's vigorous attempts, refused to give the expected reaction to the flogging.

When they met, Brains suggested that they go to one of the parlours to toast Gatlin's attempt of avoiding the flogging, which he thought was imaginative and plausible and deserving of celebration.

He apologised to him. "Sorry Gats. Had that happened last week, he would probably have moved you on. That flogging was mine, take my word for it. The backside he was seeing in front of him was mine. You should know when to keep your mouth shut. The last two were unnecessary."

Gatlin's earlier stoicism had cost him dearly, for unlike his friends who were all sitting, he was forced to stand and would not be able to sit properly for a couple of days.

"You made one mistake," said Optic. "You involved a pillar." He meant someone regarded as a pillar of society. "He knew you lied, he must have checked."

"Never mind Gat, I'm sure Gary Cooper would be proud of you," said Nugget.

He smiled for the first time since the flogging. He lifted up his ginger beer and said, "The Brotherhood. Roll on August!" They all drank to that.

21

The holidays had started and they agreed to meet in the pasture. It was only three days until Movealong started his 2.0 p.m., to 10.0. p.m., shift and plans had to be finalized.

Optic was the last to arrive and when he did, TT was with him. He was full of himself as he greeted them.

"Whoa, ruffians! What's up?"

They all ignored him and gave TT a warm welcome.

"We thought you might be here since last week," said Nugget.

"I would have, but we had school track competition," he answered.

"And guess who is the hundred yards champion and the answer to our prayers?" Optic asked smugly.

"Does TT know?" asked Lobo.

"No, I left that for you," said Optic.

They explained their dilemma and their plan.

"That's where you come in, you are fast enough to keep him close enough, to be interested long enough, to reach the hollow."

"No prob man," said TT, but I don't know the hollow."

"No prob man," said Nugget, aping him. "We have three days, we start tomorrow. By the time we're finished, you'll know it as good as me."

True to his word, Nugget walked the infamous track with TT, showed him every hole and crevice and the best way to get around

216

them. By the end of the second night, he was ready for a demonstration, and was passable.

"After we go over it some more tomorrow, he'll be ready."

The plan was simple. TT would wait near Salisbury Street and get Movealong to chase him. He would run down the hollow, hopefully, with Movealong in close attendance. Brains would be on one side of the track, with Atlas on the other. They will take hold of the rope but leave it loose on the ground until TT ran by; they will then tighten the rope for Movealong. Afterwards, whatever happens, they would all make their separate ways straight home. They'll meet on the beach next day.

Came the night and they met briefly, again in the pasture, and went over their plan in detail. The only thing left undecided was the method of persuasion to get Movealong there, and that they left to TT.

"Well!" Said Lobo, "let's go get him."

"Damn right," said Ahab. "This is our back yard, he's the stranger here."

TT took his place early and from his vantage point, watched Movealong as he made his way from the station. Predictably, he turned left on High street, and with easy measured steps, covered the ground towards Salisbury Street. He was in khaki shorts and tunic, and as he passed under the light, the peak of his cap glistened fleetingly.

When 'Movealong' was about fifty yards from his turn-around point, TT moved into sight and stood by the side of the road, undid his buttons and started to pee.

Before every race he was always charged with adrenalin and filled with nervous energy. Now, not only were they multiplied, he was also terrified.

It seemed to take a while before 'Movealong' saw him. He reached for his flashlight and focused the beam on TT.

"You there!" he shouted. "Stand still."

217

TT, without stopping to button his pants started walking.

"I said, stand still!" he shouted again. He increased his pace without running and TT matched him.

"Don't make me chase you, or you'll be sorry," he shouted again.

"Ah shut up!" TT shouted back.

The insult acted as the starter's gun, 'Movealong broke into a dead run, he had taken the bait.

They ran up the street towards the hollow. Halfway up, he made a serious effort to close the gap, and for a little while, TT was flat out to maintain the eight feet between them.

"They were right, Nugget would never have outrun him," he thought.

As they got near the turn, TT allowed the gap to narrow to about six feet as encouragement; and as a signal to his friends, he laughed loudly.

'Movealong' must have misinterpreted the laughter as another insult and redoubled his effort to catch TT as he turned into the hollow.

Still laughing, TT ran past the spot where he knew the rope was resting. The moment he went by, tension was quickly added to the rope followed by the expected result. 'Movealong' went tumbling down the track, all the time screaming at the top of his voice. By the time he had come to a stop, there was no sound of anyone else around. The night was silent.

None of them saw him when he emerged from hollow about fifteen minutes later, his clothes torn, his body bruised, leaning on a makeshift stick. He made his way slowly and agonizingly down to the surgery.

If 'Movealong' had his suspicions, he never indicated it, and though they tried to keep out of his way, they were never dispersed again.

From that moment on, TT became a bona fide member of the group.

The next day on the beach, the remnants of the excitement of the night before was still upon them. They congratulated each other at length, with TT the obvious hero, and for a while, they became 'a mutual admiration society'.

Flushed with victory, their spirit of camaraderie was intense.

Earlier, because of his excitement, Gatlin had stuttered badly, and Nugget, never missing a chance to torment him, goaded him into singing. For once, Gatlin ignored him.

"I'm not being funny, but why sing?" asked a clearly puzzled TT.

"Well," explained Nugget, "Gats here sings in the school choir, even solos sometimes and he never stutters, that's a fact."

"You mean people who stutter never do when they sing?" asked TT with genuine surprise.

"I don't know about the others, but our boy here? Not a one."

"He is lucky," said Optic. "In a real crisis, he could just sing. Me, sometimes when I dream, my eyes are fine. I used to wake up in he mornings and run to the mirror to check them. After a while I stopped looking. Then a few weeks ago, I was dreaming when my dad woke me up for school, it seemed so real, I actually went to the mirror and had a look."

He shook his head. He had a wry smile on his face.

"The whole thing was kinda screwy."

"Why was that?" asked Brains.

"Those babies man, I tell you. One was looking at the sea, and the other was trying to look at the mountain."

There was a riot of laughter that included Optic's.

"Don't feel too sorry for him," Ahab said to TT, still wiping tears of laughter from his eyes.

"He is the only one among us who could undress a girl with his eyes and not get blasted for it." Once again, the beach echoed their laughter.

It was a measure of their togetherness and the complete acceptance of TT as a member of the group that they were able to talk and laugh about their disabilities without attitudes.

22

Come Sunday, as far as the boys were concerned, all roads led to the beach. It was a blisteringly hot day and though it was more than an hour before mid-day, you could already discern a shimmering in the distance.

With his trunks already on, Lobo made good speed, eager to get to the beach to put the plan he had worked out with TT for dislodging Ahab from the table into action.

Quickly shedding his clothes, he started for the water at a dead run, only to pull up sharply after a few strides. Over to his left, about fifty yards away from the crowd and building what looked like a sand mountain, was Leona.

His excitement increased.

Her concentration was total. It was not until his shadow shielded her body from the sun that she looked up.

He thought her smile, when recognition dawned, matched the brilliance of the sun above. She wore a blue swim hat that matched her swimsuit and she rested easily on her calves, with her toes digging into the sand behind her.

"Hi!" he said, returning her smile.

"Hello stranger. I thought you would have been here with your friends before this."

"I would have, but I was serving at a wedding," he said, squatting on the sand beside her.

"Want to be sure you know what to do when your turn comes?" she teased.

"Well yes, I, I mean no!" he stuttered.

She threw back her head and laughed and he joined in.

"It was worth it to see your face," she said.

"When did you get up?" he asked.

"Last Monday. A few of us stayed behind to help Sister prepare the dorm for the new girls starting after the holidays."

"I saw you about a month ago. I went to the bank in St George's to do something for my sister. You were walking by with two other girls."

"They are my friends. We live close by and walk home together most evenings. Why didn't you say hello?"

"I didn't want to lose my place in the queue for fear of missing the last bus. By the time I got out, you were gone."

At that point his friends at the table noticed him and began shouting for him.

"Your friends are calling for you, Lobo," she smiled. "You better go."

If there were any lingering doubts about his liking the name, hearing her say it banished them forever. Not wanting to draw undue attention to her and still not having said all the things he promised himself he'd say when he saw her, he expressed the hope of seeing her soon, then swam for the table to join his friends.

No sooner had he got among them when he joined TT to put forward their plan to alternately, but consistently, attack Ahab until they wore him down. Believing her to be watching, he attacked with a zeal that might have won him the day all by himself. Not unexpectedly, a few minutes later, the plan succeeded. The mighty Ahab conceded.

Afterwards, lying on the sand, he said. "Lobe, you were on fire today, I wonder why?"

Before he could answer, Brains broke in.

"Could it be that the fair Cleopatra was your inspiration?" he asked. Their looks were questioning.

221

"Do you mean Leona?" asked Lobo.

"No," said Brains dripping sarcasm. "I was talking about that other Goddess, Venus. Who do you think I meant?"

"Why do you call her Cleopatra?" asked Lobo.

"Before she changed school, we were taking it in turn to read a play. She was only happy when she was playing Cleopatra. Afterwards, some of the kids called her that," he explained.

"So Lobe," Gatlin teased, "how long you been knocking on that door then?" Without waiting for an answer, he led the others in laughter.

"You know Gatlin," said Lobo, who nearly always defended him, "all things being equal, you might have chosen a hobby other than being a comic."

"What do you mean?" asked Gatlin.

Once again Brains broke in. "like being a trappist monk?"

"What does a trappist monk do?" asked Nugget.

"He takes a vow of silence," said Brains.

This time, Gatlin didn't join in the laughter.

Tuesday of that same week, a cousin from the country paid Juliette a visit. He was in town to be a witness in a case that was transferred to another date. Jerry was sent to fetch some ice from the cafe. He bypassed the one nearer home in favour of The New Found Out, which boasted a recently installed jukebox.

On entering, there were already two people in line and the attendant was preoccupied with a handsome young cricketer, who played for the Rimlock team from Chantemelle.

The young man followed her movement with his eyes as he tried to entice her out on a date. Then Benny Crabb walked in.

He ignored the people standing in line and walked straight up to the counter, upon which he rested a dollar bill and demanded one cigarette and change for the jukebox. The woman in front of Jerry pointed out that there was a queue, Benny glared at her without answering.

Collecting the cigarette and his change, he walked up to the instrument, deposited a coin in the slot, punched in his code and waited.

The music started and the vibration could be felt throughout the shop. The Mighty Sparrow, The Caribbean's leading calypso singer, in his usual graphic style, explained the errant lifestyles of 'Jean and Dinah'.

Benny took some matches from his shirt pocket and lit his cigarette, looked around, found a stool and was about to sit down when the young cricketer decided to enhance his chances with the pretty attendant. He fell into the rhythm, swayed, and gyrated to the music, as if offering up a sample of his dancing prowess.

As the girl smiled her appreciation, Benny called out to the young man from across the room. "You!" he shouted, loud enough to be heard over the music. The young man looked inquiringly in his direction.

"Yes you," said Benny. "If you want to dance, put in your own money, or wait until some fool feeds the machine. Nobody dances when my money is in there."

"But, but I'm not doing anybody any harm," said the young man haltingly. "I'm not taking any of the music from you."

"You're damn right about that. I'll tell you for the last time, when my money is in there, nobody dances. Now!" He moved four paces forward and narrowed the gap between them. He placed the cigarette into his mouth and clamped down on the end with his teeth. He drew hard and aimed a stream of smoke into the young man's face. With his jaw still clenched, his voice was chilling.

"Now sit down before I knock you down!"

His eyes were cold and his nostrils flared. His intimidation was total.

The young man was visibly shaken, and stumbled as he searched for the stool with his hand, as if he was hypnotised by Benny and unable to break eye contact. For what seemed a long time after he sat down the only sound in the shop was that of the record.

223

Jerry who viewed the whole incident with disbelief was surprised despite all the stories that he had heard about Benny.

"You didn't have to threaten him, all he did was dance," Jerry said to Benny, not feeling nearly as brave as he sounded.

"He can dance until he drops, just not on my money."

Benny pulled another stool and sat as close to the jukebox as he could, all the time keeping a watchful eye on the shoppers.

That night Brains sneaked out to join them and Lobo gave a dramatic blow by blow account of the confrontation, telling in detail how Benny reduced the distance between the young man and himself before giving his ultimatum.

"I tell you man," said Lobo, "it had nothing to do with me but I was scared stiff. He has menace coming out of his pores. He is a loose canon, he just doesn't care about anybody, or anything."

The next morning as he left the house for the beach. He was surprised to see Brains approaching.

"What's up?" Lobo called out in greeting when he was close enough.

"Mother has got some ladies round for measurement. She sent me out to the library."

He tried to talk Lobo into going along, but he was reluctant. "Come on man, we'll see some girls there," said Brains.

Lobo, whose mind was nearly always on Leona wasn't tempted, but he knew a refusal would only start him off about the fair Cleopatra. He relented.

They walked casually along and were within sight of the school that was doubling as the library when they saw Big John walking from somebody's yard and Lobo knew instinctively that Brains was going to tease him.

Teasing is buried deeply into the psyche of the young Caribbean male and pursued with the kind of dedication that would surprise the visitor. For a successful tease, there are certain unwritten rules that must be strictly adhered to at all times.

Never allow yourself to be a reachable target.

Always take to the tracks as soon as possible when chased.

Always accept the punishment when caught without retaliation. (Four strokes of the wearers belt, unless you escape sooner.)

And perhaps the most important of all, ignore at your peril, the one thing that perhaps has saved more lives than any general living or dead; one word, "RUNNN!"

The victims are selected for any number of reasons. Something said, or done, being old, or disabled, or different in any way. In Big John's case, it was the deed and he was the perfect target. He was responsive, mobile, and his bark was worse than his bite. He has never been known to do anything other than administer a few lashes of his broad belt, to any teaser unfortunate enough to be caught.

He was close to six feet tall, with close-cropped hair, but the first thing you noticed about him was his bulk. He was all bone and muscle. He weighed almost two hundred pounds. Although nearly forty, he was still a bachelor and lived by himself.

One evening after work, he stopped for a drink in one of the bars. Heavily imbibed, he made his way home through the rain, which gave him the idea of going torching for crabs, which are enticed out of their holes after a heavy shower.

Having had a successful torch, the next morning he informed the owner of 'the New Found Out restaurant', that he had some crabs for sale. When asked how much, he estimated the catch to be around two dozens.

Later, the restaurateur came by to pick up the crabs and followed Big John to the kerosene tin where they were kept. On removing the lid, the restaurateur froze. Inside were seven crabs and a dozen and a half frogs more commonly referred to by the locals as 'crapoud', pronounced, 'crapo,' from its patois origin.

Inevitably, the name of John Crapo was handed down through the generations, as a legacy to future teasers.

The boys hung back long enough to allow their victim to enter the road about twenty feet in front of them and followed him until they were near to the little uneven track that ran behind the surgery. Maintaining their distance of safety, they launched into a ferocious session of tease.

Big John worked for Park's Produce Company and spent the greater part of his working day lifting fifty-pound bags of spices. He also made house calls to those unable to fetch their produce, which was frequent. He would use a miller handcart, but on this occasion he was carrying the bag on his head.

Brains started out by shouting an imitation of the frog's call. "Ribbit, ribbit, John Crapo! Did you go torching last night, eh frogman?"

They failed to get a reaction. They moved closer to until they were about ten feet away.

"Well, did you crapo man?" shouted Lobo. "Were the crabs jumping last night, eh?" They both laughed mockingly.

"That's it!" roared Big John, tossing the bag to the side of the road. He had swallowed the bait like they knew he would. The chase was on.

Big John's anger propelled him forward and he was actually catching them as they made the track and gradually pulled away from him. He was in a dilemma. He wanted to teach those maggots some manners, but he must mind the bag.

He headed back along the track to the road. In the meantime, the boys had kept on running the long way around and were back to the bag before him. They sat on either side, with the bag between them. The moment he appeared at the top of the road, they lifted the bag and ran with it towards Hill Street, which took Big John away from his destination.

It was a while before the big man could control his exasperation. He shook his clenched fist at them.

"That's done it Maggots. I'm going to tan your hides. I'll show you some heavy manners!"

They dropped the bag in the middle of the road. In his frustration, Big John jumped over the bag in pursuit of the boys and stumbled, almost falling flat on his face, which brought laughter to those watching. He decided to relinquish the chase.

In this way, half an hour went by. Every time he picked up the bag, they would restart the attack and as before, Big John would give chase while threatening mayhem to all maggots.

It only stopped when Lobo had a narrow escape after falling over. As he told the others later, "I was this close to being caught." He held his thumb and his index finger almost touching. Having finally rid himself of the excess energy, Brains waited until he had cooled sufficiently, donned his choirboy face and made his way home.

Later that day, on his way to bring in the sheep from the pasture, Juliette called him into the front room and asked him to sit down.

"I hear you and Clive were teasing Big John again. You mark my words, one of these days he'll catch one of you and there'll be hell to pay.

"John is a big man with heavy hands and have you seen that belt of his? It's for protecting his back. He hits you with that and you're going to stay hit. Think on that next time you feel like teasing him."

While she was at it, she took the time to reprimand him for tying his niece to the table and demanded an explanation.

"I'm sorry Sister Ju, but I just didn't know what else to do, no matter how many times she was told, she followed me everywhere. Whenever I'm with my friends, wherever we are, five minutes later, she is there. The other day she followed us to the river where we were skinny-dipping, so I tied her up long enough to get away," he explained. Promising to do her best to stop Anna from following him, she made him promise never to tie her up again.

Running a little late, he hurried to the pasture. Suddenly the wind became stronger and the grey clouds that previously drifted lazily by became darker and seemed to be in a great hurry. Lightning, less impressive in the daylight, crackled along the horizon, followed shortly by a mighty clap of thunder, which left its echo hanging over the entire island, and perhaps even beyond. He was caught in a freak tropical storm.

As he went through the gate and entered the open field, the wind was swirling around and blowing the dust and debris about. With his hand up to protect his face, he almost missed the figure that was hurrying along about a hundred yards away. Another look and he recognised the walk, even though she seemed tense; it was Leona.

Forgetting all about the sheep, he ran to intercept her. He caught up to her the same time as the rain.

Away to the left, at the northern end of the pasture, was a huge rubber tree, which offered the only worthwhile shelter. Without a word from either of them, they ran towards it.

As the wind strengthened, her long hair was being blown every which way and her flared skirt, flapping continuously, wrapped itself around her legs. She stumbled and he reached out a hand and steadied her. Then holding hands, they ran laughing all the way to the shelter of the huge tree.

Having gained the protection of the tree, they stood close together with shoulders occasionally touching, on the blind side of the wind. When they were able to talk, brushing away her wayward hair from her face, she asked, "Where did you come from? I had no idea you were around."

He couldn't take his eyes from her face, he pointed to her nose. "You have a strand of hair on you face," he said smiling.

The residue of the rain glistened on both their faces, lending a somewhat ethereal appearance as they glanced at each other.

"Will you please?" she said. "My fingers are cold."

He reached forward and very tentatively brushed the errant strand from her face. His fingers tingled slightly as they made contact with the smoothness of her skin.

"I was late picking up the sheep so I was running when I saw you. It's the first roasting I've ever enjoyed," he said.

Clearly puzzled, she asked, "What's that about a roasting?"

"Brains and I were teasing Big John this morning and I tied my niece to the table, so –" he said.

With a look of disbelief on her face, she laughed and once again he was entranced by the sound of it.

"And I always thought that altar boys were such little angels."

She asked, and he told her about both incidents in detail. After a slight lull in the conversation, she asked, so softly that he barely heard her over the wind. "Why did you enjoy the roasting?"

He looked away from her before answering. "Without it, I'd be long gone and I would've missed you," he explained.

"Every time I'm in trouble, there you are to the rescue. I'm not complaining," she smiled at him.

He wanted to say, "I hope I'll always be there when you're in trouble," but instead he heard himself say, "Glad I was able to help."

He was disgusted with himself, he was beginning to relax and decided to take the plunge and tell her how he felt at the first opportunity.

"You have delicate fingers," she said, "like a musician's. Is that what you're going to be?"

"No, hopefully I'd work in the newspaper trade, what about you?"

"I just love books, I think I'm going to be a teacher, that way, I'll always be close to them," she smiled furtively. "Imagine being paid for doing the thing I enjoy most."

Just above her head was a hole in the tree large enough to hold a fist. He reached up and put his hand into it and pulled out a feather. "Some bird was probably nesting there," he said.

"Weren't you afraid of animals in there?" she asked.

"A little bit," he admitted, smiling.

"You know, when you smile your whole face changes," she observed.

"According to Nat King Cole, it's a cure-all, he said. "Don't you know the words of the song? *Smile though your heart is aching*."

"I've heard it, but I don't know the words," she said.

"I could write it down for you and give it to you when next we see each other," he offered.

"I know, why don't you leave it in the tree? Put it in the hole," she suggested.

A few minutes later, the rain stopped and the wind subsided. She made her way home.

Walking behind the sheep in his wet clothes, he felt as if he had grown wings and could fly if he wanted to. For years to come, that evening in the rain was his 'happy thought'.

Later, in bed, he thought at length on his inability to say to her the many things he wanted to say. After taking the trouble to tell her that he spent most of his time on the beach, he had the perfect opportunity to tell her that it meant he wouldn't miss her if she turned up. Instead, he had very timidly said, "Perhaps one day you'll drop by."

He decided to write to her. With her not being there, it might be easier to bare his feelings. Better still why not write her a poem?

The next evening, with his back against the grotto, writing pad on his knee and the pencil that she had given him as inspiration, he contemplated and agonized at length, knowing everything he wanted to say, but finding it difficult to voice it through poetry. He willed himself to concentrate.

The next afternoon Juliette was changing the curtains when Marigold walked in. They engaged in casual conversation, then, Juliette asked, "Did you see Jerry on your way home?"

"No," said Marigold. "Isn't he liming with his friends?"

"I just wanted to be sure he was nowhere near. Take a look in the pocket of his school pants hanging on the bedpost."

Marigold returned with a sheet of paper in her hand and a look of bewilderment on her face. She sat down heavily in one of the chairs.

"He has written a poem. My little brother is in love!" she said in a hushed voice. "How did you find it?"

"I was picking up his dirty clothes and was clearing out the pockets

230

as usual. That explains him wearing his Sunday clothes in the middle of the week. Go on, you read it and see if it doesn't make you want to cry."

Marigold read aloud.

> I think of things I'd like to say,
> But when we meet I cannot speak.
> I hesitate and then I stutter
> And later on, I cringe and shudder.
> An echo heard, while in the rain,
> Made me think of the flowers' refrain.
> Will I dare tell you how lovely you are?
> I think of you always, even when you're far?
> Or will I forever hold my peace,
> To ensure our friendship never cease?
> That too, I do hold preciously.
> Whatever will become of me?

Marigold sat with the hand holding the paper on her lap, while the other massaged her throat. Her eyes looked very bright.

"He's grown up Ju, and by the sound of this, he's head over heels in love. Any idea which girl it might be?"

"Not a clue. Finding the poem was the first hint, but whoever she is, I hope she feels the same way. You better put it back before he comes, he mustn't know we've seen it."

Ten minutes later, Jerry breezed into the house and into his room and breathed a sigh of relief as he found what he was looking for. He carried it around in his pocket all the next week and walked by Leona's sister's house several times without seeing her. As a last resort, he left it in the hole in the tree.

He was heartened by the fact that the copy of the song he had left her was gone. Later, he concluded that she too was gone and wouldn't return until the end of term, or so he thought at the time.

That day by the tree was the last time that he saw her. She had emigrated to the United States to stay with an aunt and further her education. A few months later, he received a letter from her. She apologized for leaving without saying goodbye but explained that it was an unexpected opportunity that was unlikely to come again and couldn't be missed.

For sometime afterwards, he went out of his way to avoid going to the pasture. The sight of the giant rubber tree where they had actually rubbed shoulders was too much of a reminder of her absence.

He wondered, not for the first time, about the necessity of yet another person he knew leaving him behind to feel such intense pain and he was confused as to why so many people had to go to another country in order to be successful. And what of those dreams of success? He'd heard otherwise, but still they went in their thousands.

They corresponded for a while, but the poem was never mentioned. The letters gradually became fewer and further apart, and eventually stopped. For a long time, he wondered what it would have felt like, to have kissed her.

The very next day after that tease, Big John suffered an accident at work and twisted his knee so badly, he was ordered to stay off his feet for at least a week. When the boys found out, they took it in turn to leave offerings on John's doorstep. Bananas, avocadoes, corn, and anything they could get their hands on that they thought useful.

Jerry had just returned from his dip in the river when Juliette called him in just as he was about to dash off to school.

"We're missing a pumpkin from the garden, do you know anything about it?"

He shifted uncomfortably from one leg to the other. His nervous smile masked the sheepish look on his face.

"I was going to tell you about it. Big john is confined to bed and we all brought him some stuff, I left him the pumpkin."

"Well I declare," she said, laughing out loud. "You boys spent all your time tormenting that poor man, now he's sick, you're bringing him gifts? Your conscience is bothering you, eh?"

"No," answered Jerry. The sooner he is better, the sooner we can start teasing him," he had a big grin on his face. She threw the dust-cloth after him as he bolted out the door.

23

About a month after Leona left, there was a meeting at the Anglican school on the Thursday evening, addressed by the charismatic leader of the Grenada Metal & Manual Workers Union (GMMWU). It was Eric Matthew Gairy, arguably one of the most influential figure of post war politics in Grenada.

Born in Grenada in 1922, he had been a primary school teacher in the parish of St David's before emigrating to Trinidad, where he spent two years and then through a contact, emigrated to the Dutch Caribbean island of Aruba, where he worked for The Lago Oil Company. In both countries, he had studied and had been involved in the Trades Union Movement.

On his return to Grenada six years later in 1949, he had rallied and succeeded in getting the total support of the workforce, particularly the agricultural sector. On the strength of that support, the self-styled 'Uncle Gairy', called on his workforce to strike. With the cocoa crop nearing its harvest, the bosses, who had never encountered organised militant trades unionism before, capitulated on all fronts.

On the strength of that victory, Gairy rode the wave of his popularity and formed the island's first organized political party. He later contested the 1951 general elections under the banner of, the Grenada United Labour Party (GULP) and captured five of the eight seats in the legislature.

As the crowd began to gather, Poole and his gang were sitting in their usual places when an airport taxi came slowly up the hill towards them. The driver beeped and some of the people in the street scrambled to safety.

At the top of the hill, he pulled over to the opposite side of the road and stopped. He turned around in his seat as if consulting with his passengers for direction.

The committee members zeroed in on the two people sitting on the back seat; two women who could be mother and daughter.

"Any idea who they are?" asked Poole expectantly.

Carla unashamedly stood up for a better look. Then her face brightened, for as the car pulled away and turned left up the hill to High Street, the older woman waved as if in recognition of her.

"I know who that is!" said Carla triumphantly. "That's Ada Moses. We went to school together. Old man Sam is her father."

"She is here to make sure she gets everything when Sam kicks the bucket," said Violet spitefully.

"Or she might just be here to help her sick father get better, which is a very Christian thing to do," said Poole, taking the high ground.

"Oh no, you're wrong Violet, Ada is not like that," said Carla.

Violet kept her eyes straight ahead and refused to concede.

"I tell you Violet," said Clifford, "sometimes I think you put pepper in your tea instead of sugar."

As the gang argued, another group of observers were equally interested in the visitors, especially the teenaged girl who boldly returned their stares with the most enigmatic of smiles. It was for the very possibility of seeing a strange girl that the boys had attended the meeting. Now, as one, without a word, they turned and followed in the direction of the car.

In the next couple of days, through the speedy and reasonably reliable teenage grapevine, they learnt that she was from Trinidad, and was here to help her mom look after her grandfather. Her name was Frangipani Bloom, but she liked to be called Frangi.

In the days following, great attention was given by the teenage males to personal grooming, not only by the group, but also by the other young men in the town. Everywhere, there were unprecedented visits to the barbers, and Sunday clothes were worn during the week.

Aware of the strong effect she was having on the boys, Frangi was enjoying every bit of her popularity and didn't seem to care who knew it.

She enrolled with the Anglican school for the duration of her stay and very quickly joined the school choir and became the third soloist, together with Lillian Blake and Gatlin.

With Frangi in town, all the talk while liming was mostly about her. Hitherto, there was an understanding among them, that if while pursuing a girl, she was inclined to favour another of the group, not only would they pass on the information, they would leave the field. This time however, all the indications were that all bets were off.

Ahab, up front as usual, put into words what they were all thinking. "As my grandma would say, 'Tout muchaflay clere pou namyay'."

"And what the hell is that sup- sup- supposed to mean?" asked Gatlin, who, perhaps because of his close proximity to Frangi, in class and in the choir, was clearly besotted by her.

"Loosely," said Brains, "all firefly must shine its own light".

And so it became official. Every man was for himself on this one.

On their way from school one Wednesday afternoon, they gathered around with the rest of the passers-by to listen to Dabo as he made outrageous claims while advertising the film, *The Bells of St. Mary*, which starred Bing Crosby.

"Don't you be late," he cautioned, "or else you might miss the first miracle, because for the first time ever you'll see a nun in the nude," he lied.

None of the group showed any interest in the film, except Nugget.

"I won't be at the lime tonight. Lily is going to the show with her aunt and I promised her I'll come," he said a little awkwardly.

They were standing under the lights, just near to where Poole and his gang still sat, when Lily and her aunt Florence walked by.

236

Although it was an exceptionally warm night, the older woman carried an umbrella and wore a wide brimmed straw hat.

Nugget waited until he saw the lights go out inside the school before he went in and sat directly behind Lily. He gave himself time to settle down and then very tentatively, reached out and held Lily by the waist.

Taken unaware, she jumped a little, turned around and stared through the dark, trying to see who had touched her. Nugget meanwhile, looked straight at the screen. Feeling easier now that Lily knew who he was, he reached out and held her hand that was folded across her breasts.

After a little while, she took her hand away, as Nugget continued to stroke her hair, rub her back and generally maintain as much physical contact during the rest of the film. Shortly before the film ended, she again folded her arms and again, Nugget took her hand.

As, The End appeared on the large screen, he tried withdrawing his hand before the lights came on. After all, Florence must never know he and Lily were holding hands. He tried to pull his hand away, but Lily seemed very reluctant to let him.

Suddenly, the hall was bathed in light, and holding on tightly to Nugget's hand was Aunt Florence, who, unknown to him, had passed her hat to Lily at he start of the show to appease someone at the back who had complained.

He looked as if he had seen a ghost and tried in vain to get his hand back. Just then, she picked up her umbrella, and proceeded to rain blows on the hapless Nugget.

"How dare you manhandle me?" she wanted to know.

Nugget stuttered. "I- I thought you were someone else I'm sorry." By this time most of the spectators were doubled over with laughter.

Breaking free at last, he bolted out of the school and into the safety of the night. Needless to say, the lime the following night was a riot.

"Surely you saw her face when she looked at you after you held her hand that first time?" quizzed Brains.

"It was very dark and I was looking straight at the screen."

"If I were you, next time I go to that cinema, I'd wear a miner's hat," said Gatlin, who was enjoying every minute of his friend's embarrassment.

"Don't feel so bad man," said Lobo, whose cheeks were wet with tears of laughter. "Just think, you might have squeezed her breasts, or did you?"

"Hush your dirty mouths!" shouted Nugget in frustration.

It was many months before the taunting stopped. One or the other would tease him with, "Did you see Aunt Florence today Nug?" or, "I saw Aunt Flo today, she had a new umbrella, did you pay for it Nug?" or, "Where is the kid?"

"Which kid?"

"The Tabanca Kid!"

They speculated at length at the reception they thought he might be given, should he ever approach the family for Lily's hand.

As the weeks drifted by, Frangi, a natural mixer had become more and more involved in the affairs of the community.

Later, she joined the girls' rounder's team. Practice sessions that in the past were ignored as a matter of course, were suddenly well attended, not only by the boys at her school, but by their rivals at the Roman Catholic school as well. Most surprising of all, was the increased membership of the school choir, most of which were young men, who before would hardly have considered it. As yet though, if she favoured anyone, she gave no indication of it.

Coming from Port-of-Spain like she did, Frangi had every right to feel insulated against the effect of 'brango', a term commonly used in the region for getting around someone or buttering them up. In Otto's words, brango took flattery into an art form.

Frangi had stayed after school for choir practice and was walking home with another girl, Rosa, who lived nearby. As they turned the corner into High Street, near to Miss Murray's shop, they came face to face with Jimsey, who was heading in the opposite direction.

Hs stopped directly in front of them, claiming their undivided attention. He smiled broadly and doffed his cap politely in greeting. "Good afternoon young ladies," he said, still holding the cap with both hands.

"Hello Jimsey," answered Rosa also smiling.

"Ah, Miss Rosa. You get prettier every time I see you." But his eyes were mostly on Frangi who was also smiling sweetly.

"Ah", she thought, "another brango artist; this should be interesting". After all, she had grown up with the best.

Now he gazed at her directly. "Bless my sight, you can only be Miss Frangi." He seemed genuinely impressed.

"Thank you Mr Jimsey."

"Oh no, please, just Jimsey." Still holding his cap in front of him, he tilted his head slightly. "Now I understand."

She wondered what his line was going to be.

"Understand what?"

"Why all the young bucks in town have declared the rutting season opened."

Despite her intuition, she found herself laughing openly. She knew she should discourage him, but she didn't.

"I have no idea what you're talking about," she said.

"Miss Frangi, you must know all the young bucks have been butting heads since you got here. Why, there's a set of twins in La Mode, Benny and Benjy, closer than two peas in a pod. When I saw them yesterday, they both had black eyes, on account of Benjy saying he saw you first."

"But I don't even know them," she protested laughingly.

"I tell you Miss Frangi, right now I wouldn't be sixteen again for all the tea in China."

He noticed a slight change in her expression.

"Don't get me wrong. Both you girls are so pretty, a person might think you were born in a flower garden, but with my face, I'd be a sure fire loser. That's why I'm glad I am not a contender," he grinned lopsidedly.

Their laughter was interrupted by the sound of Dabo's bell long before he came into view, with *The Cruel Sea,* printed in large letters on his sandwich board.

"Oh no," groaned Jimsey. "I've been waiting a long time to see this movie and they choose this week to show it. Oh well, maybe next time."

Frangi hesitated for a moment, then opened her purse and handed him a dollar bill, but Jimsey hesitated.

"Please take it. Think of it as payment for making us laugh," said a knowing Frangi.

"In that case, thank you very much. I really can't wait to see who is the lucky buck." He stuffed the money in his shirt pocket and made a beeline for Alexander's bar.

Frangi watched his retreating back with a huge grin on her face. She knew she had been brangoed but she had enjoyed every minute of it.

However, perhaps inevitably so, there was one person who did not fall under her spell and simply couldn't wait for her to return from whence she came. That was Lillian Blake, the other female soloist in the choir.

A year before, she had won the first prize for singing in the local talent contest and had assumed prima donna status on the back of it. It was therefore with a great deal of relief that the choir mistress welcomed Frangi, whom she felt would help Lillian to get things into perspective. Despite her efforts to instil civility, which many felt she wanted to fail, the girls became staunch rivals.

A few weeks later, on the second Sunday of the month, a local woman named Carmen had organized a party to celebrate the christening of her child. Such functions were social occasions when old grudges were put aside and all-comers were welcomed.

The fare generally consisted of ice cream, cakes, sandwiches and everyone's favourite, rice and peas and curry and of course, River Antoine rum for the men.

The entertainment such as it was, was always supplied by the guests themselves. Some recited poems, others told jokes, a few played instruments, from the clarinet to comb and paper and the majority sang. Many of the party pieces were already well known.

The boys, who usually drifted along when proceedings were well underway, were all there at the very start, just in case the rumour that Frangi was going to sing was true.

Old Man Chord was Master of Ceremonies. The 'old man' was added to his name, not so much for his age, but for his full head of snow-white hair, and because he nearly always wore a safari jacket.

Starting with a prayer, the function got underway and some of the less accomplished performers were called upon, on the understanding that the stars would be left for later, when hopefully, there would be a full house.

About an hour on, Chord called for order and introduced Frangi to the crowd as someone who came to us not so long ago as a stranger, but was now regarded as an honorary Grenadian, as someone with the pedigree of having performed on the Auntie Kaye show on Radio Trinidad. Someone he was sure will do justice to the popular Frankie Lane hit, *I Believe*.

Frangi was in fact an old veteran of the famous children's show held every Sunday afternoon at one o'clock.

In the week leading up to the party, the young people had talked of little else, other than the clash between Frangi and Lillian, and inevitably, their loyalties were divided.

The boys however, were quite literally behind Frangi. They stood all around and behind her, as if they were offering physical, as well as moral support. It was no surprise that after they had settled, Gatlin stood directly behind her.

At fifteen years old, she was about five feet, three inches tall, with shoulder length hair the colour of a raven's wings, which she wore in a ponytail. Her eyes were so big, they made you think of ping-pong balls. Her ample breasts were accentuated by the slimness of her waist.

She wore a man's white shirt with the collar turned up, and a pink can–can skirt of the type made popular by the Bill Haley rock 'n' roll films, and white reasonably heeled shoes, which drew attention to her shapely legs. She wore a pink choker with a silver cross, which nestled comfortably in the small of her throat. She weighed just over a hundred pounds.

At a given signal, Chord nodded to the guitar player, whose job it was to accompany the singers.

Taking her cue, Frangi eased into the song and a hush descended, which was as clear an indication as any of the esteem in which she was held. The performance was flawless and got the sustained applause usually reserved for Lillian. It was two or three minutes before Chord could restore order sufficiently to allow the show to go on.

Given his experience, many were surprised when he attempted to follow Frangi with a recital of his party piece, a poem entitled *The Charge of The Light Brigade*.

"Half a league, half a league, half a league onwards," he began. He stood with his feet about three feet apart, his knees were bent to simulate horse riding. In his left hand he held an imaginary rein, and in his right, an imaginary sword. This time instead of the usual appreciative applause, there were shouts of derision.

The crowd refused to be denied and continually chanted the name of Lillian. Cutting his losses, he promised not to disappoint his supporters, imaginary or otherwise, by a later rendition. The crowd by this time was quite wound up. They had seen Frangi throw down the gauntlet and were eager to see Lillian pick it up.

After quiet was restored, Lillian made a big show of consulting with the guitar player and went for the Jo Stafford hit, *No Other Love*.

She began with her usual confidence and made a great show of her breathing, to show that she was making the proper use of her diaphragm.

She was at a pivotal moment; the phrase which took her soaring into the high notes. She inhaled deeply and right in the middle of the most pregnant of pauses, Frangi farted, abruptly and very loudly.

242

The crowd gasped as one and all eyes were turned in her direction.

The seconds ticked by. Utter silence. She was rooted to the spot where she stood. She wanted to run, but her legs refused to obey. She wished the earth would open and mercifully swallow her up, but that too was equally unyielding. Another couple of seconds went by – "O God," she prayed silently, "please let me die."

"Pardon!"

It was Gatlin's voice, clear and precise with no hint of a stutter, as he accepted responsibility for the unfortunate indiscretion.

The crowd breathed again and many giggled with relief.

"I'm sorry," said Gatlin. "It was ve- ve- very sud- sudden."

"There is no shame in that boy!" boomed Chord. "It's a natural enough function."

Gradually, the commotion ceased, but Lillian's big moment was ruined. She gave up trying to sing the song, when she realized she had lost the audience. Frangi was so relieved that her secret had remained intact, that she had to restrain herself from hugging Gatlin as such a display might have given her away. She felt somewhat self-conscious with the boys, but given the alternative, she was more than a little happy.

Later on, taking advantage of the moonlight, they went to the calabash tree in the pasture to discuss the day's event, but more specifically, to acknowledge Gatlin as the hero they thought he was. His back and shoulder were getting sore from being patted, as he accepted their congratulations for being so alert.

"It's great that you fellahs thought I was sharp, but I wasn't. I thought everybody was looking at Frangi and I wanted the silence to stop, I heard the voice say 'pardon', and it was mine, but I didn't really do it," he said, with customary modesty.

"Oh yes you did, my man," said Brains, "and I wish I'd thought of it. You are the man of the moment, so enjoy it." The rest echoed his sentiments.

In the days following, it was noticeable that Frangi and Gatlin were walking around a lot together and it became obvious that he had the inside lane. Despite their previous resolve to the contrary, they all withdrew to leave Gatlin with a clear field. It was a bit ironical, that in the end, perhaps fate had made the final choice. Frangi's secret was never known outside the circle of friends.

About three months later, her grandfather had improved sufficiently for them to return to Trinidad. Frangi and Gatlin would correspond well into their adult lives. She never once wrote without sending her regards to his friends.

It was a month since Frangi left, and understandably, Gatlin was not his usual funny self, and together with Brains, had declined the opportunity to accompany the rest of the group in support of the local men's cricket team, Old Trafford, who were playing Invaders, in a crunch match. They were the only teams still unbeaten that season, and that was enough incentive for them to walk the three miles to La Taste. As they walked, it was noticeable that lots of people were heading in the opposite direction.

"Where are all these people going?" asked Atlas.

"Uncle Gairy has a meeting in the courtyard. It starts at one o'clock," said Optic.

"Uncle is some man eh?" said Lobo. "He even managed to get Rose Hill and Chantemelle who were always at loggerheads, to unite."

"My dad says he is the people's man. Do you know he was at a cook-up party in Paradise last week?" said Optic.

"And how would you know that?" challenged Nugget.

"Use your head! Paradise is less than two miles from where my dad works. He said there were people lined up all along the road, waiting to see him pass," Optic explained.

As they continued on their journey towards the town in small groups of three or more, all the conversation was about Uncle, as he was affectionately called by his supporters, and how he was going to change their lives.

The match, as expected, was closely fought. It swung both ways, keeping all the supporters guessing, right to the very last ball. Finally, victory went to the home team by one wicket.

Their disappointment was somewhat eased, after they hitched a ride on the back of a truck, which left them to walk just the last mile home.

As they approached, they could hear the sound of the loud speakers, but as yet, were unable to discern what was being said.

"Don't tell me that meeting is still going on," said Lobo. "It should have been finished long ago."

"Perhaps Uncle was late," surmised Ahab.

As they turned into the courtyard, they could see Gatlin who was standing with Brains at the top of the steps leading to the courtroom. He was jumping up and down with his arms raised, in an attempt to get their attention. They picked their way through the huge crowd and joined their friends.

"What's happening?" asked Optic. "Where is Uncle? And why are they still here?"

"They are still waiting for Uncle," said Gatlin.

"What's happening," informed Brains, "is that Milo the branch secretary has been making excuses since two o'clock about why Uncle isn't here yet. First he had a puncture and they were trying to find a mechanic to fix it. Then he stopped at Victoria to visit a sick union member and so on. They started leaving about an hour ago."

"But the courtyard is still full of people," said Lobo, sounding surprised.

"I have never seen anything like it. They were scattered everywhere," said Brains. "Some of them have a long way to go, perhaps that's why they left."

"Well, no point in us hanging around, lets go get a soda," suggested Nugget.

"You can't," said Gatlin. "All the shops around are sold out of everything to eat or drink. People like peas man."

They walked the fair distance to 'the New Found Out restaurant', leading to the Roman Catholic church and were sitting on the steps outside, giving the missing members a detailed account of the match they had watched earlier.

Just then, they were approached by J.V. Redhead, the principal of the Roman Catholic school. He asked them to help free a car that was stuck in the mud of the schoolyard. It belonged to one of his friends.

When they got to the schoolyard, they recognized Uncle's big American car and could tell that there were two people in it. He was sitting behind the wheel. Next to him sat a woman wearing a wide brimmed sun hat. She kept her head bowed.

They took their positions and started pushing the huge car from the hole. Lobo was directly behind the principal, who in turn was alongside Uncle, whose window was down.

"J.V.", said Uncle in a conspiratorial tone, "you've no idea the kind of day I had. I've been out preying all day long." He emphasized his meaning by spelling the first part of the word. 'P-R-E-Y'.

Although Lobo kept his position and went through the motions, he had stopped pushing.

Back at the restaurant, after he was finished telling what he had heard, there was a sense of devastation among them. They found it hard to believe that Uncle would keep a thousand of his supporters standing in the sun all afternoon to pursue his personal pleasures.

"He thought that you were too stupid to understand what he was saying," Optic said angrily.

"He thinks we're all stupid and he is right," said Lobo, who was one of Uncle's more vocal admirers.

"Well, no more," said Gatlin, with a hint of finality in his voice. "I'm going to te- te- tell Mama about this and see who she vo- votes for ne- next time."

"And I'll tell my sisters," said Lobo and so it went, until all the disillusioned former followers vowed to tell whoever would listen what they had found out.

No one would claim that the boys' disclosure was the reason why Gairy's party always found St Patrick a bit of a stumbling block.

246

Although they won the odd seat there from time to time, there was no denying the loss of support for the party.

Despite that small hiccup, which quite possibly Gairy knew nothing about, he went on to join the long list of politicians in the region, who led their party successfully for well in excess of twenty years. Prime minister, Eric Williams, of Trinidad and Tobago, and Prime Minister, Vere Cornwall Bird of Antigua, readily comes to mind.

A handsome man about five feet, ten inches tall and weighing about a hundred and sixty pounds, the charismatic Gairy became a household name throughout the islands and was generally regarded in the media as having a flamboyant dress code.

At a meeting of heads of states for the region, held in Trinidad, Gairy was the first speaker of the afternoon to address the house. He had attended the morning session dressed conservatively in a dark blue suit, with white shirt and black tie to match his shoes.

The house reassembled for the afternoon session and as expected, Gairy was called to the rostrum, but was nowhere to be found. The frustration in the voice of Prime Minister Adams of Barbados hinted at some sort of history between them.

"The Honourable Prime Minister from Grenada must have gone back to his hotel for yet another change of apparel," he said sceptically.

Hardly had he sat down again when Gairy appeared in a striking tan suit, white shirt and maroon tie, and amazingly, brown and tan shoes.

The next day, all the papers showed pictures of the suit that was the subject of that terse remark.

Despite the longevity of his political career, the boys never changed their opinion about him, although Lobo was convinced that Gairy was quite sincere in the beginning and truly had the people's welfare at heart, but like others before him and since, he had succumbed to the two P's; popularity and power.

24

The grapevine was buzzing with rumours of Benny's reign of intimidation, and if only half were true, he was in danger of running amuck. Outside Pete's tailor shop, a group, of which Benny was one, was watching a game of draughts in front of a few spectators.

The proprietor was playing a stranger and up until the halfway stage the game was fairly even. Benny wagered a cigarette on the stranger with another man.

Later, when it looked like certain defeat for the stranger, Benny reached over and upended the board, scattering the pieces all over the floor, and declaring the game as drawn, he belly-laughed his way out through the door.

On another occasion, he was walking by where some young kids were having a kick-about in the street and was struck by the ball. Without a word, he reached for his knife, punctured the ball and threw it back to them.

Lastly, but very much more sinister, was his meeting with Poole along the track leading to the river. As usual, there was an altercation. In a rage, Benny kicked Poole's walking stick from beneath him, leaving him on his backside, and threw the stick into the river.

Sitting under the light at the crossroad where the concoction was thrown, the boys having discussed these rumours reaffirmed their intentions to stay out of Benny's way.

Juliette was waiting for Jerry when he came in from school.

"After you've had something to eat, before you go to the pasture, I want you to take some fish for Granny Rose."

Eager to join in the game that he knew would start shortly, he took the bag and ran all the way there and back.

"That was quick," said his sister on his return about half an hour later.

"Please do me one last favour Jer and fill the pail with water before you leave."

Still sweating from the run, he picked up the pail, bolted out the door and came face to face with an enraged Big John. Jerry took one look at his face and realized that he was in big trouble.

Big John was still fuming after a tease. Terrified, Jerry tried to collect his wits.

"Good af- good afternoon Mr John," he stuttered, as respectfully as he could, but the big man had a wild look in his eyes and his nostrils flared at intervals.

"Oh no!" said Big John. "Oh no, it's John Crapo, remember?" And unable to control his temper, he slapped Jerry hard on the left side of his face, throwing him in a heap on the ground.

The extent of the man's frustration was visible by his demeanour. He towered over Jerry who was still sitting on the ground and with both his hands formed into giant fists, ignoring the boy's close proximity to him, he shouted, "I've got you now maggot, just like I told you I would."

Jerry knew that he had one choice, and that was to run as soon as the opportunity presented itself. He rested on the balls of his feet, and transferred his weight to his hands resting on the ground just behind him.

Big John continued to shout, "Now you're mine maggot, and by the time I am through with you, you'd wish you were a crapo."

He reached for his belt with both his hands. Jerry saw his chance and made his exit like an athlete getting off the blocks in a sprint. The big man gave chase, but the boy's survival instinct took him away to safety.

Later, with the man's finger marks still imprinted on his face, he complained to his sister in an attempt to secure some sort of justice.

"I wasn't even there when they were teasing him," he protested. "I was trying to tell him that, but he wouldn't listen."

"No, you listen Jer, I know you didn't tease him this afternoon, because you went to Grandma Rose's place, but let's be honest about this, if you had been there, you would have been right in the middle of that tease. Big John thinks you were there, so let's just leave it at that."

She bathed his face in cold water, smeared the reddened spot with Vaseline and advised him to stay out of Big John's way for a while.

Talking to his friends later, he gave them a detailed account of his encounter with Big John, and was surprised at how enthralled they were.

With the fear and the pain now gone, he took perverse pleasure in interpreting Big John's manner and intention and emphasized that he was lucky to escape with his life. The fact that he had also escaped the belting was a big boost to his street credibility.

He was still enjoying the aftermath of his brush with danger when he joined his friends the following night, only to find them steeped in an atmosphere of gloom. Taking one look at the faces on display, he asked, "What's up? Why is everybody so cheerful?" He looked at each in turn, but no one offered an explanation.

"Just what the hell is going on here?" Lobo demanded an explanation. He was barely able to contain his curiosity.

"You better tell him Atlas," said Brains. With all eyes turned towards him, Atlas fidgeted for a while. He explained that he was picking up his older brother's bicycle from the menders. He met Lily and walked with her toward the shop. Along the way they encountered Benny, who was sitting on the wall under the big willow tree near to the road.

"You!" Benny addressed him. "Run back to the shop and buy me a cigarette."

"He didn't even bother to say please. I told him that I was on an errand and that I was busy.

On my way back, he was still under the tree, but was standing in the middle of the road. He had what looked like a broken branch in his hand. He made no move to get out of the way so I rang the bell. He held his ground, so I decided to go around him. As I went past, he stuck the branch through the spokes of the front wheel and sent me sprawling in the gutter."

"Then what happened?" asked Lobo who could hardly wait.

"I couldn't believe it," said Atlas. "I asked him, 'Do you see what you have done? Are you mad?'"

"And what did he say?" asked Lobo.

"If you stop interrupting him, he'll tell you," said Brains.

"He just laughed at me. 'Don't forget,' he said, 'you're a very busy boy.' Then he walked away still laughing."

"I just don't believe it, he can't do that," said Lobo.

"He can and he damned well did," said Nugget. "Right from the word go, he has been throwing his weight around. Have you forgotten Fisherman's Birthday? Had Ahab not been there, Cecil would have lost his binoculars. Something has got to be done about him."

"You know," said Gatlin, "I think we should all stay away from Lily."

"Just what the hell do you mean by that?" Nugget demanded angrily.

"I just think she is bad luck," Gatlin explained.

"Femme fatale?" said Brains almost to himself.

"Let's keep it serious," advised Lobo.

For some time afterwards, no one spoke. It was as if they were each considering the enormity of the problem and perhaps an honourable way to avoid it.

Finally, Ahab broke the silence.

"What I don't understand is how he can do all those things and still not be arrested."

"Well," said Lobo, "some people like Cecil decided it wasn't worth bothering about, and others like Atlas here didn't have a witness. The rest are just too scared."

"So," said Optic, speaking for the first time, "this is a problem we should have considered before, but we tiptoed around it because we felt it didn't concern us. Well now it does. Atlas could have been badly hurt, but he didn't give a damn. Question is what are we going to do?"

"If we do anything, we must have a good plan of attack," suggested Lobo.

"What the hell do you mean if we do anything?" Nugget demanded angrily. "Atlas could have been seriously injured. That crook crossed the line."

The discussion raged on until the end of the lime, at which time it was agreed that they would go away and think about it over the next few days.

The following meetings were fraught with arguments and uncertainty, and as yet, no one had come up with anything feasible. It took Optic to put their frustrations into words.

"All that squawking is getting us nowhere, we keep running on the same spot. Question is, are we ready to do something about it?"

"You're damn right we're going to do something about it. He crossed the line," said Brains.

"Maybe I should do what Nugget did with Pato and face him myself," said Atlas.

"Let's all calm down and remember who we're talking about here. Benny is as mean as they come, when we move against him, it has to be a plan that gives us a chance," said Lobo.

As before, they all spoke at the same time. Optic raised both hands for quiet.

"Wait a minute fellahs, Lobo is right. When we make our move, we won't get a second chance." Despite much discussion, only one idea by Ahab merited any consideration.

"Why don't we get Benny and Big John to butt heads?"

252

"And why would Big John want to do that? He knows that Benny doesn't tease him," said Nugget who was clearly animated about the attack.

"Besides," said Gatlin, "there's no malice in Big John."

"And anyway," said Atlas, "you couldn't get Big John and Benny together."

"Oh, I don't know," said Brains. "We could put it about how Big John keeps saying all Benny needs is a good slapping."

Gatlin was uncomfortable with the suggestion.

"I thought that we were the fellahs with the white hats and Benny was the crook."

"Get serious, will you Gats? This is not a movie," said Ahab.

"No Gatlin is right and we're not running a race, let's give it some more thought," suggested Optic.

The following Saturday evening, Jerry was busy getting ready to go down to the cinema. Earlier, Dabo had done his usually brilliant advertising of the action film, *The Mark of Zorro*, which starred perhaps the most popular actor of his day, Tyrone Power. It was Jerry's turn to wait in line for tickets for himself and his friends.

His sister Marigold was preparing to do the ironing, and asked him to fire the coal pot. In his haste to get away, he fanned vigorously at the coal until the fire was glowing then placed the three irons on top of it. Just then, their neighbour Carol from across the road walked through the open door, carrying a few items of clothing. After the customary greeting, she requested the use of one of the irons.

"I have been working on this dress all day for the big dance tonight and need to take the creases from it."

"Is Ivan taking you?" asked Marigold, referring to her daughter's dad.

"That low-life? You must be joking! No, I'm going with Mary." Her tone suggested contempt for the man she was boasting about only two days before.

At that moment Juliette walked in and placed her shopping basket on the table as Jerry was about to take off.

"Glad I caught you Jer, would you look after that for me please?" she said, handing him the recently acquired fish that needed to be cleaned. The boy cursed his luck for still being around, but had no choice in the matter.

Carol, having finished her ironing, was standing in her favourite spot in front of the large mirror. She tilted her head to many different angles, smoothed her eyebrows, and touched the odd strand of her recently pressed hair. Then she pulled her dress tight across her chest and blatantly admired her breasts. With an almost inaudible sigh, took hold of her nose between her forefinger and thumb, in a vain attempt to permanently create the effect she would have preferred.

She was about five feet, three inches tall, and slim, with passable legs. By her reckoning easily her best asset were her magnificent breasts.

The two sisters, quite accustomed to the ritual, looked at each other with raised eyebrows. After a while, Juliette spoke.

"You know Carol, my grandmother told us a story once. It was about a deer that lived in the forest. He was a fine looking specimen and in good health. Every morning, he went down with the other animals to the waterhole to drink. The others would leave quickly for fear of the hunters but the deer always stayed behind to admire its reflection.

He would turn his head around and gaze in awe at his magnificent horns. When he left, he would look despairingly at his knobbly legs and wished they matched the excellence of his splendid horns.

One morning, while it was still admiring itself, it heard the sound of the hunter's horn and the barking of the hounds. It was time to run for its life, and his knobbly legs took him to the safety of the forest. Still, the hunt continued and a most dreadful thing happened. Those magnificent horns became entangled in the foliage above, and the hunter was gaining.

Then with one massive effort he freed himself and his knobbly legs that he so despised carried him to safety. What I am trying to say is to appreciate all of your attributes. Those magnificent breasts you cherish so much will one day sag, but you'll get used to it. Think of how you'd feel if you woke up one morning and you couldn't smell a flower, or a mango, or even rotting fish. Then you'll really have something to worry about, so give your poor nose a break."

When the boys emerged from the cinema, they found that all the vendors had vacated their usual pitches, in favour of the more lucrative prospect outside the Roman Catholic school, which was the venue for the big dance.

The dance, which was an annual event, was held by the Mechanic's Lodge which was the junior of the two lodges in the parish. Unlike their senior and more conservative counterparts who always insist on invitation by tickets, they simply accepted money at the door.

On arrival, the boys saw the usual crowd of spectators who came to watch and comment as the would-be dancers passed by in their finery.

Shortly afterwards, there was a commotion at the door as someone was forcibly ejected from the building. Too far away to recognize the culprit, they made their purchases of salt-fish souse rolls and ginger beer and left.

In the weeks following, Otto, an eyewitness at the incident, would tell the story of the ejection over and over again.

"The Bannermans arrived and joined the rest of the married couples at the northern end of the building. After the men had dutifully escorted their wives to their seats, they congregated in small groups for a smoke and a chat."

"It was at this point that Bulls-eye went to the bar for a steadier, which unfortunately, turned out to be a quick three or four. For any who may have missed him, he was now very conspicuous by his presence and the obvious displeasure of Mrs Bannerman, who was sitting on the last chair at the far end."

"The band struck up and the men drifted away to find their partners. For some reason that he alone understood, Bulls-eye started from the opposite end to where his wife was sitting. He asked the first woman for a dance and was refused."

"Then that fool did the dumbest thing possible. Even a bishop knows that if there are two or more women sitting together and the first one you ask refuses, the smart move will be to walk away, but not Bulls-eye."

"Down the line he went asking each in turn, and each in turn, they refused, until at last, he came to his wife, who also refused. Perhaps by then, his Dutch courage had kicked in. Very slowly, he walked back to the middle of the line and in carefully formulated words, he said, 'Ladies, I applaud your togetherness, but you know what?' At which point he gave them his back and speaking over his shoulder, he said, "all of you ladies can –"

"Like a bat out of hell constable Wells had him by the scruff of the neck and bundled him out the door before he could fully compliment the ladies."

"The vengeance of the committee was swift and final. At a hastily convened meeting, their decision was a life ban, from all of the Lodge's activities. I have it from a very reliable source from someone who was actually at the meeting, that the person who seconded the motion to ban Bulls-eye, was none other than Mrs B, herself."

Some time later, Bulls-eye was taken ill with a virus and was in bed for about three weeks. Not being especially religious, his wife was surprised when he asked to see a priest. According to Otto, it was not until Father Devas' third visit that he got to the bottom of Bulls-eye's dilemma.

"Tell me my son," said the priest, "what is it that troubles you so?"

Bulls-eye hesitated a while, looked all around to make sure they were alone, then whispered, "Father, is it true that when we die we are reunited with our loved ones for all eternity?"

There was a pleading look in his eyes, and the priest, eager to reassure him, patted him on the hand and said. "Of course my son, I give you my word that you will be reunited."

Bulls-eye covered his eyes and groaned. "Oh no, anything but that!"

All too late, the priest finally tuned into Bulls-eye's fears and hastened to repair the damage. "Don't trouble yourself my son, there is no place for that sort of thing over there. There is only a spiritual existence. There'll be no hate, no jealousy, and most especially, no talking. Only a universal spiritual love."

Bulls-eye relief was manifested by his grip as he held on to the priest. "Thank you Father, thank you!"

25

They met by the calabash tree and everyone was pleased to see TT, who was up for the weekend from St George's The mood was defiant. Nugget was the first to address the subject that'd been occupying their minds.

"We've been rolling this thing around for weeks and getting nowhere fast. Why don't we just ambush him one night?"

"Because that's not what we are about!" said Lobo sharply. "We're supposed to face our opponents, remember the power of the unicorn? Because if you do, we only have one way to go."

"Well", said the normally cautious Gatlin, doing his best imitation of Gary Cooper, "there's a snake in the Garden of Eden and I say it's time we cast him out."

There was a roar of approval and even Lobo, despite his reservation joined in.

TT spoke for the first time. "Listening to you fellahs, it seems that everything Benny does, he does out in the open. If you are going to shame him, it should also be out in the open."

They were so impressed with the idea, that they made it their criteria.

Scenarios were exchanged and rejected. Then Atlas suggested they should approach Benny in public and demand an apology like they did with Pato.

"And when he refuses, and he will refuse, what then?" said Nugget.

"Then we jump him together, like we do Ahab at the table," said Gatlin.

"If we do that, then we are just a gang, and we'll be playing Benny's game," said Optic.

It was TT who suggested a compromise. "Without any doubt, Optic is your best man on a one on one situation if you challenge him, so let him take him on."

"I don't know about that", said Atlas, who was beginning to get a bad feeling about the whole affair. "Benny would not be boxing, and he is as strong as a bull."

"Forget that!" said Lobo quickly. "That would be stupid. Benny is a bully, don't forget."

"Well," said Brains, "we have been thinking about it for a long time and that's the best idea we've had. What do you say Optic?"

Lobo jumped in before Optic could respond.

"Let's say with his trickery and his speed, Optic hits him five, six times without getting caught. That's not going to put him down and sooner or later, Benny would catch him, and you know how mean he is."

"Wait a minute," said Ahab. "What if we arrange it so that we are all there. It wouldn't take much for Optic to provoke him. Optic takes him on and we all go in to assist him?"

"I thought we decided against a mass attack?" said Lobo.

"Wait! Just wait one minute," said Brains excitedly, holding up his index finger to emphasize the minute.

"What if Optic gets him to attack him? Then we all jump in and pull them apart, all the time shouting, 'Keep it fair'. We release Optic a split second before him to give him time to prepare himself, and repeat the process every time he tries for a clinch?"

"I could live with that," said Optic, who was speaking for the first time since the suggestion was made. "If you can keep him from crunching me, I'll take my chances."

"I think that could work," said TT. "With a crowd watching, he'll have to fight fair against a boy."

259

Gatlin, unusually quiet for most of the discussion, brought them back to earth. "Ev- everybody is talking as if the only way Benny could win is to squa- squashes him. What if he ca- catches Optic with a good punch?"

"I have been hit before, all he can do is knock me out. If that happens, I'll be counting on you fellahs. No, just keep him off me and see what happens," said Optic who didn't feel nearly as calm as he sounded.

Satisfied that there was now finally some sort of a plan, they felt relieved. Lobo, with some reservations, suggested that they keep on trying for a better plan, one that was less dangerous. In the meantime, they'd try to think of ways of improving the one they had.

Despite their enthusiasm after Gatlin's war cry, Lobo could not shake off his fears about that confrontation. He had to keep stalling until they could find something better.

They met under the lights at the junction of Salisbury and Hill Street. They were able to keep an eye on Main Street, near to the spot where Leopold had picked up the coins and where they could keep look out for Movealong. They had all but given up on Nugget when he came running up to them in a highly excited state. Benny Crabb was in jail. During a disagreement with his girlfriend and expectant mother of his child, he had lost his temper again and slapped her so hard she collapsed into a heap on the ground.

Benny's dad who had witnessed the whole thing was so shocked, that he had himself made the report that resulted in constable Wells breaking his perfect record of never having logged an arrest.

"Well," said Lobo, the relief clearly audible in his voice, "we can all relax now, he'll be facing Heligar."

"That crook is going to get what's coming to him at last," said Atlas.

"Now all we have to do is get into that courthouse to see him get it," said Brains.

"That is going to be much easier said than done, no way is the

260

sergeant going to let seven of us in," said Lobo, remembering his apprehension the first time they tried.

When they met the following night, Brains was clearly excited.

"Great news fellahs, Benny's case is set for a week on Tuesday, but here's the best part. I was talking to Madge today. You know, the sergeant's daughter, she told me he is going to be away in the police school all that week. That means Corporal Tate will be on court duty. Don't you see? We could work the old school project dodge." He was very pleased with himself.

Walking from school with Nugget, Lobo was surprised to see Benny walking along the street.

"Look! There's Benny, I thought he was supposed to be in jail?"

"His mother bailed him out earlier today," answered Nugget.

"That's one strange family, the father gets him jailed, the mother sets him free. It's confusing," said Lobo.

Lobo could hear their laughter long before he could see them and he hastened his steps, eager to be a part of whatever was tickling them.

"What's all the howling about," he asked when he'd joined them.

"TT and I were just entering Miss Murray's shop when we ran straight into Big John," said Optic. "I shouted for him to run, but he got caught."

TT took up the story. "I was too slow, he grabbed me by the arm and wrestled the belt from around his waist with his other hand, while I was trying to escape. 'Please I said, it wasn't me sir.'

"Oh no!" he shouted. "No sir, never sir. Don't you remember maggot? It's Crapoman!"

Had anyone being close enough to hear them, they would have found their laughter contagious.

"Then what happened?" asked Lobo.

"After he got his belt free, he caught me once on the arm, then his pants fell down around his legs and all those people started laughing. He had to decide whether to hold on to me, or pull up his pants. I

261

got away. The last thing I heard him shout was, 'I'll get you yet maggot!'" Yet again, they doubled up with laughter. If there were any lingering doubts about TT's credentials, that brush with Big John dispelled them forever.

Afterwards, they discussed plans for Benny's trial. Brains began the briefing.

"Don't forget now, we must be there on time so we can all go in together. If we turn up in dribs and drabs the corporal will smell a rat. One more thing, make sure you are in uniform. It will look more official."

On the morning of the trial, they were early enough to be at the top end of the waiting line, headed by none other than Poole. He was standing with his pipe already smoking and had his glasses on. He had waited a long, long time for this day, and had hardly slept a wink the previous night. He wanted to be able to see Benny's expression when Heligar sent him down.

The smart talk at McCloud's was that a jail sentence was a dead cert.

The door was opened promptly at nine o'clock and sure enough, Corporal Tate was standing in the place normally occupied by Sergeant Philip. Gradually, the boys in their school uniform approached the corporal, whose cap peak almost covered his eyes.

Brains stood at the front and presented the letter as soon as they made eye contact.

"What's this?" he asked.

"A letter from Mr Mark Corporal. We are on a school project," Brains lied, looking every inch the choirboy.

The corporal read the contents, folded the paper and handed it back to him.

"Behave yourselves now. Remember where you are." He waved them forward.

Half an hour later, the magistrate, smartly dressed in a navy blue suit, white shirt and the customary black tie and shoes, opened the door that led to his seat on the bench. As always when seated, he took

262

a long look around the courtroom and once again, his eyes lingered on the boys. He turned to the corporal. "corporal, why are these children here?"

"They're on a school project sir," the corporal informed him. Satisfied, he continued his scan of the gallery. When he spoke, his tone contrasted his boyish appearance.

"I know that this is an emotional case for most of you, but I will not have these proceedings marred by unruly behaviour. This is The King's court, so I shall expect you to behave accordingly."

At last, things got underway and as was hoped, Benny's case was the first to be heard.

Benny's girlfriend, whose name was Mable, was offered and accepted a chair and was asked to tell her story. She said that Benny wanted her to go to the shop, but the sun was very hot and she felt dizzy, she couldn't handle the heat. She had told him so and offered to go when it was cooler, but he has a temper. He got angry and slapped her, but she was all right.

Heligar thanked her and turned to Benny, his voice even. "And you, what have you to say for yourself?"

Benny took his time answering. "Well, every time I tell her to do something, there's always an excuse, and –"

Heligar cut him short. "Is it true that she is having your baby?"

"Yes sir, but –"

The magistrate addressed Mable. "How far along the way are you?"

"Almost seven months, sir."

He turned his attention back to Benny. "Given your girlfriend's condition and the fact that it is your baby, why are you expecting her to fetch and carry for you? Right now, you should be helping her. Whatever you think she is to you, she is a person in her own right and shouldn't be subjected to your brutality. That's why there are laws to prevent people like you from physically abusing others."

He paused and a murmur escaped the crowd as their excitement rose.

From his seat, Jerry noticed the reflected smoke in the mirror, as it swirled slowly towards the ceiling, reminding him of the mists that surrounded the mountaintop before being dispersed by the morning sun. The sharpness of Heligar's voice got his attention.

"I can find no excuse not to send you to prison."

"Oh no sir!" shouted a clearly perturbed Mable. "Please don't send him to prison, sir."

Her emotional appeal was accompanied by the wringing of the hat she held in her hands.

"Jumping catfish!" exclaimed Poole in total disbelief of what he had heard.

There was shock and consternation on most of the faces in the room. Heligar shook his head. It never ceased to amaze him, these women's perversion for defending men who physically abuse them.

He gave Poole a long penetrating look as he addressed Mable again.

"And what will you have me do with him?"

"Please sir, could you just fine him, sir," she pleaded. He turned abruptly from her and faced Benny.

"It was my intention to send you down for the maximum term for your cowardly attack, especially on a woman in her condition. Now her plea that I should fine you instead places me in a real dilemma. If I do as she asks and order you to pay a fine, it would be counter productive. Whatever you pay to the court should hopefully have gone to her, in her time of need. Miss Mable here said you had a temper. If you did you wouldn't be in the fix you're in now. Contrary to popular belief, people only react violently when they lose their tempers and your presence here suggests that you frequently do. I therefore place you under restriction, not to indulge in further violence of any kind for a period of one year. Given your volatile nature, that would take some considerable restraint. But make no mistake, if you re offend within that time, whatever sentence you are given for that crime, a further year will be added to it for this offence. Now get out of here, and Mr Crabb, don't come back!"

Inside, the sound of Benny's laughter as he descended the stairs was the same as if he had coughed in their faces.

The crowd was in shock. Lobo was devastated and the tightness in his chest reminded him of being under water too long. Now our troubles have really begun, he thought.

The verdict so affected Poole that he had to be assisted from the court. Gone were his jaunty steps of just over an hour ago. With the exception of Benny's mother and girlfriend, the entire town wanted him sent down. Everything seemed set for a prison term, yet he walked away with a ban.

"At times like this, you wonder if there really is a God," said Poole as he made his way home. Suddenly, he felt like lying down.

Later, there was an unusual quietness among the boys who were normally very talkative. A feeling of gloom hung over them.

The conversation went round and round. Some blamed Mable and the others blamed Heligar. Then Brains made a point that had crossed all of their minds at some point.

"The fault is neither Mable's nor Heligar's. Even if he had been sent down, we still had a problem with him for what he did to Atlas."

At length, they rallied to formulate a plan, and after long discussions decided on the coming Saturday, only four days away.

They reasoned that the many shoppers around would hopefully shame Benny into fighting fair and more importantly, as Gatlin had suggested, with any luck, he would have had a few beers which should slow him down. Optic tried to inject some humour by saying.

"With my biggest fight coming up soon, I'd better get to bed."

Lobo was fully stretched out on his back with his hands clasped behind his head and for once he was glad of the darkness that enveloped him; the same darkness he used to be so afraid of. Once again, he pondered their situation in much the same way as he had before the trial. Brains was right. The thought that they were obliged to face Benny for what he did to Atlas had occurred to him, but concern for Optic had induced a convenient amnesia in all of them.

They had a moral obligation to face Benny. The spirit of the Brotherhood demanded it, but there had to be another way. What was it?

Despite their show of bravado following Gatlin's war cry, there had to be some nagging doubts at the back of all their minds. Benny's bulk was very intimidating. One good shot and only God knew the rest. Not for the first time, he wondered how all of this got started and he remembered the first incident and Puff Jake's downfall. Jake was ashamed and was content to let the matter drop. Then there was the Pato Incident with Nugget and the giant conceded, because he knew he had crossed the line.

The Paperman incident followed, but Duffy had withered and presented no threat. Even 'Movealong' chose peace after being out manoeuvred, then Brains had out-foxed the principal in their battle of wits, but Benny was in a different category, he was meanness personified.

What if Optic got lucky and did to Benny what David did to Goliath? Would Benny retaliate? The answer to that was obvious. If Optic got hurt, it would be his fault. He was the one who suggested the power of the unicorn. There has got to be a better plan than the one they had, but what was it? The question revolved in his head.

He thought of Optic and all his successes, but he knew he had never fought anyone with Benny's strength or meanness, and who quite probably had never heard of the Marquis Of Queensbury, and his boxing rules.

He turned over and bashed the pillow a couple of times, but sleep was no nearer.

"I wish it would rain," he thought. When Ambrose went away at school and he had trouble sleeping, the rain when it came always calmed him and helped him to sleep.

The music when it started was nothing special. In fact, it was a minor irritation, sounding like someone practising musical scales. Jerry closed his eyes and tried to concentrate. He was trying to think of a way to convince the group to wait for something better. The only good thing in their favour was that Benny knew nothing of their intentions.

The music came from a lone saxophonist known as Crombie, a member of the local band. Like his many predecessors and still more of his contemporaries all over the world, Crombie was a heavy smoker and drinker. From time to time, in an effort to exorcise his dark moods, he played into the night, long after the lights that guided the men home from the bars were put out. Then, as if it were important to him to have the night all to himself, he poured his heart and soul out through his renderings.

After finishing his scales, he started with the Harry Bellafonte hit, *Scarlet Ribbons*. It was a popular song and the boy had heard it many times before on the radio, he couldn't help but put the words to the tune in his mind.

'I peeked in to say goodnight,
Then I heard my child in prayer.'

As soon as he was finished, with hardly a break, he launched into *I Believe*. He broke all the rules. Notes that were short, he held on to forever, as if trying to make a point.

The music soared into the still night, piggy-backing on the gentlest of breezes and reached all the stressed, anxious and troubled souls like himself, lying in their beds and seeking divine assistance. It invited them to tune into his exorcism and maybe even their own fears.

On and on he played for about an hour. He spent a long time on *Someone To Watch Over Me*, and once again, Jerry sang in his mind.

'There is someone that I'm longing to meet'.

The mood was melancholy, but the melodies soothed and rejuvenated their troubled spirits like balm on an angry wound.

His mind went back to the problem.

"TT was right," he thought. "Optic was our best man for the job, he was second only to Ahab at the table, but this was on land. If only?"

Suddenly, he sat bolt upright in his bed and laughed out loud.

In the next room his two sisters were lying in bed listening to the music.

"Jerry is dreaming," said Marigold when she heard the laughter.

"I'll take laughter instead of whimpering any day," answered Juliette sleepily.

When he eased back onto his pillow, he had a broad grin on his face. He could hardly wait for tomorrow.

As always, Hoagie Carmichael's *Stardust*, was the final rendition of the night. By now, most of them were safely tucked in and in the land of nod, but the few that were still awake knew that the performance was at an end until the next time. Lobo breathed easily, there was not a single worry line on his forehead.

Years later, when asked what his favourite instrument was, without stopping to think, Jerry promptly replied, "the saxophone."

The beach, well away from the main road was almost deserted at this time of night. They sat in a circle around the fire, which was roasting two breadfruits. Only the exploding sparks from the flames and the breaking of the waves, together with their subdued conversation disturbed the night.

Quite deliberately, Lobo, obviously in a jaunty mood, was the last to arrive.

"Hey, Lobo! What's up man?" greeted Ahab.

"What's up? I'll tell you what's up." He put both hands in his pocket, and tilted his head before speaking.

"What would you say if I told you that I had a plan that would give us a great chance to fix Benny's wagon?"

"Now wait a minute, Lobe, we already have a plan and it goes into action two days from now," said Nugget with a hint of finality.

Lobo raised both hands in a calming gesture.

"Please!" he pleaded. "Just hear me out. If afterwards we don't agree to a man, then we go on Saturday, no prob."

They made room for him to sit but he remained standing. He turned to Ahab.

"Can you remember what you said on the table before that swim we did from Rathan's Bay?"

"Sure I do. I said what I always say. Out there, I'm the King and the Table is my throne," said Ahab confidently.

"I also remembered you saying, 'Come one, come all'. Did you say that?"

By now, anyone could tell from their studious expressions that they had already grasped the thread of the conversation.

Ahab felt their eyes upon him, he looked at their faces and suddenly realization dawned.

"Damned right I said it, I always say it," he said. His expression suggested surprise that they should doubt him.

"Question is, did you mean it?" said Brains.

"Damn right," he said again, "I meant every word."

"Isn't it time the fish went on the fire?" Gatlin wanted to know.

"That's Ahab's department," Atlas reminded them. They suspended discussions while Ahab tended to the fish.

"Pass the butter," someone said. They ate and got back to business.

"No disrespect to you Optic. We all know that you're our best man for the job on land, but I think Ahab would have a better chance in the water. I can't think of a better leveller," said Lobo, looking at each in turn.

Gatlin's sensitive nature shone through once again, he asked, "Is that alright with you Optic?"

"Sure man," said Optic. "I don't mind admitting that monster scares me. One problem though, how are we going to get him to the sea?"

"Oh, we'll have to think about that one for a while, but you are wrong Optic, we have more than one problem, lots more," said Lobo.

It was settled, Ahab would face Benny in the water at a time yet to be decided.

At the next meeting, suggestions were many and varied. Someone suggested sending Benny a fake message to meet a friend on the beach, but they couldn't think of such a person.

Nugget, who lived closest to him, said that Benny often went to the beach about four in the afternoon, but that was discarded because there were hardly any of the locals on the beach that late. Just when it looked like getting hopeless, Brains said, "Easter is only two weeks away and everybody goes to the beach on these holidays, chances are, so would Benny."

"Besides," said Lobo, "let's not forget he is bound over and not likely to start trouble, so we have time."

They were unanimous in their acceptance. All that was left was the strategy. Casting out time was almost at hand.

They made full use of the time they had leading up to the holiday. Their preparation was methodical, with lots of attention to details. There was a practice session every day after school in the water, with Ahab taking on two opponents simultaneously. The emphasis was placed on pinning him under water as much as possible, so he could learn how to relax instead of resisting. That way, according to Optic, he would conserve energy.

They still had the problem of getting Benny to the beach. Even if he did go there on the appointed day what was to say he wouldn't choose the same time. It would all have to be down to potluck.

Two days before their anticipated confrontation, they chose the calabash tree in the pasture as their meeting place, secure in the knowledge that they could not be overheard. Although the moon was only in its second quarter, it produced enough light for their purpose. TT, home for the Easter holidays, took his place among them on the grass.

"Now we know that Ahab is in good physical shape," began Lobo, "but we mustn't forget that Benny is one hell of an adversary, so let's talk about tactics. As with Optic, we'll be around and ready to jump in and separate them if things get really out of hand." All eyes were turned on Optic.

270

He took a little while answering and just for a moment, his glasses reflected the pale light of the moon as he moved his head slightly. His voice was furtive.

"The most important thing is to get him into deep water where he can't swing his arms to punch you. One more thing, you're not in a race. Take as much time as you need to wear him down. Don't forget, you have surprise and preparation on your side. Because of the ban, he may even have to be goaded into this fight, but given his short temper, that shouldn't be a problem."

"We are going to make that crook say, Boss," said Nugget, amid some laughter. Lobo raised his voice to get their attention.

"Let's take this thing seriously or forget about it, because Benny will. And it's not 'we'. If this thing is to work, Ahab alone has to do it. We are there to make sure of fair play and offer moral support."

"Relax Lobe," said Brains. "We all know how serious this is, but we have done all that we can. Tomorrow, Ahab will have one last practice. Then we just hope that Benny turns up."

TT broke his silence. "You fellahs have been practising a lot. I don't think one more day is going to make a difference. Besides, Ahab may be injured and you would have to cancel."

TT had spent a lot of time around the docks with his dad and had done his share of diving with the other kids amid fierce competition, when tourists threw coins into the water along the esplanade.

He continued, "When this thing gets started, he'll be in a rage and he'll come at you hard. Try and get him in deep water, so if he tries to hold you down, he will also be under. Then, it will all rest on who lasts longer."

"So, are we just going to go down to the beach and hope that he turns up?" said Atlas.

"That's right, unless you want to give him a personal invitation," suggested Nugget.

They agreed to meet back at the calabash tree following night for the final briefing.

271

Gatlin unfolded the newspaper package he was carrying and exposed several pieces of a broken mirror.

"What's this?" asked Nugget and before Gatlin had a chance to answer, he carried on. There was a broad hint of sarcasm in his voice. "Don't tell me, these are signalling devices, right?"

"If it's good enough for the cav- cavalry, it's good enough for us," insisted Gatlin.

After a bit of ribbing, they passed the pieces around. Optic coordinated the operation.

"Nugget lives closest to Benny. He is going to keep an eye on him until one o'clock, if he makes a move before that, he'll signal Atlas, and so on. If not, we'll meet at the beach afterwards."

Ahab who had been unusually quiet had fidgeted all evening. Gatlin placed a hand on his shoulder.

"You all right man? You've been very quiet."

The others rallied around, clapping him on the arm and his back.

"What's up A? You having second thoughts?" queried Brains with some concern.

"Nothing like that man. It's the waiting. I just can't stop thinking about it."

"Try not to think about it so much Ahab. I know it's hard but try. You can't match him for strength, but you are better in the water and much fitter. Try and keep him deep and concentrate on holding him under water," suggested TT.

Atlas made a grim observation.

"Once he loses his temper, he'll come after you for real, so you have to forget about fighting us at the Table and be prepared to be really mean."

Optic started to speak, addressing Ahab's competitive side.

"This time it's not sport, it's the most dangerous challenge we have ever undertaken, and you're the man in the front line so don't compete with him, just concentrate on keeping him under water."

272

He lapsed into silence for a while as if considering the wisdom of what he was going to say next.

"Jersey Joe Walcott is my favourite boxer of all time. I first read about him in one of those boxing magazines that my dad brought home. He was light for a heavyweight, but he was so good. His amazing footwork and speed inside the ring made him very hard to hit and he was climbing fast in the ratings.

"Eventually he got his big chance to fight the champion, Joe Louis, better known as The Brown Bomber.

The night of the fight Jersey Joe, clearly the underdog, boxed very cleverly. By the time the fight reached the halfway stage he was so far ahead on points that all he had to do was avoid being knocked out.

"The crowd became very excited, some of it must have rubbed off on Jersey Joe. Instead of keeping to the plan he decided to try and beat Louis at his own game and started trading punches.

"The inevitable happened and Louis knocked him out in the thirteenth round. He only had to survive another two to win. He had ignored his corner's advice to stick to the plan and he lost the chance to be world champion."

"In other words," Brains jumped in, "make him fight your fight, you don't fight his."

Judgement day, when it came, brought with it a mixture of apprehension, nervousness, optimism and excitement. They were all assembled at the beach.

They posted a man at the top end near to the road to be sure of an early warning, with a promise of relief in half an hour, each man to take his turn until Benny showed up. Then, anxious to save energy, they sat around in their bathers and waited.

The beach resembled a fairground without the rides. Scattered everywhere were families enjoying picnics and picking their way among them were three donkeys laden with children.

Further down, away from the crowded area were several ball games being played by both sexes and the inevitable male versus female tug of war with a ratio of two to one in favour of the women.

Overhead were two massive kites, and in true traditional fashion each sported several razor blades tied onto the tails. This helped the owners who were doing a good imitation of two puppet masters as they engaged in a battle of wits to control their kites in the high winds while at the same time trying to cut the other's kite loose. It's a highly developed skill admired by many of the older people.

It was impossible to ignore the noise pitched high above the sound of the waves crashing against the shore. The pleasurable screams of the children running in and out of the water, parental cries of guidance to errant offspring, the strumming of a guitar accompanied by three or more singers and for sheer nuisance value, the constant squawking of the seagulls in their greedy search for food. A cacophony that would sound the same on beaches the world over.

Five o'clock came and went and still Benny didn't show. The beach emptied quickly as families began packing away their picnic things.

"I think it's time we went home," said Brains, voicing the thoughts of the others.

"It'll have to be next Sunday before we try again. Remember, we are playing against La Mode tomorrow," Lobo reminded them.

Without having entered the water, mentally exhausted and hungry, they made their separate ways home.

Ahab opened the door and walked into his grandmother's question.

"That you Lynton?" She didn't wait for him to answer. "Your dinner's gone cold, but you already know that."

"I'll be all right Mama," Ahab said, trying to calm her before she really got started. He had hardly eaten a thing all day, yet he wasn't hungry. He was nervous and tense and excited, but not hungry.

Ever since Lobo had come up with the plan that he, Ahab, should face Benny in the water, he hadn't been able to think of anything else. It wasn't that he was afraid, he was cautious and apprehensive but not afraid. In the water, he wasn't afraid of anybody.

He remembered when his love affair with the sea began. He was about three years old before he stopped falling over and skinning his knees. He was tall, gawky and clumsy. The doctor told his dad that he was growing too fast and that his joints were weak. He then advised walking the boy on the beach in the hope that the sand would strengthen his legs.

In the months following, except in bad weather, they never missed an opportunity. It wasn't until two years later that the father relented and allowed the boy into the sea.

From that memorable first moment of entry, he felt himself transformed into someone slick and graceful and who enjoyed a special affinity with the sea. He couldn't remember learning to swim, it seemed that he always could.

Afterwards, his exercises became concentrated in the water and the benefits were obvious. It wasn't long before his friends named him Ahab, after the infamous captain of Moby Dick fame.

He thought about Benny and all the rumours, some of which he knew to be true, and was caught up by the romance that all boys attach to adventure and hero-worship. There was a part of him that very much wanted to be the hero who vanquished Benny. The Brotherhood was in trouble and he was its chosen champion. He was determined to continue the tradition set by the others, of successfully defeating an opponent. He decided to miss the lime that evening he needed the time on his own to think. Whenever it happened, if it happened, he must be ready.

He dreamt the fight went on and Benny carried him high over his head from the water and dashed him onto the sand. He jumped up and tried to run away but his legs were leaden. Benny blocked his path and bared his teeth, which glowed like burning coal. His hair, standing straight up reminded him of barbed wire, and his eyes opened wide, were red. Black smoke spewed continuously from his nostrils. He leaned forward and flexed his fingers, which had nails like long, sharp knives.

"I'm going to cut your heart out, Mongrel!" Benny had threatened.

The crowd, led by Heligar, bayed their support.

"Ben nee! Ben nee, Ben nee." He had shouted for his friends but he was alone. He woke up with a start, drenched in sweat and his heart was pounding.

"Whoa," he breathed, sitting up abruptly. His mind cleared slowly. "Jesus!" he breathed. "Man, you're something else, but I got to tell you, nobody cuts my heart out in the water fellah and on land, you got to catch me first."

26

The visitors were late. The home team had lost the toss and Lobo was poised on his mark with the new ball ready to start the innings, when a rider was seen approaching fast. His demeanour clearly indicated urgency. As he got closer, they recognised Gatlin, who had ridden right through the playing area. The rest of the gang gathered around him but Gatlin was very animated, and had difficulty making himself understood.

"B-b-b −"

"Easy now Gat", said Lobo. "Calm down and tell us what's happening."

He tried again with the same result. Nugget held on to the handlebar and pulled the bike further away from the other players.

"Sorry about this fellahs, back in a minute," he shouted over his shoulder to the two batsmen from the visiting team, then joined the others who were all there with the exception of Brains. He massaged Gatlin's neck with one hand.

"Gat", he said gently, try and sing it." They all looked sharply at him and realized that he was deadly serious.

"Go on Gat, try it," he encouraged.

To the tune of, *Jingle Bells*, sung quietly so only they could hear, he informed them that he had just seen Benny with a bath towel thrown over his shoulder, going to the beach about ten minutes earlier. The singing seemed to have calmed him.

"I must ta – take the bike back now, I did promised," he said.

"All right, said Lobo. "Alert Brains and the both of you join us as soon as you can."

They apologized to the opposing team and promised to play the match at their convenience. They explained that something had come up which couldn't wait. Picking up their belongings, they set off at a run towards the main road."

The visitors, sensing that something unusual was about to break followed at a respectful distance.

Poole sat in his chair near the window overlooking the road, but was oblivious to everything that was going on before him. He was thinking of his fourteenth birthday, the first time he was allowed to go out on the boat with his father.

He could not remember a time when he didn't want to be a fisherman like his dad, but always, he'd told him, "You will wait until you're fourteen, like I did".

It took a little while to learn to control his stomach, but being out in all weather he was soon rated an able seaman and never minded even when he had to rise very early, or go sailing in the dark.

"When the tide is your task master boy, you have no choice", his father used to say, over and over again.

Poole thought of the first time he had accompanied him in darkness so dense he could barely see his hand in front of his face. As they stumbled trying to set the fish traps, he had asked his dad, "How are we going to find them again? We can't see anything".

"Oh yes we can", he had assured him. His dad went on to explain that the stars marked the spot, as did the church steeple and the light that was always left on in Wildman's attic window for just that purpose.

"Thing to remember though," said his dad, "is what the eyes cannot see, the hand cannot take".

Poole met his wife, whom he loved dearly, and married her two weeks after his twenty-seventh birthday. He hardly had time to get

278

over his hangover after he wedding when he was called for a trip to the sister island of Carriacou, which, since the days of the pirates, operated a thriving contraband business in alcohol and tobacco.

They chose an out of the way cove that they had used before.

The waves, always big in that area, pounded the nearby rocks and sent huge fountains of frothy spray onto the cliffs above. All the sails had already been taken in and they rode in on their momentum. Someone shouted a warning as a rope snapped and sent the boom swinging out of control, but it was much too late. It struck Poole across the shoulders, and flung him unconscious, onto the nearby rock.

He opened his eyes and found himself lying flat on his back on the sand and the pain in his right leg was making him see white lights. There was no doctor in the nearby village and someone was sent to fetch the local fix-all, who informed them that Poole's thigh was broken and did the best he could to set it with what he had available.

Without shifting his gaze, Poole reached for his leg just underneath his right knee and vigorously massaged it with both hands, then, changing to his thigh, he stroked it gently. Then, again with both hands, he lifted the leg to a more comfortable position before straightening it out before him.

In time the leg mended, but the pain never went away. He had returned to work as soon as he could and struggled valiantly for another ten years, but eventually admitted to himself that he could no longer pull his weight. Reluctantly, he ended his love affair with the sea and kissed goodbye to his dream of working on a schooner and sailing among the islands, goodbye. Now, he visited them in spirit, through the letters of his only son, who went on to achieve both their dreams.

As he sat at the window, he knew that Benny was the real cause of his foul mood. No matter how hard he tried he couldn't control himself around him, they were like kerosene and matches. Benny's laughter as he went down the steps of the courthouse still infuriated him. He found it hard to believe that he had walked with just a ban.

Suddenly, the loud gobbling of a turkey directly beneath the window startled him. Almost immediately, another one answered some distance away.

"Damn birds"! Fretted Poole. "Now they're going to be at it for the next half hour before they decide which is top turkey." He reached around the corner for his boots.

"Did you say something husband?" asked his wife from the kitchen.

"Just thinking aloud wife. Nothing for you to worry about," he answered in that peculiar way they had of addressing each other.

She was surprised to hear him moving around since he had been so inactive recently.

"What are you doing?" she asked.

"Think I'll catch some air and stretch my legs." He reached for his new walking stick and checked his pocket for his pipe. As he came into the yard, he looked up at the sky from force of habit.

"Not a single cloud," he said to no one in particular. As he hobbled towards the road he called out over his shoulder, "See you later wife!"

"See you later husband," she answered from her place by the kitchen window.

She thought of the man he used to be and it broke her heart to see him limping so badly. She remembered the day he came walking jauntily to her father's house with a bunch of wild lilies and hibiscus hidden inside his hat for fear of being ribbed by his friends if they saw him. If only Benny hadn't come back, she thought.

He walked through the courtyard and headed for the cemetery entrance, towards his favourite spot just behind the Anglican church overlooking the ocean. Without knowing why, he changed his mind and turned towards the road leading to the beach. He knew that he Boucheree would be overcrowded; he just had to find somewhere quiet. He walked along until he turned into Beach Road, lodged between Dwarica's store and Springle's bakery. He took the cobbled path sloping downwards from the main road and picked his way diligently across the uneven surface. His right hand, still tender from breaking in the new stick, was badly jarred as it slipped over the smooth cobbles beneath, causing him to swear under his breath.

He was so preoccupied with his slow progress, that he was startled by the sudden appearance of a group of boys, who hardly seemed aware of his presence. Finally on the beach, he looked around for somewhere away from the crowd, with a bit of shade.

The boys were about a third of the way towards the beach when Optic called a halt.

"Hold it! Hold it one minute," he shouted. After they had stopped, he advised, "If we keep this pace up we'll be tired by the time we get there. Besides, we don't want to draw attention to ourselves".

"But if we don't hurry, we might miss him," said Ahab.

"If we get there tired, what good is that? You tell me," said Optic.

They continued at a brisk pace, with little conversation passing between them.

Preoccupied, they almost knocked old man Poole over. Once on the beach they changed into their bathers and tried to spot Benny in the crowd, while they waited for Brains and Gatlin to arrive.

Although the beach was not as crowded as the previous day, picnickers still dominated it.

"Over there!" exclaimed Nugget, pointing.

"No pointing," hissed Optic, forcing his hand down. "Just tell us where he is."

"He is over by the tug of war. He is sitting on the sand. He is over on the women's side." They all saw him, just as Brains and Gatlin joined them. Optic took over as a matter of course.

"Okay, now we wait until he goes into the water." He looked over at Ahab and held his gaze. "Now is the time man, this is it. Lobo was right. You've got ten times the chance I had, but if for any reason you've changed your mind, just say so and we'll think of something else."

"No man, not a chance," said Ahab. "Just kind of nervous and a little anxious, but I'm not scared."

"Scared is not such a bad thing, it makes you careful," said TT. "If anybody can do this, it's you, so scared or not, be careful."

Then it was Lobo's turn.

"Listen Ahab, this whole thing was my idea, so if anything happens to you out there, I won't be able to live with myself, but I really believe you can do this. You're our champion and we'll be there to keep an eye on things. Just one thing man, you don't have to be like Samson, you don't have to die with your enemy."

They each in turn added their own words of encouragement. So far, everything was going to plan.

Benny luxuriated in the freedom of the beach, but cursed the holiday that brought the noisy brats and geriatrics to clutter it. He'd always liked the sea and as a boy had even thought of becoming a fisherman, but it was always the same with those damned old men, forcing their opinions on you even when you didn't ask for it. "Do this. Don't do that. It's always being done this way," or, "It's bad luck at sea". He'd had it with them and had told them what they could do with the job, now that the world was his oyster. Never mind, he thought, this is the life and tomorrow is another day.

He rose from the sand, held his hands high above his head and had a long, luxurious stretch then he hopped into the water and allowed his body to fall in causing a big splash. When he surfaced, he had covered some twenty feet from his point of entry.

This was what he'd missed most while he was rotting in Careara.

"He's in the water now," said Atlas excitedly.

"So here we go," said Nugget. "It's casting out time!"

Optic walked alongside Ahab. "Don't forget man, stick to the plan. You have trained for this and he hasn't. Hell! He has no idea this is coming and you are in better condition than he is, but he is as strong as a bull and just as mean and he grew up near the sea, so he's no slouch in the water. Remember, when he tries to hold you down, don't try to wrestle him off, hold on to him, keep him close, less chance of him using that hammer of his and try not to use up extra energy. If he tries to make for shore, we'll block him, now let's go!"

They all made the sign of the cross.

As they approached the water, Gatlin ran forward and slipped into Gary Cooper mode.

"You pluck his feathers good and I'll have words with Nina, you hear?"

Nina was his attractive twin sister and the object of the attention of many of his friends.

They waded into the sea and Ahab swam towards the spot where Benny was lazily swimming, a little to the left of the Table. He waited for the first riser and stood on what he thought of as his throne.

Standing there, he felt again the familiar feeling of invincibility that was so much a part of his connection with the water. Only this time it was different, he would not be fighting mock battles with his friends. He looked at Benny and just for a moment, his resolve wavered.

"He is as strong as a bull and just as mean," Optic had said, but somewhere within him, he felt that this was something he had to do for himself.

"Hell, this is the reason I woke up this morning," he thought.

For a moment, he was tempted to jump on top of him and finish it as quickly as possible then discarded the idea immediately.

"This is a serious cause. It's for the Brotherhood." Ahab reminded himself. He took a deep breath, measured the distance and jumped into the water, making a splash of his own no further than two feet from where Benny was swimming.

Surprised and annoyed, Benny wiped the water from his eyes and focused on the intruder. He whirled around to face Ahab.

"Get the hell out of here and take that damn racket with you!"

Ahab was just out of arms reach.

"The sea is for everybody. If you don't like it here, then move someplace else," said Ahab with a calmness that he didn't feel.

283

"To hell with Heligar," thought Benny. "If it wasn't for him that mongrel wouldn't be here." He was getting frustrated and his irritation showed.

"I won't tell you again so git before I change my mind," he said without moving his jaws.

Ahab shivered slightly as he felt the surge of adrenalin through his body.

"There is a snake in the Garden of Eden," Gatlin had said. Now it really was casting out time. Question is, is he ready?

"And I'll tell you again, you don't like it here? Then scram!" He said boldly, looking Benny straight in the eye.

Benny was finding all this hard to believe.

"The hell with Heligar!" He said out loud.

He lunged forward, quickly closing the gap between them. Ahab twisted away but Benny caught hold of his left arm. The water was up to Benny's chest and Ahab's neck. Benny tried to pull him closer but Ahab ducked beneath the water, forcing Benny to follow him down, if he wanted to maintain his hold.

After a while, Benny released him, but kept a watchful eye for his reappearance. Ahab broke the water at his back and surprised him, as he leapt forward fast enough to get Benny in a choke lock. By now, his friends were close enough and shouting their encouragement.

Gradually, the crowd on and around the beach became aware of the disturbance.

"Benny is beating somebody up in the water," shouted one young woman to her friend, and before long, the entire beach was alerted.

Somebody had mentioned Benny's strength, but none of them had imagined just how strong he really was. He lifted Ahab whose hand was still around his neck and with an effort lunged backwards. He flung Ahab about six feet away. Turning quickly, he was beside him when he stood up. Though Benny was somewhat handicapped by the water he still struck Ahab hard enough to knock out his tooth.

The water crimsoned with Ahab's blood. He could hear his friends shouting for him to back away and after the stars faded, he made out lots of people trying to get a closer look.

Poole had found a good spot in the shade of a frangipani tree away from the crowded beach, but close enough to hear the joyful squeals of the children and the deeper murmur of attendant adults. After he had filled his pipe with tobacco, he loosened the laces of his boots and removed them then he painstakingly straightened his legs. Then he lit his pipe.

Over the water, away from the bathers, a flock of pelicans circled.

He looked up into the sky. It was the third quarter of the moon. He thought, "Must be a school of jacks".

Shortly afterwards, the pelicans were joined by some squawking gulls and the feeding frenzy began.

His attention was drawn, not so much by the noise that came from the beach but the tone of it. The squeals of delight only a short time ago had turned to shouts of apprehension. From their gesticulations, it soon became clear that there was a struggle of some kind going on between two men in the water and somewhere in he middle of all the noise, he was sure that he had heard Benny's name.

Poole lifted both hands to his face.

"Jumping catfish! Another mother's son is going to be damaged by Benny."

He very quickly rolled his trousers legs up to his knees, removed and placed his jacket on the ground with the boots lying on top of it to prevent it being blown away by the strong breeze.

Without much regard for his bad leg but still with the aid of his stick, he made good progress down the slope to the sand. He waded into the sea and closer to the action.

Ahab could see lots of people around and most were shouting, but their voices were disjointed by the noises all around him. Benny inched up to him, but he held his ground, noticing that Benny was too deep in the water to swing his arm. His underestimation cost him

285

dearly, as Benny, well schooled in the art of street fighting, swung his right elbow with devastating effect. Ahab felt as if his left temple had exploded and the stars were once again behind his eyes.

The water engulfed him, the cool soothing effect helped to revive him and he was thankful as it streamed from his head and mingled with the stinging tears brought on by Benny's vicious elbow. Yet again, Benny had stained the sea with his blood and as Optic would have said, "He hadn't laid a glove on Benny as yet."

Just this once, he wished he had Optic's cross-eyed ability to confuse people about where he was or wasn't really looking.

Heartened by his previous success, Benny raised his voice for the benefit of those around them.

"This is your last warning. Now, get going!"

"Ahab, make for the shore, give it up!" screamed Lobo.

"That's good advice. If I were you, I'd take it," snarled Benny.

"Well I'm not you! And this is my last warning to you. Beat it!"

Again, Benny leapt and got his hand around Ahab's neck and was about to apply pressure when Ahab struck backwards with his elbow, and busted Benny's nose.

The exhilaration made him slightly light headed. He had never experienced that kind of satisfaction before. It proved that Benny was human after all. The water was bloodied for the third time but this time it wasn't his. "Now," he thought, "you'll have something to show."

"See! You're not so tough. Now your blood is in the water the same as mine." He taunted Benny.

Benny looked in disbelief at the discolouration in front of him and there was menace in his eyes. He clamped his jaw together and growled. "That's it mongrel. I'm done fooling around with you. Now I'm going to break your back."

Benny advanced on him and Ahab, buoyed by his recent success, stood his ground. He repeated his elbow tactic but Benny had anticipated it, easily took hold of the arm and immediately, forced the baffled Ahab towards the beach. He laughed without humour.

"Now you're up a gru gru tree with no way of getting down," he said. The tree was of the palm family and was distinctive because its stem and branches were covered with thorns.

Ahab tried to wrestle his arm from Benny's grasp, taking a punch behind the left ear as he did so. He tried to dive beneath the water, but Benny held on fast with his left hand.

"Not this time mongrel, this time, you're mine."

Benny shaped to punch again but Ahab kicked out sharply and connected with Benny's knee. He winced with the sudden pain and released his hold long enough for Ahab to get away.

"Come on Ahab, make for the shore," someone shouted, but he knew that on land Benny would probably take them all. He ignored the advice.

"Stick to the plan!" The corner shouted, but he wanted to beat Louis at his own game, with the inevitable result. Louis knocked him out in the thirteenth."

Optic's words rang in his ears. He realized he had been doing just that.

"Remember, you have trained and he hasn't."

Ahab acknowledged he wouldn't like to fight Benny if he was prepared.

"When this thing starts, he'll be in a rage. He'll come at you hard. Get him into deep water," TT had advised.

"The water is my domain," Ahab thought. "This is my time to prove it. Benny is the trespasser here, not me."

There was some numbness behind Ahab's ear and the spot where his tooth used to be throbbed continuously.

"If I can only keep away from those clubbing punches, I'll be all right," he told himself.

Like two wrestlers in the ring, they lunged at each other. When they surfaced, Benny had the advantage with both his hands on Ahab's shoulder. He couldn't resist gloating, "Say Amen mongrel. You were just too stupid to listen."

With an effort, he pushed Ahab underneath and held him. Ahab, with hands and feet, assisted by the buoyancy of the water, took them deeper, then quickly placed both hands behind Benny's neck, wrapped his legs around him, and held on.

Benny increased the strength of the strangle hold, but quickly realized from his lack of resistance that the boy was trying to hold him under. He released his hold but even so he couldn't free himself. He panicked and struggled frantically to get away.

Ahab held on until he felt uncomfortable before letting go.

Benny shot upwards coughing and spluttering and gasping for air. Ahab surfaced and remained close by, he was breathing normally. They stared at each other and for the very first time he thought he detected doubt in Benny's eyes. He approached him and Ahab back-stepped deeper in the water. Benny hesitated and then stopped. His reluctance to go deeper wasn't lost on the Ahab.

"So," he thought, "there are lines you won't cross after all."

He decided right there that should he need to run, it would be towards the ocean.

Ahab's confidence rose and he decided it was time to take TT's advice to hold Benny under. He took a deep breath before he disappeared. Benny looked frantically around before falling forward in the water as his feet were dragged from under him. Ahab held on to them and kept him under. Benny tried desperately to break free, then kicked Ahab savagely in the head and scrambled to the surface, leaving the stunned Ahab to regain his focus.

Poole was waist deep in the water and jostling for his place with the rest of the spectators. As he'd approached, he could tell that the young man had been getting the worst of it, but things seemed to have changed for the better. He roared his encouragement.

"Hold him under son. That's it, make the tyrant pay!"

The boys who were very concerned at the way things were going suddenly perked up and became very vocal in their support.

"Be careful Ahab!"

288

"Stay out of reach Ahab!"

"Go for it Ahab!"

"Pluck his feathers, Ahab!"

They were as one in their words of encouragement.

Ahab repeated the holding under tactic, this time wary of Benny's kicks, and as before, he held on until he became uncomfortable before letting go.

Benny came up coughing and made a determined effort for the shore, but the Brotherhood members blocked his path long enough to allow Ahab to catch up.

They latched on to each other and Benny tried mercilessly to rip off Ahab's right ear, until he was wrestled beneath the water again. This time, Ahab ignored his aching lungs and held on as long as he could. "Let's see what kind of condition you're really in." He held on until his aching lungs forced him to release a terrified Benny, who, in his desperate search for respite, sought the sanctuary of the Table.

Ahab almost jumped for joy. Of all the places in the entire world this was where he had the most control. He caught the first decent riser to come his way and in the same movement, wrapped his arms around Benny, and allowed the momentum of the wave to take them into the water.

Benny was exhausted and several times made for the table, only to be pulled back to the last place he wanted to be. Ahab swam around and waited for the next riser. Benny held up his hand in a pacifying gesture. His lack of condition had told on him and he was bending forward with his mouth wide open.

"Wait," he gasped, as he laboured to breathe, "just one minute."

"Why?" asked Ahab, "would you like it better if I had a big belly?" And without waiting for an answer, he charged Benny head first, and butted him hard in the stomach knocking what little wind he had left out of him.

Trapped within the rolling surf, Benny collided with a nearby rock hidden beneath and skinned his shoulder. He scrambled up the table, but lacked the energy to stand up.

Very slowly, he sat down, and resumed pleading.

"Let's talk about this," he gasped.

Yet again, Ahab taunted him.

"Would you prefer me on a bicycle, or better still, if I walked with a stick?"

He shaped to attack and Benny shouted, "Wait a minute." Then more urgently, "Please!" he begged.

"Did you wait to throw Cecil's glasses in the sea? Did you wait before you took the cinema ticket?" Ahab demanded angrily.

Benny seemed shattered. He repeated his plea.

"Please, no more, I beg you!"

"Alleluia!" shouted Poole. "Make him say it again."

The riser loomed.

"I didn't hear you!" Ahab shouted.

"I beg you, no more," spluttered Benny between coughs.

Ahab moved closer and took hold of his right leg, but he did not struggle, his exhaustion had taken its toll and all the fight seemed to have gone out of him.

"Out here, I'm the tough guy. Now say it!" shouted Ahab.

Once again, Benny raised his hand for understanding.

"All right, all right," he said meekly. "Out here, you're the tough guy."

"Alleluia!" Poole shouted again.

"Ahab held his place and watched Benny as he eased himself into the water and ran the gauntlet of derision from the spectators, as he made his way to the shore. Very quickly and very quietly, he left the beach.

They carried Ahab shoulder high to the shore and all the way up the cobbled path to the main road, truly believing that the power of the unicorn was upon them, and like a bunch of young colts in love with life, they joked, and frolicked, and sang the praises of the Brotherhood.

Poole was wet all over from having done his first somersault in the water in over twenty years, when Benny actually begged to be left alone. He hurried out of the sea and up the slope, brushed the sand from his feet before putting on his boots, donned his jacket and made his way home, quite oblivious of the cobbles.

They were on cloud nine on their way to the New Found Out, for their usual conquest celebration, when they bumped into Jimsey on his way to his favourite haunt, Alexander's bar.

Like almost everyone else in the town, Jimsey had heard of Benny's humbling. His face lit up at the sight of them and there was no mistaking the admiration in both his voice and demeanour. He had a broad smile on his face and he opened both his arms wide to take them all in.

"Gentlemen, I haven't felt so exhilarated since D-day, and I will be greatly honoured if you will allow me to show my appreciation by buying you all a drink to celebrate this momentous occasion!"

"Why, thank you Jimsey," said Lobo, he looked at the beaming faces around him. "We'll be delighted."

Under the bright lights of the restaurant Ahab looked as if he had been through the wars, and in their opinion, he had. There were cuts and bruises all over his face and his body ached all over. He knew from experience that by the morning, he would be black and blue all over.

Having taken their orders, Jimsey returned with eight beers, and one ginger beer for Brains, who, once again because of his condition refused the opportunity to experience the taste of real beer.

After they had settled down with every man holding a bottle, Brains claimed the right to be first. He stood up and turned to face Ahab. Ahab, clearly feeling self-conscious had a lopsided grin on his swollen face.

"You don't have green eyes, but you showed courage and heart. We're proud of you." He held his bottle aloft. "Ahab!" he shouted. "Ahab!" they repeated, and tasted beer for the first time. After that, they took it in turn as each expressed his congratulations. Optic was next to go.

"I'll admit I was worried, but once you went back to the plan, you were flying. Something else, I never would have taken him. You are the best!"

Nugget showed his pearly whites.

"You're something else man, you can be my deputy anytime."

Atlas waited until the laughter died down. He continued the western theme. "He'll carry your brand for as long as he lives. Thanks man."

Lobo knew what he wanted to say but he took a while to speak.

"You dug us both out of a big hole man, and I owe you. He was a lot better in the water than we thought, but you were equal to it. You are the true King of the Table. King Ahab!"

Gatlin insisted on being last, or so he thought. TT was next to go and his congratulations were more general. "Now you understand why I spend so much time up here, you fellahs are the best." He turned to face Ahab. "As for you man, you are something else."

Gatlin stood up and took a floppy white hat from his back pocket, much like a baby's bonnet, offered it to Ahab and stood to attention.

"You deserve to be the fellah in the white hat. Permission to call you boss, BOSS!"

As usual, there was plenty of laughter. From that day onwards, he never called Ahab anything but Boss Ahab.

After they had settled, Jimsey's generous side shone through and he repeated the round, then requested their permission before adding his congratulations to theirs.

"You share a kindred connection with men such as Ivanhoe and Audie Murphy. Years from now, I shall boast of having shook your hand, young Ahab."

All eyes were on Ahab. His speech was slightly slurred, but not from the effects of the beer.

"This belongs to you as much as it does to me. I couldn't do it without you. Last night I dreamt that Benny was trying to kill me, I called out, but you fellahs were not there. Well, you sure were today." He lifted his bottle, "THE BROTHERHOOD!"

All, including Jimsey, repeated, "THE BROTHERHOOD!"

Jimsey then excused himself and left them to finish alone. Although none of them particularly liked its taste, they enjoyed the feeling of light-headedness brought on by the beer. This was a special night they would all remember vividly, a night when they truly believed in their invincibility.

Poole walked into the house and the rapid sound of his stick against the floor alerted his wife to his haste and she was immediately alarmed.

"You all right husband?" She tried to keep the anxiety from her voice. As he came into view, she gasped. "My word, what's happened to you?" she exclaimed, with her eyes on his wet trousers and dishevelled appearance.

He approached her chair and she stopped her darning long enough for him to kiss her fully on the mouth. His eyes shone with excitement.

"This is a great day, a very special day, wife. I heard him with my own ears!"

"Heard who, saying what?" she asked, puzzled. Before he could answer, she pointed to the direction of the bedroom. "You should get out of those wet things, or you'll get pneumonia. Then you can have something to eat, while you tell me all about it."

He ate heartily and gave her a detailed account of Benny's downfall, all the time emphasizing the bits that were unflattering to him. When he was finished, he dressed in his Sunday suit, removed a floorboard, extracted some money from a jar and checked his pocket for his pipe.

"Think I'll go have me a drink to celebrate the occasion, wife. I have waited a long time for this day."

He went past several bars on Main Street and walked the extra distance to McSwill's bar on the waterfront, where he knew his friends were drinking.

Poole's mood was jaunty as he entered the bar. He stood for a little

293

while in the doorway to allow his eyes to get accustomed to the bright light as he tried to locate his friends. He locked eyes with Clifford from his place by the corner.

"What's up with Poole, I wonder? He seems full of himself," Clifford observed to Vernon.

Poole looked down at the bottle that was still standing on the bar and noted the brand on the blue label, which depicted a schooner with bloated sails and had the word Rivers printed across the top and boasted over-proof rum. The aroma filled the bar.

"There you are, hiding in Abraham's bosom," he said. He had a big grin on his face.

"What's happening?" asked Vernon. "Why are you all dressed up? And what are you doing down here at this time?"

"All in good time. Now, let me buy you fellahs a drink."

He pounded the bar even though the attendant was close by. "Barkeep!" A drink for me and my friends, large brandy for me and whatever poison they're having."

They both switched to whiskey.

He pulled up a stool and made room for his bad leg. Still in a high state of excitement, he again recounted in detail the incident at the beach, answering questions as he went along.

"I tell you fellahs, this is a great day. Did I tell you that I actually heard him beg? When something like that happens, you just know there is a God."

"Right," said Clifford, "then the next time something disappoints you there'll be no God".

"Oh, you don't understand. I was sitting at home with no thought of going out but those beautiful turkeys drove me out. Then I was going to my usual spot behind the church but changed my mind for no reason that I can think of and headed for the beach, just as Benny was going to get his. I tell you, this is no coincidence. It was as if fate intended me to be there."

"Did he really say please?" asked Vernon, wanting to believe it.

"Yes," said Poole reflectively.

He had a faraway look in his eyes. Then thinking aloud, "It was like running before the wind with a full sail and a bumper catch."

A smile that spread across his craggy face was the look of a man who had had the last laugh.

"I don't care if I never see the other one, this was the one that counted."

"I have no idea what you are talking about," said Clifford.

"Don't you remember that first day he came back? That day he picked our bones dry? He said there were two things I would never see; him saying please, and a green donkey."

27

In the days following, Ahab became a reluctant hero, as his humbling of Benny was blown out of all proportions. One alleged spectator swore that Benny's hands were clasped, as he prayed to Ahab to spare his life.

As for Benny he kept a lower profile and with his aura of invincibility shattered, became just another hard case with his share of altercations.

His humiliation, though in no way as spectacular as David's slaying of Goliath, as Otto had suggested, bore a small but significant similarity.

About this time, Heligar was transferred to the capital and a few years later, became 'the Attorney General for the Windward Islands.

Perhaps as a direct consequence, Benny re offended and was arrested and charged for assaulting his girlfriend, whom he had struck yet again.

Despite her explanation at the trial of a misunderstanding, he was jailed for two years, one for each assault. On his release, he gradually faded into obscurity.

The Benny bending incident was their biggest and last adventure that they had together. With constant reminders from their teachers, those that were leaving at the end of the school year worked hard for their school leaving certificates.

Brains, to the consternation of the principal became a teacher and worked for three years, before transferring to the civil service, to honour his father's wish of having a son for a civil servant.

TT worked in a store for two years, then afterwards joined the Dominican Police Force, where he spent most of his early years with the athletics team.

Gatlin's grandmother died that Christmas and shortly afterwards, together with Nina, they joined their mother who was by then living in Brooklyn in America.

Nugget was a long time adjusting to life without Gatlin and became disruptive. He joined his father in Trinidad and became a motor mechanic.

Ahab served part of his apprenticeship as a stevedore, before working on a schooner from Martinique and, through a contact, landed the plum job of working on a cruise liner out of Bermuda.

Within six months of each other, Optic and Atlas travelled to Canada.

The fact that one lived in Toronto and the other in Montreal did not prevent them from being godfathers to each other's children.

Brains, the only one to remain resident in Grenada was the point of contact through which the others stayed in touch.

At the end of the following school year, Lobo followed Brains into teaching, just around the time his mom returned home after having one of her breasts removed due to cancer. The doctor at the American hospital was hopeful that she was cured.

With her coming came a feeling of security and well-being; there was an extra warmth within the home.

Jerry spent a lot of his time reading to his mother because of her failing eyesight, her two favourite books Black Beauty and Joan Of Arc. They talked a lot about the things she had seen, the people she had met and the places she had visited with the family for whom she worked, but her greatest joy she told him, was the welfare of her family.

"Don't ever forget", she said to him one day, "it is your duty as a parent to make sure that your children get one rung higher up the ladder than you did". She put her hand gently on the side of his face. "We did that with you Jer. I think in you we've found an acorn that looks like growing into a big tree."

She was very proud of him and never missed an opportunity to inform anyone who didn't yet know, that her son was a teacher.

Two years later, Ambrose wrote him from London and invited him over. At first the objections were strong, especially from Juliette, whose pride in him probably exceeded that of her mother's. She always made sure that he had a clean shirt for every working day.

"What do you want to go to London for? You have everything you need right here", his doting sister had reminded him, but all his friends except Brains had left and even he was in St George's. Besides, the wanderlust was rampant within him.

Eventually, his mom relented, probably because she understood his need better.

"I knew you would leave the nest one day, but I hoped it would be later rather than sooner, but I understand. Besides, there are many more opportunities over there, and I know you are going to take them. Tomorrow, we will begin the preparations."

In the week preceding his departure, there was a subdued atmosphere within the household and Juliette's apron tail was always damp with wiped away tears. On the Sunday of his departure, the whole family went to high mass to pray for his safe arrival, and afterwards at breakfast, hardly anything was eaten.

When it was finally time to leave, he said goodbye to friends and neighbours and kissed his family. His mom hugged him to her and blessed him.

"Remember son, things change but values are constant". She walked into the other room allowing Juliette the final goodbye.

She handed him a brown paper bag.

"I got you some things to protect you from the cold in England, Vicks to rub your chest, an inhaler for stuffy nose, aspirins for headaches, Canadian Healing Oil, and —"

"Juliette, let him go now." His mom called from the other room.

She hugged him tightly, her head rested comfortably on his chest, and his chin rested comfortably on the top of her head. He was the son she never had and it was hard letting him go. He kissed the top of her head and she released him reluctantly. The tears were swimming around her eyes, but she was trying hard not to cry. She lost that battle, one of a very few. He walked all the way to the car without once looking back. He didn't want them to see his tears.

Ten years later, Jerry returned home for his first holiday; a surprise holiday. The car stopped directly in front of his childhood home and aroused Juliette's curiosity. She looked out just as the taxi pulled away and there was a look of disbelief on her face. She stood rooted to the spot as if she couldn't move.

Jerry put down the suitcase he was holding and quickly covered the distance between them. In one swift embrace he lifted her briefly from the ground. She held on tightly to him and he was surprised how small she seemed. She reached up and stroked his face very gently with her calloused right hand and for once she didn't fight the tears of delight that rolled down her cheeks, grey was now the dominant colour of her hair.

She disengaged herself for a better look at him.

"Let me look at you. A full grown beautiful man!"

Her tears that were still visible did not seem out of place next to her broad smile. He couldn't stop smiling. He knew that had he returned looking like Quasimodo, she would still have thought him beautiful.

Every Sunday for the duration of his stay, they walked the long way around from church just as he had done with his mom.

On the very day of his arrival he went down to the riverbank and collected some wild lilies for his parents' graves. Having placed them, he walked over to his favourite spot near the grotto overlooking the ocean. He sat as of old, with his back against the stone and listened to

299

the squawking of the seagulls and delighted in the marksmanship of the pelicans.

On the water was a majestic three-masted schooner with purple and white sails billowing in the stiff breeze as she tacked into the wind. In the schoolyard a pair of doves were picking at insects hidden in the grass.

Living through the hustle and bustle of London, there were times when he wondered if indeed, this spot with its beauty and tranquillity still existed. His mind went into overdrive as the memories tumbled over each other, accompanied by a cocktail of emotions.

He sighed with relief and felt a great sense of belonging to this place where everything was the same, as if time itself had lingered here.

As he stood to leave he walked over to the stone upon which were the two L's that he and Leona carved. Though faded, they were still visible. With Leona still on his mind, he headed for the pasture and the giant rubber tree.

He took the south path and stayed long enough to stroke the gnarled exterior of the calabash tree that he regarded as an old friend, then slowly made his way to the rubber tree and more importantly the posthole.

He knew that his action was illogical but he had often wondered if she would look there, should she ever return. He put his hand into the hole and felt around, but it was empty, probably long since found and used by other hopeful lovers.

The next morning, he caught the very first bus and headed for the capital and Brains. His office was in an old colonial building in the heart of town and boasted plenty of room in the reception area. Lobo approached the attractive secretary and asked to see Mr Rawlings. She looked over her shoulder to a closed door on her left, with C. Rawlings written on it.

"Do you have an appointment?"

"No, I'm afraid not. He doesn't even know I'm on the island," said Lobo smiling.

"I'm sorry, but I'm afraid you must have an appointment," she said as she reached for the appointment book.

"Please, let me explain. I don't mind waiting and I'm sure if you tell him I'm here, he'll see me," he pleaded.

"Take a seat," she said, finally returning his smile, "and I'll see what I can do."

Hardly had he sat down when the door opened and a man emerged and handed a sheet of paper to the secretary.

Before she had time to go into the office the door reopened and Brains also handed her a bit of paper, turned sharply and returned inside. Lobo thought that their eyes had met briefly, but couldn't be sure.

Suddenly, Brains emerged quickly from his office and strode forward and stared at Lobo and as if both had been given an invisible signal, they ran towards each other and embraced, much in the way of women and jumped around making foolish noises.

They became aware of the many faces around who seemed very amused by their jubilant reunion, and retired hurriedly to the haven of his office.

The questions flowed back and forth, and an hour went by like a minute. Brains looked at the clock on the wall and decided on an early lunch.

"Boy, I don't know how I'm going to go through there. In all my years here, I've never shown any emotion, then today we behaved like two big girls."

They laughed like old times. The secretary opened the door and looked in.

"Oh, Miss Noel, I'm glad you came. Please cancel all my appointments this afternoon, and rearrange them as best you can. I'll see you in the morning."

They sat at the Turtle Back restaurant, where most of the diners were busy feeding the fish in the harbour through the floor boards, which was a special feature of the restaurant.

They chatted right through the lunch crowd, then moved over to the bar where Lobo made the incredible discovery that Brains had remained a teetotaller.

After a little while, he surprised Brains with his question.

"Has Leona ever been back?"

Brains' expression betrayed his thoughts.

"You mean the fair Cleo? Well, what do you know? Don't tell me you're still carrying that torch. She has been here twice. The last time was last year. She spent the two weeks with her sister in Sauteurs."

"No, nothing like that," said Lobo and he went on to explain the poem and the hole in the tree.

"I couldn't help wondering if she may have looked in there, but I guess that's silly."

"Why is it a silly idea?" You looked in there, so might she."

Brains spent that weekend in the country and on the Saturday they went into the nearby town of Grenville. They parked the car and were walking the opposite way up a one-way street when a man emerged from a shop and stopped to light a cigarette.

"Think you know who that is?" challenged Brains.

Apart from a few more wrinkles, a full head of grey hair and about a stone heavier, which was expected anyway, he was still the same.

"As I live and breathe, it's Big John."

The man walked towards them and when he was almost level, lifted his hat in the old-fashioned way of greeting.

"Hello Mr. John, it's really nice to see you. How have you been," said Lobo smiling broadly.

Big John addressed Brains but his eyes were on the stranger. "Hello Mr. Rawlings, I'm afraid your friend has the advantage of me." His smile was equally broad.

"I'm Jerry, the butcher's son, lived on High Street."

"Oh!" said Big John, as his hand went instinctively to his mouth. "You mean," and he held his hand about chest high to indicate a small boy. Then recognition dawned and he actually laughed out loud.

302

He extended his right hand.

"Well, God bless my eyesight, I'm pleasured."

They all three chatted for a while and as Big John was about to take his leave, they each extracted twenty dollars from their wallets and offered it to him. After an enthusiastic "Thank you," he walked away, blowing smoke into the air.

Lobo turned back to Brains and saw the old fanatical look in his eyes.

Clearly apprehensive, he whispered urgently, "No Brains, don't do it!" Even as he spoke, Brains was shouting. "Ribbit, Crapoman!"

They both got on their marks and were ready to run to save life and limb, but there was no sound of running footsteps. They looked back to see Big John with a big grin on his face, he lifted his hat as before in a farewell greeting, patted his pocket with his recent gift, and headed for the nearest bar.

"Are you crazy?" asked Lobo as he moved from one leg to the other. With the adrenalin pumping through his system, he was finding it impossible to stand still.

"I'm sorry man," said Brains, laughing nervously, "but having you here and bumping into Big John like this, I just couldn't help myself."

"I know," admitted Lobo after a little while. "I was just giving him time to get a little further away before I called him."

That incident became known among them as 'the last tease', and they'd always recall it whenever two or more of them met.

Several years later, for the only time, Brains made seven international telephone calls and passed on the sad news of Big John's death. He went to bed one night and never woke up.

Each in turn asked the same question, "Can I help?"

But Big John had taken the precaution of paying for his own funeral, down to choosing his own coffin. He had a huge turnout.

Epilogue

A few years down the road and Jerry was sitting in the front room with his daughter, Jade. Five years old and very precocious, she was always asking questions. He was trying out one of Sister Ju's tricks.

On the table was freshly made stir fried vegetables with baked fish fingers.

"What's that you are eating Daddy?" she asked.

"Nothing that you would like, Butterfly."

"Why not?"

"Because children don't like it, it's for grown-ups."

"Give me some," she said, and opened her mouth wide.

"Don't open your mouth so wide and what must you say?"

"Give me some please."

"Well all right but I told you, children don't like it."

He put the food into her mouth and watched with satisfaction as she chewed, then swallowed.

"See? I told you," he said.

She opened her mouth again.

"What?" said Jerry acting surprised, "you want some more?"

She nodded her head.

"All right then, last time."

They carried on like that, taking alternate mouthfuls until the plate was empty. She climbed and sat on his lap.

"Daddy?"

"Yes Butterfly."

"Tell me a story about Mr Leopold."

"Which story?"

"The one about your present, with the animals."

"Do you remember how many animals there were?"

"Four. One whale."

"And?"

"One lion."

"Good girl, what else?"

"One elliphant."

He laughed and gave her a squeeze and wondered how long it was going to take her to get the word elephant right.

"That's my girl, well done Butterfly."

"Daddy?"

"Yes Darling."

"Was Mr Leopold an angel Daddy?"

"I'm trying to keep an open mind."

"What's an open mind?"

"I'll explain it to you when you are older."

"You promise?"

"Cross my heart and hope to die."

"No, I don't want you to die." Her arms tightened around his neck.

"Cross my heart then."

She reached up and kissed his cheek.

"What was that for?"

"That was for Mr Leopold."

"Don't forget, you still have one animal left. Do you remember what it is?" He knew it was her favourite. Her face lit up as she said proudly.

"A unicorn!"

Many thanks are due to the following people:

Shaaira: For her invaluable technical assistance.

Harry, Lenny and Sam: For their patience in guidance in getting me through the maze that I find the computer.

Acknowledgement:
To Beza!
May you derive as much pleasure reading this, as I did reading your poems.

Wilfred LB Fraser was born in the Caribbean island of Grenada in November 1935. He was educated at the St Patrick's Roman Catholic School and later worked at that school as a teacher, before emigrating to England at the age of 21. Fraser's ambition was always to become a writer, particularly a sports journalist, and with this in mind he enrolled on an evening course at the Working Men's College at Mornington Crescent. But life in those days was a struggle for survival and when he married and started a family, he substituted the classes for overtime.

Once retired from the Post Office, the London based resident never lost sight of his dream and resumed studying at Hackney College where he completed courses in English literature and creative writing. The Brotherhood of the Unicorn is his first published work.